6/17

WHAT MAKES A FAMILY

WHAT MAKES A FAMILY

COLLEEN FAULKNER

THORNDIKE PRESS
A part of Gale, Cengage Learning

Farmington Hills, Mich • San Francisco • New York • Waterville, Maine
Meriden, Conn • Mason, Ohio • Chicago

GALE
CENGAGE Learning®

Copyright © 2017 by Colleen Faulkner.
Thorndike Press, a part of Gale, Cengage Learning.

Thorndike Press® Large Print Women's Fiction.
The text of this Large Print edition is unabridged.
Other aspects of the book may vary from the original edition.
Set in 16 pt. Plantin.

LIBRARY OF CONGRESS CATALOGING-IN-PUBLICATION DATA

Names: Faulkner, Colleen, author.
Title: What makes a family / by Colleen Faulkner.
Description: Large print edition. | Waterville, Maine : Thorndike Press, 2017. |
  Series: Thorndike Press large print women's fiction
Identifiers: LCCN 2016058079| ISBN 9781410498458 (hardcover) | ISBN 141049845X
  (hardcover)
Classification: LCC PS3556.A93 W47 2017 | DDC 813/.54—dc23
LC record available at https://lccn.loc.gov/2016058079

Published in 2017 by arrangement with Kensington Books, an imprint
of Kensington Publishing Corp.

Printed in the United States of America
1 2 3 4 5 6 7 21 20 19 18 17

WHAT MAKES A FAMILY

1
ABBY

"She looks dead." My fifteen-year-old daughter leans over her namesake to get a better look.

"She's not dead." I sound more certain than I am. Sarah's observation is pretty accurate. My grandmother already *looks* dead. Of course I know she's not because the hospice nurse just left. The nurse would have known if Mom Brodie were dead, even if none of us were sure.

I take a step closer, coming to stand beside my daughter. I can't take my eyes off the collection of skin and bones in the bed that barely resembles my grandmother . . . or any other human being, for that matter. I suppose this is what I'll look like someday if I'm lucky enough to live to be a hundred and two. I stare at her comatose body; her eyes are closed, her thin, gray lips slightly parted. Her arms are pressed to her sides, making her look awkward, as if she's about to march up and out of the bed.

My grandmother's marching days are over. Cancer. *Eaten up with it,* is how Birdie put it. Whatever that means.

With great care, I take Mom Brodie's hand in mine, almost afraid it will shatter if I squeeze it too tightly. Her hand is cool to the touch, her skin wrinkled and so thin that I can see the gnarled blue lines of her veins like the protruding roots of the old oak tree where I used to swing on a tire in the backyard.

Sarah leans closer, studying the shrunken body lost in the folds of clean sheets that smell the way only line-dried clothes can. Like sunshine and something more elusive. Less tangible, but nonetheless present. The scent of the bedsheets instantly takes me back to my childhood on the island. This house. A part of me wants to embrace it, to bury my face in the pillow and inhale the perfume of all it means to be a Brodie. A part of me wants to run from the house, screaming.

The truth of the matter is that I'm not ready for this.

I've been preparing myself for years, of course. I *knew* Mom Brodie would die. We all die. Typically, before we reach three digits. I can usually be impartially logical about things like this, but not here, not now. I want to shake her awake and holler, *not yet, not yet.* I want to beg her not to leave me. I want to be her little girl one more time and curl up in the bed beside her and smell her peppermint breath and listen to her talk about people on Brodie Island, some I know, some who are long dead. Some I suspect might be born totally of her imagination. I want her to read one more chapter of *Robinson Crusoe* to me.

"*Mom,*" Sarah says in the teenager tone that makes it clear she thinks I'm an idiot. She's not in the least bit upset by her great-grandmother's condition. All my worry about bringing her here for this vigil was for nothing. "She *definitely* looks dead. And kind of . . ." Sarah takes a step back as if studying a piece of artwork on the wall of a museum. She wrinkles her heavily freckled nose. "Kind of *flat* . . . like Tiger after he got run over by that car."

I brush the tears from my eyes and lower my grandmother's hand to the bed. Back to marching position because that's the way the nurse left her.

I can't believe I was concerned it would frighten Sarah to see her great-grandmother this way. Clearly, she's not distraught. "She's not dead," I say, trying not to sound impatient. But what mother doesn't lose patience with her teenage daughter? Particularly when said teenager is comparing her great-grandmother to a dead cat. And Tiger wasn't even *our* cat; she was the neighbor's. "Not yet."

I pull the flowered sheet up a little higher, covering my grandmother to her knobby chin that's spiked with gray hairs. Mom Brodie has always been modest. I don't think I've ever seen her bare arms above the elbows, or legs above the kneecaps. She always wore a calf-length flowered house-dress, with a full apron in a competing flowered pattern over it. Now she's in a baby-blue hospital gown.

I fight a sob that lodges in my throat. I need to be strong for Sarah. For my Sarah. To show her that dying is a natural part of living.

But they're both my Sarahs. I need to be strong for them both.

Releasing the sheet, knowing there is nothing really to be done, nothing I *can* do, but be here for them both, I exhale and step back. My mother ordered the bed from a medical supply store on the mainland last week when my dad decided to bring his mother home from the hospital to die. I've heard about the bed in great detail in phone conversations with Birdie over the last couple of days: the extravagant cost, what insurance will and won't pay, its electric high/low elevation feature, and the trouble over making it with sheets from the linen closet. I talk to my mother often on the phone, but never about things that matter. Never about things I imagine mothers and daughters *should* talk about. The things I hope my daughter and I will always be able to talk about. Birdie and I only discuss trivial stuff like the features of a leased hospital bed. It's Mom Brodie who's been my confidant since I was a little girl, and now I can never talk to her again.

"It's just how a body looks when . . . when it's slowing down," I tell my daughter. I cross my arms over my chest and stare down at the silent, motionless body that really *could* be a corpse. The only indication Mom Brodie is still alive is the slightest rise and fall of the sheet over her.

I can't believe Mom Brodie is really dying. I was awake all last night going over it in my mind, trying to grasp it. How could she die and leave me? Who will I be without her? Because more than anything else, more than a daughter, a wife, or even a mother, I'm Sarah Brodie's granddaughter. She's been my identity since I was aware of my

11

existence and my relationship to others, somewhere around four years old. She's been the identity of all of us Brodies.

And what *about* all the others? What will Brodie Island be without the matriarch who's reigned over her for more than eighty years? Will the island just vanish, like on the TV show *Lost*? Will all of the descendants of the Brodie family disappear in the blink of an eye with Mom Brodie and the island? What about those of us who live on the mainland? Will my life end when hers ends?

When I speak to my daughter again, I use my parent voice. The tolerant, understanding one, not the irritated one. "I told you it would be this way. The body's organs all slow down, almost as if going into hibernation, and then eventually . . . they just shut down. She'll stop breathing." I take a deep breath and go on. "Her heart will stop beating and that will be the" — my voice catches in my throat — "and she'll die in her sleep."

Sarah takes one more good look at her great-grandmother and then backs away from the bed. She glances around the room with its ugly, dated wallpaper and too many pieces of mismatched furniture pushed against the wall. It used to be Mom Brodie's sewing room when I was a little girl, back in the days when many of the women on the island still made their own clothes.

Sarah looks at me with an innocence born of not yet having lost a loved one, and I have the sudden urge to hug her tightly. I don't. I stand there, hugging myself. Sarah has made it clear that she needs me to respect her *space.* No touching unless invited, which is hard for me. I'm a huggy, touchy person, particularly with my children. Maybe because my mother never was. I've never been to a psychiatrist, or even had counseling, but I'm pretty sure that would be the conclusion at the end of a long billing cycle.

It was Mom Brodie who hugged and kissed me, growing up in this house. She was the one who wiped the blood off my scraped knees and gave me a grape Popsicle to ease the emotional suffering of a fall from the chicken house roof. She was the one who told me it was okay when I didn't win the state spelling bee in the seventh grade when I misspelled *totipotency.* Mom Brodie was the one who took me to the movies, driving me all the way to Salisbury, the night Billy Darlen escorted Tabitha Parker to my junior prom instead of me. I still have the blue dress I never wore.

From the bedside table, Sarah picks up a photograph of Mom Brodie and my grandfather, Big Joe. It's a faded black-and-white photo, him in a porkpie hat, slender, dark tie and suit, and her in a flowered dress and hat. The most interesting thing about the photo is that Mom Brodie appears to be wearing lipstick; she never wore lipstick. The photo was taken in the mid-forties, I would guess from the style of their clothes. I don't know that I've ever seen the photo before. I wonder where my mother found it.

Sarah regards the photo for a moment. "She was really pretty."

"She had freckles like yours," I tell my daughter. Sarah's freckles are a constant source of worry and complaint these days. She's heavily freckled across her nose and cheeks, unlike me, who just got the usual ginger curse of a splattering of freckles everywhere.

Sarah sets the framed photograph down beside a glass of water and several prescription bottles.

I wonder absently why the pills are still there. Mom Brodie is past the point of swallowing pills. We have an eyedropper of morphine to ease her passing.

Sarah looks up at me. "Did we miss dinner? I'm hungry."

"Supper was at five."

"Five? Who eats at five?" Again, she wrinkles her nose, far too indignant for such a trivial matter. My children seem to thrive on indignation, this one in particular.

"Your grandmother and grandfather do. We always had supper at five. Everyone on Brodie Island eats at five. It's . . . the farm way."

Sarah ambles to the doorway. In the last six months, she's gone from moving like a giraffe, with awkward, long limbs, to moving lithely, like some kind of freckled jungle cat. Her newfound grace is harder for me to accept than the stilt-leg phase was. She looks so adult-like all of a sudden with her poised presence. So . . . *sexual* that I find it startling. Sarah wears no makeup, her pale red hair is piled on top of her head like a bird's nest, and she's wearing a paint-splattered T-shirt. Her freckles, which I think make her model-beautiful, are the first thing anyone sees. She *looks* like a woman, and I wonder when that happened and where I was as it was happening.

"No one who has field hockey practice eats at five," she points out. "Doesn't anyone play field hockey at Brodie High?"

"There is no Brodie High anymore." I walk to the foot of my grandmother's bed, wondering if she can hear this inane conversation. If she could open her eyes and see

15

Sarah, would she ask who stole my sweet baby girl and left this nimble feline in her place? Or would she even notice?

My grandmother and Sarah were never close, not the way I had hoped they would be. My husband Drum says it's my fault. (Not in an accusing way. He's not that kind of husband. But he *is* the kind who calls it as he sees it. No sugarcoating.) He thinks that my avoidance of my mother has kept our kids from having deeper relationships with the rest of my family. He might be right, but I don't have time to feel guilty about that right now. There are more pressing guilt trips for me to take this weekend.

"Everyone goes to Princess Anne for middle school and high school," I explain. "Just the little kids go to school here, now."

Sarah shrugs. "You said it was a crappy school, anyway." She walks out of the tiny room that's beginning to feel claustrophobic. "Birdie!" she calls down the hall. "You have anything to eat?"

"That's Mom-Mom to you," I tell my daughter. "You shouldn't call her by her first name."

"You do. And it's not even her name," Sarah throws over her shoulder. "If I was going to be disrespectful and call her by her first name, I'd have to holler *hey, Beatrice!*"

16

I don't respond, and Sarah vanishes from my view, down the hall. I know I should call her back and ask for an apology. Drum says I shouldn't let her talk to me that way, but sometimes . . . I just don't have the energy to fight her on every little thing. *Pick your battles.* That's what Mom Brodie always told me, and I've tried to live by that. You pick your battles, not just with your kids and your mother and your boss. You pick your battles in life. You keep in mind what's really important and what's not. Ask yourself, "will this matter in five years?" It might be one of the sagest pieces of advice she ever gave me.

I return my attention to my grandmother. Mom Brodie hasn't moved since we got here, and I have to stare for a minute to confirm that she's still breathing. I'm relieved she is. I'd feel bad to have to call the nice hospice nurse who just left. She's the one who will *call* Mom Brodie's death when it comes. Gail. She lives all the way in Salisbury, though, and it's Thursday night. I'd hate to have to ask her to turn around and drive back.

I sigh and walk to the single window in the room, unlock it, and give it a shove. I don't care that the air conditioning is running in the house; my mother probably has the vent closed in the room. She closes them all the time, to save on the electric bill, which makes no sense to me, but then little my mother does makes sense to me.

It takes two tries to ease the window up a couple of inches. The house is more than one hundred years old, built by my great-grandfather Joe Brodie, Sr., Mom Brodie's father-in-law. A house this age always needs work. I don't know why my parents don't have the windows repaired. Or replaced.

They certainly have the money to do it. I don't know what they're worth. It's not something we Brodies talk about — money. Because my grandparents lived through the Great Depression, my mother wears her Keds knockoffs until the rubber soles fall off them, my father carries a ten-year-old wallet, and they wash and reuse Ziploc bags. I suspect their net worth is in the millions.

They could build a new house if they wanted. Something single-story and smaller, more manageable. That had been the plan at one time. My brother, Joseph, the fourth, and his family were going to take this house, and Dad and Birdie were going to live in the new house. Then Joseph's marriage fell apart and so did the house plans, I guess.

I take a deep breath, closing my eyes. It's still August, and we're in the heat of the late summer, but I exhale and inhale deeply, filling my lungs with the briny, salt air of the Chesapeake Bay and all that it means. The good and the bad.

I stand there breathing in the evening air, listening to the insect song and the distant croak of frogs. I can't imagine ever living anywhere but on the Eastern Shore of the Chesapeake Bay. Drum keeps talking about moving to the ocean, maybe a little place on the Delaware shore. He doesn't understand what it's like to be conceived, born, and bred here. He doesn't understand that the bay is in my blood.

Realizing I'm not alone in the room anymore, *we're* not alone, Mom Brodie and I, I open my eyes and turn quickly to the doorway. It's my mother. For her size and weight, she's stealthy. She can walk soundlessly when she wants to; she's like a big mouse in a flowered apron. She listens in on conversations not meant for her ears. She's a shifty one, my mother. Always has been. I remember once, as a teenager, demanding furiously why she was listening in on one of my phone conversations, why she was so prying and underhanded about it. She said it had been the only way to survive in this house, growing up. I never quite understood what she meant, but I never asked her to explain, either.

It was my grandmother who brought Birdie to Brodie Island. As Mom Brodie told the story, she found Birdie in an orphanage in Baltimore and brought her home to help with housework. Growing up in this house, she was some sort of cross between a hired girl and a stepdaughter, I guess. I never really understood it; my grandmother's pat explanation had always been "things were different here in those days." My mother never gave any explanation at all.

As the years passed, Mom Brodie realized she had the perfect opportunity to raise a good Christian woman to become her son's wife. Mom Brodie taught Birdie how to cook and clean and grow a garden and be a good wife to a Brodie man. And when my mother turned eighteen, she married Mom and Pop Brodie's only living child, my dad.

"She doing okay?" my mother asks.

I study her.

Birdie is short and round and lumpy, the way women who eat biscuits and bacon for breakfast in their sixties are. She has a helmet of old-lady gray hair, pale blue-green eyes, and a sour puss. That's what Mom Brodie used to call it. A sour puss. Right to Birdie's face. Mom Brodie was the only person I ever knew who called my mother on her behavior, on the terrible things she says sometimes.

Birdie wears her usual uniform: faded stretch pants, a nondescript, beige top, and a full, colored apron over it. And cheap, canvas shoes with stained toes. My mother is by no means an attractive woman. Some might call her ugly. No amount of makeup or designer clothing could make her beautiful. She looks older than her years. Always has. But a nice pair of capris, sandals, and a decent haircut would go a long way. I gave up years ago trying to get her to dress better, maybe use a little foundation to even out her ruddy complexion.

"She doesn't seem to be in pain," I say. My voice sounds breathy and far off. I feel as if I'm on the verge of a crying jag, but I don't know why. I didn't feel like this until Birdie came in.

Birdie walks to the bed and straightens the sheet beneath my grandmother's chin. The sheet that doesn't need straightening. The interesting thing about the gesture is that it seems tender. And tenderness isn't something I've ever seen in my mother. That's not to say she isn't a good person, because she is. In a lot of ways, she's a better woman than I'll ever be. Any of us Brodies will ever be. She's a good Christian with respectable morals. She's the first one to volunteer in her Methodist Women's Circle, the first one to send a card for a new baby, and the first in line at a viewing. But tender, my mother is not.

"Air's on," she says, pointing her chin in the direction of the window. It's an accusation; I hear it in her tone. Birdie is all about *tone,* and she's the master of it.

"You need to lower the thermostat, open some more vents. Something." I close the window slowly, already missing the smell of the bay. I think maybe I'll go for a walk later. After I've gotten a chance to talk to Daddy for a few minutes. After Sarah retires to our room to text her friends. "It's hot as hell in here, Birdie."

She ignores my "swear word," as she calls it. I guess Birdie knows something about picking her battles, too. The thought is intriguing, but I'm too upset and too tired to contemplate the complexity of it right now.

"I don't want her to catch a chill," Birdie says. She's still looking down at my grandmother, studying the wrinkles on wrinkles of her face.

It's on the tip of my tongue to say *It's not as if it's going to kill her,* but I don't say it.

I'm really not that person. That spiteful person who says mean things just to be mean. Not usually. That would be my sister Celeste's modus operandi. But there's something about my mother's constant judgment that puts me on edge . . . and sometimes pushes me over.

"What made you decide to put her in here?" I ask, walking over to stand beside my mother, who is several inches shorter than me. "Instead of her room?"

Had it been my choice, I'd have wanted Mom Brodie to die upstairs in the bedroom she's slept in since the day she arrived on the island as a new bride at eighteen years old. If possible, I'd have tucked her into the bed she shared with my grandfather for forty years before he died in the bed in his sleep of a heart attack.

"Stairs," my mother says. The puss again. "Arthritis is acting up." She rubs her hip. "Change in weather coming I imagine."

"Well, I'm here to help. To do whatever I can to make things easier." I gaze down at my grandmother's face, and I feel the tears well up again. I don't want to cry in front of my mother. Birdie doesn't cry. "Celeste, too. She texted me. She's on her way." I give a little laugh. "Of course we know what that means. She could be here in five minutes or five weeks."

"I'll be glad to have her here to help me. Celeste. She works too hard," Birdie frets. "I worry about her."

I hold my tongue on the issue of my sister's ability to be helpful. The facts behind the *works too hard* statement, too. I'm not here to fight with my mother. For once, I feel as if I need to play nice. We should be on the same side. All of us: Birdie, Celeste, Sarah, me. The Brodie women. We're here for Mom Brodie, to help her pass quietly, without pain and with the dignity she deserves. The same dignity I hope someday my children and grandchildren will give me. Looking down at my grandmother, I realize this is where I want to die, too. In this house. Maybe even here in this sewing room.

"I gave her some macaroni and cheese and some fruit salad. Sarah." Birdie tugs at the bedsheet again, this time retucking it under the mattress, sealing Mom Brodie a little tighter in her sheet tomb. "Didn't want chicken and dumplings."

"She's a vegetarian."

Birdie sniffs. "So she said. Nothing but nonsense. God put chickens on this earth for us to eat. 'Every moving thing that lives shall be food for you,' " she quotes.

24

"Genesis," I say.

"Nine three." Satisfied with the sheet, Birdie stuffs one hand in her apron and pulls out a crumpled tissue. She leans over and gently wipes beneath my grandmother's nose. "Mrs. Brodie will need to be bathed tomorrow. She was always one for takin' a bath."

"I can do it," I say.

She looks at me doubtfully. "It's a privilege to do for family when they're this way." She shakes her head. "But that don't mean it's easy. See a woman like her unclothed, like a newborn babe."

"I can do it. Celeste and I will do it. You've got enough on your hands."

My mother still gets up at five every morning. She tends to her chickens and makes my father a full breakfast: eggs, scrapple, pancakes, and bitter, black coffee. She usually handwashes the dishes even though she has a dishwasher, and then she straightens up. In this day and age she still has a designated day to do things: laundry on Mondays and dusting on Tuesdays. Mid-morning, five days a week, Birdie tends to our friends and neighbors who she deems are in need. She's all over the island in her tan Buick. She drives women to the doctor, delivers homemade chicken noodle soup to

25

the sick, and sits with the elderly to relieve caretakers. Every day of her life she either feeds my father lunch at the house or delivers it to him in a brown paper bag wherever he is on the island, here on the farm or in town. The afternoon brings more cleaning, an hour in front of her soap operas, and then she makes supper and cleans up all that. The next morning, she gets up and does it all again. I don't know where she gets her energy or her stamina. I can't imagine that there's another sixty-six-year-old woman who gets done what my mother can get done in a day.

"You have to wonder," Birdie says, breaking the silence of the room.

"What's that?" I ask.

She lifts her chin in the direction of Mom Brodie. "What's going on in her head. You think she knows she's dying?"

2
SARAH AGNES

I hear their voices, my Abby's . . . Birdie's, but they seem far away. I'm not myself. I feel all light and floaty. My old bones ached before, when I was in the hospital. But now that I'm home, it's the oddest thing. I feel just fine. Better than I've felt in years.

I told my son, my Little Joe, that I needed to come home. Home to die. That's what I meant, even though I didn't say it. No one would say it, but I could tell by the look on Little Joe's face that that's what we were talking about. On the faces of the doctors and nurses. Like a volt of buzzards sitting on a house roof waiting for chicken killing. When you hear people whisper *make her comfortable,* you know your days on God's earth are numbered. And there's no sense fighting it. Ashes to ashes, dust to dust and all that.

Abby and Birdie's voices drift in and out. At first, I try to listen, to follow what they're

27

saying, but it doesn't seem important that I know what they're saying, only that they're here.

I let go . . . let them drift away from me. Or maybe I'm the one drifting.

The shadowy room fades and then brightens with a brilliant radiance, like a dozen sunrises spilling over the Tidewater at one time. My, oh my, it's a sight for sore eyes.

I smell sunshine . . . and popcorn and cotton candy. Like an outgoing tide, the scents pull me up and out of the bed, and I float to another time. Another place.

I smile. I know exactly where I am, even before I open my eyes.

I remember that moment as if it were only a moment ago, instead of eighty-five years. Give or take.

I've been three people in my lifetime, but that day I was still Sarah Agnes. Born Sarah Agnes Hanfland, outside of Gary, Indiana, in 1917. I'd fudge that later. My Joe went to his grave never knowing I was barely sixteen when he married me. It was one of those *what he don't know won't hurt him* kind of things. I think God will forgive me for the fib when I meet him at the pearly gates; He knows I did it more for the Brodies than myself. Some would think I was too young to marry . . . but I wasn't. I was a woman grown, and I knew my own mind as sure as anybody ever does. Maybe I was never all that young, or maybe the hard times made me what I was.

But that afternoon, the spring of 1931, two years into the Great Depression, when I smelled the sunshine and the popcorn and I stared up at that big Ferris wheel and heard the calliope music, I was still Sarah Agnes. A little girl, as innocent as a hatching chick. A shell of a woman.

"My mama will whip my tail if she catches me here," Cora whimpers. She's my best friend in the world, and I love her like a sister, but she sure can be a scaredy-cat and a whiner.

"Hush up," I warn her. "Nobody'll even know we been here if you don't tell them."

Cora's eyes get bigger, and she makes a little squeak of protest, but she doesn't argue. Which means she'll do what I tell her, at least for now. I give her a reassuring smile and whisper, "Come on," as if I go to carnivals all the time. I just hope I don't look as scared as she does.

We're both kind of star struck. We squeeze each other's hands tightly as we stare up at the Ferris wheel that looms overhead like a magnificent alien creature. Or God. Because for me, it was a religious experience, seeing that Ferris wheel, realizing there was a world beyond Bakersville. This is the first time a carnival has ever come to our little town that's barely more than a crossroad in endless acres of brown fields and clouds of dust. The gossip in school is that the carnival show was headed for Gary when one of their trucks broke down, and that's why they stayed. In any case, it's a miracle they are here.

Johnny Alber's Uncle Dandy owns the garage in town. Johnny told us on the playground yesterday that the truck engine had to be rebuilt, and it would be a week. Parts have to be delivered, maybe from Chicago. Johnny said his uncle was glad to have the work. Carnies paid top dollar for a tire or a spark plug. He said his cousins might get shoes for what the carnies would pay to get their jalopy going again.

Shoes are something we talk about a lot on the playground. Those that have them do. Some kids, the ones without, the ones we whisper about, mostly have stopped coming and stay home where nobody can poke fun at their bare feet. I'm in between. My shoes are a size too small, and my papa put cardboard in the bottoms to cover the holes in the soles, but nobody would dare tease me about it. They know better.

But who cares about pinched toes. The carnies are in Bakersville.

Carnies. That's what Johnny called them. And you could tell it wasn't a nice word by the way he said it. That's what my papa calls them, too, from behind his newspaper. "Carnies in town, Madge," he says. Smoke from his pipe rises above the newspaper. I never see his face, just hear him from behind a newspaper. He's gone most of the time these days, looking for work. He used to be a salesman. Grease. He carried a leather case filled with little jars of different kinds of grease: axle grease, ball-bearing grease, household grease for hinges and such. Now he goes town to town, looking for odd sales jobs to put bread on the table.

It's a big table. After we lost our house, we moved in with my grandmother and grandfather Hanfland, me and Papa and his wife, Madge, and my new little brother. Then Papa's sister Lorraine and her four kids moved in, too. Her husband, my Uncle Pat, got caught robbing a gas station last year. He's in jail so Papa has to feed his kids, too.

"Best keep the children away from that carnival trash," my father warns from behind his newsprint wall. "Sixteen-year-old girl, kidnapped last year in Terre Haute.

31

Parents said she was riding the Caterpillar one minute; the next she was gone. Never found her. Most likely dead or worse."

"Or worse," Mrs. Hanfland echoes from her post at the kitchen sink. That's what she says I have to call her, my stepmother, Mrs. Hanfland.

I wanted to ask what could be worse than dead; I couldn't imagine what she was talking about. I was so innocent then; I knew so little. They should have told me more; I should have asked more questions. But in my grandparents' house, children were to be seen, not heard.

I blink and inhale the exotic scent of the carnival world that has sprung up out of an abandoned wheat field. Goose bumps rise on my arms at the blare of the calliope and the shout of barkers beckoning to passersby and waving their prizes. It's all so wonderful, better than Christmas and my birthdays mashed up together. Better than ice cream with fudge sauce and whipped cream on top. I never tasted that, but a girl in my class bragged about having it when she went to Chicago with her mother to get new school clothes. Whipped cream with a cherry on top. She was probably lying, though. Her *new* dresses looking like they came out of the mission charity bin at church. Nobody in Bakersville has the scratch to take their kid to Chicago and buy clothes and whipped cream with a cherry on top.

I feel my hand, sweaty in Cora's, as we stare up at the Ferris wheel, watching it slowly turn. Sun glimmers off fresh gilded paint and jewels on the massive spokes; I wonder if they're real diamonds.

"You think they're open yet?" I whisper. I can't stop gazing upward. The sky is a perfect blue; not a cloud of dust to be seen, which is a miracle. It seems like the dust storms have been worse this spring. Not enough rain. People in Bakersville talk about how the worst is yet to come, drought, they say. Too much sin, my grandmother Hanfland insists. That's why the stock market crashed, too, she says. That's why people lost their jobs. That's why crops have been poor. She says she wouldn't be surprised to see locusts.

But there's no plague of locusts today. Today it's a perfect spring day that's neither too hot nor too cold. I'm so glad I wore my best dress to school this morning. It's a shirtwaist with a blue and green plaid bodice and a blue skirt and hardly looks worn. Cora's wearing her best dress, too, but hers has a big patch on the front. I told her just to hold her hand over it and no one would see.

We cooked up this scheme yesterday after everyone was talking on the playground about the carnival. About sneaking off after school today. I knew my stepmother wouldn't let me go. Not without my papa's say-so and he's gone again, to Canton. He heard some factory was hiring grease monkeys, men to grease big machines. It probably won't pan out; the jobs never do. But by the time he gets back to say I can't go, the carnival will have pulled up and pulled out. And Cora . . . well, her papa is the Baptist minister in town, so it goes without saying, she'll never get permission to come.

Cora's hand is cold in mine. "We should go," she whispers, still staring up at the great God-wheel in the sky. "Someone who knows us might see us. We won't be able to sit for a week after the switchin' we'll get."

"Stop whining. Just look at it. Isn't it the cat's pajamas?"

As we stand there in the middle of the mowed-grass path in the field that has become a paradise of sights and sounds and smells, two boys my cousin Calvin's age walk by and give us the once-over. One whistles and winks at me.

"See," Cora hisses in my ear, grabbing my arm with her free hand. She's afraid of the boys. She's afraid of everything. "It's not safe."

I wrinkle my pretty, freckled nose. I know it's pretty because people have told me so. And my grandmother says I'm too pretty for my own good and that girls who look like me get what they deserve. I don't know what she means by all that, but I know that since Aunt Lorraine got me a brassiere this spring, her son Calvin's friends have been looking at me. Early bloomer, that's what Aunt Lorraine calls me. Cora doesn't need a brassiere yet, so I guess that means she's a late bloomer, like the asters in my grand-mother's garden.

"I wish I could have a ride," I say, feeling like I'll die if I don't get to sit on one of those glittery benches and ride high in the sky. I'm fairly certain that right now I would rob a gas station like my uncle or trade my salvation for a ride on that Ferris wheel.

"You gotta have a ticket," Cora tells me. "And you gotta have money to have a ticket. We don't have any money."

What she says is true, but I don't care. I *have* to ride that Ferris wheel. "We can at least go have a look-see," I say.

Cora doesn't answer. I let go of her hand. "Fine. Go home by yourself then." I walk away, but I'm not looking at my friend

35

anymore.

A boy has caught my eye. No, not a boy like my cousin's friends with their peach-fuzz chins. Older than that. This is a man. He's taking tickets from a father and his son who wear matching wool newsboy hats. As the man takes their tickets, he looks at me and not them. He's the most handsome man I think I've ever seen, as foreign to my girlish Indiana eyes as the Ferris wheel. He's wearing a jacket made of black leather and a flat hat cocked on his head that later he'll tell me is a beret he bought in Paris. My beautiful man has a thin black mustache above his upper lip.

"Sarah Agnes," Cora whispers loudly. She's staring at the Ferris wheel man, too. She sounds as if she's about to have an apoplexy. Her feet are still glued to the ground where I left her.

I take a step closer to the Ferris wheel. The man's eyes are still on me, and I feel as if he's drawing me toward him with a golden thread, leading me to the destiny I know is mine.

The man and the boy in the matching hats have climbed onto one of the benches on the Ferris wheel, and they're slowly rising up and out of my line of vision. I feel my face getting hot. The way the man in the leather jacket looks at me . . .

I walk toward him, feeling like I'm floating on a cloud.

"Bonjour, mon amour," he says in French.

Of course he speaks French. I only know what French sounds like because Aunt Lorraine took me to the picture show in Gary to see *All Quiet on the Western Front* for my fourteenth birthday a month ago.

I feel as if I'm melting in my shoddy oxfords as his gaze meets mine. He has dark brown eyes . . . eyes so deep you could drown in them.

"Would you care to ride?" He says it in English, but with a French accent, and I feel dizzy, like I've already ridden round and round on the carousel I see in the distance.

"I . . . I don't have a ticket," I hear myself say. I feel Cora standing behind me now, so close the hem of her dress is brushing against mine and her breath is hot on my back.

A mosquito lights on my ankle, but I don't even swat it. I just stand there, looking at him, and hoping he'll let me ride the Ferris wheel. *Let me ride it. I'll die if you don't let me.*

He glances around, as if looking for someone, and then reaches out and takes my hand. His touch makes me feel like the time I got shocked trying to turn on an electric lamp in the parlor of our old house. Only that time it was one big sting. Now, I feel like a current is moving from his fingertips to mine, and it makes me hot in my belly.

"Lucky for you, *mon amour,* it is free today for girls with red hair." Still holding my hand, he reaches back and pulls a big lever, and the Ferris wheel stops. The father and son rock gently, high in the sky, almost to the top. "What's your name?" the Frenchman asks. His voice is silky, his words only for me.

"Sarah Agnes," I manage, the words sticking so hard in my throat that they don't sound like my own when they come out all breathy. "And . . . this is my friend," I add boldly. "Cora. Could . . . could she ride, too, even though she doesn't have red hair?"

"Bonjour, mademoiselle." He nods in her direction, but he never takes his eyes off me. "Of course your friend can ride."

He lifts the bar on the bench that will take us high into the sky, and I'm almost disappointed when he helps me up because I'm torn between wanting to ride up into the sky and wanting to stand here and have him hold my hand forever. Cora hops up next to me fast, and he lets go of my hand to lower the bar.

The man high above us is shouting something. I think he wants to know why he's not moving.

The Frenchman snaps the bar into place. "Enjoy your ride, *mon amour.*" He winks at me, and I realize this is the second time in five minutes that someone of the opposite sex has winked at me, and I somehow feel transformed. I always suspected my life in Bakersville was a mistake. A monumental error. Not really on God's part. I know God doesn't make mistakes, but somehow . . . I just know I'm not where I'm supposed to be. I know Sarah Agnes Hanfland isn't who I'm supposed to be.

The Ferris wheel slowly begins to turn, and I'm lifted, miraculously, up and away. In any other circumstances, the ride would have been the most amazing thing I've ever done in my ordinary, boring life, but now it's completely overshadowed by this Frenchman. This beautiful Frenchman. We're a good story over him when I lean down and shout, "What's your name?"

"Henri," he calls back.

And then he smiles a smile that's for no one but me, and I know in an instant that he's the love of my life. And I'm his. *He's* my destiny. This is what I've been waiting for. *He's* what I've been waiting for.

The ride is a blur. From the top, where I'm higher than I've ever been, even higher than the silo I once climbed, I see the field and the carnival with its midway and rides and a bunch of tents, big and small. I see the buildings of the town, and even our house, and the people look like miniatures. But in my mind's eye, all I can see is Henri and the way he looked at me. Part of me wants to stay up here forever. But a part of me can't wait for the ride to be over, just so he can take my hand to help me down.

Eventually, Henri slows the wheel and stops it. Again, he takes my hand. Cora jumps down on her own, but I barely see her.

"You should come back, *mon amour.*" He eyes Cora, then looks back to me. "Alone . . . ?"

"Sarah," I murmur. "Sarah Agnes. I'm Sarah Agnes."

He cocks his head to one side, his eyes still holding mine. "You don't seem like a Sarah Agnes," he tells me with his French accent. "I think I will call you . . . Sarry."

"Sarry," I whisper. *"Oui."*

"Sarah Agnes, come on," Cora calls anxiously. "We should go. We have to go." She sounds like she's on the verge of tears. "I just saw my brother. We have to go home. He'll tell on us both."

I look at her and back at my Henri. "I'll be back," I whisper. "I promise."

And then my fate is sealed. Henri lifts my hand and kisses my skinned knuckles, his gaze never leaving mine.

"Sarah Agnes," Cora whines.

I let go of his hand, even though I don't want to, and Cora grabs my other hand and pulls me away. "We have to go home," she whispers harshly under her breath. "We shouldn't have come. My papa is right. It's a bad place. Full of sin and, and . . . sin."

I barely hear her as she rushes me off. I barely see the midway beginning to fill with people. All I see is my Henri.

3
ABBY

I spoon the last bit of creamy broth from my bowl of homemade chicken and dumplings into my mouth and savor the rich, salty taste of it. I never make dumplings at home, and I never eat them except when I come home to Brodie Island. Otherwise, I'd *be* a dumpling. Birdie makes some of the best chicken and slippery dumplings I've ever eaten, and if there's one thing I know as a girl born on Maryland's Eastern Shore, it's slippery dumplings.

Licking my spoon, I look up at Birdie. She's hovering around the kitchen table, watching me. It used to bug me that she does this, pacing the kitchen linoleum, watching us eat, but never eating herself. Mom Brodie would do the same thing, but she'd sit down with us. Sometimes she'd even take a spoon from the kitchen drawer and stick it in my bowl and have a taste. Having rolled out the dumplings with her own rolling pin, and being my grandmother, she believed she had a birthright to the last dumpling in my bowl.

Thinking of Mom Brodie with her spoon in my bowl, me a teenager and her already in her late sixties, makes me smile. But it's a bittersweet memory because I know she'll never do it again.

I look up at Birdie again, then around the familiar room. It's a typical farmhouse kitchen on the island, though bigger than most. And the appliances are more expensive. There's a big, six-burner Viking gas stove, dating to the early eighties. A porcelain farmhouse sink my great-grandfather salvaged from the original Brodie house, built in the mid-eighteen hundreds right here on this same spot. Mom Brodie once told me that they used the timbers from the old house to build the new. The Brodies are a frugal bunch; at least they were before my generation, when according to Birdie, everything went to hell. Only she says "heck." My mother is the leader of the Dorcas Circle at the Methodist church where we were all baptized and will eventually be funeraled. Birdie doesn't curse.

I study the green medallion wallpaper that must be as old as me. And then the sturdy hickory table that seats twelve. My grandfather didn't put a dining room in the house. We're not dining room people. But the kitchen is bigger than the kitchens and dining rooms combined on the street where I live in Oxford.

I can hear Sarah's voice drifting in from the back porch; she's talking to someone on her cell phone. I can't make out what she's saying, but I hear giggling. Drum is concerned that she has a boyfriend and she's not telling us. I'm letting him bear the weight of that worry for now.

I watch my mother. She uses the hem of her flowered apron to wipe an imaginary smudge from the door of the white refrigerator. "You must be tired," I say, pointing at the chair nearest to me. Her chair. There's an interesting hierarchy in the Brodie house when we all sit down to eat dinner together, and it's all about your designated chair. "You should sit. Rest."

"He'll be back soon, I expect. Your father." She ignores my suggestion that she join me at the table. "Had an errand to run in town, he said. Done?" She sweeps my bowl and spoon out from under me, not waiting for me to answer.

I sit back in my chair, that's actually Daddy's chair when we eat together. The head of the table, his chair since my grandfather died all those years ago. The only chair I've ever seen my father sit at in this kitchen.

I wipe my mouth on the paper towel. In my house, we use cloth napkins and cotton dish towels. There's nary a roll of paper towels to be found in my house. Drum is big on protecting the environment. Having grown up here, it was hard for me to get on board when we were first married, but I've adjusted. For the most part, I follow my dear husband's "rulebook of recycling" as my kids call it. But secretly, I'm enjoying the rough feel of the paper towel on my lips. There's something childishly satisfying about it. (I secretly hoard Chick-fil-A napkins in my car.) Recycling hasn't caught on, on Brodie Island yet; there's no recycling pickup. We have a drop-off site, my brother's pet project, but then everything has to be hauled to the mainland. My siblings and I joke about the fact that Brodie Island's twenty-five miles from civilization and twenty-five years behind.

Birdie takes my bowl to the sink and washes it and my spoon and lays them in a dish rack to dry. She rarely uses the high-end stainless steel dishwasher Daddy bought her a couple of years ago for Christmas. She seems to distrust dishwashers; she says

45

dishes are cleaner when she washes them by hand.

I play with the ceramic pepper shaker in front of me that looks like a rooster; I line it up behind the hen salt shaker. The salt and pepper come out of holes poked in their heads. Birdie collects chickens. I wonder if they're the same salt and pepper shakers that I remember from my childhood. They have to be. Surely there can't be more than one set of these hideous things.

"I should check on Mrs. Brodie," Birdie says absently. "Do you think I should keep a bowl of chicken and dumplings out for Celeste? She doesn't eat enough. She's too scrawny. I worry about her."

My sister is always on some crazy Hollywood diet. She's done them all: cabbage soup diet, ice diet, cookie diet. I don't think she tried the cotton ball diet, but only because, when she told me about it, I threatened to bury her in private and not publish the obituary she's written and revises regularly. Celeste doesn't need to diet. She already has to stand up twice to cast a shadow. That's what Mom Brodie always says. *Said.*

"Celeste probably won't want any chicken and dumplings," I say. What I don't say is that what my sister *would* probably like is a

46

fifth of vodka. Right now, the idea appeals to me, as well.

My mother and grandmother are proper Methodist teetotalers. My father is usually a geographical teetotaler. He abstains when within a mile of his mother. My brother and I are drinkers; we've been known to stop at the diner in town, get a Styrofoam cup of sweet tea, pour out the sweet tea, and fill it with beer to have at a family picnic. Celeste is probably an alcoholic. I've seen her drink straight vodka from a flask from her handbag in the back pew of church on Easter Sunday. Secretly, I admire her a little bit for that kind of rebellion. I'll give her one thing. She's got some cojones. And the thing about Celeste is that she doesn't care what anyone thinks about her. I hate that. And I admire it.

"I thought she'd be here by now," Birdie fusses, looking out the window over the sink. She gazes out through the red gingham curtains, bordered in chickens, onto the back lawn that leads down to the bay. It'll be getting dark soon. "You think she had a flat tire?"

Celeste doesn't have a car. Hasn't had one in years. You never know what she'll arrive in. You can't hire a taxi or get an Uber to bring you to Brodie Island all the way from the dinky Salisbury airport. She's come in a hired car, on the back of a motorcycle, and once in a black stretch limo. Another time she rented a red Mustang convertible.

"She has a cell phone," I say. "She'd call if she had car trouble."

My mother turns to me and leans against the sink. "She won't live out the week," she says.

It takes me a moment to realize she's talking about Mom Brodie and not my sister. I sigh and sit back in my chair, feeling sorry for myself again. "That what the doctors said?"

"I want you to be nice to her. Your sister. No bickering," she instructs.

We're back to Celeste again. She's my mother's favorite. Growing up, Celeste was her favorite; I was Mom Brodie's. "I'm not the one who starts it."

"You're the oldest," Birdie answers, as if that's reason enough.

I look away, strangely close to tears again. I promised Drum I wouldn't fight with them. With my mother or my sister. Not this week. This week I swore I would keep my mouth shut and go along with whatever they say. I just have to get through this; that's what Drum said. *Get through it and come home to sanity and my black bean burgers.*

48

"Why do you always do that?" I ask, looking at the rooster pepper shaker. I give it a push, propelling it across the table. "You always take her side."

"She looks up to you."

I make a face. "She does *not.* I edit boring textbooks for a living. I work in sweatpants and a Mickey Mouse T-shirt. She's a New York City actress." I gesture with a flourish. "She's the one who's rich and famous."

Celeste is neither rich nor famous, but everyone on the island either thinks she is, or, like her, pretends she is. Celeste *was* an actress, once. In her *heyday,* she played the best friend of a major character on a marginally successful soap opera. It ran for four years. That's her claim to fame. And it went off the air six or seven years ago. Since then, the only acting she's done, as far as I know, is a few regional commercials selling recliners and attic insulation. At forty-one years old, she shares an apartment with two roommates she found on Craigslist and works at a department store in Brooklyn, at a makeup counter. I'm not judgey about the job. A job is a job, in the economy of today. It's the fact that she pretends to be a successful, working actress that bugs the hell out of me. And the fact that my mother believes the lie.

Aye . . . and there's the rub, my Drum would say. Though I'm pretty sure Will Shakespeare said it first. Drum works as a chemical engineer, but his undergraduate degree was in British literature. He knows the Bard well. He also totally gets my mother, which I'll never understand. She's a mystery to me, and I've known her for four decades.

I press my fingertips to my forehead, suddenly feeling profusely guilty. "I'm sorry," I say softly. "I don't mean to . . . be cross with you. I'm just upset. About Mom Brodie."

My mother doesn't say anything. She just stands there looking at me, her face blank. I feel tears burn the backs of my eyelids. I wish she'd come over and hug me. I wish *someone* would hug me.

I hear the back door open and glance up. Saved from this awkwardness that is me and my mother. It's existed since she gave birth to me in the bed she shares with my father. There was no bridge between Brodie Island and the mainland in those days. Birdie had Celeste and me, and the little boy who didn't survive, right here in this house where my father was born. We entered the world by way of a midwife. Mom Brodie didn't trust doctors when it came to "women's business."

"I didn't hear Daddy's truck," I say, starting to get out of my chair. Feeling my spirits lift.

My brother bursts through the doorway, surprising me.

"My favorite sister!" he hollers, looking genuinely happy to see me.

The fact that he also calls Celeste his favorite sister doesn't bother me.

Joseph throws out his arms to me, and I feel myself relax in them. He's a good hugger, the kind who makes you feel like things are going to be okay. Of course I know very well they're not going to be. I mean, this week can only end one way, and that's with all of us dressed in black standing graveside.

"You okay?" he whispers in my ear.

I nod several times, fast.

"Yeah?" He leans back, looking into my eyes, still holding on to me. He smells good: of soap and grain and the salty air.

I start to tear up again and fight it. Why am I so emotional? I want Mom Brodie to die. I've been praying for this for months, since she was diagnosed with cancer. I want her to be free of her pain and these earthly coils and all that.

But I guess I don't really want her to die.

51

I just don't want her to be sick anymore. Or old.

Joseph lets go of me and turns to his mother, the only mother he has ever known. "Mom." He walks over to her, folds his tall frame downward, and kisses her cheek.

She seems embarrassed by his show of affection. Why, I don't know. He sees her every day of his life, and he still kisses her hello and good-bye.

"Stewed chicken and dumplings?" she asks.

"Of course." He comes back to the table and pulls out the closest chair. Birdie's chair.

He's really upset the chair hierarchy if Birdie decides to join us. His chair is across the table, to my father's right and one seat down. Mom Brodie sat to my father's right my whole life. This weekend will be full of never agains. . . .

"Heard anything from Blondie?" he asks.

He calls our sister Blondie. Has since she dyed her brown hair blond when she was in the eighth grade. Birdie came unhinged. There was some sin wrapped in dyeing your hair, though exactly which one I can't remember. Celeste has been a bleached blonde ever since.

I meet his handsome gaze, my lips pulled

tight with amusement. "She's supposed to be here anytime."

His blue eyes twinkle. My little brother is a handsome man by anyone's standard. His eyes are as blue as a summer sky on a clear day. His skin is the color of the coffee my Drum makes for me in the morning: strong with a big splash of soy creamer. Joseph has a cap of dark, curly hair that he keeps short under his Husqvarna ball cap. Joseph is biracial. He's the love child of my father and a laborer who worked in our cannery here on the island. I never knew Aisha, who everyone called *Esha,* just of her. I have a vague memory of Daddy and me running into her in town one day before Joseph was born. Me with an ice cream cone, him sipping a Coke as we strolled down the sidewalk talking about baseball scores and the Orioles, probably. Over the years, I've wracked my brain, trying to recall if there had been an exchange between them suggesting the relationship they had, but I can't. And I was around thirteen, so maybe I wouldn't have seen it even if it had been there. I was pretty innocent in those days, even for a thirteen-year-old. I like to think Brodie Island kept us innocent. At least most of us.

Esha died giving Joseph life thirty-two

years ago. And so my father did what farmers have been doing on the Eastern Shore for the last three hundred years. He brought his illegitimate son home on the seat of his pickup and handed him to his wife. And Birdie did what farmwomen have been doing on the Eastern Shore for the last three hundred years. She took the baby, called him her own, and to my knowledge, never questioned her husband, the unequivocal head of the household.

Drum says that's crazy. Just because we kids never heard our parents discuss Esha, or my father's infidelity, doesn't mean they never did. Drum says we can never know what goes on in a husband and wife's bedroom. I suppose he's right. I think I understand my parents' relationship, but I probably don't.

Joseph looks into my eyes, and his mouth starts to twitch, too. He knows the joke. He knows Birdie will fret and fuss over Celeste's impending arrival. Possibly for days, until our dear sister graces us with her presence.

"Mom, how's Mom Brodie?" Joseph asks our mother, over his shoulder.

I wonder if Birdie has ever seen the irony in the fact that Joseph is the only one of us who calls her Mom.

"Same." Birdie stands in front of the

microwave, watching the bowl of dumplings go around in a circle.

Joseph turns back to me and takes my hand in his. He doesn't say anything; he just looks at me. He knows how important Mom Brodie is to me. He knows my heart is breaking. Joseph is one of the nicest guys you would ever want to meet. He's right up there with Drum MacLean, the best husband ever. Which makes me insanely curious as to why Joseph's wife Marly is filing for divorce. I have a hunch it's over infidelity. Joseph's got the charm my grandfather Big Joe had. Everyone says so.

I figure I'll get the dirt this week. Joseph and I don't talk that often on the phone. I haven't heard any details of the breakup except through the Birdie lens. I don't feel like it's a reflection of the relationship between my brother and me. He just doesn't like talking on the phone. When we get together, it's as if no time has passed since the last time we were sitting on the back porch, feet propped on the porch rail, watching the sun set over our beach, over Brodie Island. The world.

"She looks so small," I say quietly. "She's lost so much weight." I stare at the chicken salt and pepper shakers. "I always thought of her as a big woman. Not fat, but . . . you know, substantial, strong. At least in my mind."

He squeezes my hand.

The microwave beeps, and Birdie brings Joseph his chicken and dumplings in the bowl I just used. She uses the edge of her apron as hot mitts. He gets the spoon I used. She goes to the counter and brings him a paper towel she's ripped off the roll.

He reaches for the pepper rooster. "I could eat chicken and dumplings every day of my life," he declares.

"She didn't like dumplings," Birdie says. "Marly. Hard-pressed to trust a woman that doesn't like a dumpling."

"We're not divorcing over dumplings." Joseph adds a bunch of pepper and shovels a big spoonful of dumplings into his mouth.

They smell good, and I think about having another helping. I'm entering the mourning process. I have a right to comfort food, don't I? But I wonder, if I ask for another helping, what Birdie will do about the bowl situation. Will I have to wait for Joseph to finish so she can wash it and give it back to me?

Sarah walks into the kitchen from the porch, her phone in her hand rather than to her ear, where I sometimes fear it's permanently attached.

"Speak to your uncle," Birdie orders.

"Already did."

Joseph winks at my daughter.

Sarah sweeps through the kitchen. "Going upstairs, Mom. Text me when Aunt Celeste gets here."

Sarah likes Celeste; she thinks she's exciting and unpredictable. "Or I could call up the stairs," I suggest to her back.

Her gazelle legs carry her through the room and out the other door.

I meet my brother's gaze. "This is what you have to look forward to," I tell him. He has a little girl. Ainslie. She's four.

"I can hardly wait," he says through a mouthful of dumplings. "Where's Dad?"

"Home soon. He had to do something." Birdie.

"Ah," Joseph says. "That's right. He's tracking down Loopy. One of the corn combines is belching smoke again."

I eye our mother, waiting for her reaction. Loopy is our mechanic. Has been since I was a kid. He fixes whatever needs to be fixed on the farm: machinery, the washing machine, a leaky faucet. He's also the town drunk. Or at least the best one . . . worst one. Which means Daddy is probably at The Gull. Which means our mother is going to be ticked come ten o'clock when she's ready to go to bed and Daddy isn't here. I've never seen Daddy drunk in my life, but he likes a beer at The Gull. He likes several if he's there with Loopy.

Joseph is scooping up the last bit of broth from his bowl. He's inhaled the chicken and dumplings. "I can call him, Mom. Tell him Abby's here."

I see a flicker of pain in my mother's eyes, and I feel like such a jerk for picking on her. Even in my own head. Daddy's mom is dying. He should be here with her. Birdie shouldn't be the one to bear the burden, especially considering the tenuous relationship she and Mom Brodie have shared over the years.

Birdie turns her back to us and flips on the water faucet. "He'll come home when he's good and ready, I expect."

Joseph, always the peacemaker, lifts his bowl from the table. "Are there more dumplings, Mom?"

4
BIRDIE

I leave the water running and lean over the bathroom sink. I stare at the reflection in the mirror. A wrinkled, pudgy-faced woman stares back at me. An ugly woman. I lean closer, wondering if someone is playing a trick on me. When did I get so old?

I slowly push on the faucet handle to turn off the water and drop my toothbrush into the cup on the counter. Mrs. Brodie's toothbrush catches my eye. It's red, not a proper color for a toothbrush. She always wanted a red one when I went to the five-and-dime. The five-and-dime has long been closed downtown, but I still remember trudging in, telling the boy behind the counter that I needed a red toothbrush. Had to be red for Mrs. Brodie. I stare at her toothbrush and wonder if I should throw it away. She still has a full set of teeth, Mrs. Brodie. Not me. I got an upper plate years ago.

59

The brush really should go in the trash. She won't be needing it. I reach out, but I can't bring myself to take it from the cup. Not yet.

But when I do, it will just be my toothbrush and Joe's. Two toothbrushes. And I'll be the lady of the house. The dame. The mistress. The queen of everything, as my Celeste says. Finally. Fifty-seven years. That's how long I've lived in this house. Fifty-seven long, hard years I've dreamed of sitting to Joe's right instead of his left at the kitchen table. Fifty-seven years I've waited for him to ask me what's for supper instead of asking his mother. Even after I took over the cooking, thirty years ago, he still asked her.

I take the hand towel from the rack and wipe my mouth. I go to the door, open it, and flip the light switch. In the dark hallway, I see the light on under Abby's door. I don't hear voices. She and Sarah must be reading, or one's asleep and the other's reading. I want to go down the hall and knock on the door, say good night, maybe "God bless."

There's a lump in my throat, and I'm tearing up again, and I don't know why. I'm not a crier. I can count the number of times I've cried in my life. I stare at the door. Seeing Abby and Sarah's faces would make me feel better. But what would they think if I just showed up at their bedroom door at ten o'clock at night?

It's not what I do.

But I still stand there and stare at the line of yellow-white light. I smell the wood polish on the wainscoting and the faint scent of my minty toothpaste on my breath. Sarah's gotten tall since I last saw her, and thin and so pretty. How did I have such pretty daughters, such a gorgeous granddaughter when I'm such an ugly toad? Brodie blood, I suppose. Mrs. Brodie was a beautiful woman, even when she got old.

I turn away from the light and shuffle in my old slippers down the hall to my bedroom. Little Joe's still not home. Not home to see his daughter and granddaughter. Not home to tuck his mother in and say good night. He hasn't been around much since we brought her home earlier in the week. He's scared, I think. I don't hold it against him, though. Coming into life and going out, it's not men's business. It seems fitting to me that because women bring life into the world, it's our place to see it go out.

In my bedroom doorway I stop. I consider going down to check on Mrs. Brodie one more time, but I don't want to. My knees are sore. Stiff. One more time down and up these stairs might be my undoing. Joseph set up a baby monitor he brought from his house. I'll hear Mrs. Brodie if she stirs.

Still, I have to force myself to walk into the bedroom and not turn and go back down the stairs again.

In my room, in the dark, I lay my robe over the footboard. I sit on the edge of the bed and drop my slippers to the floor. I hate it when Joe doesn't come home. I hate lying down to sleep without him.

But I hate having him in my bed at the same time.

I think about the first time I ever got into this bed with Joe. Eighteen years old. I was so scared. And really, there was no reason to be. Joe was kind to me and quick, and it was over in no time. Really nothing for what the fuss is all about. But the thing is . . . I didn't want to be in this bed with him. I didn't want to be his wife. I didn't want to live my whole life here on Brodie Island, barely ever catching a glimpse of the world beyond the bay. I didn't want to mostly because Mrs. Brodie wanted me to. Of course I couldn't say no. I couldn't have refused to marry Joe. No one ever told Mrs. Brodie no.

I get up, pull back the chenille coverlet,

and lie down on my side of the bed. Moon-light filters from around the edges of the drapes. I stare up at the tin ceiling panel I've been staring at for forty-eight years. I wonder where Celeste is. I know she'll come along in her own good time. She always does. But it's important that she be here, that she comes in time to say good-bye. Good-byes are important.

I close my eyes, feeling hot tears brim in them. Mrs. Brodie's breath was so shallow when I went to tuck her in and say good night that I held her hand mirror to her mouth to see if she was still alive. I was so afraid the mirror wouldn't cloud. I was afraid it would.

Against my will, a sob escapes from my throat. I can't believe she's dying. Which is stupid, of course. Stupid Birdie. Stupid, ugly Birdie.

All these years I've known she would die before me. There were times I *wished* it would come faster. But now that the day, the hour is almost upon me, I'm scared. Who will I be when she's gone? As long as I can remember, beyond a few shadowy recol-lections of the orphanage, Mrs. Brodie has defined my identity. What I am is what she's made me.

And I've hated her my whole life for it.

5
ABBY

After stopping to check on Mom Brodie, who doesn't look like she's moved since I said good night last night, I walk barefoot into the kitchen. I'm wearing a pair of Drum's boxer shorts with four-leaf clovers all over them and one of Sarah's oversized T-shirts. The smell of coffee has lured me from my bed. Ordinarily, I'm not an early riser. It's one of the privileges of having survived my children's formative years, and being self-employed. But when I come home to Brodie Island, I feel guilty lying in bed, even past seven, knowing my mother has already been up for hours, made breakfast, planned the day's meals, and probably scrubbed a floor or two. The energy the woman has continually amazes me . . . and makes me feel inadequate on so many levels.

I'm surprised to not find Birdie in the kitchen . . . but my sister pouring coffee from the old-fashioned percolator on the back of the stove. I never heard from her last night. She's dressed in black leggings and some kind of swishy, patterned kimono-looking thing, thinning hair in a chic chignon and makeup on her face. At seven-twenty in the morning.

"Coming in or going out?" I ask. Then I laugh because the joke never gets old with her. Luckily, she laughs, too. She doesn't look like she's slept in days; the heavy makeup doesn't cover the black circles beneath her eyes. I'm the big sister, but she easily looks ten years older than me, and that thought makes me sad because what she looks like matters a lot more to her than to me. I'm one of those forty-something women who wears jean shorts, flip-flops, and my long red hair in a ponytail. Makeup is for church and meetings with the high school principal.

"What's with this thing?" Celeste asks, pouring black coffee into her mug from the ancient percolator. "Didn't we get Birdie a coffeemaker last Christmas?"

"And the Christmas before. I think there's at least three, still in the boxes, in the pantry." I reach up into the cabinet to get a mug. My choice is between a black lab with a mallard duck in its mouth or an advertisement for a commercial fertilizer. I go with the fertilizer.

Celeste leans in to me, and I give her a peck on her cheek. For all my grumbling, it's good to see my sister. She smells heavenly of expensive perfume. Samples she pilfers from work; she always gives them to me for Christmas. Of course I rarely remember to use them. "I'm glad you're here," I tell her. "She wanted to call out the state troopers last night when you didn't show before bedtime."

"I ran into Daddy. We had a drink."

"You *ran* into him? The Gull's not exactly on your way here." I wonder how she got here; I didn't see a car I don't recognize in the driveway, but I don't ask.

"Sure it is." She takes her mug to the table; it's one of those old white ones, spider-cracked with age, that looks like it's probably been in the house since the Great Depression. Which is entirely possible. "I came on the bus. Stops right across the street."

I don't say anything about that, either. I pour my coffee that will take a quarter of a cup of sugar and the same amount of whole milk to make it drinkable. Celeste's financial circumstances must be even worse than usual. Sometimes she takes the bus to Salisbury, but *never* over the bridge. Never to Brodie Island. She always arrives in style.

"Daddy already gone?" I go the fridge, take out the gallon of milk, and watch it glug into my coffee cup.

She beats me to Daddy's chair. "Yup."

"Birdie?"

"Someone died. Or is sick, or something. She took a coffee cake from the freezer. She should be back soon."

I nod and grab a spoon and my coffee to take to the table. I slide into Birdie's chair and reach for the white sugar bowl that's right next to the hen and rooster salt and pepper shakers. "Seriously," I say. "Are you already up and dressed or did you just get here? And if so, where have you been all night? The Gull closes at one."

She blows across the surface of her black coffee that I know will be so hot coming off the stove that it will take the skin off your tongue if you're not careful. Birdie likes her coffee hot. "Have you seen her?"

"Her" and "she" usually refers to our mother, but I know that in this case, Celeste is talking about Mom Brodie. The secret language of sisters. I dump a heaping spoon of white sugar into my cup. No white sugar in my house; Drum prefers raw sugar, or better yet clover honey. I hate honey in my coffee; it ruins the taste. If I wanted clover in my coffee, I'd pick some from the yard and throw it in. "I just looked in on her. She's still holding her own."

"But she's definitely going to die this time?" Celeste asks.

I add another spoonful of sugar, not caring for Celeste's tone, but understanding where she's coming from. "She's going to die." I stir slowly. For years Birdie has been blackmailing us into coming home more often than we like, holding our grandmother's impending death over us. Based on age, not illness. It's been going on since I was in undergrad. "I don't know how she's hung on this long," I say. "She's skin and bones. Waiting for us to get here, maybe," I add.

"I can only stay until Wednesday, Thursday at the latest." Celeste tucks a lock of her thinning hair that's fallen from her chignon behind her ear. It's obviously been freshly bleached and looks so brittle that I wouldn't be surprised to see it lying all over the floor instead of attached to her head that looks too big for her body.

"Audition," Celeste explains.

Which means she has to work at the department store. *Sister language.*

I stir the sugar in the bottom of my cup. "Birdie says Mom Brodie needs to be bathed. I told her we'd do it."

Celeste frowns, although it's hard to tell; Botox, I suspect. Or cryogenics. "Birdie can't do it?"

"I thought we would . . . so she doesn't have to." I cut my eyes at Celeste. "You know how the two of them are. I think Mom Brodie would be as embarrassed as Birdie, if she knew. I thought we'd spare them both."

Celeste's now looking at me as if I've grown a unicorn horn from the center of my forehead. "We're supposed to bathe her, *like in the tub?*"

"Not in the tub." I blow on my coffee and take a tentative sip. Even with the cream and sugar, I suspect it would take the paint off the peeling front porch steps. "Not in the tub. Just a sponge bath."

"Crazy question. If she's dying, why does she need a bath?"

I try not to be irritated with Celeste, not in the first five minutes I'm with her. I know she's not exactly a nurturer, but I was hoping for a smidgen of compassion. "I can do it." I take another sip of my coffee/paint remover. "You look like you could use a nap."

She sighs. "Fine. At least let me finish my coffee."

69

I lean back in my chair, my fingers around my warm mug. "Deal. Now tell me how Daddy is."

Birdie's still not home when I fill the plastic pink washbasin I found in a "patient's belongings" bag with warm water. In the same bag, I find liquid soap. From the linen closet upstairs, I've fetched a washcloth and a couple of towels. I don't really know how to give a comatose person a sponge bath, but how hard can it be?

Harder than you would think. I realize that when I stand over Mom Brodie's bed, looking down at her. It's such an intimate thing, to bathe an adult, the elder you've loved and admired and adored your whole life. And humbling. It's a humbling thing.

She looks very peaceful . . . and still a little dead. So I just stand there, looking down at her.

"You could just tell her we did it," my sister suggests. She was out on the back porch smoking a cigarette while I prepared the bath. I can smell the smoke lingering on her clothing. Celeste lives on coffee, cigarettes, and vodka.

I ignore her and lean over the bed. "Mom, it's Abby," I say softly. "I'm going to wash you up, okay? And then . . . you'll feel better," I add lamely.

She doesn't answer. But she keeps breathing.

I feel a little shaky as I fold back the sheet and blanket to expose her withered body.

"Birdie steal that hospital gown?" Celeste asks, remaining in the doorway.

"Believe it or not," I say, dipping the blue washcloth into the warm water, "the church has a bag of them members can borrow for home health care." It's Brodie Island. We don't do nursing homes. We take care of our own.

"So what you're saying is that someone probably already died in that thing."

Sometimes my sister's funny. Sometimes she crosses the line. She hopped, skipped, and jumped over it this time.

I ignore her and give my attention to my grandmother. I start with something easy: her face and then her arms and hands. As the minutes tick by, I relax. Even though her skin is thin and wrinkly, I don't feel like this is any different from washing a newborn baby. A sleeping baby. I find myself glad I can do this for her. She certainly washed my naked body and my bare butt many a time.

When I roll down the gown to wash her breasts that barely resemble breasts anymore, it makes me think about the life she's led. I don't know a lot about her days growing up; she never wanted to talk about it. I always wondered if she had a skeleton in her closet, like had her father been abusive, or had she been born out of wedlock? I'll never know now. What I *do* know is that she was born in Indiana to wheat farmers, an only child. She was a young girl during the Depression. She lived through the stock market crash, and more wars than I can count right this second. She met my grandfather at a Methodist tent revival in 1933, and he asked her to marry him that first night. He brought his eighteen-year-old bride home to Brodie Island. She had enough miscarriages that she didn't know how many. She's lived long enough to see her husband and every friend she ever knew die.

And this will be me someday, I think, gently stroking the fragile skin at her collarbone. If I'm lucky.

When I reach her waist, I fold the cotton hospital gown back up to cover her, for modesty's sake, even though it's just us girls here. I'll get her a clean gown later. I fold the hem of the hospital gown up to her waist above her Depends. As I dip the washcloth in the warm water, I glance at my sister, who's still standing in the doorway, as if keeping an eye out for Birdie while we have a smoke. Of course, when we were kids, it was Celeste smoking, and I was standing watch. I've never smoked a cigarette in my life, and only a couple of joints. I prefer the vice of a good pinot noir.

"Sarah come?" Celeste asks, averting her gaze. It's interesting that our grandmother's body makes her uncomfortable. There was a time in her life when she'd sleep with anything with a Y chromosome. And did.

"Yup. Still asleep. She got permission from her field hockey coach to miss practice all week."

"No school?"

"Not until after Labor Day."

"Ah. Reed gone back to college?"

"Never came home this summer, except to get the futon out of the basement. And his bonsai tree. He and his friends rented an apartment in Philly. They had to sign a year lease, so they decided they might as well move in. He has a summer job in the bio department, a lab thing." I don't bore her with the details of the neuroscience research he's working on at UPenn. It wouldn't mean anything to her, and she'd start a conversation about my *brainy* son needing to live a little, find a girlfriend, sow his oats.

I dip the washcloth into the warm water, wring it out, and slide the sheet down to expose my grandmother's bird legs. And that's when I see it, high on her thigh. For a moment I just stand there, washcloth poised in my hand, midair. "Celeste," I say, unable to look away. "Did you know Mom Brodie has a tattoo?"

6
CELESTE

"Holy shit." I stand next to Abby and stare at the skeleton in the bed. Mom Brodie doesn't even look like a human. She looks like one of those creatures that comes out of the tomb in *The Mummy,* with Brendan Fraser, back when he was skinny and hot. The first movie. Not the others. They sucked.

"That *is* a permanent tattoo, right?" Abby whispers.

"Well, I don't think it's done with a Sharpie marker." I turn sideways to get a better look, butting my pretty, perfect big sister out of my way. She drops the washcloth into the washbasin, and I hear it splash.

"That's definitely a tattoo." I'm fascinated and horrified at the same time. I wish I had my reading glasses, but they're hidden in the depths of my overnight bag. I never wear them in front of anyone, not even my family. "It . . . it's a garter I guess."

"A garter?" Abby repeats.

"Yeah." I point, but I don't touch it. Touch her. I swear she looks dead, and I don't do dead. I can barely manage living. "You know, like in the old days. To hold up your silk stockings."

I can't take my eyes off the tattoo, even though the skinny, fleshy thigh creeps me out. (Maybe because it looks a little too much like my flabby thigh.) It's a good tattoo, done by an artist, not by a friend one night when everyone got too drunk. I know those tattoos. I've got a fairy on my butt cheek that kind of looks like a gargoyle now.

"Mom Brodie has a tattoo?" Abby says, sounding as if she might cry.

"Mom Brodie has a tattoo?" Sarah bursts into the room. "And nobody told me? Why doesn't anyone ever tell me these things?" she demands. She seems pissed to be left out of the loop, and excited about the tattoo at the same time.

My sister cuts her eyes at me. "I don't think you should have told her."

"Told her!" I roll my eyes. "I didn't *tell* her anything. She was eavesdropping."

"I wasn't eavesdropping," my gorgeous goddess teenaged niece tells me. She looks at her mother. "Mom, I was *not* eavesdropping. You know that's not my style. I was just walking down the hall." She gestures with her slender hand. "And I hear Celeste say *loudly* 'that's definitely a tattoo.' If you say it loud enough for other people to hear, that makes it public knowledge."

"I've asked you. Call her *Aunt* Celeste," Abby says.

"And I told her to call me Celeste. I don't like that 'aunt' stuff." I tug on the hem of the teen's T-shirt. "She can't tell you what to call me. She's not the boss of everything."

My sister opens her mouth to say something, then closes it and looks down at our hundred-plus-year-old grandmother again. "Mom Brodie has a tattoo," she says, still sounding as if she doesn't believe it, even though we're all staring at it.

"Right," I say with just the right intonation, the way young people do. I've been working on word choices, trying not to say things that date me, like *cool* and *neat.* I've almost got the *"yeah, yeah, yeah"* down pat.

"It's beautiful," Sarah breathes, standing between us. She's braver than I am. She reaches out and runs her finger along the ruffle of the garter, which I want to do, but it scares me. Old people scare me in general, the way they smell, the way they look at you, the way they seem to know your worst

77

thoughts. All your failings. And Mom Brodie was as good at that as anyone I've ever known. Not that I know a lot of old people. Like I said. They creep me out.

"How long do you think she's had it?" Sarah whispers in breathy awe.

I fluff up my bangs, hoping they can't see the bald spot on the right side of my head that's widening. "She sure as hell didn't get it on Brodie," I say.

It might be one of the most beautiful tattoos I've ever seen. It's a ruffled garter, three quarters of the way up her thigh, in pale blue, not the ugly green ink you usually see in old tattoos. My guess is that it was once a navy blue. There are two little birds, with curly ribbons in their beaks, weaving them around the garter.

"They're bluebirds," Sarah says, speaking with such reverence that you'd think we were in a damned church. "Does it go all the way around?"

Abby looks at me. I put up both my hands. I'm sure as hell not picking up Mom Brodie's skinny leg to look. I'm not touching her. I don't care how much money she's leaving me.

My sister reads my thoughts.

"Let's have a look," Abby says. She lifts Mom Brodie's leg at the knee, bending it, and ducks her head to look.

I'm going to take her word on it.

"It goes all the way around," she says. "And there's another bluebird." She gently straightens out our comatose grandmother's leg.

Sarah looks down at her mother, a carbon copy with the red hair, only taller and prettier, if that's possible. "But how did she get it?" she breathes. "When?"

"Sure didn't get it in the last decade," I say. "Or last eight." I look at my sister. "She had it when she came to Brodie. Had to have."

Sarah wrinkles her freckled nose. She's covered with freckles, the kind that cluster in patches across her nose and cheeks. Very chic. She says she wants to be a physical therapist, but she could be a model. She's got legs that go on for a mile. And her pale face with that blaze of freckles across her nose and cheeks . . . beyond amazing. She could do runway couture.

"But you said she was a child bride. She married Great-Grandpop when she was eighteen," Sarah says.

I shrug. I need a cigarette. And possibly a drink. I'm hoping Joseph will meet me for lunch at The Gull. I already texted him, but he hasn't texted back. I need the dirt on

Mom Brodie's will. Abby won't want to talk about it. She'll be all righteous and say we shouldn't discuss it, not with Mom Brodie on her death bed. But honestly, what does it matter? Mom Brodie's *going* to die. It's not like us talking about it is going to make it happen any faster. And I know very well we're in her will because, five or six years ago, a legal secretary called from Clancy Jacobs's office, the only attorney on the island, to get my mailing address. Her name was Tootsie or Tootie or something like that. She said "Mr. Jacobs was doing some work for Miss Sarah." There's only one *Miss Sarah* on Brodie Island, at least whose name is said like that, like you're saying Princess Di or something. Mom Brodie was writing her will, all right (which was about freakin' time since she was already in her nineties), and I'm in it. I just need to know how big I'm in it.

"I'd lay ten to one, Mom Brodie had that when she married Pop Brodie." I chuckle at the thought. "Pop Brodie thought he was getting some sweet little Methodist virgin and what he was actually getting was a little minx."

Abby cuts her eyes at me again. Obviously she doesn't like the idea of her saintly Mom Brodie possibly being anything but what

Abby has built up in her head over the years. She doesn't know as much as she thinks she knows. Like the fact that it was Mom Brodie who paid for my abortion when I was in the eleventh grade. (And a couple more when I didn't tell her what the money was for.) Or about the picture of the young woman in a feathered bathing suit Mom Brodie kept taped inside the silk lining of her Bible. I found it looking for money once. Old people always hide money in Bibles. And cookbooks. Birdie used to keep her pin money in a *Betty Crocker Cookbook* until she caught me snitching it.

I asked Mom Brodie who the girl in the picture was. She said a friend, but it had to be her. To wear a bathing suit like that in those days was not an everyday thing. (And made of feathers? Who wears feathers swimming?) So the sweet Methodist virgin Pop Brodie thought he married, wasn't, and Mom Brodie's got the racy tattoo to prove it. It occurs to me that she might even have one on her butt, but there's no way I'm looking for it.

"It's the only thing that makes sense," I say. "She got it before she got married."

"So Pop Brodie knew she had it?" Sarah breathed.

I shrug again. "Maybe. Maybe not. Who

knows? That generation did it with the lights out."

My sister throws me a disapproving look.

"What?" I walk away from the bed, losing interest in the tattoo. "You're kidding, right?" I ask my sister. "You think she doesn't know people have sex?" I lift my chin in the direction of her daughter. "*Please* don't tell me you haven't had *the talk* with her."

"Of course she knows about sex," Abby answers, a little snippy. "I just think it's . . . inappropriate to talk about our grandmother's sex life . . . in front of her."

"What? Her?" I point at Mom Brodie. "She's in a coma. She doesn't hear a thing." I shake my head. Abby might be the smartest person I know, but she sure can be stupid. "She's already gone, Abby. Her body just hasn't caught up with her head yet."

Abby turns her back to me and carefully covers Mom Brodie with the blue sheet. "I don't think we should say anything about this to anyone."

"You mean Birdie?" I ask from the doorway, giving a laugh. I'm headed out for a cigarette. I might try to hold off on the vodka a while longer. It's early, even for me. "That would be rich, wouldn't it?"

Abby sighs. Apparently the bath is over

because she's tucking Mom Brodie in like she's a baby going down for a nap. "Obviously Mom Brodie didn't want us to know about the tattoo; otherwise, she'd have told us about it. Or showed it to us."

Sarah, who's now standing between us, nods. "I agree with Mom. We shouldn't tell anybody, at least not yet. Not until we know more about it."

"Know more about it?" I make a face. "How are you ever going to know anything? She's the only one who knows." I point to the sleeping *queen of everything.* "And I've got news for you two. She's not talking."

Sarah turns to her mother. "Maybe I can find something on the Internet. There're hundreds of sites about tattoos. Lots of pictures, about the history and stuff."

"And how do you know that?" Abby asks.

Sarah looks at me — as if I'm going to save her — then back at her mom. "You can Google anything, Mom."

I smile. Good save. Sounds like she might have been tattoo window-shopping. So maybe my niece isn't quite as angelic as she seems.

"I'm serious. Don't tell Birdie. Or Daddy." Her patient tucked in, Abby picks up the washbasin.

"I'm having a cigarette." I head down the hall.

"I'm not kidding, Celeste!" my sister hollers after me.

7
SARAH AGNES

No one notices us at the carnival. I told
Cora we wouldn't get caught. She still cries
all the way home. She has to wipe her runny
nose with the hem of her dress before she
goes in the house.

I stop at the library after I leave Cora.
When I get home, no one asks me where
I've been. Not Grandmother, or my aunt,
and certainly not Mrs. Hanfland. It will be
years before I realize no one asked because
no one cared, but when you're fourteen
years old and you've never been anywhere
or done anything, you don't necessarily see
things for what they are. Especially when it
comes to love. I'll learn that lesson, too.

With the tiny, battered book I got at the
library, I go to the attic. I don't have a
bedroom of my own anymore. I used to in
our old house. Now I sleep on the couch in
the parlor. I don't even stop in the kitchen
to eat my supper. It's boiled turnips and

cornbread. Last year's turnips that are getting wrinkly. No butter, no milk. I hate turnips, and I hate cornbread without drippings or butter or jam. It's like eating bricks of sawdust.

No one says anything about me passing up supper; more for them, I guess.

In the attic, I settle cross-legged on the feed sacks under the window under the peak of the roof. I've made myself a cozy place to read and daydream, where I can be alone. It's the only place I can hide from these people I live with. I know they're family. Well, *supposed* to be my family, but I have my suspicions that they're not. Maybe they're just waiting until I'm older to tell me the truth. Maybe I was an orphan, and my father and my mother took me in. I don't think I'm a princess or President Hoover's secret daughter or anything like that. But maybe I'm the daughter of a rich Chicago family. Maybe they lost all of their money and put me up in the orphanage as a baby so someone would feed me. Or maybe my parents are famous jazz musicians, and they couldn't take care of me with all the late-night gigs.

I think maybe I'm not really a Hanfland because I've never felt like I fit in here. Not with these people, not in this town. I've never been to Chicago, but I think maybe that's where I came from. Sometimes I dream about moving to Chicago. If I got a job, I could buy pretty hats and silk stockings and marry a really handsome rich man and live in a big house with maids. And if I married a rich man, I'd make him take me to the picture show every night.

Under the attic window, while the early evening light is still good, I open the book. It was the only French book in the library, which isn't really a library because it's in the back of Mrs. Abbiati's market. Mrs. Abbiati said she only had the one book on how to speak French, but she had two on Italian. She told me Italian was better. She said if I learned to speak Italian maybe I could go to the Vatican and meet the pope. But she's Italian, so I guess that's something she would think of.

I took the French one. I want to be able to say something in French when I see Henri again. And I *will* see him again. I was actually playing with the idea of going back to the carnival tonight. After dark, when it would be easy to slip out of the house. I've never snuck out before, but I'm such a ghost in this family since Mrs. Hanfland married my dad that I doubt anyone will notice I'm gone.

On the first page of the *Speak French Francophone Language Teacher* there's an introduction. In English, thank goodness. It says I can "manage to speak the language studying only a few minutes a day with the Hugo plan." It says I could have learned to speak French years ago if I had known I could *"without hours of boresome study."* And "The secret to the Hugo plan is its simplicity and naturalness," and I'll be speaking in my first lesson as if I was in France. I don't read the rest of the foreword about how people have been so pleased with the book. I'm too excited.

I stay under the window, practicing my first words of French until it's almost too dark to find the ladder to climb down. I snitch a block of dry cornbread from the pantry and make my bed on the couch with the pillow and blanket I keep underneath. No one says good night, and I lay in the dark, fully clothed, the book on my chest, and whisper, *"Bonjour, monsieur. Ravi de vous rencontrer."* Good evening, sir. So nice to meet you. *"Qu'est-ce qui t'amène?"* What brings you here?

I debate what to learn next. *Can you tell me where is the best place to buy croissants?* doesn't really seem all that useful, but I work on it anyway because I like the sound on my tongue. *"Pouvez-vous me dire où le meilleur endroit pour acheter des croissants?"* I've never had a croissant. I'm not even sure exactly what it is, but I can imagine, if it's made in France, it must be good. They probably eat them with strawberry jam, or maybe even whipped cream. I think whipped cream must be French.

I wait until the house is quiet and my grandfather has gone down the hall the last time with the kerosene lamp. We used to have electricity, but it got turned off months ago. Papa said it was temporary. That he'll have it turned back on once he gets a job. I don't think he's going to get a job. No one has jobs anymore. The stock market crashed, and then all of a sudden hardworking people didn't have jobs anymore. Or shoes. Or food. We're lucky because my grandfather gets a small pension from the railroad. He gets enough money for us to eat turnips and now and then a mess of chicken necks and pan gravy.

Once everything is quiet and my grandmother has stopped coughing and my cousins have stopped crying and gone to sleep, I slip out of the parlor, carrying my shoes. I'm scared when I go out the door, but by the time I reach the field where the lights

are still bright and the calliope is still playing, I know it's what I was meant to do.

8
ABBY

I'm brushing my teeth when Drum calls me back. It makes me smile to see his name come up on my phone. I spit and wipe my mouth before I answer. "Hey."

"Hey, yourself," he says, and I'm surprised by the little shiver I feel when I hear his sexy voice over the phone. It's hard to believe we've been married twenty years and he can still do that to me. For me.

"Sorry. Just got your message. Department meeting this morning," he goes on. "What's up?"

"Hang on," I tell him. I grab my toiletries bag and go down the hall to my bedroom and close the door. Birdie's down in the kitchen making egg salad for Daddy for lunch. I told her I would run it out to him. Sarah's in the living room looking through family photo albums, and Celeste went to get cigarettes. In my car.

Mom Brodie is sleeping/comatose right

where we left her.

"You're not going to believe this," I say, closing the bedroom door behind me with my hip. And even though the door is closed, I keep my voice down. Just in case Birdie's sneaking around. "Mom Brodie has a tattoo."

Drum laughs. "No way."

I drop the toiletries bag on the bed Sarah and I are sharing. It's covered with a homemade quilt, but not the nice kind made by the Amish in Lancaster, Pennsylvania, in one of those cool patterns like a double wedding ring. It's the kind you buy at a church bazaar that's made of scraps of hideous polyester fabric. Sarah and I have been laughing about it since she discovered it on one of our previous visits, the orange pieces with Popsicles on them, next to the blue goats with strawberries pattern.

"Swear to God," I tell him, stepping out of my sleep shorts and into cotton bikini panties. It's eleven, and I'm finally getting around to getting dressed. I skipped the shower. It's one of the things I like about being home. No one showers *every single day,* like in the real world.

"Queenie?" He likes to call her the queen or Queenie, but he doesn't mean it in a bad way. He always liked her, even after she caught him when we first started dating smoking pot on her back porch and threatened to put the joint out by dumping a bucket of water over his head. Drum never smoked weed on her back porch again. Ever.

I grab a pair of knee-length shorts off the bed and shimmy into them, capturing my cell between my chin and shoulder. "Celeste and I were giving her a sponge bath this morning — well, *I* was giving her a bath — and we found it."

"A tattoo. Like a Tweety Bird on her shoulder?" Drum can barely contain himself. I knew he'd get a kick out of this. "No, wait," he says. "Let me guess. A butterfly tramp stamp. Lower back, just above her butt cheeks."

Now I laugh. It seems a little sacrilegious to be talking about my grandmother's butt while she's dying downstairs, but I can't help thinking, if our roles were reversed, she'd see the humor in it, too. And this is too good not to share with Drum.

Drum and I sometimes joke about getting matching tattoos. We're either going with a Harry Potter lightning bolt on our foreheads, or a dotted line around our necks with the words *couper ici,* meaning "cut here," in French. Although lately, Drum's been leaning toward a troll doll in his armpit with his armpit hair for the doll's hair. I'm *not* going with the troll doll. Final answer.

"Hang on. I have to put my bra on."

"You could leave it off, and we could talk dirty to each other," I hear him say as I set the phone on the bed long enough to pull on my racer-back bra and hook it in the front.

I grab my Carey's Crabs T-shirt and pull it over my head. It's old and worn; there's a stain on one sleeve where Sarah wiped her blueberry pie mouth on me years ago, but I'm not ready to give it to the ragbag in our garage. I love my Carey's Crabs shirt; it feels like home. Mr. Carey's been dead for years, but we still buy our crabs from his son and grandsons down at the public dock.

"This is going to sound crazy, Drum," I say when I pick up the phone again. "But it's beautiful. Her tattoo. I wish you could see it. It's this . . ." I sit down on the edge of the bed, pressing my bare toes into the ancient carpet. I've been begging Birdie for years to pull it up. There's amazing hardwood under it. But she refuses. She has it in her head that hardwood is for people too poor to be able to buy carpet. She calls it "wall to wall" as if it's still 1954. "It's a garter, on her thigh."

"Holy hell," he breathes. "I thought you were kidding. Queenie really has a tattoo?"

"This isn't just *a tattoo*. It's . . . a work of art. I've never seen anything like it. It looks like a ruffled garter that would hold up a silk stocking. On her upper thigh. There are these little bluebirds, three of them, that have ribbons in their beaks, and it looks like they've wrapped the ribbon around the garter. All in blue and green. It's so beautiful," I repeat. "Maybe the prettiest tattoo I've ever seen."

Drum gives a low whistle. "Wow. And I'm going to go out on a limb here and assume no one knew she has a tattoo?"

I make a face as I pull open the heavy drapes on the French doors that lead out onto my second-story balcony. "Of course we didn't know."

"Birdie?"

"I'm sure she doesn't. I mean . . . it's probably safe to assume she doesn't. It's not like Mom Brodie would have ever hiked up her dress and said, 'Hey Birdie, wanna see my tat?' Mom Brodie hadn't been bathed since they brought her home from the hospital, so Birdie wouldn't have had the opportunity to see it. We didn't tell her," I add quickly.

"You didn't tell her about the tattoo?"

His tone is incredulous, as if I've crossed some major line in the sand. And maybe I have, but this is new territory for me. "Uh-uh," I say.

"Why not, Abs?"

"I . . . I don't know."

He makes a little sound like a sigh. As if he's disappointed in me. I hate it when I disappoint him. When I disappoint anyone. I've got that firstborn child thing about always wanting to please people.

"Abs, you complain that you and your mother aren't close, but you never tell her anything."

"I tell her things," I defend. "I talk to her at least twice a week."

"You know what I mean. Sure, you tell her what the kids are doing, what you're making for dinner, but you never tell her the important stuff. Stuff about you. Parents want the personal stuff. The who-you-really-are stuff."

I twist my mouth, considering his words. This isn't the first time he's said this to me. But I'm not ready to engage. Talking about Birdie is always prickly between us. My mother does that to all of us. "You know how the two of them are, Mom Brodie and Birdie. I just . . . I figure Mom Brodie kept it secret for a reason. It's not my secret to tell, Drum."

"But you told me."

His areas of expertise are chemical engineering and unclogging toilets, but the man I married also has Vulcan logic. Which I love and hate, usually at the same time. I frown and feel around on the floor with my bare foot for my Rainbows. I keep the old leather flip-flops in the closet as part of what Drum calls my "Brodie Island uniform." "Of course I told you. I tell you everything."

"You didn't tell me when you backed into the recycling bins at the end of the driveway and dented the bumper on the Honda."

"I'll tell you everything *important,*" I amend. I don't care that he's brought up my little fender bender. It really wasn't a big deal. I was more upset about it than he was. I just hate it when I do ditzy things. Because I'm not a ditz. "And I got the bumper fixed, didn't I? And, if I recall correctly, I got the ding in the door fixed, which *you* did with a shopping cart at Whole Foods."

He chuckles. "Okay, okay. My point is, are you not going to tell anyone else about your grandmother's little secret? Your dad? Joseph?"

"That would be weird, wouldn't it?" My bare feet in my flip-flops, I pace in front of

97

the bed. "Tell a man his dying, one-hundred-and-two-year-old mother has a provocative tattoo on her thigh?"

"I don't know. He might appreciate it. It certainly says there's more to Mom Brodie than any of us realized."

"That's for sure." I reach the wall, which needs painting, and turn and go the other way. "I don't know about Joseph. I guess we'll tell him. He'll get a kick out of it. You know how he loves his tattoos."

"Does Celeste want to tell Birdie?"

"I'm sure she does. Pot-stirrer that she is. We didn't really get to talk about it. Sarah walked in while we were bathing her and —"

"Wait, so *Sarah* knows her great-granny has a tat?"

I smirk. "She was so excited. She wants to do some research on the Internet and see if she can find out anything about it. It looks old."

"Well, it's got to be. Mom Brodie sure as hell didn't get it on Brodie Island. Is there even anybody who does tattooing on Brodie?"

"Just JD Morris, in his trailer. They're not bad, but they're not of this caliber, and he's Joseph's age."

"How old was Mom Brodie when she

married your grandfather? Eighteen?"

"Yup." I catch a glimpse of myself in the mirror. My long red-blond hair is pulled up in a high ponytail and then looped through the band to shorten the tail. The diamond studs Drum gave me for our anniversary in my ears. No makeup. I look pretty damned good for my age if I do say so myself. I swear it's the sun here or the salt air or something. I always feel as if I look better here than in my real life. I feel better, more like myself, which is crazy because I hate it here. . . . Love it here. Hate it here.

Talk about being a ditz. I pick up my sleep shorts and tee and toss them on the bed. "How's your day going?"

"Fine." He sighs. "It's fine. I . . ." He exhales, and I hear a change in his voice, in his demeanor. I know what he's thinking. We've been together that long.

"No one's said anything about the will," I say quietly.

"I wasn't going to ask. I just . . ."

It's my turn to sigh. My dear, sweet, never-asks-for-or-expects-anything husband is having a bit of a midlife crisis. He's a full-time professor of chemical engineering at a small college on the Eastern Shore. He used to like his job, but he's gotten burned-out over the years. About a year ago he came to me with the idea that he wanted to retire early, move to the beach or, worse, to Brodie. And become a glassblower. It's his hobby, which he swears he could make a living at, given a little time. My dad has even been in on it, saying they can convert one of the outbuildings right on the Brodie farm for Drum to use as a studio.

The thing is, we don't have the money to make that kind of life change, not with Reed just a sophomore in college and already talking about a PhD. Like his dad. And before we know it, Sarah will be heading off. I mean, I make a decent living, but not enough to support all of us for who knows how long.

A couple of weeks ago, I came home to see Mom Brodie, and she whispered to me when I kissed her good-bye that she was leaving me "a little pin money." Pin money is an old phrase I grew up with. Once upon a time, it meant money a woman kept for herself for personal use. I think it dates all the way back to a time when straight pins used in sewing were expensive and considered a luxury. In my grandmother's day, most farm women sold eggs or baked pies to sell to have their own pin money. I got the impression, from the way Mom Brodie said it, though, that she wasn't just talking about money to buy myself an extravagant pair of shoes. I think she meant *money* money. But it's hard to say.

My family's wealthy. Really wealthy, though I've never seen numbers, and no one would ever have the bad taste to bring it up. Except maybe Celeste. Brodies own almost the entire island between my father and his cousins. My great-grandfather and his brother had a crabbing business and the farms. And because they had their own canneries, they cut out most of the middlemen. They also owned everything on Main Street and the boats and trucks that carried their goods on and off the island. My dad and his cousins went their separate ways in the sixties. The cousins kept the stores, the trucks, the boats. Daddy kept the farms and the canneries. The cousins sold their waterfront land early on, but Daddy hung onto it and ended up making an amazing deal in the nineties. And he didn't sell all of the beachfront, so God only knows what he's worth. But Mom Brodie had her own money. Grandpop Joe had enough forethought to know it would be smarter to leave his wife well-to-do in her own right, so as not to put pressure on her or their only son. But to my knowledge, other than for birthday and Christmas presents, she never spent much.

So . . . depending on what she leaves me, we *could* be making some life changes. But I don't know. I don't know about the whole becoming a glassblower thing. My Drum is not a flighty man. And he's certainly not impulsive. But a *glassblower*? It sounds a little farfetched and way too hippie-dippie, even for my Drum. Do we really upset our whole world so he can pursue his hobby?

"You okay?" I ask. I felt bad leaving him home alone this week. He's been so quiet the last couple of weeks and . . . a little sad. I worry about him. We discussed his seeing our family doctor. Talking to her about his depression. Well, *I* talked about it. Drum just sat there and folded laundry.

"I'm fine. I better go." He hesitates. "I better go," he repeats. "Lucy keeps walking by my office door. I think she wants to talk to me about adding that thermodynamics night class this semester. I don't want to teach it, but I guess I can't avoid her forever."

"Don't agree to it, Drum. Not if you don't want to. Stop being such a nice guy and bailing other people out." I'm quiet for a moment, waiting for him to respond. He doesn't. "Call me later?" I ask.

"Sure. You going to take a pic of your

granny's tat? Text it to me?"

I laugh because it sounds so funny the way he says it. And so bizarre. And it's both, I guess. "I don't know," I say, going to the bedroom door. "Isn't that a little creepy? Taking a picture of my comatose grandmother's thigh and texting it to you?"

"Not as creepy as my *looking* at a text of your grandmother's thigh," he says.

"Good point. Love you." I make a kissing sound.

"Love you, babe."

I smile as I disconnect. There was a time when I hated it when he called me *babe.* It seems so . . . misogynistic. But he never meant it that way, and now after twenty years of marriage, I like the fact that he still calls me anything that's in the least bit affectionate. We're getting to that age where friends and coworkers are divorcing. Hell, some of them are divorcing now for the second time. I'm a lucky woman to have a man like Drum, and I know it.

Drum's older than I am. Fifteen years. I met him at a pub crawl in Baltimore my senior year of college, which is funny because that wasn't my thing. Pub crawls. It wasn't his either. We were both there because friends had trapped us into the evening of drinking and carousing, which wasn't all that fun because we were sober. I was just coming out of a two-year relationship, not looking for a date, certainly not looking for a husband. Drum was single, too. He'd had several long-term relationships, but never been married. Which is amazing, considering what a catch he was. He's always said he was waiting for me; he just didn't know it.

It was funny because when we bumped into each other, ordering a drink at the bar, I don't think I even noticed how much older he was than me. I was too taken with his smile. He said he noticed right away that I was quite a bit younger than he was because he couldn't understand why anyone as young and beautiful as me would be interested in an old hippie like him. It was love at first sight for sure. For both of us. My breakup with my old boyfriend hadn't been traumatic; we'd just drifted apart as we matured, so I think I was ready to fall in love. Drum and I talked until closing, abandoning our friends. We exchanged phone numbers, dated a few weeks, and after graduation I moved in with him, to the horror of my parents. We married six months later. Never a day, or a moment of regret. For either of us. And now here we are, still together, still in love, still trying to figure out how to do this life thing.

Downstairs, I check on Mom Brodie and resist the urge to lift the sheet and blanket and peek at her tattoo. My grandmother, my proper Methodist Circle grandmother, has a racy tattoo. I just can't get the idea out of my head. Where did a girl who met her husband at a Methodist tent meeting, at eighteen years of age, get a tattoo on her thigh?

I wander down the hall and find Birdie in the kitchen. She's wearing a pink and green, full, flowered apron and leaning over the counter dicing hardboiled eggs. She must have a dozen.

"How was your morning?" I ask. "Get your errands run?"

"Took chicken salad and coffee cake to Mrs. Barton. Laid up with the gout again. That worthless son of hers, lives next door and can barely carry her a can of Campbell's."

I perch on a stepstool we keep in the corner of the kitchen. The cabinets run all the way to the eight-foot ceiling, and so they're tall. And Birdie's short. She drags the stool around the kitchen to get what she needs.

"Sarah's in the living room looking at picture albums. Wanted pictures of Mrs.

Brodie. She wants to make one of those slide things for the funeral. You know, where they put pictures up on the screen. I don't know that Mrs. Brodie would like that. Pictures of her on a movie screen."

I prop my feet on the lowest step and hug my knees. "Oh, I think she would. You know how Mom Brodie was. She always loved to have her picture taken."

"Vain," my mother says, her back still to me as she chop, chop, chops the eggs. " 'So I'm allotted months of vanity, and nights of trouble are appointed me.' "

"What's that from?" I wrinkle my nose. I used to know my Bible quotes cold, but over the years I've drifted from my Methodist roots. I still feel as if I'm a spiritual person, but certainly not religious. Organized religion makes Drum itch. But he meditates every morning before he goes through his yoga routine.

"Job."

"Ah. Right." Of course, my mother would quote Job. It's her favorite book in the Bible. She loves all the suffering.

I hear my daughter's footsteps, and she comes into the kitchen, carrying an ancient picture album. "Hey Birdie, these pictures are kind of stuck. You sure it's okay if I take them out? There's like glue on these sheets, and the pictures got glued in. I might be able to peel the plastic off and just leave the sticky back. Then I can just scan them on Grandpop's scanner in his office."

"Do what you want with 'em," Birdie answers. "You want egg salad?"

Sarah cuts her eyes at me. She's barefoot in a tank top and wearing short shorts that border on Daisy Dukes, in my eyes. But she doesn't even know who Daisy Duke is. "I don't do mayo, Birdie." She turns to go.

"Who doesn't *do* mayonnaise?" Birdie says, mostly to herself as she goes to the refrigerator and takes a jar with the blue label out.

Sarah is almost out of the kitchen when she turns back to us. "Birdie, what was Mom Brodie's maiden name?"

Birdie shuffles back to the place at the counter where she's chopped the eggs and tossed them in a Pyrex bowl. I can tell her feet are bothering her. Plantar fasciitis. I keep suggesting better shoes and maybe orthopedic inserts might help, but she won't go for it.

"Hm. Can't say I recall."

I get the eye cut again from my daughter. It's her "what the hell?" look that's almost identical to her father's. "Where could I find out?"

Birdie sighs and takes a wooden spoon and begins dropping big lumps of mayo into the bowl. "I don't know."

"Would Grandpop know?"

Birdie taps the spoon on the side of the bowl. "Doubt it."

Sarah thinks for a minute. "Do you have her marriage certificate?"

"Might. Have to ask your grandfather. It might be in the safe deposit at the bank."

Sarah looks at me. "I don't even know what that means."

I laugh. "Banks used to have a room full of metal boxes. You could rent them and keep important papers in them."

Sarah cradles the album to her chest. Her breasts are small like mine, only she doesn't mind. When I was a teen, it bothered me that I wasn't large-breasted. Over the years, I've come to appreciate my little boobs. No sagging.

"It was mostly to preserve them in case of a house fire," I explain. "Back in the day where there were a lot of house fires."

Sarah nods slowly. I can see she's taking in the information. Then she looks at me and says, "Denim axe examined," and makes her exit.

"I don't even know what that means,"

Birdie declares, watching her granddaughter go.

I laugh and wonder if Birdie realizes she used the very same words Sarah had used. "It's a palindrome."

"What?" Birdie says, taking on her cranky tone. The one she uses when she thinks someone is getting "uppity" with her. I feel as if I can never win on this subject. If I explain "big words" she gets insulted and accuses me of thinking she's stupid. If I don't explain, she thinks I'm being "uppity," too.

"It's a sentence that reads the same forward or backward. She's been doing it for months. You asked me about it the last time we were here." And the time before that.

My mother screws up her mouth. "Why on earth would a teenage girl just blurt something like that?"

I chuckle and shake my head. "Because she's a teenage girl and she likes palindromes." Birdie stares at me, perplexed. "Come on. I did the same silly stuff. Remember the summer I was fifteen and memorized a bunch of Shakespeare's sonnets? You'd ask me if I wanted breakfast and I'd answer 'Pity the world, or else this glutton be, To eat the world's due, by the grave and thee.' Which is particularly funny

109

because Shakespeare was not talking about appetite."

My mother goes back to making her egg salad. I let it go and watch her add even more globs of mayo to the bowl of chopped eggs. "What time is the hospice nurse coming?" I already know the answer; it's just a way to make conversation with my mother. And a better choice than asking if she knows Mom Brodie has a tattoo.

"Between two and four."

"I'll be back by two, then."

"I would certainly hope so." Birdie adds relish to the egg salad. "Don't take that long to carry your Daddy his lunch."

"No, but I thought I'd go for a ride. Maybe go find Joseph."

She pulls a load of white bread out of the breadbox on the counter. "What for?"

I shrug, refusing to feel like I'm a kid again, being grilled by my mother. "I don't know. Because he's my brother? I'm worried about him. The divorce."

"I told him not to marry her." She lays the egg salad on thick on the bread. "Thinks she's better than us. Her being a doctor."

I hold my tongue. I had my doubts the marriage would work, too, but not because I didn't like Marly. And certainly not because I thought she thought she was better

110

than us, whatever that means. My concern with their union was based more on the type of people they are. Joseph is a simple man with simple needs. His whole life is this farm. This island. And his family. He's one of those people who says, "Why would I ever want to go to Paris?" And he sees everything in such black-and-white. There's no gray with Joseph. Which I suspect will change as he gets older. I know I certainly see more gray with each gray hair that appears in my hair.

Marly's a go-getter. She's driven. She's ambitious and not in a bad way. I just worried that they would never see eye-to-eye once the wild sexual attraction wore off. And we all know it does. And apparently, as Birdie would say, "those chickens have come home to roost."

I glance out the window over the sink. My car's still gone. I can either take Birdie's Buick or the old pickup. Daddy gets a new pickup every eight years, or so. His one extravagance. But he always keeps the old one as "backup." I'll take the pickup. I kind of like driving it. It reminds me of my teenage years. Birdie would never let us drive her car, and we were never allowed one of our own. It was Daddy's truck I drove when I snuck around with my girlfriends, drink-

111

ing underage, calling to boys on the sidewalk in front of the diner, and laid in the bed, staring up at the stars down by the water's edge, dreaming of the life I would lead.

I watch Birdie put the sandwich in a Ziploc bag and add an apple and a Little Debbie oatmeal pie to the bag. My daddy has a sweet tooth. He loves his Little Debbies. He'll eat three oatmeal pies in one sitting if Birdie doesn't get to the box first. She worries about his cholesterol, which is high, and his weight, which is too heavy. And this is one subject we agree on. I think Daddy should take better care of his health. But I also think we're all born with free will, and she can't hide all the Little Debbies on the island from him.

Birdie holds up the brown paper lunch sack.

I pop off the stool and cross the kitchen to take it. As I reach for it, I meet my mother's gaze, and I realize she looks sad, and it's on the tip of my tongue to ask her if she's okay. But of course she's not okay. There's a woman we've all known our whole lives dying down the hall. Even with the conflicted relationship Birdie and Mom Brodie have had, this has to be hard for her. A part of me wants to give Birdie a hug. Just a quick one. But my mother never hugs me. I'm afraid it will make her uncomfortable. It will sure as hell make me uncomfortable.

So I take the lunch sack, grab the keys off the hook near the back door, and sail out. "Back soon."

9
BIRDIE

"Abby's gone to take Joe his lunch. Egg salad." I pull up the chair to the side of the bed and sit down. I put the plate on my lap and pick up half of my sandwich. I take a big bite. It's good: fresh eggs from the henhouse, just the right amount of mayonnaise and store-bought pickle relish, and a pinch of salt. I didn't know how to make egg salad when I came here. It was Mrs. Brodie who taught me. "Celeste went to buy cigarettes in Abby's car. Be lucky if she sees that car again." I take another bite. "Nah, her clothes are upstairs. Big bag of makeup and such in the closet. Using something in a bottle to make her hair grow. It won't work. She wouldn't leave without her makeup."

I take another bite and chew. "Mrs. Barton's down with the gout again. Joe says she drinks, but I don't believe it. Sends her best."

114

I look over at Mrs. Brodie. She hasn't moved a muscle since one of us moved it for her. I wonder how long this will take. Her passing. A few days I hope. Not that I want her to suffer. But I like having the girls here. When she dies, they'll all go home and leave me here alone in this house.

I watch her chest rise and fall. She doesn't look to be in pain to me. She just looks like she's sleepin'. Kind of peaceful-like. "Abby thinks Joseph's going through with the divorce. I know you liked her. Marly. But I told you she thought she was too good for him." I make a sound between my teeth. "And now they've got that sweet little one. Families today, they think they can just divorce if they don't like the same pudding." I take another bite of the egg salad and reach for the coffee I've set on the nightstand. Wash the bite down with a good swallow. Coffee's just the way I like it. Strong and cooled down. Some people have to have the coffee hot. Joe'll put his in the microwave if it's not hot enough. Mrs. Brodie was the same way. Of course everyone thinks I'm the one who likes it hot, but I don't. I make it hot for them. I'm used to my coffee sitting while I do one thing and then another.

I set the mug back on the nightstand and

look over at Mrs. Brodie again. I wonder if she's wonderin' where her son is. Doesn't seem right, her being his mother and me being the one sitting here. "Joe's down at the cannery. He's thinkin' about letting the fire department burn it down. Training. You know. They have to teach the new boys how to put out a fire. Won't cost him a thing. Place got cleaned out years ago, but he said he just wanted to have a good look around. Make sure nuthin' was left behind he could use around the farm or sell at the junkyard."

When he told me he was heading to the cannery this morning, just to have a last look before she's ashes, I think it was on his mind that he met *her* there. Esha. I know it was on mine. *She* picked tomatoes for us first, then worked on the line in the cannery. Once she caught his eye. Probably had his way with her there in his office, too.

I never asked.

Can't say I'll be sad to see the place go up in flames, down to ashes. Good riddance, I say.

I taste the bitterness of his fornicating in my mouth, and I take another gulp of coffee to wash it down. You'd think after more than thirty years I'd be over it. I used to pray on it all the time. Ask God to take away my resentment. He never did. I used to pray

He would let me love Joseph the way I love my girls. The fruit of my husband's sin. That didn't happen either. Not that I don't love Joseph, because I do. In my own way. Any woman loves a baby she walked the boards with at night when he had a fever, the boy who brings her home a Christmas ornament made of a paper cup with his picture glued on it. The boy who calls her "Mama."

I wonder if Big Joe ever laid with another woman. There was talk in his younger years. But if there was ever any truth to it, I never saw it. And Mrs. Brodie never spoke of it. Not even when our Little Joe come walking into the kitchen carrying that little black baby wrapped up in that blanket with the teddy bears all over it. I burned that blanket. Threw it right in the old wood stove we used to have in the kitchen.

He was such a sweet thing. Joseph. Scrawny and small. Not like my girls who came out all plump and pink. And he never cried. Not like Abby and Celeste. I swear, I think they both screamed for the first year of their life. I remember looking at Abby one night thinking I understood how a mother could smother her baby with a pillow. Just to make them stop that racket. Not that I was ever tempted. But I understood it.

I smile thinking about the feel of Joseph in my arms. I hated that little baby so much. Hated Little Joe for bringing him home when the mother died. But Joseph found some way of wiggling into my heart until one day I realized I didn't care what color he was or who the mama had been who birthed him. Far as I was concerned, he was mine. Funny, he's the only one of them who calls me Mom.

I finish my sandwich and my coffee and get up to straighten Mrs. Brodie's blanket. I let down the shades so the bright light doesn't hit her in the face. Then I stand over her and look down. "Brought you something." I point at the teacup and saucer I set in the middle of the pill bottles on the nightstand. "That old teacup you like. Thought you might . . ."

I don't finish my thought, because it seems silly, now. I brought it down because she always loved that old teacup. Never drank tea or coffee out of it. Just kept it on her dresser. Put earrings and such in it sometimes. I thought about bringing in one of her books, too. Mrs. Brodie was always a reader. We've got books floor to ceiling in the living room. Had to have bookshelves built in. And books in her bedroom and on the front and back stair landings. And under beds and in closets. But I thought she'd rather have the teacup. In case she opens her eyes. She'll see it. Because I don't reckon she'll be reading anymore. Not on this earth, she won't.

I turn the handle on the teacup. It's got a stamp on the bottom. MADE IN ENGLAND. I don't know where she got it; she's had it as long as I've been here. "Nurse's coming later," I tell her. "Just to listen to your heartbeat and such." I hesitate. "She says your breathing might get funny. That you might get restless. If you do, I've got medicine for you. It'll calm your nerves. Comes in a dropper like we use to give the cats their wormer. So you don't have to worry about swallowing a pill or anything." I'm quiet for a second. The whole house is quiet.

"Sarah's been asking me questions all morning. Abby's girl. About you. Wanted to know your maiden name." I stare at the wallpaper, fighting the lump in my throat. "I feel bad, Mrs. Brodie. I don't remember it. I know I must have known it. Once upon a time."

I sigh and pick up my empty coffee cup and the sandwich plate. More dishes to wash. Always more dishes to be washed. "She's picking through the old photo albums. The ones you put together. I don't know why she's all of a sudden so interested. But who knows the ways of a teenage girl?" I give a little laugh. "The sweet Lord knows I was an odd one at her age." When I was fifteen, I got the notion in my head to run away. I was going to go to Hollywood and be an actress like Julie Christie. Mrs. Brodie had taken me to the movies for my birthday, and that was when I saw Julie Christie in *Doctor Zhivago.* She was so beautiful up on that big picture screen. We had gone all the way across the bay to Baltimore. Mrs. Brodie took me out to eat in a fancy restaurant and shopping, too, but the movie was the best part.

I never got the nerve to run away, but I dreamed about it for years. Until Little Joe and I married, and he got me in the family way.

I slowly make my way to the door. My feet aren't too bad off today, but I woke up with a stiff hip. At the door I turn back to her. "Soaking chicken in buttermilk to fry up for supper tonight. Just the way you taught me. Having baking powder biscuits and limas. Joseph is coming. And Little Joe promised to be home on time. So the whole family will be here." I look at her thin white hair and remember the color it used to be. Same color as Abby's, pretty near. Prettiest

120

hair I ever saw. That's the thing I remember most from the day Mrs. Brodie came for me at the orphanage.

"Sorry you can't have any. The chicken. But you'll be able to smell it, I guess. If you can smell anything . . ." I fall quiet because I feel silly saying that. I know I'm just babbling. Chances are she can't hear me. But just in case she can . . .

"I'll be back to look in on you shortly," I say. I start to say "call me if you need something," but then I realize how stupid that is.

In the hallway, on the way to the kitchen, I poke my head in the living room. It's always been Mrs. Brodie's room more than mine, with all those bookshelves lining the walls and her knickknacks. Sarah's sitting on the floor in front of the brick fireplace, leaning over a picture album. She's got them stacked around her.

She glances up after a minute. "Birdie. You startled me. I didn't hear you." She waits, looking at me. Expecting something.

I run my thumb over the lip of the coffee mug, looking for something to say. "So . . . looking at family pictures."

"Mmm-hm." She nods and holds one up. "Is this Grandpop? Or is it Great-Grandpop? They look so much the same, I can't tell."

I walk into the living room to get a closer look, leaving the mug and plate on the end table. I've left my reader glasses somewhere. On the kitchen counter, likely. I wish I had them so I could get a better look. "Let me see."

I take the photo from her. It's a square one, the way they were printed in the fifties and sixties. "This is your great-granddad, all right. Big Joe. Before I knew him. Taken on that dock right out there." I point toward the bay, the lifeblood of the Brodie family since they came to the island in the 1600s. Back then they were farmers and fishermen, too.

I hold up the faded picture toward the light coming through the east windows. Big Joe's wearing dark pants and a white T-shirt, the arms rolled with a cigarette pack in one cuff. He's barefoot and wearing a smile that I imagine turned heads in his day. He was a good-looking man. Not plain like my Joe. He was a charmer, too, but not the pull-the-wool-over-your-eyes kind. The kind that made you feel as if you were pretty and smart . . . even though you knew you weren't. I always liked Big Joe. I took it hard when he fell dead of a heart attack.

I hand her back the photo. "Early 1950s,

from the look of him."

Sarah holds the photo in her hand, studying it. "Big Joe met Mom Brodie in New Jersey, right? At church?"

"1933 or '34. Revival meeting. They used to be big in those days."

"What's a revival meeting?"

I settle myself down on the edge of the sofa, liking the idea of talking to my granddaughter this way. Just the two of us. I don't remember ever talking to her like one person to another. Mostly we just talk about what she will and won't eat. Sometimes I tell her to bring down her dirty wash. "It's . . . like Sunday services, only bigger. Longer. We used to call them camp meetings. Someone would put up a big tent, and preachers would come and preach, and there would be singing and altar calls and . . . it was like a big party."

"A church party?" my gorgeous granddaughter asks.

I think on it. "Something like that. We used to have one every summer here on Brodie when I was a girl. Not just for locals. It was before there was the bridge. People would come in boats. Some would stay and sleep on the beach. Put up tents."

I loved the tent meetings. I looked forward to them all year round. Mrs. Brodie always made me a new dress for them. I got one every summer. And she'd roll my hair up in rags to make it curly. Or try to. Humidity never let me keep those curls, but I loved them the short time I had them. And Mrs. Brodie let me go hear every preacher. They had traveling preachers come through, like in the old days, they told me. I went to every singing, too. No cookin' or cleaning for me that week. Mrs. Brodie brought in girls out of the fields to work in the house.

"I was hoping I might find Mom Brodie's maiden name on one of these old pictures." Sarah picks another one up off a pile next to her bony knee. She's pretty all right, but could use some meat on her bones. Of course, she don't eat meat.

"You think Grandpop would know where her birth certificate or her marriage certificate is?" Sarah asks me.

"You can ask him come suppertime. But I know we haven't got any birth certificate. Burned up in a fire when she was a girl." I nod, remembering. Mrs. Brodie never shared much of her life before she came to Brodie, but she did tell me that once. "We're all going to have a big supper together," I tell Sarah, excited about the thought of seeing my children around the table again. Us a family again. It's too bad my grandson

124

Reed couldn't come. He's a good boy. Sweet. Smart as a whip, like his dad. Which makes him a bit of an odd duck. But that's okay. I'm a bit of an odd duck myself.

Spotting one of Mrs. Brodie's Hummel figurines cockeyed on the mantel behind Sarah, I get up and go to straighten it. There must be two dozen of them in this room, all staring me down. I never liked them much, but it made it easy to know what to get Mrs. Brodie for birthdays and Christmas. Little Joe always left gift-giving to me. I just used his credit card. I use his credit card for everything, even though I got one of my own now. With my own name on it and not his. What he doesn't know won't hurt him.

I give the little girl with the sheep staff on the mantel a push and she spins round to look at me. I glance down at the pile of photo albums, and a turquoise cover catches my eye. "Where'd you get this?" I ask. I reach down and snatch it up.

She shrugs, looking up at me. "I don't know. One of those shelves, I guess." She points to the bookcase against one wall. "What is it?"

I feel my heart all fluttery in my chest and sweat beads up over my upper lip. I've always been a sweater. It used to embarrass me in my younger years. Mrs. Brodie was always handing me a hanky from inside her sleeve and telling me to wipe my face. It doesn't bother me much anymore. It's not like I stink. I just get wet.

"It's mine," I hear myself say. I hold the scrapbook tight against my chest. It's my own fault she found it. I must have left it down here last time I was working on it, around when Mrs. Brodie took sick this last time. I don't know how I could have been so dumb as to leave it for just anybody to see. Of course it wouldn't have been likely anyone would have picked it up. Little Joe sure wouldn't have given two toots. But this one, my granddaughter. She's a nosy one.

"O . . . kayyy," Sarah says, drawing out the word, sounding like I'm talking crazy. She looks down at the picture album in her lap, and I feel like I've been dismissed. Mrs. Brodie used to do the same thing to me. When she was done talking to me, she'd just go back to what she was doing without a how-do-you-do.

"I don't like my stuff touched," I tell my granddaughter, and I turn around quick and walk right out of the living room, leaving my dirty dishes right on the end table. I don't stop 'til the book is tucked safe in my drawer under my nighties.

10
ABBY

I pull up next to my dad's new red truck in front of the old cannery and throw the pickup into park. The gears grind a little, but it's been doing that for at least a decade. It's got a three-on-the-tree. One of the last F-150s made with shift on the column. Drum says he imagines it's worth something. Not as if my dad would sell Old Blue. I grab the lunch sack off the seat and climb the rickety steps to the loading dock; the floorboards creak beneath my feet, and I wonder if they're even safe to walk on.

I hear a dog bark, and my father's black Labrador retriever comes barreling through a hole in a wall right for me. My dad's definitely nearby.

"Daddy?" I call as I walk through one of the open bays.

The dog keeps barking excitedly.

"Hey, Duke," I greet. This is Duke the Seventh. Daddy always has a black Lab; has since he was a kid. It goes everywhere with him in his truck. Sleeps on the floor beside his bed at night. Mom Brodie used to jokingly call the Dukes Daddy's black angel; she said she never worried about his safety, no matter what time of day or night or where he went on the island. One Lab dies; Daddy gets another. Always black, never yellow. And names him Duke.

The big black Lab makes a circle around me, barking another greeting, and then takes off again. This Duke is young, only two, and full of youthful puppy exuberance. He's big, too. Bigger than the last Duke, with a big, broad head and powerful hindquarters. He scatters bits of torn newspaper and other junk that litters the wood plank floor.

The cannery is where women once washed and cut tomatoes and put them into tin cans to be sealed and shipped to the mainland. The tomatoes came in this set of bay doors in the back in farm trucks from the fields and left canned, in cases, out the doors on the far side where the old docks are. The place is mostly empty now; everything salvageable has long been hauled off. There are a few splintered wooden crates, a broken lawn chair, which is clearly a recent addition, a truck tire of all things, and just some other worthless junk. But I remember, in my mind's eye, what the place looked like when I was kid. Long after this kind of hometown cannery had closed on the Eastern Shore, Daddy kept ours open. He said he had some families who had been working for the Brodies for five or six generations. Where would they go if there weren't tomatoes to pick and can?

I remember the rows of wooden tables where the women stood, in long aprons, peeling hot tomatoes. The tables were just cut from oak from the woods near our house and slapped together, but Drum and I managed to save one we found in the barn when we were first married and too poor to buy furniture. Eight-foot long and refinished, it's still the centerpiece of our dining room. I wouldn't part with it for the world.

I accidentally kick a rusty Fanta soda can with the toe of my flip-flop, and it startles me. "Daddy?" I call again, walking further into the open warehouse. A bird flutters over my head and flies out a hole in the roof. Duke has disappeared through a hole in the exterior wall, and I hear him in the distance barking. He barks at ducks constantly. Daddy says he got a dud with this one. Who ever heard of a dog raised on a Chesapeake Bay island that barks at ducks?

They're as common here as seagulls. Duke barks at them, too.

"Abby?" My dad comes out of the room on the far end of the building, once his office. He's wearing his ever-present green and yellow John Deere ball cap. "Girl!" he calls.

I hurry to him, dodging a piece of timber that's fallen from the ceiling and a pile of unidentifiable excrement. I throw my arms around him, and he squeezes me tightly. I rest my head on his shoulder. Daddy's shorter than I am, and round and soft and balding. He was never a good-looking man, even in his younger years, but I don't see the thin, gray hair, or the gut, or the fact that his dark eyes have faded. I see the man. I see his heart. And I see the happy childhood he gave me. I was always Daddy's girl and never attempted to hide it, and neither did he. I think he was always trying to make it up to me for the fact that Birdie didn't know how to be a mother, didn't know how to give me what I needed. What I wanted so desperately from her.

"Sorry I missed you last night, and again this morning. If I didn't know better, I'd think you were trying to stay out of the house."

He mumbles something like, "Don't want

to be underfoot."

I release my grip on him, reluctant to let go of the smell of him and his warmth. I think about the bluebird tattoo on his mother's thigh, and I know there's no way I can tell him. Ever. "I'm sorry about Mom Brodie, Daddy."

He nods and looks away, but not before I see him tear up. My daddy's a crier, which is funny because he's also the strongest man I've ever known. He's our rock. Always has been.

"I just hope the good Lord takes her fast," he says, pulling a neatly ironed and folded clean white handkerchief from his pocket. He's the only man I know who still uses white handkerchiefs. He might wear the same pair of work pants four days in a row, but he puts a clean handkerchief in his pocket every single morning. A clean, ironed handkerchief my mother's put in the top drawer of his old chifforobe. "I know she hates to be that way. She was never one to lie in bed, not even when she caught something."

My own eyes get teary. I hate to see my dad this way. Hurting. Knowing there's nothing I can do for him but be here for him. "She's not in pain," I tell him. "She just . . . seems like she's sleeping."

"She hasn't eaten a thing since we brought her home Monday. Hasn't taken any water in two days. Birdie tried to get her to drink —" He stops and starts again. "But she wouldn't." He wipes his eyes and then blows his nose with the handkerchief. "I can't imagine she can go long without water."

I press my lips together, looking into his lined, suntanned face. Mom Brodie says there's Native American in the Brodie line; she always said that was why the men tanned so dark. "I don't think it will be long," I whisper.

My father adored his father, but he had a special relationship with his mother. Maybe because they've lived together in the same house his whole life. Maybe because they're so much alike in so many ways. I don't know. But there's a bond between them that seems to go deeper than just mother and son. Mom Brodie used to tell me that *Brodies feel deep.* I never understood what she meant by that, but as I get older, I'm beginning to understand. We feel strongly about our convictions. We love hard. We're also too slow to forgive. No one can hold a grudge as long as a Brodie.

"Not long, Daddy," I say softly.

He sniffs, wipes his nose, and stuffs his handkerchief into his pocket. He looks up, taking in the big, dilapidated building around us. "I'm letting the fire department burn her down. It's not safe. I run some teen boys out of here a couple of nights ago, again. Partying. They do it all the time. I find beer cans. Cigarette butts." He looks up over our heads. "Ceiling comes down on them, someone gets hurt, I'd never forgive myself."

"They shouldn't be here, Daddy. There're no trespassing signs up everywhere."

He shakes his head. "Time it came down. Long past time."

My gaze drifts past him, and I spot a faded wooden sign that's at least six feet long and three high. *Brodie* is painted in black and gold on it. It's leaning against the office wall. It had hung on the wall outside on the loading dock for longer than I've been alive. "You found the sign." I'm filled with an overwhelming sense of nostalgia.

"Was turned facedown on the floor," he says. "Thought it was long gone."

"What are you going to do with it?" I ask.

"Thought I'd put it in my office back at the house, or maybe hang it on the back porch. Against the house."

I nod and then hold up the brown paper sack. "Birdie sent your lunch."

"What is it?" he asks. We walk side-by-side through the building, toward the back on the bay.

"Egg salad."

He makes a face as we walk through a hole in the wall big enough to drive one of our trucks through. The sunshine is bright and hot, and it sparkles off the surface of the bay. In the distance, I can see the bridge that now links Brodie to the rest of the world. Something I'm not entirely sure has been a good thing. Because along with the positives, like better prices in the grocery store and improved access to medical care, negatives have made their way across that bridge: drugs, crime, a loss of innocence that came so naturally in a place as isolated as Brodie Island had been.

The smell of the bay is rich and briny. I see Duke bounding along the reedy shore, his big paws splashing in the water.

"I hate egg salad," Daddy says.

We both laugh. My mother likes egg salad. She doesn't care that Daddy and I don't. That none of us do. But she never just comes out and says we're getting it whether we like it or not. She just keeps making egg salad sandwiches. It's a little joke Daddy and I have shared for years and years. She makes him egg salad sandwiches, and he feeds them to Duke.

"There are Little Debbies in there, too. And a Granny Smith, I think."

We walk to the end of the loading dock, and he leans on a sun and wind-bleached rail. I stand beside him and look out over the bay. In the cannery's heyday, boats came in and were loaded with cases of Brodie canned tomatoes. The boats carried them to the mainland where the cases were loaded on trucks and shipped up and down the Eastern Shore of Maryland and Virginia.

"Celeste said she saw you at The Gull last night."

Daddy pulls an oatmeal cream pie out of the brown bag and hands it to me. I take it. He pulls the second one out and tears the cellophane and takes a big bite. I nibble on mine. They're pretty sweet. Too sweet. But they remind me of all the good things in life, and I savor each oaty, creamy bite.

"I'm worried about her," he says.

I frown and watch two female mallard ducks paddle in and out of the reeds near the end of the crumbling dock that no one has used in twenty years. I love talking to my dad, but not about my sister. And we talk about her a lot.

"She doesn't look good," he continues. "She's drinking too much. And she's . . . she's sad, Abby."

I want to tell him she just puts on that act for him. To get him to feel sorry for her. To get him to give her money without having to ask. But I know what he's talking about. It's not all an act. I've noticed it over the last year or so. It seems as if it takes more energy for her to pretend as if everything is fine. As if she's successful and happy and still beautiful. And not aging like the rest of us.

"You know how she is. She gets sad sometimes." I shrug. I don't want him to worry about Celeste. He's got enough to deal with, with Mom Brodie dying. "She takes medication for it."

My sister's been on and off anti-depressants half her life. Drum and I sometimes joke that we'd have to take them if we lived her life too, but it's not as funny as it used to be. Her wild, unpredictable behavior went over much better when she was in her twenties, and even in her thirties. The drinking, the random men. Now it's just . . . It makes *me* sad.

"I've been telling her it's time to make changes," he says, chewing on a mouthful of oatmeal pie. "I think maybe . . . she ought to come home to Brodie. Live with us a spell."

I laugh out loud. "Celeste would rather be

six-foot under alongside Mom Brodie than come home, Daddy. Than to admit she's beaten and live with you and Birdie."

He thinks on that for a long minute. One of the ducks disappears under the dock, and I wait for her to reappear.

"Would that be such a bad thing, living here?" he asks.

I glance over at him. He's not talking about Celeste now. He's talking about me. And Drum's dream of retiring. Here. On Brodie Island.

I choose my words carefully before responding. This isn't the time to talk about me picking up my whole life and moving to Brodie. "I don't think she belongs here; she never did. She needs the bright footlights of the city . . . even if she's not standing in them anymore."

He exhales. "I'm afraid she's not going to take the news well."

I'm still eating my oatmeal cream pie. Daddy's finished his and is crumpling the cellophane wrapper in his hand. It crackles between his fingers. I watch Duke lumber toward us. He's got a two-foot-long, wet stick in his mouth.

"What news?"

He exhales again, loudly. It's his sign that I'm not going to like what he has to say. Or *someone* isn't going to like it. I've always teased him that he'd be a lousy poker player; he's got the worst poker face ever. Unlike my mother, who can smile sweet as pie and curse you under her breath. At least her version of cursing.

"Clancy came by the diner this morning. Had coffee with me."

The family attorney. The only attorney in Brodie. He's got an office in the back of his house just off Main Street, the same office his father used before him. The Jacobses have been on the island since the nineteenth century. Been lawyers and judges and law enforcement for just as long.

"Uh-huh. What'd Clancy have to say?" You have to be patient to have a conversation with my dad. He takes his time to say what he wants to say. And when he speaks, he speaks slowly, as if considering each word. He talks like a man whose family has been here since Maryland was a colony, with an accent that's fading fast on the mainland. When Drum and I first started dating, he was fascinated by the Eastern Shore inflection I barely noticed. He did a little research and discovered that men and women in this area spoke in a very similar manner to men and women in Cornwall in the UK. Or rather the way they spoke there three hundred years ago. Somehow the Eastern Shore and Brodie Island have remained a capsule of that time and place where their settlers came from in the seventeenth century.

"Clancy wanted to warn me that Mama came in to see him nine, maybe ten months ago."

"*Warn* you?" I wait, still eating my oatmeal pie. When my dad doesn't want to have to tell me something, it takes him even longer to get it out. Duke comes to stand in front of me. He drops the stick, looks up at us, and picks it up again. "I'm not playing fetch with you," I say. "Not right now, boy."

He drops the stick again, seeming to understand exactly what I'm saying. He tilts his black head at me and looks up with big, puppy eyes. "I'm not playing," I repeat. Then I toss the last bite of my snack cake high in the air. The Lab leaps and catches it in his mouth, midair.

I look at my dad. "So Mom Brodie went to see Clancy. Professionally, you mean?"

Daddy nods. He's got the apple out of the bag now, and he's rolling it between his hands. He has small hands, hands scarred and tanned from years of hard outside work. I love my dad's hands; they aren't any bigger than mine, just thicker. Meatier.

"And what did he want to warn you about?"

"Changed her will," he says.

"Okay." I lift one shoulder. I recall her whispering to me about her pin money. "Her prerogative," I say. "And I don't know what her will said before."

He looks down at Duke, who, realizing the snack cake is gone, picks up his stick and walks away with it.

I wait on my dad.

"She didn't ask me my opinion," he says finally. "She just did it. And she didn't tell me once it was done."

"So you didn't know she'd made changes." I'm a little surprised, and I imagine he is too. Maybe a little hurt. Mom Brodie and Daddy were always a team. He never made major business decisions without consulting her, after Grandpop died. And she always consulted him on anything beyond simple household matters, which were always her domain.

I frown, knowing I'm creating wrinkles across my forehead every time I do it. Permanent wrinkles. "You know that's not really legal. Clancy telling you Mom Brodie's personal, legal business."

"He knows she's dying. Everybody on Brodie knows it. I was at the diner an hour

140

later than usual this morning, so many people coming by to pay their respects."

"Jeez, Daddy. She's not even dead yet," I mutter.

"They don't mean any harm by it. Everybody loves your grandmother. Respects her. She did a lot of good here. For the people of Brodie."

I'm fascinated by the sense of responsibility Mom Brodie and my father feel for the people who live and work on Brodie Island. And not just the people who work for us. For anyone who makes their life here. I suppose my mother feels it too, but I've always gotten the sense she feels an obligation to them, not a responsibility. It's not the same thing.

Again, I wait. I wish I had Duke's stick to prod my father into just spitting out what he has to say.

"She . . . Mama . . . I guess she thinks Celeste isn't responsible."

"She isn't, Daddy."

"With money."

I suddenly get a bad feeling, realizing where this is going. "Oh, no," I murmur.

He nods. "She cut her out. Your sister." He doesn't look at me when he says it.

"*Out* out?" I ask.

"Out out," he repeats.

I lean on the rickety rail, copying his stance: forearms against the splintered wood, legs apart, shoulders hunched.

"The way Clancy tells it, Celeste isn't getting a cent. Just . . . some pieces of old jewelry."

"Maybe they're worth something," I say hopefully, thinking my sister would run, not walk to the nearest pawnshop. There's no such thing as sentimental value to her. No such thing as sentiment.

My father stares out at the bay. "Good chunk of change. In the will."

Now I'm curious. I can't help myself. "Who . . ." I feel guilty, even before I speak the words, so I swallow. "You think we should wait and talk about this after . . . after she's gone?"

He just keeps staring out at the bay. A skipjack, one of the few commercial sailing ships left, glides across the water. It looks like the *Miss Claire.* Most of the skipjacks left in the Chesapeake Bay dock at Deal Island, nearby. Skipjacks are commercial fishing vessels that dredge for oysters in the winter. They only still exist because of an old law that prevents motorboats from dredging the Maryland state oyster fishery. Daddy says it's only a matter of time before the law changes, and that will be the end of the skipjacks.

I watch the *Miss Claire* move slowly through the dark, green-gray water. She's sloop-raked with a boom the length of the boat and a sharply raked mast. Her mainsail is a simple triangle with a jib mounted on the bowsprit. The sailboat's strange construction allows for enough power, even in light winds, to dredge for the oysters.

In the far distance, beyond the *Miss Claire,* we can see the shore of the mainland. When I'm here, the mainland, the real world seems far away and not quite . . . real. Drum says Brodie Island is the most enchanted place he's ever been, a place and people almost untouched by time. I tell him he's touched in the head.

"Do you think Celeste was expecting money?" I ask my dad. But I already know the answer.

He looks at me. Tugs on the brim of his ball cap. "What do you think?"

I sigh and stand up. "You going to tell her now or wait until after Mom Brodie dies?"

"I'll wait; it will mean holding off the storm."

I can't help myself. I smile. My sister can throw a hell of a fit. She doesn't just scream; she throws things. Mostly accusations, but occasionally a shoe or a glass of iced tea. A disagreement over whose turn it is to use the washing machine can quickly become a discussion of who got more candy in his or her Christmas stocking in 1985. And how I'm Birdie and Daddy's favorite. Always have been. Which isn't true. I'm Daddy's favorite, but Birdie can barely tolerate me.

"You could talk to Birdie about when you ought to tell Celeste. She's pretty good about measuring Celeste's temperature."

"I don't like to bother Birdie with such things."

I hesitate. My parents have been married for almost fifty years. Who am I to tell them how a marriage should be? But I just feel like it needs to be said. Even if I'm wrong. And that's one of the best things about my father. Even when you're wrong, he's willing to listen to you. "You know, Daddy, when Mom Brodie dies, you're not going to have her to talk things over with anymore. Birdie's going to be the head of the house. She . . . in some ways she's going to have to take over Mom Brodie's position on the island. She'll be the matriarch of the family. You need to start including her in things. In decisions you make."

My dad looks at me, and I think he's going to agree with me. But instead, he says, "You best get home. Your mother might need help with Mama."

I sigh. I don't feel sorry for my mother often; she creates her own discontent most of the time. But for once, I feel like Daddy's wrong. Drum and I talk about everything. Sometimes we argue, but even when we know an argument is coming, neither of us avoids a subject. It's the way we've kept our marriage sound.

But I don't argue. That time and place thing. And this isn't it. "You'll be home for supper, right? Sarah's been going through old photographs. She's been asking a lot of questions about . . . Mom Brodie," I say carefully.

I have no intention of telling him about his mother's tattoo. And I know Sarah won't either. Like her namesake, she's a woman to be trusted with a secret. Drum always says she's the one to trust with the knowledge of where the bodies are buried.

"Only natural. A girl gets to be her age, and they start trying to figure out where they belong in the world. Best way to do that is to know where you come from. I'll answer her questions best I can. You know Mama never talked much about growin' up." He covers my hand on the railing with his. "Thank you for dropping things at your place and coming. Glad you could be here.

It's what she wants. The way she wants to go. All of us gathered 'round her." His voice is thick with emotion, and I'm afraid he's going to start to cry again. Which means I'll cry.

"Me too," I say, blinking back tears. I give him a quick kiss on his weathered, farmer's cheek and head for the pickup.

11
Sarah Agnes

He's waiting for me at the foot of the Ferris wheel, just like I knew he would be. *"Bonjour,"* I say to him, my face feeling hot.

"Bonjour." He smiles, looking into my eyes as if I'm the only girl on the midway. The carnival is busy, despite the late hour. "Would you like to ride?" he asks me, holding my hand.

Not trusting myself to speak because my words sound all breathy, I just nod. Standing close to Henri like this, I can smell his aftershave, and it makes me light-headed. Is this what love feels like?

He turns to a man standing nearby, smoking a cigarette. "Hey, Spotty. Can you send us up?"

Spotty looks me over the way the boys from town looked at me this afternoon, only he makes me feel a little uncomfortable. He's a tall man, a long drink of water, Papa would call him. And covered with freckles.

Like me. Only his hair's not red. It's blond and shaggy. He's wearing red pants. I've never seen a man in red pants. "Sure this is a good idea, Hank?" he asks, his cigarette dangling from the corner of his mouth, bobbing up and down. He's still staring at me. "She looks young."

"How old are you, baby? Seventeen, right?" Henri asks, draping his arm over my shoulder.

"Eighteen my next birthday." My voice sounds squeaky now. I look down so he can't see my eyes, but I feel my face growing hot from the lie.

"See. Almost eighteen," Henri says.

"Fine. Just don't let Jacko catch you."

I look up at Henri, suddenly frightened for him. I don't want him to get in trouble. Not on account of me. "We don't have to. I don't have to ride," I tell him.

"It's fine. Spotty's a worrywart. *Oui,* Spotty?" Henri pulls the long lever on the Ferris wheel that's slowly turning over our heads, and it slowly comes to a halt. There are a couple of passengers, but their cars are nearly at the top. Henri helps me into the blue car. It swings as we get in, and Henri reaches across my lap to secure the metal bar. When he moves back, he does it slowly, looking into my eyes. And I see his.

The prettiest eyes I've ever seen.

Then Henri gives Spotty a thumbs-up, and the car lurches and swings, and suddenly we're moving up, up in the air.

"He called you Hank," I say, looking up earnestly at him. "Why'd Spotty call you Hank, Henri?"

Henri shrugs. "These birds, they don't speak *Français.* You know." He brings his finger beneath my chin and tips it up so he's looking right into my eyes. His breath smells . . . mediciney. "But you, *mon amour . . .*"

High above Bakersville, the bright colored lights of the carnival flashing in the darkness, I get my first kiss. It's too amazing for words. Utterly heavenly. And it's such a doozy that I'm still holding Henri's hand, staring up into his eyes when we hop off the Ferris wheel. Then we stroll down the midway, crowded with men and women and a few children who've come to Bakersville from miles around. I don't see anyone I recognize; most of the people have to be out-of-towners so late in the evening. But I wouldn't care if someone I knew *did* see me. I'm not like Cora. I'm not like anyone in this town. I'm not afraid like they are. Afraid of everything. Which is why I don't belong here.

Henri buys me cotton candy, and he plays a game where he throws metal rings onto wooden sticks. He makes the hardest throw and wins me a Kewpie doll with a painted blue dress. I hesitate to take her when he holds her out to me; I don't want Henri to think I'm a child. But she has rouged lips so I decide it's okay to take her. We walk by several other booths where you can play all sorts of games and win fancy prizes. Henri knows everyone, and he waves and greets the people working there. They all seem to like him.

I feel like I'm spinning in circles, even when we're walking hand-in-hand straight through the trampled grass. The colored lights on the game booths blink on and off, and men call out to passersby, trying to entice men and boys to win prizes for their gals. Then we come to a big red and white-striped tent where men are lined up along a rope. Loud, racy music comes from inside the tent.

"What's in there?" I ask.

"Girls." He grins. "You know." He shakes his hips.

Then he laughs, and I laugh like I know what he's talking about, even though I don't. I know from the sound of Henri's voice and the sounds of the men in line that neither my papa nor Mrs. Hanfland would be the people to question. And something tells me Cora won't know, her being the daughter of a preacher.

Just past the tent, Henri backs me up against a metal pole and kisses me again. His kiss is long and hard, and, when I pull away, I still taste his tongue that touched mine. "I should go," I tell him.

"Not yet. Come see my place." He points into the darkness. "I got a little jag juice." He winks at me and kisses me again quick on the lips.

"Jag juice?" I say.

"Foot juice. Giggle water?"

Then it dawns on me. He means whiskey. Or some kind of hard drink. That's what I smelled on his breath. Tasted when he kissed me. Prohibition is still the law of the land, though my papa is always reading from the newspaper about how people say it's not going to last much longer. My father doesn't drink, far as I know. I don't know anyone who does except for Old Mr. Clopper who's the town drunk and sometimes sleeps on our back porch if Granny doesn't catch him.

"I should go," I say, hugging my Kewpie doll to my chest. It's gotten cold out, and I wish I'd been smart enough to wear my

151

coat. "Home." But I don't want to go home. Not ever again. "How long . . ." I look into Henri's eyes, even though I can't really see them in the dark. I don't need any giggle juice. I already feel giggly inside. "How much longer will you be here? The carnival?"

"Hard to say. Day or two. We pull up on Jacko's whim. He runs the joint. He's the big cheese." Henri pulls a cigarette from the brim of his cap. "Fag?" he asks me.

I shake my head. "But you'll be here tomorrow? Tomorrow night? Right?"

"Likely," he tells me. He strikes a match, and for a moment I see his face clearly. And I know I can't live without him.

"I'll come tomorrow night. After my family's asleep."

"I don't want you to get into trouble, *mon cher.*" He says it with a lazy sound to his voice. I know he says it because it's the right thing; of course he doesn't want me to get into trouble. But I also know he wants me to come back. That he feels the same way about me that I feel about him.

We're in love.

Henri exhales cigarette smoke and then leans down and kisses me again, wrapping his arms around me, and I think to myself, *Take me with you.*

12
CELESTE

I slip into Abby's bedroom after I see her shut the bathroom door down the hall. My niece is seated cross-legged on the bed, her laptop in front of her. "What's up, Pussycat?" Then I see that she's wearing a mink stole over her skinny-ass shoulders. Real mink. "Hey! Where'd you get that?"

She looks up. "What?" She looks down at herself. "Oh, this old thing?" She grins and looks at me again. "Cool, isn't it? I found it in the hall closet downstairs. I was looking for pictures of Mom Brodie. There are plenty of pictures of her, hundreds. She must have liked having her picture taken. But not a single one of her in a bathing suit or even shorts."

"That's because she never wore a bathing suit or shorts. Give it to me." I hold out my hand. "It's mine."

Sarah slips the mink stole off her shoulders. "Birdie said it was Mom Brodie's.

Look. It's got her name embroidered inside it."

She reveals the silk inside lining of the brown stole, and, sure enough, Mom Brodie's name is on it. Like every other ef-ing thing in this house. On this island. Even when my grandmother's name isn't embroidered on something, everyone acts like it's hers. She always acted like it was all hers: the house, the land, the people who worked for us. Like she was Cleopatra or something. I once tried out for the part of Cleopatra. Off-off Broadway. I had planned to play the part Sarah Brodie style. I didn't get the part. But if I had, and I should have (I think the director was intimidated by my beauty), I'd have nailed it.

I never understood why my grandmother was so high and mighty. Or why Birdie always thought she was all that and a bag of chips and has always kowtowed to her. I mean, Sarah Agnes, she came here with nothing. Everything she became was because of my grandfather. Because of the Brodies. I wonder if Birdie would be so smitten if she knew about the tattoo on Mom Brodie's thigh. That might take her down a notch in my mother's eyes.

I snatch up the stole. "She gave it to me."

My niece wrinkles her gorgeous freckled

nose, and I want to yank on the pile of tangled hair on top of her head. I want to yank a little out and see if I can somehow weave it into my own hair.

"Your nose is growing, Celeste. Birdie said I could have it. She said Mom Brodie wanted me to have it because it's got my name in it."

I slip the mink around my shoulders, and it feels good despite the heat that won't let up today. "You're not a Brodie."

She closes her laptop. "Am, too. Sarah Brodie MacLean. It's on my birth certificate. And I've got it embroidered on my field hockey letter jacket."

I like the fact that my fifteen-year-old niece won't take any crap off me. "You should speak better to your elders," I tell her.

She ignores me and flips open the laptop again, looking down. "That mink isn't yours. It's mine. Birdie said so, and you better not walk out of the house with it. Guess what I found?"

"What?" I sit down on the edge of the bed. My feet are killing me. Brodie Island black dirt is not conducive to four-inch heels. I should have ditched them when I went into town, but you never know who you might

meet. Even at the mini-mart, getting cigarettes.

"Look at all these pictures of old tattoos.
Tattoos women used to get." Sarah brings
up photos on the screen. "These are from
the twenties and thirties."

"I didn't even know women got tattoos in
those days," I say, fascinated by the images
that scroll by under Sarah's skillful thumb.
"Find anything like the garter?"

"Not yet. But I'm thinking it has to be
from the thirties. Wouldn't you think?
Before she married Great-Grandpop?"

She glances up at me, and I realize something. When my niece looks at me, she
doesn't see me for what I really am: old and
wrinkled and balding. A failure. She sees
me as someone else. She sees more than I
really am, ever will be, and for some reason
it hurts. I feel like I'm disappointing her.
The same way I disappoint all the Brodies.

"What year were they married?" I ask,
fluffing my hair. The humidity is bad for it.
It's so thin that the moisture in the air
makes the carefully constructed hair tent I
build collapse. I've been thinking long and
hard on it, and I've decided that with the
money I inherit when Mom Brodie kicks
the bucket, I'm going to get hair plugs. The
real thing. I've already done the research. I

want a face-lift, too, of course. And a boob job. But plugs are expensive. I'll do the plugs first; a full head of hair is what I need to get my foot back in the door. My acting career's stalled, but I know with a good tune-up, I'll shine at my next audition. I've already got an appointment with a plastic surgeon in Manhattan. He's supposed to be some kind of doctor to the stars. Celebrities fly from Hollywood to New York to have their work done, just to get away from the paparazzi.

"Not sure when they were married," Sarah says, not looking up. "Birdie wasn't exactly forthcoming in her answers. If Mom says it's okay, I'm going to ask Grandpop if I can look through Mom Brodie's important papers. There's got to be a marriage certificate or baptism record or something." She keeps tapping away on the keyboard. "Right? They're something an old lady would save."

"Why are you asking your mother's permission?" I slide the mink off one shoulder, taking my shirt and bra strap with it, and gaze at myself in the wavy mirror over the old bureau. It would look great over a glitzy, strapless dress. I can imagine myself dancing in some fancy place. Maybe with the old coot, Bartholomew. He seemed very interested last night. "It's time you start standing on your own two feet," I tell my niece. "Thinking for yourself. Acting on your own."

She glances at me over the laptop screen. "I don't want to cause any trouble. Everyone's upset enough as it is . . . you know, with Mom Brodie dying."

I roll my eyes and bare the other shoulder. I definitely need a spray tan. And maybe hair extensions. Women always look young with longer hair: Halle Berry, Sofia Vergara, Jennifer Garner. And they look hot. With longer hair, I bet I wouldn't have to let old coots buy me drinks. I could let the young, hot guys buy me drinks. "I'm telling you, it's time you were an independent woman," I tell my niece. "You've got a mind of your own; use it."

She returns her attention to her laptop. "Mom and Dad still pay to maintain this mind."

Christ, she sounds like Abby. Always so *practical.* And such a goody-goody. It's annoying as hell.

My cell phone, tucked in my padded bra, vibrates, and I check it. I smile when I see who the text is from. I can't believe the old coot actually texted me. I wasn't sure he even knew how to use that fancy latest model iPhone of his.

"Who's that?" my niece asks.

"A rich old man who wants to whisk me off to Europe," I tell her, texting something coy back.

"You're such a liar."

"Sarah Brodie!" My sister walks into the bedroom. "Don't speak to your aunt Celeste like that." She looks at me. "Daddy home yet?"

I stick my tongue out at my niece and then turn to my sister. "He's with Mom Brodie. Birdie said supper's in ten."

Abby pulls her T-shirt over her head, and I stare at her. She's got an amazing body for a forty-five-year-old. Put a different head on her, and she could pass for thirty. And her face doesn't look a day over thirty-five; I must have gotten her crow's-feet. I look away, disgusted. Why was I the one who got the bad genes? Standing in my bra like that, I look like Mom Brodie, minus the tattoo. My skin's all wrinkling and lumpy, bumpy. No matter how much I lay off the carbs, I've got more cellulite in my little finger than my sister's got on her whole body.

"Little warm to be wearing Mom Brodie's mink, isn't it?" Abby asks me.

"She's trying to steal it from me." Sarah doesn't look up from the laptop. "Birdie

159

said it's mine. Mom Brodie wants me to have it because it has my name in it."

Abby pulls a white T-shirt down over her head. "You'll wear a mink stole, but you won't eat chicken?"

Sarah wrinkles up her nose like her mother's and says the most absurd thing. "I didn't kill the mink."

"You didn't kill the chicken frying downstairs, either."

I look at my sister, then my niece, then my sister again, enjoying their little tiff. Abby always stays so calm with her kids. I'd want to slap them. Often. So it's probably just as well I never had children.

"She can't do that, can she?" I get up from the bed, wincing. I consider going native and heading downstairs to supper barefoot like my sister always does. Let the open blisters on my heels dry out. "Birdie can't just give away Mom Brodie's shit."

"Do you really want that old mink stole?" My sister tosses her dirty shirt in a pile next to the door. "Sarah, could you go downstairs and see if Birdie needs help getting supper on the table?"

My niece looks up eagerly, but doesn't move. "You guys going to fight?"

Abby cuts her eyes at her daughter. She doesn't say a word. Sarah takes one look at

160

her, closes the laptop, and leaves the room, shutting the bedroom door behind her.

"*Are* we having a fight?" I ask my sister, thinking I must have missed something.

"Not to my knowledge." Abby is fiddling with her earring. "I just want to make it clear that we understand each other. We're not telling Birdie or Daddy about the tattoo. We're not telling anyone."

I don't say anything. I don't feel strongly about it one way or the other, but I don't like to commit too soon. Or be accused of being a traitor later, unless it's absolutely necessary. I kick off my heels and sigh with pleasure as I sink my feet that are as knobby as Mom Brodie's into the ugly blue rug. "You said that this morning."

"And you didn't agree you'd keep your mouth shut." Abby's tone takes me off guard. "Nothing good can come from telling them, and it could be . . . hurtful."

"You mean they might realize that Mom Brodie wasn't the saint they think she is."

Abby hovers near the door. "I don't think Birdie ever thought Mom Brodie was a saint. They were always at each other's throats."

"Sure, to her face. But behind her back," I say, "she was always, Mrs. Brodie this and Mrs. Brodie that. You know, I never got why

161

Birdie called her Mrs. Brodie. I always thought it was weird."

My sister crosses her arms over her chest. She looks concerned. But I get the feeling it's not about how our mother addressed our grandmother, or even the tattoo. Adjusting the stole over my shoulders, I walk to the old bureau with the big oval mirror on it, like I'm strolling the runway. I could have been a model, if I'd been a little taller. I've got the walk. I pick up a compact of cream blush. I pop it open and add a little to the apples of my cheeks. "Birdie said you took Daddy his lunch. I came back from getting my cigarettes, and you were gone. I was going to go with you."

"I didn't know I was supposed to wait for you. Didn't you have lunch with Joseph?"

I learned a long time ago that you don't have to answer a question, just because it's asked. "Daddy say anything about the will?" I ask, glancing at Abby in the mirror.

She starts chewing on her bottom lip. She hasn't learned my little trick concerning unwelcome questions. "He did."

I turn around so quickly that the stole slips off one shoulder. "And?"

"He just said that Mom Brodie updated it recently and that Clancy said it's good to go. Probate won't be a big deal."

I smile and turn back to the mirror, patting one cheek and then the other to plump them up. "Sounds like we're getting our money quick, doesn't it?"

Abby opens the bedroom door. "Let's go have supper. I hear Joseph." She hesitates in the doorway. "Put the mink back in the closet, Celeste. It's Sarah's."

"*Hiss,* says the mother cat." I pretend to bare claws.

Abby doesn't even smile. "There's a list on the refrigerator of stuff she wants us to have. Who gets what. I can't believe you missed it. She left you the diamond stud earrings."

"As long as I don't get that stupid frog bowl."

"Oh, you're getting the frog bowl, all right." Abby laughs and walks out of the bedroom. "I told her you wanted it."

13
BIRDIE

"Heavenly Lord, be with us now . . ."

While everyone else's head is bowed and Little Joe is saying grace, I peek at my family gathered around the table. Joe sits at the head of the table not looking like himself without his ball cap. Of course Mrs. Brodie's chair is empty. But everyone else is here: my Abby, my Celeste, my Joseph, and my Sarah. I wish Reed, Abby's boy, were here, too. He's a good boy. I don't understand him. He's like a boy from outer space to me, but he's sweet like his father, and he never looks at me like the rest of the Brodies do. He never expects anything from me, which means I never disappoint him. Reed's needs have always been easy, ever since he was a baby. As long as he had a dry diaper and a full tummy, he was content. Joseph was mostly that way, too. And Little Joe is, too.

So maybe it's girls that always expect too much.

My gaze drifts to Mrs. Brodie's empty chair as Little Joe asks God the Father to look over us in our time of need and give us comfort in knowing that Mrs. Brodie will soon be with Him. Mrs. Brodie's chair is almost glowing, and I blink, knowing it must be my imagination, or a lightbulb in the lamp overhead that needs changing. I've always been a God-fearing woman, heavy on the fearing part, but honestly, I've never felt much like He was with me. That Mrs. Brodie's chair is lit up shouldn't surprise me. I have no doubt God is with her. Always has been. It's why she's lived such a blessed life.

I keep staring at her chair from under my lashes. I came close to sitting in it when everyone walked into the kitchen and sat down for supper. I stood right there in the middle of the kitchen, bowl of mashed potatoes in my hand, and stared that chair down. Because it's mine now. Or will be. It's my rightful place, next to my husband. My whole life I've waited for Mrs. Brodie to leave it to me, and finally it's happening. But now I'm scared. I don't even know if I want the stupid chair. Especially with it glowing like that.

"Amen."

I don't realize grace is over for a second, not until I hear the clink of a serving spoon in a bowl. I drop my hands to my lap and look up, feeling guilty. I should have been praying and not gathering wool. No one seems to have noticed. They never do.

Everyone starts talking at once, which is the way my family does. I only get bits and pieces. Celeste says something to Sarah, and Abby's putting her two cents in while talking to her daddy. Then Celeste is complaining about the skin on the chicken and saying she wants a piece of baked breast. "Isn't there a baked breast?" she asks no one in particular.

My granddaughter says, " 'Tis but a tub. Sit." Just blurts it out. I know it's one of those silly word things she likes, but I'm a little worried about the girl, and I have half a mind to talk to Abby about her. Fifteen-year-old girls don't just say " 'Tis but a tub. Sit." I wonder if she needs to see a doctor.

"Dad, I ordered the part for the combine." Joseph is putting two pieces of fried chicken on his plate. Thighs. He likes dark meat like me. My favorite is wings, though. Nobody else likes them, so I always get the wings. He looks across the table at me. "Chicken smells great, Mom. I've been looking forward to this all week. Think you've outdone yourself."

I look down at my empty plate, feeling my cheeks get warm under the praise. "Biscuit?" I say, picking up the plate and holding it out for Little Joe.

He takes two.

"Overnight it?" Little Joe asks, dishing out a heaping spoonful of peas onto his plate.

"Yeah, but shipping's free," Joseph says.

"Have you got any real vegetables in the fridge, Birdie?" Celeste asks. "Something that's not a carb?"

"Maybe a head of lettuce," I answer. "Carrots."

Celeste is fiddling with her hair. She's going bald, just like her daddy. I don't care how much she fluffs it; she can't hide it. "Carrots are carbs, Birdie. Don't you know how much sugar is in a carrot?"

I don't say anything. I put a biscuit on my plate and pass the plate to Abby.

"Hey, Grandpop, Birdie tell you I've been looking through photo albums?" Sarah calls across the table.

I'm impressed by my granddaughter's maturity, by how well she carries herself. Speaks. (When she's not blurting out those weird sentences.) She seems like a girl who's not afraid of anything or anyone. I give

Abby and Drum credit for that. They're good parents.

"That right?" my Joe says, passing me the mashed potatoes. He's put a big pile on his plate. Doc Moses says he needs to lose weight, but Joe works hard. A hardworking man has a big appetite. Brodie men all have big appetites. And you can't give them a green salad and call it supper.

I spoon some potatoes on my plate and pass them on, watching Sarah shake her head when Joseph tries to put a drumstick on her plate. She laughs and pushes at the piece of chicken on the end of his fork like it's a dog turd or something.

"Ewww," Sarah squeals. "Stop, Uncle Joseph! Haven't you seen *Forks Over Knives*?"

"What's that?" he asks her, still trying to make her take the chicken.

"A documentary on Netflix." Abby. "I don't know that I agree that we should all become vegans, but it will make you think. You should watch it sometime."

"There more butter, Birdie?" Little Joe asks without looking at me.

I push my chair back, and it scrapes the floor loudly. Duke yipes like I've taken off his leg instead of just bumping it. "Dogs shouldn't be at the table," I say to no one.

"Grandpop. Do you know where Mom

Brodie's marriage certificate is? Birdie says she doesn't have a birth certificate."

"House fire, when she was a little girl," Little Joe responds. "But there's a marriage certificate. Imagine it's in my office somewhere."

"Birdie thought it might be at the bank."

"Nope, she brought all her stuff home to go through it. After they told her she had cancer."

Sarah rests her chin on her fist, her elbow on the table. "I was wondering what year she and Great-Grandpop got married."

I open the refrigerator and pull out a stick of butter. I unwrap it as I carry it to the table. It looks strange to see Mrs. Brodie's chair empty, and it sets me off-kilter. She never misses supper. I put the stick on the butter dish in front of Little Joe and mumble something about checking on Mrs. Brodie. I love having everyone here, but it makes me anxious, too. All the laughing and talking between them, and I can't think of a thing to say to anyone.

I go down the hall. In the sewing room, I turn on the bedside light. I notice a couple of red and white peppermints beside the teacup and the baby monitor and the pill bottles. Abby must have left them there. She and Mrs. Brodie were always eating them together.

"Just checking on you," I say. I smooth the light blanket beneath her chin. I stand there for a minute looking down on her. She's still breathing. "Made fried chicken and dumplings for supper. Added a little paprika to the flour for the chicken, like you showed me. Hope I didn't put too much in."

I look at her as if I think she's going to say something back, but she doesn't of course. It's funny. There were times when I would have given anything to make her stop talking. Always criticizing me. Always telling me what I should say. What I should do. What I shouldn't have said or done. Now . . . I just wish she'd say something. Anything. Even if it's just to tell me the chicken's got too much paprika.

"Sarah found my book," I hear myself whisper. I have no idea why I'm telling her. "You know, my Arizona book. My own fault. I must have left it in the living room and then forgot about it in all the hubbub of your getting sick. It's called the Grand Canyon State. Arizona. You probably know that. But did you know it's also called the Apache State? Like the Indians. Native Americans," I correct myself.

I stand there, quiet for a minute. I can

hear everyone talking in the kitchen. Laughing. The sound didn't change when I left the room. "I don't think she looked at it, though," I go on. "It was just lying there on the floor. I don't think she noticed it. I'll be more careful, now on." I watch Mrs. Brodie's chest rise and fall. I find myself trying to match my breath to hers, but it's so slow, it makes me dizzy.

"Well . . ." I say finally. "Guess I'll go have my supper. You need anything, you just holler."

Later, I lie in bed in the dark, listening to Little Joe unbuckle his pants over on his side of the bed. He sleeps in his underdrawers. Always shuts the light off before he undresses.

"You check on Mama before you came up?" he asks me, throwing his pants over the chair. Then he adds his shirt, and I smell his state of undress. Not that he stinks. Little Joe has always been clean, not like some farmers who barely take a sponge bath on Sunday mornings. Joe showers regularly. Uses deodorant. But he has a man smell about him that I find strangely comforting. Especially since I don't worry anymore about him pulling off his underdrawers. That ended after I had my hysterectomy ten years back. I didn't tell him I wasn't doing

171

my wifely duty anymore. That I wasn't doing *it.* I guess we just came to a silent agreement. Husbands and wives our age don't
do that anymore, anyway.

I wonder sometimes if he misses it,
though. And if he tried with me, how I'd
respond. I think maybe I'd let him, just
because he likes it. And it's really not that
awful, and it's over quick enough. A small
price to pay when the man keeps a roof over
my head.

I make a sound of affirmation. "And
turned out her light. Just left the night-light
burning. Plugged it in over by the door. And
the baby monitor's on." I nod to the white
receiver on my nightstand. Its little light
glows green. I hesitate. "You tell her good
night?" I ask him.

He sighs and sits down on the edge of the
bed, and I feel the mattress shift. "It's hard
to see her like that, Birdie. She . . . she looks
like she's already gone."

"But she's not, Joe." My words seem to
hang in the darkness. I want to tell him that
he ought to be sitting down there right now,
holding her hand. Helping her pass. I want
to tell him how lucky he is to have had his
mother all these years. But I know he
wouldn't understand. I guess you have to

be an orphan to appreciate a mother or a father.

He peels back the sheet and gets into bed beside me, and I feel him settle his head on his pillow. We both lie there, staring at the ceiling.

"Sarah gone to bed?" he asks.

"Light was still on, but the door was shut."

"She sure has gotten pretty, hasn't she?" I hear the smile in his voice. "Reminds me of Abby at that age."

"Prettier than Abby was," I say, and close my eyes.

We're quiet again, and I feel the familiar heat of his body beside mine. He and I have been sleeping in this bed side by side almost five decades. I wonder what it would be like to not have him here. His father died of a heart attack around the age Little Joe is now. It could happen.

I wonder if I could sleep without him. The only time we haven't slept together is when one of us was in the hospital, me for my hysterectomy, him when he got an infection in his arm from a cut from a piece of machinery. And after Joseph was born, when I told Little Joe if he crossed the threshold of our bedroom while I was in it, I'd shoot him with his own shotgun. Back then, he kept it loaded, propped in the corner of the room. People used to do that in those days, keep loaded guns ready for robbers. Now we have a gun safe in his office.

"Abby say how late they'll be?" Joe asks me.

"Knowing Celeste, last call." They'd gone to The Gull for a drink, our three children. It made me feel good to see the three of them together, laughing and arguing in the kitchen over whose car they were taking into town. But it made me a little sad, too. They asked their daddy if he wanted to go. He knew better than to say yes. He saw the way I looked at him when they asked. But they didn't ask me. Not that I'd go. I've never set foot in there but once, and that was when the devil got into me and I went in and told Little Joe to get on home because all three of his kids were down with a stomach virus and I'd cleaned up enough vomit and diarrhea for one day.

"How did Celeste seem to you?" Joe shifts his weight in the bed and starts cracking his knuckles. He always cracks his knuckles the last thing before he goes to sleep. "She seemed good to me. She seem good to you?"

"She's puttin' on a good face," I answer. "Don't know how good she's doing. She doesn't look like she's getting enough to

174

eat. She's nothing but bones."

"She said something at dinner about an audition next week. Some TV show or something. Sounds like she's getting a lot of auditions. She's bound to get a part sooner or later."

I don't know what kind of lies Celeste's been feeding him. I missed that bit of the conversation at dinner. But I don't say anything. If Joe wants to go on thinking his daughter is some big, fancy actress, who am I to burst his bubble? Instead, I say, "I imagine she's worried about money. Rent keeps going up. That health insurance she gets on the Internet, it keeps going up and up, too. I think the money will ease her mind. What Mrs. Brodie leaves her."

He makes a grunting sound and rolls over, his back to me. I roll in the other direction and reach out to set the alarm to get up and check on Mrs. Brodie in two hours. The digits glow red. It's nine thirty-two.

14
SARAH AGNES

"Do you love me?" I breathe.

"Of course I love you, *ma belle,*" Henri whispers in my ear. His breath is warm, and the sound of his voice makes me dizzy.

Ma belle. Belle means beautiful. I remember that from the French book hidden in my old box where I keep my clothes and stuff. Last night, after I got home from the carnival, from meeting Henri, I stayed up most of the night, reading and studying. There's a good chance I'll get slapped when Mrs. Hanfland realizes how much kerosene I used in the lamp, but I don't even care. It will be worth the slap.

I gaze into Henri's eyes. He thinks I'm beautiful with my ugly red hair and uglier freckles that are spread across my nose and cheeks like some kind of disease. That's what Mrs. Hanfland says. I look diseased. Afflicted.

Henri and I are lying in the grass on an

old horse blanket just beyond the bright lights of the carnival. In the distance, I hear the calliope music and men laughing, but it seems as if they're very far away. I can faintly smell popcorn and candied apples, and the smell of horse is strong on the blanket, but mostly I just smell Henri. He smells like tobacco and men's cologne and . . . a chance to be happy.

He leans over me and brushes his lips against mine, and I touch his chin with my fingertips the way he showed me. The way he likes me to do.

Henri asked one of his friends, Bilis, if he would run the Ferris wheel for a little while so he and I could go for a walk. Henri has a lot of friends here; everyone likes him. Bilis is the shortest man I've ever seen; he doesn't come nearly to my shoulders. He's got a regular-sized body, but short legs and short arms. I knew it was rude, but I couldn't stop staring at him when he came over to talk to Henri. He was wearing wool tweed pants and a matching jacket, even though it's getting warm for wool. And his hat matched, too. He was the nicest dressed man I think ever came to Bakersville. And when he spoke he had an accent, but not French like Henri's. It was something else. I asked Henri where Bilis was from, and he said

England. Bilis has a British accent, which is divine. Of course not as divine as Henri's. Nothing is any more beautiful than a Frenchman speaking French.

Henri told me that Bilis is a dwarf. Henri said Bilis was born that way, short like that. I've never seen a dwarf before, and the whole thing about God's making us in his own image occurs to me. I wonder . . . what if God is a dwarf?

But the Bible doesn't say anything about that, so I realize that's probably silly.

Bilis told Henri he'd run the Ferris wheel for a few minutes, but he'd better make it snappy. He said something about Jacko, but I didn't catch it because I was too busy staring at him, at his little feet and little hands. The funny thing is, he isn't bad looking, though he does have an enormous nose.

On the midway, after we left Bilis to take tickets at the Ferris wheel, Henri bought me cotton candy and we walked, holding hands, to get the blanket out of the back of a big truck. Henri said he wanted to lie out and look at the stars, but I think mostly we came for kissing. I like kissing Henri. I like how it makes me feel. I like the sounds Henri makes when I kiss him.

Henri didn't just have kissing on his mind, though. He unbuttoned the front of my dress. (I wore my second best so I could wear something different on our second date.) He wanted to touch my bosom, inside my brassiere. I knew I shouldn't let him, but he was nice and so sweet and . . . I liked it. So I let him. But I know better than to let him touch me under my skirt. I set him straight on that.

So now we're just lying here under the stars, and Henri is holding me tight, moving his hands lightly over me. It's warm out tonight, but him touching me makes me shiver.

"How much do you love me?" I ask him.

"To the stars and back!" He gestures to the sky. Then he sits up and reaches for his cigarettes. I watch him in the darkness. He strikes a match, and I smell the sulfur, then the pungent smell of burning tobacco. He breathes it in and offers me the cigarette. The *fag*. That's what he calls it. A fag.

I shake my head. "Oh, no, my father would —" I feel my cheeks go warm as I catch myself. What kind of woman will Henri think I am if I'm talking about my papa? What he will and won't let me do. Henri won't think I'm a woman at all. He'll think I'm a little girl, and that won't work, not for my plan. "I don't smoke," I say quickly.

I sit up beside him. "When do you think you'll go? Tomorrow? The next day?" I ask anxiously.

"I told you; I don't know, *chéri*. When Jacko says we pull up stakes, we pull up the tent stakes," Henri says lazily. Then he looks at me. "Why? You want me gone?" He smiles his handsome smile, and I know he's teasing me.

I laugh and boldly put my hand on his chest and kiss him. "No. In fact . . ." I hear my voice tremble, but only just a little. "I think you should take me with you."

Henri doesn't do what I expect him to do. He doesn't pull me into his arms and cover my face with kisses and say he was going to ask me to come with him. To marry him and travel all over the country with him, seeing the sights.

My chest gets to feeling tight when he doesn't answer right away. "You love me, right? You want me to go with you, don't you?"

He still doesn't answer right away, then he asks, "You don't think your parents would miss you?" He blows smoke.

I shake my head. "They don't care about me. They don't love me. But you love me, Henri, right?"

"Of course, *mon chéri*." He kisses me, first

180

gently, then harder, and he pushes me onto the blanket, and for a minute I can't resist. He stretches out over me on the blanket, and I feel his body against me, hard where I'm soft.

He kisses me until I can't breathe, and I feel like the sky overhead and my life are spinning faster and faster. When I feel his hand on my bare thigh, I put both hands on his chest. "Henri," I pant. "Do you want me to come with you or not?"

He rolls onto his side and takes another puff of his cigarette. "You're eighteen, right?"

"Almost," I say. It's the baldest-faced lie I think I've ever told, but I'm getting better at it. "I . . . I can work if I come with you. In the carnival, right? Take tickets or sell candy apples or . . . whatever Jacko needs. And . . . and I can live with you." It occurs to me that I don't know where he sleeps when he travels. "Do you stay in hotels?" I ask.

He laughs. "Back of that tent truck. It's cozy, though. Got a mattress and all."

I sit up again. The stars are bright tonight, and the sky seems so big. And suddenly my tiny world seems big. And full of wonder and possibilities. "So I can come with you?" I playfully take his beret and pull it onto my head, wishing I had a mirror right now.

He seems to think about it for a minute, maybe because marriage is a big commitment. But when you love someone, you love them, right? You can't live without them.

"Sure, doll, you wanna come along?" He shrugs. "Free country."

"Hank!" a voice in the dark calls. "Hank! You out here?"

Henri grinds his butt out on the bottom of his shoe and tosses it into the grass. "Yoo!" he hollers, raising his hand.

I hear someone in the grass and see a small figure approaching in the dark. I stiffen and start buttoning my dress, my face hot with embarrassment.

Bilis stops a few feet from the blanket, but I know he can see me buttoning my dress. I can feel his eyes on me.

"Jacko says to get your bloody arse back to your post." The little man tips his hat to me. I don't think I like the word *dwarf*. It makes me think of Snow White, and in books her dwarves are like gnomes or something.

"Pardon my French, Miss," Bilis says.

I think that's such a strange phrase, *pardon my French,* especially since Henri is French.

"Come on, chap. Business is spanking," Bilis says in his British accent. "I gotta run my ballyhoo for the coochies."

Henri takes his beret off my head and puts it back on. "Who's runnin' my joint?" He stands and puts out his hand to me. I take his hand and come to my feet, still fussing with my dress.

"Jacko," Bilis answers.

Henri swears under his breath. I don't even know the word, but I can tell by the way he says it that it's a swear. He grabs the horse blanket off the ground. "You should go," he tells me, not really looking at me.

"Okay." I lift up on my toes and kiss his cheek. "I'll be back tomorrow night with my things. You won't leave before tomorrow night, will you? You won't go without me?" I grab his shirt. "Don't leave without me, Henri!"

He runs his hands over my buttocks and heads for the bright lights, walking right past his friend.

Bilis just stands there looking at me. Long enough to make me uncomfortable. "How old are you?" he asks me.

"Eighteen." It comes out smooth.

He doesn't say anything, but I can tell when he speaks again that he doesn't believe me. "Hank's right. You should go home, girly. To your parents. A place like this, carnies like us, they're not for the likes of a good girl like you. Pretty girl."

I don't say anything because I don't know what to say. So I just walk off, but as I cut across the field, heading home in the dark, it occurs to me that Bilis is the second man who's told me I am pretty today. Which makes me think maybe I wasn't meant to move to Chicago and marry a rich man. Maybe God means me to be a carny.

15

ABBY

The music pounds in my ears, and I remember why Drum and I don't go to bars, even now that the kids are old enough that we actually could, if we wanted to. It's not that I can't appreciate the Commodores' "Brick House"; it's just that the music is so *loud*. I can't hear what anyone is saying. And I didn't come for the music or the alcohol. I came to talk with my siblings without our mother listening in. It's always been a tradition, the three of us coming together at The Gull. We do it whenever we're all here for a family event, which doesn't happen as often as it used to.

Celeste hollers something to me, and I shout back, "What?"

She makes a motion as if raising a drink to her mouth. She's going to the bar. Which doesn't mean she's actually buying a round. She'll put it on Daddy's tab. She always does. He swaps Red Willy beer for rent.

Daddy owns The Gull, or at least the land it sits on. I lost track long ago of Daddy's wheelings and dealings with people on this island.

"Dogfish Head 60 Minute!" I tell her. "Or Yuengling, if they don't have it!"

Joseph makes a face at me as if I'm an idiot. "What?" I demand, motioning with my hands. "Hope springs eternal."

"She'll take a beer!" he tells Celeste.

"At least something in a bottle!" I shout. "No canned beer!"

Celeste holds up two fingers to me, her eyebrows, which are drawn in, going up questioningly. In her opinion, there's no need to order one drink at a time. It's a waste of energy to walk back to the bar so soon for the second. I hold up one finger.

She points at Joseph sitting next to me at the high-top.

"Surprise me!"

Celeste sashays off in a pair of ridiculously high, sparkly heels that look even more ridiculous in The Gull. The place is the definition of a dive, with the smell of stale beer and cigarette smoke, even though it's been years since anyone could legally smoke inside. It still had a dirt floor up until ten years ago.

I fan myself with a plastic-coated menu.

The food is mostly bad, except for the crab cake. Red Willy might make the best crab cake I've ever eaten. *Anywhere,* and I've eaten my share of crab cakes and then some. And he won't share the recipe. Passed on from his great-grandmother, and he swears he's taking it to his grave, no matter how often I ask him for it or what I offer to give him in exchange. Knowing how badly I want the recipe, Celeste actually once offered Red Willy sexual favors. She was kidding, of course (or half kidding), but Red Willy wouldn't even trade his crab cake recipe for a BJ.

I fan myself harder, thinking I must be heading toward menopause. Which is just peachy. Where are the years going? I'll blink again, and I'll be lying in Mom Brodie's bed, breathing my last breath. There's an old air conditioner sticking out of a window, but I doubt there's much cool air coming out of it. "I need to talk to you," I tell Joseph when Celeste walks away.

He cups his hand over his ear. The Commodores are winding down.

"I talked —" I cut myself off and get up, pointing at a booth in the back, near the ladies' bathroom.

Joseph rises and follows me. As I slide onto the green Naugahyde bench, I spot my sister in her short skirt and flowered kimono getup. She's facing the big mirror and a blinking *PBR* sign behind the bar, but I can tell by the sling of her hip that she's talking to the old guy on the barstool beside her. By the way he's looking at her, she's definitely caught his eye. I don't recognize the man. He's clearly not local. I'm pretty sure he's wearing a silk ascot. Must be someone staying at one of the rental condos on the beach. The tourists find The Gull quaint. And they keep it in business so we put up with them.

I tilt my head in Celeste's direction as my brother slides in across from me. "Wanna lay money she doesn't make it home tonight?" I say. It's quieter in the corner because the speaker mounted on the wall behind me is dead, except for the occasional crackling sound it makes. The downside of this booth is that I can smell toilet bowl cleaner every time someone goes into the bathroom.

"Nope." Joseph grins and sits back. "Bad bet."

I lean forward on the table. My forearms stick to something, and I lift them, making a face. "So . . ." I tell my brother. Smokey Robinson's voice fills the bar. "Tears of a Clown." "Houston, we have a problem."

"You know that's not the quote," he tells me. "Tom Hanks got it wrong."

Joseph is one of those guys, like my husband, whose brain is full of useless trivia. You never want to play against either of them in Trivial Pursuit. You want to be on their team. I wait because I know that's the only way to deal with either of them. Joseph's going to tell me how Tom Hanks got the line wrong, and why, whether I want to know or not.

"Haise said, 'Okay, Houston.' Then Swigert said, 'I believe we've had a problem here.' Then Lovell said, 'Houston, we've had a problem.' Ron Howard changed it for dramatic effect in the 1995 movie *Apollo 13*." He thinks for a minute. "Although the line might have been changed before that. *Apollo 13* was a remake."

"Probably the screenwriter, not Ron Howard," I quip, showing him I know at least a *few* tidbits of useless information. I mean, I would have had to pick up a couple along the way, having been married to Drum for twenty-two years.

"So what's up?" he asks me.

I shake my head, thinking about my conversation with Daddy today. Then my little chat with my sister before supper. I feel bad that I lied to her about the will, but

Daddy was clear he didn't want her told. Not yet, at least.

This is going to be bad. I can just feel it. *Bad.*

Joseph goes to lean forward and flicks something off the table to the floor. The Formica table's not just sticky; there's food on it. *Gross.* I catch the waitress's — Sadie's — attention. She's been working here since she graduated from high school with me. It used to make me feel awkward coming in and having her bring me my fries, but I got over it, eventually. She's tickled that we always tip well, and I find it nice to see her. It's nostalgic. Her brother used to buy us beer when we were underage.

I point at the table.

Sadie comes right over, whipping a damp rag from her apron pocket. She's wearing blue, sparkly eye shadow. I didn't know anyone made blue eye shadow anymore. "Good to see you, Abby. Real sorry about your granny. She was always sweet to me."

Not dead yet, I think. "Thanks," I say.

"You want to order some fries?" she asks me, but her eyes are all over Joseph. "Hey," she says.

"Nothing right now. Celeste is grabbing us beers."

"Sadie." Joseph smiles at her and adjusts

the brim of his ball cap. "How are the kids?"

She's got four, all from different fathers. She had the first girl two days after we graduated high school. I remember her big belly in her graduation gown. I think she lives with her current boyfriend and his mother in my cousin's trailer park.

"Good." She nods. "Roy Junior's got a job at the chicken plant in Onancock. Full-time. Bus picks him up other side of the bridge. It's a good job. Debeaking."

Joseph nods appreciatively as Sadie gives the spot on the table in front of him one last swipe. "Heard you and your wife split up," she says. "Sorry to hear it. We should go out sometime." She smiles a toothy grin and tucks her bar rag back into her apron.

My brother smiles at her as if he's definitely going to call her. He isn't, of course. He likes his women smarter than he is and a little chubby, which makes me adore him. Poor Sadie is not, as Mom Brodie would say, the brightest bunny in the hutch, and she's stick-thin. (And the missing tooth isn't doing her any favors.) Joseph likes his women with meat on their bones. What's not to love about a man who likes a little butt and gut?

"Isn't she with John J?" I ask when Sadie walks away. John J has got to be at least ten years older than us. He's a crabber. "I heard she moved in with him."

Joseph nods. "Last I heard. But she's still on and off with his brother."

"Then why would she —" I cut myself off. *Theirs not to reason why . . .*

Joseph gives a good-natured shrug and meets my gaze. "So what's the problem you wanted to talk to me about?"

I spot Celeste coming our way and nod in her direction. She's dancing to "Ain't No Mountain High Enough," singing louder than Diana Ross and ever so slightly off-key. I think she was nipping from her flask on our way into town, riding between Joseph and me in Daddy's old pickup. "It must be 1970s Motown night," I quip.

Joseph gives me one of his killer smiles. He's got the prettiest teeth and never needed braces like Celeste and me. "Every night is 1970s Motown at The Gull." We both laugh as Celeste makes it to the table.

"Cheers!" she declares, setting four open cans of Bud on the table. "Right back with the tequila shots!"

"I am *not* doing shots," I call after her as she dances away, swinging her hips like she's a hula dancer. My shots days are long over. I push a can of Bud across the table toward Joseph when she's out of range of hearing

192

again. "Daddy told me this afternoon that Mom Brodie cut Celeste out of her will."

He's just tipping his can, and he uprights it. "What?" He wipes a dribble of beer from his lip with his thumb and swears under his breath, using one of the words that used to get him soap in his mouth when Birdie caught him. "You've got to be kidding."

I shake my head.

He shakes his head and gives a low whistle. "How much *was* she getting?"

I shrug.

He knits his eyebrows. "Who's getting the money, then? Just you?"

"Maybe you," I say, though honestly I have no idea. Mom Brodie loved Joseph. I never had any doubt about that, and he didn't either. But he was still illegitimate, and something like that never sits well in the United Methodist Women's Circle. Ever. "I didn't feel like I should ask. You need to talk to Daddy."

He sits back and takes a drink of his beer. He's clearly upset. "Celeste will be devastated."

I reach for one of the beers. I hate Bud, and I hate beer out of a can worse. One of the luxuries of being in a higher federal tax bracket is being able to afford beer in a bottle. I'm not even much of a beer drinker.

193

I prefer wine. But I like beer with pizza, and of course when I pick crabs. I drink it when I come to The Gull with my brother because it's that or shots. The wine Red Willy serves makes me wish I could still order Boone's Farm. I take a swallow of the beer, and it's just as nasty as I think it's going to be. I make a face.

He reaches for my beer. "I'll drink it if you don't want it. You're such a snob, Abs."

I pull the beer can out of his reach, thinking I should have had a nip from Celeste's flask. "You need to talk to Daddy and see what's going on. I think Celeste needs to know. I don't think we should just spring it on her after the funeral."

My little brother's thinking now. I know those fine lines around his eyes. "And let me guess, Dad doesn't want to tell her before Mom Brodie dies."

"You know Daddy. He avoids conflict any chance he gets. I think if he had it his way, no one would tell her until *he's* dead."

The thinking face again. "Do we know how much money we're talking about?"

"No idea," I say. "Could be a hundred dollars. Could be ten thousand."

Celeste hollers to someone as she comes toward the table carrying three shots, and

Joseph and I both slide back in the booth again.

"Ain't no mountain high enough," Celeste sings, sliding in beside me. She smells good. And she looks pretty good, all dolled up. We had to wait fifteen minutes in the truck while she "put her face on." "So what shall we drink to?" she asks.

"You." Joseph grabs his shot glass, and I resolutely reach for mine, thinking I'm going to need it to get through the next few days.

I would have won the bet, had Joseph taken it. Celeste didn't leave the bar with us when we headed home at eleven thirty. She tried to get us to stay, but I'd already had enough to drink by then, and I wanted to get home to be with Mom Brodie. I just had the feeling she wasn't going to be with us much longer, and I wanted to hold her hand. I wanted to tell her how much I love her again, and I didn't care if she could hear me or not. I'm usually a happy drinker. Tonight, the fact that I was a little tipsy seemed to be driving me into melancholy.

"I'll catch a ride home!" Celeste hollered after us as we went out the door. She was dancing with two young guys I only vaguely recognized. But the old guy on the barstool had just bought her a drink, so there was no telling what the evening's outcome would be.

Joseph and I rode home in the old pickup, mostly in silence, except when we belted out a little Adele. We briefly discussed Mom Brodie's will, and he said he'd talk to Daddy in the morning before he went to pick up Ainslie. Then we'd talk later. We were having a good old-fashioned Brodie crab feast tomorrow, although it would be low-key. Just our immediate family, no friends, no cousins. Lettice, the mail lady, would not be invited to stay.

When Joseph pulled into the back driveway, he didn't cut the engine. "Don't you want to come in for a sec?" I ask, opening the passenger door. "Tell Mom Brodie good night?"

"I think I'm going to head home. I'm beat." He grips the steering wheel, staring straight ahead. "I saw her after supper."

I hesitate. He's as bad as our dad. Daddy stuck his head in the door this evening to check on his mother, but he didn't say anything to her. He didn't go into the room; he certainly didn't touch her. I don't know what it is with Brodie men that makes them so scared of dying. It's like they think if they get too close to her, they might catch what

she's got. Like cancer and old age are con-
tagious.

I get out, close the door, and lean in the
window. I don't have anything else to say, I
just . . . I feel like Joseph and I get so little
time together. And we're almost never
alone. Seeing him like this, being with him,
makes me realize he's one of my best
friends. Not the kind you call to tell them
that you burned the spaghetti sauce or to
get a brownie recipe. He's my friend the
way Drum is my friend. The kind who
knows you inside and out . . . and loves you
anyway.

I meet my little brother's gaze. "So you'll
talk to Daddy about the will? See what he
wasn't telling me?"

"Will do," he says.

I watch him back up and out. We've got
this grand horseshoe driveway out front,
and we never use it. We all pull around back
near the porch. I can't remember when the
last time was that I used the majestic front
door.

Birdie's left the back door unlocked for
us. She likes the last one in to lock up. We
never used to lock our doors at all, but one
morning a couple of years ago, Birdie came
down to the kitchen to find that someone
had let themselves in and eaten half a cherry

pie off of the counter. Whoever it was put his or her plate in the kitchen sink. Also had a carton of milk. Had to be some teenage boy. Likely one of the Carlton grandsons; there were four of them, each one ornerier than the other, and they lived half a mile away, if they cut across Brodie land.

Inside the back door, I debate whether or not to throw the dead bolt. Celeste said she'd be home, but I doubt it.

I leave it open. Hope springs eternal and all that.

Inside, first I check on Sarah. Sound asleep in the bed we share. I brush my teeth, pull on the T-shirt I slept in last night and a pair of Drum's pj bottoms I keep in a drawer in the room, for him or me. I walk through the dark house; I don't need a light. This is what Mom Brodie calls our dream house. The place you dream of most. This is her dream house, too. Only when she walks the halls in her dreams, she says she sees it the way it was in the first days when she was still a teenager and it was the 1930s.

I walk into Mom Brodie's room a little light-headed, still feeling my beer/tequila too-old-to-be-out-drinking buzz. I'm surprised to find Birdie there, asleep in a chair. For a moment I stand there in the doorway, looking at my mother by the glow of a night-light she's plugged into an outlet by the door. It's not a modern night-light like the kind we used to use in the kids' rooms. It's actually a lamp that takes a small wattage bulb. A lamp from my childhood that I remember well. It used to be on a table on the landing at the top of the staircase. Daddy always turned it on, last thing before he went to bed. After he came into our rooms and said good night. My father came to tell me good night until the day I left for college.

Birdie, asleep in the chair, is wearing a sleeveless sack of a nightgown that comes past her knees. White or maybe pale pink with tiny flowers on it. Two buttons at her throat. I can't imagine where she got the thing. I don't think anyone has made a nightgown that looks like that in forty years. It's the same kind of nightgown Mom Brodie wore until she turned hers in for a hospital gown. It might *be* the same night-gown. On her feet, my mother's wearing a pair of pink, terry-cloth mules that look as if they've seen better days. Her ankles are swollen.

I smile, touched that Birdie would choose to sleep down here in a straight-backed chair, to be with Mom Brodie. Standing here in the semidarkness looking at her, I feel a sudden sense of shame. This tiniest detail tells me I've missed something in the relationship between my mother and her mother-in-law. Something big.

My mother has always complained about Mom Brodie; Mom Brodie is "domineering, haughty, nitpicky." I've been hearing it since I was a kid. All true. And Mom Brodie wasn't above throwing a criticism my mother's way; though, thinking back, Mom Brodie was duplicitous about it. She never came right out and said my mother complained too much. She just said things like "Birdie makes things harder on herself, so quick to criticize." But standing here, looking at the two of them, it occurs to me that maybe I've missed some of the nuances of their relationship.

Growing up, I honestly thought my mother couldn't stand my grandmother. As I got older, I realized it was more complicated than that, but seeing my mother asleep beside Mom Brodie's bed — with my dad snoring upstairs — I'm reminded that nothing is ever as simple as we'd like to make it. Particularly when it comes to relationships. Family relationships.

I walk into the room and lay my hand gently on my mother's shoulder. She's warm, and she smells of Ivory soap. My

200

mother always smells clean, even when she comes in sweaty from the garden. "Mom," I whisper softly. There's a catch in my throat, and I feel tears well in my eyes.

She startles, straightening her legs and arms as if I just flipped the switch on the electric chair. "Wha . . . what?" She looks up at me.

I lower my hand. "What are you doing down here?" I ask, wondering why on earth I just called her Mom.

I never call her Mom, or Mommy, or Mama. Since I could speak, I've been calling her Birdie. Mom Brodie said it was one of my first words, and everyone thought it was so funny because that's what they all called her. No one corrected me. Not even my mother. So when Celeste was born, she imitated me and called her Birdie, too. I have no recollection of when Joseph started calling her Mom. I just remember being in high school and me saying Birdie and him saying Mom.

Birdie wipes her mouth with the back of her hand and slowly heaves herself to her feet. She peers down at my grandmother. "She all right?"

I almost laugh. Of course she's not *all right*. She's dying. But I don't say it because I don't want to start anything. It's after midnight, and Birdie should get to bed because she'll be up before dawn.

"She's fine," I whisper, glancing at my grandmother just to be sure she's still breathing. That would be a hell of thing for the two of us to be standing here chatting and Mom Brodie had passed away and we didn't know. "You go to bed. I'll sit with her."

"I think someone should stay with her," my mother whispers, nearing the bed. "I feel like she . . . she's barely hanging on." She tugs on the sheet beneath Mom Brodie's chin, and I don't know why I do it, but I lower my hand to cover hers. I stare at our hands. Mine is bigger, smoother; my fingers are long and tapered and covered in freckles. Birdie isn't freckled; we get them from the Brodies. Her hand is small and pudgy and covered with liver spots.

"I'll stay with her," I repeat.

Birdie nods ever so slightly. I feel like she's holding her breath. I must be making her uncomfortable. I know my mother doesn't like to be touched. I'm not sure why, but Mom Brodie said she came from the orphanage that way. I think Mom Brodie suspected she'd been abused, maybe even sexually. I actually tried to have a conversation once with my grandmother about it, and she told me to keep my thoughts to myself, that dredging up that sort of thing would only hurt people who have been hurt enough. I don't necessarily agree with Mom Brodie's sweep-it-under-the-rug theory, but the fact that she didn't believe that to be true about everything made me respect her wishes. I never brought the subject up with my mother.

I squeeze Birdie's hand and step back, out of her personal space, and I hear her heave a sigh. Relief? I'm forty-five years old, loved dearly by so many people, and yet it still hurts me that my mother doesn't want my touch.

Birdie straightens her glasses, shuffling toward the door. "Door locked?"

I nibble on my lower lip, looking at the chair I think I've just agreed to spend the night in. "No. Celeste's still out."

Birdie makes a sound of disapproval. "You should have brought her home with you. She needs to be home with us. A time like this."

"She didn't want to come home with us." There's a definite tick of annoyance in my voice. I'm tired of being responsible for Celeste. "She said she'd be home later."

My mother makes another sound of disapproval and disappears into the darkness of the hallway.

I take another look at Mom Brodie, then at the chair my mother was sleeping in, and I head down the hall. Daddy's got a comfy recliner in the living room that he sits in at night to watch TV. If I'm going to keep the death watch, I'm dragging in the damned chair.

16

CELESTE

"Let me out! Stop the damned truck! Stop it!" I holler frantically, beating Louie in the arm with my fist. I'm bordering on hysterical now, fighting tears. I've been in more jams with men than I can count. And you never cry. I once hooked up with a guy on an Internet dating site who, though he looked good on paper, turned out to be one of those crazy survivalists. I walked into his place, and he confiscated my cell phone and then took me on a tour of his armed bunker, locking me in with him. But I've never been scared before. Not like this.

I'm getting too old for this crap.

Louie, who's got to be around my brother's age, slams on the brakes, and the truck fishtails on the gravel road. He makes some kind of smartass comment under his breath about me being an old bitch. He and his brother Leo have been laughing, but seem to finally realize I'm serious. The laughter dies down. Before the truck has come to a complete stop, I'm shoving Leo. "Let me out! Let me out, or I swear to God I'll call the police. Jesus, I'm a Brodie. I know every one of those boys on the force. You two will be in jail cells in Eastern Correctional by lunch!"

Leo throws open the door, and I shove him hard, and he stumbles out of the truck. He's drunker than Louie, which is probably a good thing, because I'm not sure Louie would have let me out. With my shoes in my hand, I half fall, half jump from the truck. Louie takes his foot off the brake, and the truck lurches forward. I go down on one bare knee, hard, and wince.

Leo runs after the truck, and I hear his boots scrape the gravel as he manages to jump in. I hear them both laughing as the door slams shut and they peel away, throwing up stones. A couple hit me, and I cringe, still fighting tears. *Never let them see you cry. Never let them see your pain.* I want to throw my shoes at them, but they're Jimmy Choos, and there's no way I'd take the chance of breaking one of the heels off. I *acquired* them at a party I crashed in the Hamptons last summer. Women were kicking off their shoes, throwing off their clothes, and jumping into a pool. They were

206

all too drunk or high to pay any attention to me. I'd wished I'd had a suitcase with me instead of just a tote; I walked away with quite a haul. I sold all the clothes at a fancy uptown Manhattan resale shop, but I kept the Jimmy Choos. Figured every girl deserves to splurge on herself once in a while.

"Assholes!" I fling at them, instead of the shoes.

I doubt they hear me. They've got their country music blaring again. Where the hell's a cop when you need one? Of course the *force* on Brodie is only four men; one is older than my daddy and another one was dancing in The Gull with me a few hours ago, drunk off his ass, so it's a good thing I didn't need one of them.

"Assholes," I whisper as I slowly get to my feet. It's still dark out, but dawn is coming. It's that strange time of early morning when you can *feel* the sun rising, even though you can't see it yet.

"Assholes," I repeat, my voice catching in my throat. Tears fill my eyes, and I rub them with the back of my hand. I'm just about sober now. Also probably a good thing, otherwise I might have ended up in a three-some I hadn't agreed to. Or worse. I'm usually such a good judge of character. I wasn't tonight. Louie was all fun and flirting with three beers and a couple of shots. But he got ugly once he downed a pint of tequila.

I reach into my bag slung over my shoulder, feel for my flask, and pull it out. I caught Louie going through my wallet when I went to the bathroom. Joke was on him. I have seven dollars in ones, an expired driver's license, no credit cards, and a Macy's gift card I found in Birdie's junk drawer yesterday.

Feeling a little dizzy, I walk over to the side of the road and sink down in the grass on my knees. Alone in the dark, I fight a sob rising in my throat. I sniff loudly and yank at my kimono. I tore it, and not on the seam. I can't believe I ruined my butterfly kimono. What an unbelievably crappy weekend this is turning out to be. I wipe my bloody knee with the hem of the ruined kimono.

I don't know why I came home. No one really wants me here. Mom Brodie is already dead. Her body just hasn't realized it yet. What was I thinking? Family support? Who am I kidding? They'd all be happy to see me just disappear. The prodigal daughter. I bet my smarty-pants sister doesn't think I even know a word like that. She was always the smart one. Joseph was always the good-looking one. And then he had the bonus of being the bastard mixed-race child.

Something pokes my eye, and I rub at it. Eyelash. I peel off one of my fake lashes. I use the kind where you just glue a clump here and there. They almost look real, but they take a lot more glue than the full set, and I think I'm allergic to the glue.

I shake the flask. It's three-quarters full. I filled it with shots guys bought me, when no one was looking. I unscrew the cap.

I should have stayed in the Big Apple. I have auditions coming up. Well, the possibility of auditions. Birdie and Abby don't want me here. And with rent due, I really shouldn't have taken these days off.

But if my inheritance is decent enough, and I think it will be (Mom Brodie has to be rolling in dough), I can quit that lame job. Take a little break, get my *work* done, and then come back strong. Concentrate on my auditions. Maybe pick up an acting class. Just to stay current.

I take a gulp of the vodka, and I feel myself calming. A second, and I stop shaking.

I can't believe I got myself into something like this. And on Brodie Island, no less. What's this world coming to?

Everything was fine. Louie and Leo seemed like gentlemen. Well, not *gentlemen,* but decent enough. And they were into me. I was having a great evening, even after Abby and Joseph did the Cinderella thing.

After we left The Gull, me and Louie and Leo, we went to one of their friends' houses near the dock. Not exactly a house, more like a shitty shack, but there was music and everyone was dancing and laughing and having a good time. A couple of people were smoking crack, but whatever. It's not my thing, but I've never been into throwing stones.

When we got back in the truck, it was Leo who asked me if I wanted to go back to their place and party some more. I was actually considering it, then Louie made a comment that made me think his idea of partying included nonconsensual sex. When he mentioned his roommate liked *cougars,* that was when I lost my shit. I don't know if I was angrier about his thinking I was going to have sex with him and his friends or about the fact that he called me a cougar. What a jerk-ass.

I search for my cigarettes in my bag, then my lighter. I light up and inhale deeply. I really thought Bartholomew was going to invite me back to his place. I met him the night we came in. He said he was going to be around all week. Not heading out until next Sunday. He was a sweet old guy.

But about a half hour before last call, I was out on the dance floor when I saw him get off his barstool. He waved, and, before I had time to slip away from the nitwit brothers, he was gone. Thought I had him on the hook, and then he was gone.

The barest glow of sunlight begins to appear in the east, and I turn to face it. I stare out over the water, sipping my vodka, watching, waiting. And when the sunrise comes with the bridge in the foreground, it's as breathtakingly beautiful as it ever is.

Brodie Island knows how to do sunrise better than anywhere else.

I just sit there for a few minutes, smoking my cigarette, staring at the beauty. When the bridge comes into full view, I shift my attention to it. I hate that bridge. I feel like they never should have built it. I mean, I get progress and all, and it was certainly a pain in the ass when I was kid to take the ferry or a boat to the mainland. But the difficulty getting to the mainland made Brodie Island special. It made us different from everyone else. It made me feel special, being born and raised here.

The bridge brought trash like Louie and his brother. And crack cocaine. And a sadness I don't remember seeing on Brodie when I was a kid. I sigh and put out my cigarette and flick the butt into the road.

The bridge, a steel and concrete monstrosity, seems to be beckoning me this morning. I play with the idea of walking to it. Going up to the highest point and standing on the rail. I think about what the water looks like below, swirling . . . calling me. I think a lot about suicide. But never with a pill or an electric cord around my neck. Certainly not with the little .38 I sometimes carry for protection. When I fantasize about putting an end to all this bullshit, I always imagine standing on the top of that bridge. I know just the place. All I'd have to do is climb up on the rail. Take one step and splash. It would all be over. It would be so easy.

Slowly I get to my feet. Pick up my shoes. Sling my bag over my shoulder and then slip the strap over my head so it's easier to carry. The sun's barely up, and it's going to be another hot day.

I look at the bridge and then at the road that leads home. It's probably a mile walk. I only stand there for minute and then turn for home.

Why would I kill myself now? I'm on top of the world. I'm about to inherit a fortune.

17
SARAH

I stand beside the chair in Mom Brodie's dying room, looking down at my mom. She's sleeping. Her mouth is open, which makes her kind of funny looking, but at least she doesn't snore like my dad. I guess she slept here all night. When I woke up this morning, I realized she'd never come to bed. For a second, I thought maybe she had stayed out all night with Aunt Celeste. Aunt Celeste does it all the time. Here, and even when she comes to our house. She used to borrow Mom's car to go out. Only Mom doesn't let her anymore since Aunt Celeste left the car in a no-parking zone overnight in Annapolis and it got towed. We didn't hear from Aunt Celeste for three days. Mom thought she'd been carjacked, murdered, and buried in a shallow grave. She hadn't been; she was just with some guy on his boat. So that was good. But Mom had to pay like three hundred and fifty bucks to get her car back.

Of course I knew very well Mom hadn't stayed out all night. She's never done anything like that. And if she *was* going to stay out all night, she wouldn't do it without texting me. My mom and dad and my brother and I have this cool agreement. Our parents don't do things they don't want Reed and me to do — like not text if we're going to be later than expected.

Well, that's not totally true. They *do* do a few things we're not allowed to do. My dad smokes weed even though we all pretend he doesn't. We're not allowed to consume illegal substances of any sort. I used to smell marijuana on his clothes, first thing in the morning and at night before he went to bed, but now I don't because he switched to a smoke-free vaporizer. Cuts back on the carcinogens. And of course my parents have sex. A lot. And Reed and I are supposed to be saving ourselves for marriage, or at least until we fall in love with somebody we know we can't live without. Dad added that addendum. He and Mom had sex before they were married, so I guess that's why.

Anywho . . . Mom would text me if she was staying out all night with Aunt Celeste getting Grandpop's pickup towed.

I hear Birdie banging around in the

kitchen. Sounds like she's emptying the dishwasher. I know I should go in and help her. But once I go into the kitchen, I'm going to get sucked into going to the henhouse with her or something crazy like that, and I want to talk to my mom for a sec alone before things get crazy. And I'm sure they will; they always do when Aunt Celeste is here. Once she brought this guy home to have sex with in her bedroom, and Birdie walked right in and told him to get out. I heard them because I was in the bathroom. Nobody said a word the next morning at breakfast about it; we talked about how good Mom Brodie's pancakes were.

I glance at Mom Brodie. She looks just like she did when I went to bed last night. Like she's dead. She hasn't moved. Which she wouldn't if she was dead. Which Mom insists she isn't. I look down at Mom, who's still sleeping away, oblivious to the racket in the kitchen, and walk over to have a closer look at Mom Brodie. I watch her chest, and I think maybe I see her breathing, but I'm not totally sure. If I had a mirror, I could hold it over her mouth and see if it fogs up. I saw that in a movie.

"A Santa at NASA," I say softly.

I don't know why I say it. It just comes to me, and I feel like maybe Mom Brodie might appreciate it. Last time I was here, three weeks ago, she asked me first thing when we walked into the kitchen to tell her a new palindrome. And she said "make it a good one."

I'd been tempted to tell her "A slut nixes sex in Tulsa" (one of my favorites), but I knew Mom wouldn't appreciate it, so instead I gave Mom Brodie, "Degas, are we not drawn onward, no? In union drawn onward to new eras aged." It was the best long one I know that's not totally stupid. Mom Brodie clapped her hands together and said she was so glad I was smart and not just pretty. She said pretty's good, but it won't always be with you. She said smart was forever and then told me she'd had Birdie get me some Perrier at the market and that it was in the refrigerator on the back porch. She knows I like bubbly water, and I guess she doesn't think it's a waste of money like my grandmother does.

There wasn't any bubbly water in the outside fridge this time. I checked.

I look over my shoulder at Mom. She hasn't moved. I guess I should be checking to be sure she's not dead, too. But that's stupid. Her cholesterol numbers are good, and she eats fairly healthy although I know she buys Smarties and hides them in the bathroom and eats them in secret. I see the wrappers sometimes when I'm dumping the trash cans.

I stand there debating what to do. I want to have another look at Mom Brodie's tattoo. I haven't found anything like it yet, but I've definitely found some cool lady's tattoos from back in the day. Do I wake Mom and ask her if it's okay? I think about what Aunt Celeste said about thinking for myself. I mean, it's not like I'm going to be taking a lot of life lessons from her, unless it's how *not* to live your life . . . but she has a point. I don't have to get Mom's permission for *everything*.

I lean over the bed and make the decision for myself. "Do you mind if I have another look?" I whisper to Mom Brodie.

I'm not really expecting an answer, but I wait anyway. Just in case. I mean it would be rude to look at somebody's thigh without asking, wouldn't it? I don't want anyone sneaking into my room, picking up my sheet while I'm sleeping, and looking at my naked legs. That's creepy.

"Just a quick peek," I tell my great-grandmother.

I ease along the side of the bed. The weird carpet feels rough under my bare feet. We don't have carpet in our house. Just hardwood and some little rugs here and there.

Watching Mom Brodie's face, and listening for Birdie, I lift up the edge of the blanket and sheet. Birdie likes to tiptoe around and listen to conversations she hasn't been invited to. And if I leave my phone anywhere, she looks at my texts. I don't know what she's looking for. Sexts to my boyfriend? I don't even have a stupid boyfriend. (Probably never will because boys don't like girls who are taller and smarter than they are.) I once asked Mom to ask Birdie to stop infringing on my privacy. Mom said I'd get better results not leaving my phone on the kitchen table when I go to the bathroom. Which wasn't exactly the response I was hoping for.

I guess I should appreciate the fact that Mom and Dad aren't snoopers. It's part of the mutual agreement thing. They don't read Reed's or my texts, and we stay out of their drawer next to their bed. I have friends who have parents who go through their phone messages and backpacks and closets all the time. And for no reason. It's not like they're doing anything dangerous or jeopardizing homeland security; they're a bunch of geeks like me.

I still hear the pot banging and dish clinking. Birdie sure is loud about putting away the dishes. Sometimes I think she does that kind of thing for show, like to get us to look at her or feel sorry for her or something. The thing is, when I *do* try to help out, she just keeps telling me how I do everything wrong.

She's a weird duck, my grandmother. Of course, not any weirder than Dad's mom. We don't see her very often, though. She lives in Florida on a golf course and plays eighteen holes every day. She makes a point of telling me that every time I talk to her. She even writes it on my birthday card. *Happy Birthday, Granddaughter! Hope you have a great day! I know I will! Playing 18 holes!* She also uses a lot of exclamation points in her correspondence, which makes me naturally suspicious of her. And she's got a face like one of those shriveled apple-head dolls you can buy in Appalachia. Too much sun on those eighteen holes, I'd guess.

With no one looking, I make my move. I pull back the covers, and there it is. The bluebird garter. It's just as pretty as I remembered it. Maybe prettier because now I see a couple of details I didn't notice before. Like the way the shades of the ink were done to give a 3-D look to the ruffles on the garter. On impulse, I pull my phone out of my sports bra. I'm dressed to take a run before it gets too hot.

I snap two quick pics, feeling guilty because what kind of weirdo takes pictures of her one-hundred-and-two-year-old great-grandmother's wrinkly thigh? I cover her back up again. I'm careful to lay the sheet and blanket just right so they don't look like they've been disturbed.

Then I go back to the head of the bed, and I lean over my great-grandmother. "Thanks, Mom Brodie," I whisper.

I wait a second. Nothing. I glance down at the nightstand. The pill bottles are still there, but there's also a teacup and saucer. I think it's Mom Brodie's; I've seen it in her room. Someone must have put it here for her. I think for a second and then open the drawer. I root around until I find a pad of paper and a pen. I write a palindrome on the little piece of blue paper, roll it up in a scroll, and leave it on the nightstand. I don't know why; it just seems like the right thing to do. I put the pen and pad of paper back in the drawer.

I go to my mom. "Mom." I put my hand on her shoulder.

She wakes with a start and stiffens in the chair, looking over at Mom Brodie. I see panic in her sleepy face. "Is she —"

"No, she's not dead," I say, feeling bad

that Mom thought that was why I was waking her. "She's fine. Well . . . you know what I mean."

My mom runs the back of her hand across her mouth. "I need coffee."

I look down at her; she's got a funny look on her face. And she didn't take her makeup off last night. She's got mascara smeared under one eye. Usually, my mom looks so pretty in the morning, even when her hair is sticking up in the back. I grin when I realize I recognize that look, although I can't say that I've ever seen it on my mom before. But it's what Celeste looks like every morning. Celeste's pretty scary when she first gets out of bed. "Mom, were you overserved last night?" That's what I hear my friends' parents say. They don't say they got *drunk;* they say they were *overserved,* which we think is funny. How does that make getting shit-faced sound any better?

Mom looks at me and scowls, flinging off an ugly crocheted blanket and getting out of the chair. "No."

That's when I realize she's been sleeping in Grandpop's recliner. The one that's usually in the den. "You bring that in here?" I ask, pointing at the chair. "By yourself?" The thing is monstrous.

Another scowl, only this time she pushes

221

up the sleeve of her T-shirt (*my* T-shirt) and flexes to show me her fairly puny bicep.

"Why didn't you just come to bed? You wouldn't have woken me. You know me. Dad says I'd sleep through an earthquake."

"I didn't want her to be alone." She leans over Mom Brodie. Double-checking the breathing thing, I'm sure.

But there's something in her tone that makes me stop being a smartassed teenager for a minute. I go to my mother, stand beside her at the bed, and put one arm around her shoulders. She wraps her arm around my waist and rests her head on my shoulder. I'm taller than she is, now.

We just stand there for a minute looking down at Mom Brodie. Not saying anything. Because what are you going to say? She's dying, and I wish she wasn't? She's dying, and I'm sad?

But standing here with my mother in a half hug feels good. Comfortable. It's nice and cool in the room, and the sun is coming in through the windows, and my mom smells good. Her smell makes me feel safe. Like I'm not dying today.

And I'm loved.

I lower my arm. Mom kisses my shoulder before she straightens up.

We don't hug and kiss the way we used

to. And I don't sit on her lap much anymore. She was starting to make me feel smothered. I mean, I like it sometimes, but I'm old enough to not want my mother being all clingy. And I'm old enough to start learning how to live beyond her shadow. Not that I think I'll ever be totally out of it. Or want to be. My mom's my best friend. I don't tell her that, of course, because then she'd be back in my personal space again.

"You don't want her to be alone when she dies?" I ask.

Mom nods and smooths the white hair on my great-grandmother's temple.

"You think she's going to die soon?"

Again my mom nods.

"But how do you know that? She could live weeks like this, right? People do it all the time, in a coma. You see it on TV."

"Not at home, they don't. Not without medical intervention. IV fluids and a feeding tube."

Then I realize what she means. Mom Brodie can't live if she doesn't get water and food. Now I feel stupid that *that* didn't occur to me. Mom told me we were coming to be with Mom Brodie when she died. There's a hospice nurse coming every day. Birdie's asking me if I brought a dress for the funeral. Of *course* she's going to die soon.

Like maybe *today* soon.

And then she'll be gone, and I'll never be able to tell her a palindrome again or snitch peppermints from her apron pocket. And she'll never squeeze my hand and tell me that when she looks at me, she thinks she's looking in an old mirror because I look just like she did when she was my age.

All of a sudden, I feel really bad. And sad. And totally overwhelmed. I can barely deal with picking out an outfit to wear the first day of school. How am I supposed to deal with Mom Brodie, the queen of everything, dying and leaving us?

And how did I not know all this was going to make me feel this way?

I didn't come out and say this to anyone, not even to Mom, but truthfully, the only reason I came to Brodie Island in the first place was to see a dead body. Because I never saw one before. But now I realize that if I want to see a dead body, that means Mom Brodie has to die. It means we have to lose her. Forever.

I feel like I can't catch my breath. I need to get out of here.

I need to go for a run. That always makes me feel better. When I run, that's when I

224

can think about stuff. Try to make sense of stuff. After a while, I don't feel my legs burning or hear my breathing; it's just me and all the crazy stuff in my head that I need to make sense of. My dad's a runner, too. He says the same thing.

"I . . . I just wanted to tell you I was going for a run," I say, moving toward the door, snatching up my sneakers off the floor. I'm going to feel stupid if I start crying. And Mom's going to think I'm such a baby. That she shouldn't have brought me with her. That I can't handle this. But I can. I just need to get it all straight in my head.

"I've got my cell with me." From the doorway, I look back. "Mom, you know anything about a book Birdie has?" I ask softly. "Like a big scrapbook? It was with the photo albums. Blue. Aztec kind of print on the cover."

She looks at me quizzically. "No. Why?"

I shake my head, thinking how weird Birdie was about it. I mean, weird even for her. "Just wondering." I turn away again, then look back and call to Mom Brodie, but Mom, too. "Love you."

18
SARAH AGNES

So one day I'm a fourteen-year-old school-girl living in a little town in Nowhere, Indiana, and the next day, I'm eighteen years old, riding on the seat of a tent truck with the man who has changed my life forever. We're headed to South Bend, and I'm so excited because I've never been to South Bend. I've never been anywhere.

"You leave your parents a note?" Henri asks me. He's smoking, his left arm propped in the open window, his right hand on the big steering wheel. The road is dusty, and I wish he'd put up the window because I keep coughing, but I don't ask him to. For now, I'm just happy to be with him. Happy to be starting my new life.

"No," I tell him. The road is so full of potholes that I feel like I'm on some sort of carnival ride being jostled until I think my teeth might be coming loose. "I thought about it, but what would I say? When my father gets back he might try to come after me if he knew I went with you."

Henri suddenly looks worried. He glowers at me with his dark eyes. "You think he would?"

I stare straight ahead at the truck in front of us. The back is painted with advertising for the bearded lady and monkey boy attractions. I asked Henri about them this morning because I didn't see anything about them on the playbills that had blown around town. He said the monkey boy joined a different carnival last fall, and the bearded lady was still part of the outfit but she'd been visiting her sick mother all week. I asked him if she was for real, and he winked at me and told me she was for real, all right. Henri said there was actually a whole show that was usually a part of Rudebaker's Carnival, and that we'd be meeting up with them in another week or so, once the carnival season got rolling. He said there's also a family of cannibals, a giantess, and a snake man who would be joining us. I wanted to ask him where a bearded woman or a snake man could live off-season. But I'd already asked so many questions, and I didn't want Henri to think I was an ignorant girl, so I dropped the subject. I could always ask him later, or maybe ask the bearded lady myself.

Henri throws his cigarette butt out the window. "Give any thought to a job?" he asks me.

"A job?" I ask.

"Everyone's gotta pull their weight, *mon petite,* even a pretty girl like you." He reaches across the seat for me, and I slide over to ride beside him.

"I . . . Right. I thought maybe I could sell cotton candy, or . . . popcorn?"

He smiles down at me. "*Mon chér,* those are Mama Baker's concessions. She runs it; just pays Jacko his cut. She doesn't need anyone to sell her cotton candy. She's got her daughter, Matilda." He nods. "She's about your age, I think. You might like Matilda. She's a nice girl. Ugly as home-made sin, but a nice girl."

I nod. I know I told Henri I would work to pay my keep if he let me come with him, but I guess I was thinking that maybe he earned enough for both of us. It wasn't that I minded working. I just wasn't sure what I was qualified to do. Especially since I hadn't completed the ninth grade yet. "Well, I . . . I guess I'll talk to Jacko," I say slowly. "Ask him if he has a job for me."

Henri frowns. "Best you stay away from

Jacko for a few days. He might not like the idea of your tagging along."

"But I'm not tagging along, Henri." I look up at his handsome face. "I'm with you now. We're together." We hit a pothole so big that the whole truck tilts, throwing me up against Henri, and for a second I think we're going to tip over. But Henri hits the gas, and the engine whines, and we come out of the hole, and we're behind the bearded lady and monkey boy truck again. "Right?" I ask, looking up at him. "You love me, and I love you, and we're together." It's on the tip of my tongue to suggest we go ahead and get married now, but I don't say it.

Henri tightens his arm around my shoulder and kisses my cheek. "Of course we're together, *mon amour;* I'm just saying everyone works. It's not my rule; it's Jacko's, and he's the operator. He lays down the law."

I think for a minute. "Maybe I could take tickets with you for the Ferris wheel."

He shakes his head. "The ladies don't usually take tickets. Folks in these small towns wouldn't like it. Some places, we've already got the preachers breathing down our necks. They got ideas about what a woman ought and ought not to do. We can't afford to get kicked outta towns once we put down stakes. Jacko's got overhead. Show's got to go on, and all that."

I notice for the first time that his French accent isn't as strong as it had been earlier in the week. In fact, this morning he almost has a Southern sound to his voice. I know it's Southern because he sounds like the butcher we used to have in Bakersville who was from Arkansas. Mr. Clements. My grandmother always made fun of his accent after we left his shop. Called him Confederate trash. That was back when we were still buying meat. He was nice. He used to throw in beef bones for soup, with my grandmother's order for chicken necks, but he closed shop and left town around Christmas.

I look up at Henri. "But women must take some kind of jobs. I saw a couple this morning when everyone was loading up." I left home this morning before dawn with nothing but a pillowcase with my clothes and met Henri just as the carnival was loading to pull out of town. "They must do something."

He stares straight ahead and smiles this strange little smile that I don't really understand. "That they do."

"Well, what do they do?" I ask him. "I can do what they do."

230

"I don't know about that," he says slowly. "They're coochie girls, *mon amour.*"

"Coochie girls?" I have no idea what that means. I'm beginning to see that these carnies have a whole language that I don't know.

Henri smiles down at me, but I get the feeling he's laughing at me to himself.

"You know, the girly show," he says.

I shake my head, still not understanding.

Then he just smiles and points to the dirty dashboard of the truck. "Grab me another fag, will you, Sarry?"

That's when I probably should have gotten out of that truck. If I had, I could have made it back to Bakersville, walking probably. I'd have gotten a switching from Mrs. Hanfland and my father when he got home, too. But it wouldn't have been too late to go home.

Of course it never crossed my mind that day to actually go home to Bakersville. It never crossed my mind the rest of my days.

19
BIRDIE

"Can I talk to you, Birdie?"

Little Joe startles me, and I whip around, a head of cabbage in my hand. I'm making slaw. Having crabs this afternoon out on the back porch, maybe in the yard, if it's not too hot. But I like to make some salads, maybe hotdogs, when we have steamed blue claws. A person can get hungry picking crabs. It takes a lot of energy. Besides, I don't eat 'em. Crabs eat dead things. To me, it would be like eating a roasted turkey buzzard for Saturday dinner.

I stare at my husband for a minute, not even sure what to say. I can count the number of times in my life he's said he needed to talk to me.

Something's up. Something more than his mama dying in the other room. But I already knew that. He's been acting peculiar all morning. First, he slept in near to seven, which he never does, then after breakfast, he took his coffee to his office and shut the door. Which he almost never does, either. He usually does his office work afternoons. And takes a nap in there on his couch, but he doesn't like people to know he's slowing down. That he needs a nap. So we both pretend he doesn't nap. And I don't wake him while he's napping.

I could hear him on the phone this morning. His office is next to the laundry room. If I stand at the old table in front of the dryer where I fold clothes, I can hear him on the phone, or with the occasional visitor. Only this morning, he was talking quiet. Real quiet. I thought about trying to listen through the office door, but he doesn't like that. I guess he can see my feet, because he knows when I do it and he hollers, "Go on about your business, Birdie."

So when I realized this morning that I wasn't going to be able to tell who he was talking to on the phone or what it was about, I threw the load of towels in the dryer and came back to the kitchen to unload the dishwasher and start with the salads for the crab feast. And make more breakfast and clean up more breakfast. Seems like no one wants to sit down and have breakfast together; they all want to eat when it suits them. Late risers, my daughters and granddaughter, all of them. Which means breakfast can stretch near to midday.

Abby slept with Mom Brodie last night. In Joe's chair. I don't know how she got it in there. Maybe Joseph moved it last night. I didn't hear them come in. Of course Celeste didn't come in 'til after dawn. No surprise there. It used to bother me that my daughter is a slut, but I guess I've gotten used to it. Can't make a silk purse out of a sow's ear; that's what Mrs. Brodie always says. And a mother sow loves her little one just the same, doesn't she?

"Sarah just went through. Going for a run," I tell my husband, stalling for time. I'm not good at talking with people. Not even my family. Especially when it's the kind of conversation a person feels like they have to announce before they get to it. I don't like that. It scares me. A person just ought to say what they want to say. I hold tight to the cabbage. "Wouldn't have breakfast. Not a bite. Running. For no reason. Going nowhere." I shake my head. "Never understood it. Never will."

He pushes his hands deep into his work pants pockets. "Celeste up?"

I shake my head. "Still 'sleep." No need for him to know she just went to bed not long ago. "Abby's in the shower."

He looks up, like he can see through the ceiling with X-ray eyes. Then he tilts his head toward the porch and walks away. The dog falls right in behind him. Always does. Mrs. Brodie says they all follow him around, Dukes living *and* dead. I don't know if I believe in ghosts, but I darn well know I don't believe in ghost *dogs*. I think Mrs. Brodie used to say things like that just to get me riled. She knows I'm easily spooked.

I follow my husband and his dog. I take my cabbage with me. I don't know why. Something to hold on to? This has to be bad. Otherwise why would Joe want to talk outside? But I can't think what it could be. He never says much to me about the farm, about his businesses. Never has. That was always Mrs. Brodie's department. They used to sit in his office and talk and laugh. I had to learn things about what was going on secondhand through the wall while folding his drawers.

He opens the back door and then the screen door, and Duke shoots out. We keep doors closed in the summer now. It's not like it used to be with screen doors and windows wide open, to let the salt breeze off the bay blow through and air the house out. Air conditioning running. I don't care for it. Air conditioning. But Mrs. Brodie insisted on it. Central air.

Little Joe holds open the door for me and waits for me to pass. His forehead creases, furrows so deep it could be one of our plowed fields in the spring. "Birdie, what you doing with that cabbage?" he asks me.

I feel awkward. "Slaw."

"I meant . . ." He shakes his head and follows me out. Closes the doors behind us as we go out in the yard.

I think about setting the cabbage down on the table, but now that he's said something about it, I don't.

Outside, Joe just stands there. Hands in his pockets like they're glued in.

We've got a nice view of the bay from the backyard. Million-dollar view Celeste calls it. On a morning like this, the water spreads out all sparkly in front of us. Almost looks pretty. But I don't usually see it that way. It scares me. I'm not like the Brodies, who seem to be born with salt water in their blood. All my brood could swim by the time they could walk. Little Joe taught them right out there in the shallow water. Scared the liver out of me. I can't swim, and people drown out there every year. And then crabs eat the bodies if they don't wash up fast enough. Crabs Little Joe wants to put on my table.

I can see the bridge, far off. I remember when it was built. Folks got on one side of the argument or the other. Either they hated every beam of steel that rose in the sky, or they loved it. I never knew which side I fell on. In a way, I felt protected without an easy way across the water. People and things that scared me couldn't come across a bridge that wasn't there. But in other ways, I felt so trapped on Brodie, even when I was a little girl. After the bridge was built, connecting us with the rest of the world, it occurred to me that it wasn't just a road onto Brodie. It was a road to get off. A road that could take a brave soul away from this. To a new life. A better life.

A braver soul than me.

Duke barks and takes off across the lawn. Seagulls. I've never seen a dog that will chase a gull like this one. Oh, he'll chase a rabbit. Or a skunk. I've had to bathe him more than once in tomato juice after a tangle with a skunk. But who ever heard of a Labrador retriever that chases seagulls? They're water dogs. Like the Brodies. They live and breathe this bay. Water dogs aren't supposed to chase seagulls.

"Clancy rang me this morning," Little Joe says. He tugs on the brim of his John Deere ball cap. Always wears John Deere even

237

though lots of companies give him free ones all the time.

I think it's funny he says that because the phone didn't ring this morning except when Mae Bower called to ask me if I could bring banana bread for tea, next Naomi Circle meeting at the church. Means Joe called Clancy. But I don't say anything. I learned that lesson a long time ago. No need to tell everything you know.

"About Mama's will."

I nod. Not sure I knew she had a will. The land and the house and the businesses passed to Joe forty-odd years ago when his daddy died. I imagine Mrs. Brodie has a little money of her own, but how much could there be? What would she need her own money for? Her name's right on our checkbook with mine and Joe's. Always bought whatever she wanted. But she's the one who told me to tuck a little away for myself. Showed me how to take a little from here and there and tuck it away in the bank. For a rainy day. "A girl needs her own money for a rainy day," she used to tell me.

I guess Mrs. Brodie's rainy-day money is what Joe's talking about. I don't know why, but I smile to myself. The old bird. I guess she was talking from experience.

I look at Joe. His eyebrows need trimming.

Next time I cut his hair — what little he's got left — I need to trim his brows. If I don't, they get to looking like caterpillars. Like the big, thick white ones. The kind you see on the sidewalk every blue moon.

"She didn't tell me she changed it, Birdie. I didn't even know she met with Clancy."

Something about the tone of his voice makes me meet his gaze. He's got his mama's eyes. They were bright blue once. Now they've faded to a gray color. But they're still Mrs. Brodie's eyes.

I always thought Joe had nice eyes. It's the first thing I remember about him when I came to Brodie, even though I was just a little girl nine years old. They were kind eyes. He was kind to me. First night I sat at the table, Mrs. Brodie told me to keep my mouth shut when I chewed. Then she told me to stop shoveling my potatoes. She said there was plenty more and she'd make more if need be, but she didn't want me eating like a wolf at her table. Which was funny, thinking back, because that's what it was like at the orphanage, come suppertime. Eating with a bunch of wolves. If you didn't eat up fast, some boy would reach right across the table and take your potatoes right off your plate with his hand and gobble them down. It's not like we went hungry at the orphanage, but there were sure no seconds. A girl who liked to save her mashed potatoes for last to savor them ended up going without.

I remember fighting back tears at the table that first night here in the house. It wasn't so much what Mrs. Brodie said. I think I was just overwhelmed. Then Joe looked at me, and he winked. And smiled. And then I ate my potatoes slow, and I learned to keep my mouth shut when I ate. But I never forgot that kindness.

"What did she change in her will?" I ask.

As the words come out of my mouth, I daydream for just a split second that he's called me out here to tell me she's left me something. Maybe her diamond wedding ring, or a little money. Or maybe her car. She's got an old Cadillac. She keeps it in one of the sheds out back with a cover over it to keep it clean. It's a fine car. White, with a blue interior. I wouldn't mind driving it. Maybe Mrs. Brodie left me something because she realized that even though we're not blood, I've taken care of her like she was. Especially these last few months since she got the cancer. Maybe she thought someone who changed her diaper ought to get a little something,

I wait for Joe to go on, and finally he gets

240

around to it.

"She's cut Celeste out." He turns to face the bay again, clearly upset. His voice barely sounds like him. "Completely."

I rub my forehead with my free hand. I can't find my voice. Mrs. Brodie can't do that. Not to my Celeste. Not to my little lost bird. I try to make sense of what Joe's saying. "So . . . she's . . . she's leaving what she has just to Abby?" When I say it, I know very well my name's not in that will, but still there's just a little part of me that . . . hopes.

"Joseph, too. Abby and Joseph."

I look down at the cabbage. It's a decent one for summer. I won't pick mine until early October. I wonder where cabbages are growing in August. Somewhere else in the world, I guess. When I came to Brodie, we ate mostly from our own garden, but anything we did get from the market came from Brodie, or maybe Snow Hill or Salisbury. Now, fruits and vegetables come from California, Mexico. Even Peru. The wonders of a bridge.

I take a step toward Joe, looking up at his back. How could Mrs. Brodie do that to my baby girl, I think, when Celeste's the one who needs it most? And leave money to Joseph, who will inherit all this land someday?

Who will inherit the Brodie empire. "She left something to Joseph and not Celeste?" I ask.

"Joseph is my child. Same as Abby and Celeste, Birdie."

But not mine, I think. But what would that mean to Mrs. Brodie? All that matters to her is Brodie blood. It's all that ever mattered.

Joe's words aren't mean, but they're stiff. He gets like that when we talk about Joseph. Not that it happens that often, once every couple of years. And then when we talk about Joseph, we don't *really* talk about him. Not about how he got here and what Joe did to bring him into this world.

When I close my eyes, I remember the night, like it was only a day ago. A Thursday night. I was washing dishes at the sink after supper. A plate. I was taking a scrub brush to it. Cheese from macaroni and cheese. Abby was at the kitchen table doing her homework. Mrs. Brodie was beside her, reading a magazine. Celeste was in the den. She was supposed to be doing homework, too, but Celeste was never much for homework. She was singing into a microphone we gave her for Christmas. She was singing one of those nasty Madonna songs. I'd just told her to cut it out or I'd wash her mouth

242

with soap. But she just kept it up, "Like a virgin . . ."

Joe'd been gone two days. He'd called the day before, just to say he was all right. He didn't say where he was, and I didn't ask. He'd been disappearing on and off for almost two years. Just hours, never a night before though. I knew he had a woman on the side. I'd even heard rumors of who it was. A colored girl that worked in the cannery, then started doin' office work. Mrs. Brodie knew it, too, I think. She never said anything to him that I heard, but when he'd come home late, she'd give him a look that would melt paint off the side of a barn.

"It's money . . . a lot of money," Joe goes on, pulling me back from that night when he handed me that little baby and said, "He's my son, Birdie," like he was going to cry. And then he walked out of the kitchen, leaving us all to stare at the bundle in my arms.

I stare at him and shake my head. "What do you mean . . . a lot of money?"

He says something under his breath. A number. And I pull the cabbage to my chest and hug it. "Where did she get so much —" I cut myself off. No need to go there. One thing could lead to another, and then the focus could end up on me and not where it belongs right now. Which is on Mrs. Brodie. And Celeste, my poor Celeste.

"Is . . . is there something that can be done?" I ask him. "To give Celeste back her money? Because it's not right, Joe!" I raise my voice. I don't think I've ever raised my voice to him in all the years I've known him.

He stares at me for a minute. I can't read his face. He's shocked for sure, but there's something else there. "Mama had Clancy write a new will. She was of sound mind," he tells me. "It's her right to leave her money to whom she pleases. Hell, Birdie." He points to the Labrador retriever that is trit-trotting down our dock. "She could have left it to Duke if it suited her."

"That's the stupidest thing I've ever heard," I snap back. "A woman doesn't leave money to a dog!" I shake my head. "It ain't right. It ain't right, and you know it, Joe."

"She left Celeste a letter. Giving her reasons, I suppose."

I hear a splash, and we both look up. That dog has gone to the end of the dock and jumped into the bay. Right about now, I could do the same. Only I can't swim. The idea is appealing. I've played with that thought time to time over the years. It moves in close, then into the background again. I can feel it creeping in. "What's the letter say?"

"I didn't read it. Not mine to read. Clancy gave it to me, sealed in an envelope. Gave me her new will, too. To replace the one she gave me years back. Mama told him to. I'm supposed to pass the letter on to Celeste after Mama's gone as a way of explanation for what she did." Joe takes in a breath, lets it go. "I suspect it has to do with Mama's not approving of the way Celeste has led her life. The way she's spent her money." He's quiet again, but I wait. "I think she borrowed money from Mama that maybe she didn't pay back."

"We don't know that," I say, but even as the words come out, I realize I probably don't know as much about it as I think I do. I'll give Mrs. Brodie credit; she didn't talk about money, and she never spoke of whom she lent it to. I know she loaned people money, not just Celeste, but town folk, because they'd walk right up to her in the market and hand her repayment, saying "Oh, thank you, Miss Sarah, this, and oh, I don't know where I would have turned, Miss Sarah, that." And I can't say I've always thought my youngest daughter was smart with her money, but who am I to make that judgment?

245

"I guess Mama thought money would go to waste in Celeste's hands," Joe says quietly.

"And that's that?" I demand. "You're not going to do anything about it?"

He looks at me, all sad like. "I can't change Mama's will, Birdie. It's legal and binding."

"So that *is* that, then," I say.

And then I walk right across the yard and into the house. I set the cabbage on the counter and go down the hall and up the stairs. I go to my bedroom, and I close the door and lock it. I dig through my nightie drawer to the bottom, and I pull out my scrapbook. And I sit on the edge of the bed and open it to the first page. And I trace the outline of the state with my finger. "Arizona, the forty-eighth state to enter the union," I whisper. "Capital, Phoenix. State bird, cactus wren. State flower, saguaro blossom." I flip forward several pages until I find the picture of the saguaro blossom I cut out of a *National Geographic* I found at the beauty parlor.

Looking at the cactus blossom calms me. Helps me pull myself together so I can go back downstairs and make my slaw.

20
SARAH

I knock on the office door that's almost shut, but not quite. "Grandpop?"

" 'M'on in," he calls.

As I push open the door, Duke chuffs, but he doesn't get up from where he's sprawled on the hardwood floor. No ugly blue carpet here. Grandpop pulled it up years ago.

I've got my laptop tucked under my arm. After I took a shower, when I got back from my run, I came downstairs and checked on Mom. She was drinking some of Birdie's nasty coffee and waiting for the hospice nurse. She seemed preoccupied, so we didn't really talk. We just had one of the obligatory mother-daughter exchanges.

"How was your run?" She was staring out the window at the bay. She didn't look at me.

"Good."

"Have enough hot water? Birdie's been running the washing machine and dishwasher nonstop since dawn."

"It was fine, Mom."

"I saw the palindrome. I like it. She'd like it."

I nodded, and then I wandered out of the room, feeling guilty all over again that I'd taken a pic of my great-grandmother's thigh. I mean, it's not like I Snapchatted it or anything. But I think this is one of those cases where you know it's inherently wrong, even if your mom didn't say, "Don't take a picture of your great-grandmother's thigh tattoo while I'm asleep."

I walk into my grandfather's office, which is always a pleasant surprise. It's not what you would think it would be. I mean, he looks like an old farmer. He wears pants and shirts that are the same dirt color, like a uniform a guy in a factory would wear. Every day. And always a hat that advertises a seed or tractor company. He's married to a woman who looks like an old farmer's wife. But his office is . . . nice.

The walls are a medium green, with wood trim everywhere. He has a big wooden desk that must be older than he is and a bunch of filing cabinets and a leather couch. A *nice* leather couch. And a cool coffee table with leather inlay that looks really old and really expensive. And a faded Oriental-style rug that I know came from Turkey at the turn of the last century because he told me so. But the most interesting object in a room with seed catalogs, farming magazines, and the old farmer behind the desk, is an antique violin on a display stand in the corner of the room.

I stand inside the doorway. "I was wondering . . ." I shift my weight from one bare foot to the other.

"You can close the door." He points.

We both smile. He knows Birdie's a snoop. Of course he does. He's married to her. I don't really have anything to say that's private, but I close the door anyway because I like the idea of being alone with him. We don't get to be alone that often. And he's an interesting guy, my grandfather. My dad says he's complicated, which I always thought was an interesting phrase. But now that I've seen Mom Brodie's tattoo, I think I understand what Dad means, because Mom Brodie is sure more *complicated* than I thought.

The door clicks shut. It's got an old-fashioned brown glass doorknob and a big square lock that must have once had a long key. Most of the doors still have the old knobs. Only the bathrooms have newer doorknobs and, therefore, locks. I think

Mom said she put the upstairs one on herself to keep Birdie out. But Grandpop added a dead bolt on the office door. To keep out snoops, I'm sure.

I walk slowly toward his desk and lower my laptop to the coffee table. The room smells like old papers and coffee. And a dog that's been in the bay this morning. But not in a bad way. "I'm really sorry about your mom."

He smiles at me from behind his desk. He's got a big computer screen to one side, and his hands are resting in front of a keyboard. "I appreciate that, Sarah."

I glance at the violin. "Is it okay if I pick it up?" He always lets me. Has since I was little, but I ask anyway.

My grandfather doesn't play the violin. No one in the house does. It was his grandmother's. It was made in Boston in the eighteen hundreds. She was from there, and when she came to marry a Joe or John Brodie (I can't remember which), she brought it with her.

I have to step over Duke to get to it. He doesn't move, just opens one eye. I pick up the violin very carefully and lift it to my shoulder as if I know how to play. I pick up the bow and drag it ever so lightly across the strings. The delicious sound that comes from the violin makes the hair stand on the back of my neck. I love violin music.

"I wish I'd taken those lessons you offered that summer," I say. I think back to those days when I was in elementary school and Reed was in middle school. We used to come here and stay weeks at a time in the summer when I didn't have field hockey and Key Club and Reed wasn't playing travel lacrosse. Life was so easy then. I was never afraid, and I always felt loved. I didn't worry about the nuclear bombs North Korea is building or viruses that could potentially wipe out the human race.

"Never too late," Grandpop says. "To learn. I know a man who gives lessons in town twice a week."

I set the violin back gently on its stand. Then the bow. "Long way to drive for music lessons."

"You could move here," he suggests. "Got plenty of room. Your mom and dad could have her room, and you could have Joseph's old room." He's just joking. And not.

I walk to one wall and study a bunch of black-and-white framed photos, mostly of people. Them and some of the Dukes. "That you?" I point to a handsome man wading in the bay. There's an old rowboat in the background. He's wearing pants and

251

a shirt with the sleeves rolled up and a big straw hat on his head. It looks like it might have been taken in the backyard. The man is grinning like he's the happiest guy on earth.

"My dad," he says.

I look at another. It's Mom Brodie leaning against a car from, maybe, the fifties. She's wearing pants and a shirt and an apron like Birdie wears, the kind that almost looks like a really long tank top. Only it ties at the neck and the waist, in the back, and is really ugly. There's a scarf on her head, tied like a turban, and she's laughing, her head tilted back, stray locks of hair blowing in the wind. I know it's her because she looks so much like me. Or rather the other way around.

"Do you think you could find Mom Brodie's marriage license?" I ask, studying a photo of one of the Dukes dragging a wooden bushel basket of blue claw crabs by the handle. I don't know which Duke it is. "You said you might have it."

"If I do, I know it's one of two places." He gets up and goes to one of the metal cabinets. It's a little rusty around the handle. He pulls open a drawer.

I turn back to the pictures on the wall. "I know Mom Brodie was born in Indiana.

How'd she get to New Jersey, where she met your dad?"

"I don't know. Or maybe I did, and I've forgotten." He closes a drawer and opens another. He sounds like he's thinking it through. "Visiting a cousin, maybe?"

"You ever meet the cousin? Or . . . anyone else from her family?" When he doesn't answer, I turn away from the photos to look at him. "A brother? A sister?"

"She was an only child. Parents were musicians from . . . Chicago, maybe. No, I can't say that I ever met any of her relatives." He's holding a file in his hand. "I guess she didn't have any."

"But obviously she *did.*" I walk toward him. "The cousin she was visiting in New Jersey. Or was she living there with her? Him?"

"It was a girl. But maybe she was just a friend. My memory's not what it was. I can hardly remember what I had for breakfast this morning. Why all the questions?" He sets the file on top of the file cabinet, opens it, and begins flipping through papers.

"I don't know." I shrug. I'm not good at lying, so I want to be careful what I say. People know when I'm lying. Especially my mom. And for all I know, she got her superpowers from her dad. "I know it's a little late, but I guess I'm curious about her life. About who she was before she came to Brodie Island." All true. "Maybe because I was named after her?" Not a lie, either.

"It's never too late to show interest in your family." He frowns. "It's not here. Maybe the fire box." He leaves the file on top of the cabinet and crouches down to pull a big, heavy box out from under a table. It's got a combination lock.

"What's in there?"

"Stuff I wouldn't want to lose if there was a fire. Stock certificates, a few photos, insurance papers, bank information, car titles, promissory notes," he rattles off. I like the way my grandfather talks to me. He never acts like I'm a kid. Never did, not even when I was one. "Some cash money. For emergencies."

I nod. Now I know why it's locked. Celeste. She takes money. Last summer she took a twenty out of the pocket of my jean jacket hanging on the back porch. She told me she didn't, but she was lying. I guess she'd take money from her father's safe, too, if it weren't locked.

He rolls the little dials on the thingy and opens the heavy, molded lid. "I don't think Mama's childhood was a happy one," he says. "It was the Depression. Life was hard, particularly in the Midwest. Brodies were pretty cash poor in those years, but we had plenty of food, between what we grew and what we took out of the Chesapeake Bay. There weren't many jobs. Kids went hungry. Without shoes. Clothes. I imagine being a professional musician was hard. I think that's why Mama never told us much about it."

I think about the tattoo. That is *not* the tattoo of someone with an unhappy childhood. Or at least, unhappy young adulthood. It's the tattoo of a woman who knew how to live, or at least dreamed of that life. I think the tattoo also has sexual connotations . . . or at least sensual. I think my great-grandmother knew what it was like to love someone. I'd bet my college fund that Grandpop has stashed away that Mom Brodie was *not* the innocent virgin when she got married that everyone assumes she was. Why else would she hide that tattoo for eighty-some years with flowered aprons and a position on the Methodist church council?

I wonder if it's a possibility that she might have been a lady of the evening. That's probably what they would have called it then. Maybe she was one of those women working in a speakeasy in Chicago? Because, so far, what I've found on the Internet is mostly pictures of tattoos that prostitutes and exotic dancers had. Which might be another euphemism for a prostitute. Wouldn't that be something to write about in my college entrance essay, how I'm the great-granddaughter of a prostitute? Something like that might even get me a scholarship.

A slut nixes sex in Tulsa. That's the only prostitute palindrome I know.

I smile to myself and look at my grandfather again. "Your dad just met her at this tent revival thing and what? Married her on the spot?"

He nods, standing up with an old manila envelope in his hand, the kind with the metal tab. "I guess it was something like that. He once told me he took one look at her and fell in love. Knew he couldn't live without her." He carries the envelope to his desk, sits down, and dumps the contents.

"Love at first sight. *Really?*" I rest my hands on my hips. It's my new favorite pose, hands low, fingertips on my pelvic bones. My friend Maggie says it makes me look sexy and badass at the same time. "You believe there's such a thing?" I ask my grandfather, my tone indicating that clearly I think it's bullshit.

"You're young to be such a cynic."

"My dad says the same thing." I walk toward the desk. "I'm serious, Grandpop. Do you really think it's possible to fall in love with someone the first time you meet? Like before you even know what kind of person they are?"

"I think anything is possible in God's world."

The God explanation always annoys me because I feel like God's just the excuse adults use when they can't or don't want to try to explain something. But I let it go because I'm not up for a God discussion with anyone today. I push a little green metal tractor on his desk with my finger. It's an antique. Been here as long as I can remember. "Was that the way it was when you met Birdie? Love at first sight?"

He reaches for his reading glasses on the desk. They're the kind without frames. They perch on the end of his nose. He doesn't look at me. "Your grandmother was a little girl when she came here. I was a teenager."

"That's not really an answer," I point out.

He glances at me over the top of his glasses. "I don't suppose it is." He's quiet for a second, like he's trying to think of what to say. "Even though I'm older, your grandmother and I kind of grew up together."

I run my finger over one of the rubber tires. "You think Mom Brodie brought her here with the intention of marrying you two? I mean . . . was it like an arranged marriage or something?"

He laughs.

"What? We talked about arranged marriages in my history class last semester. People used to arrange marriages for, like, political reasons. Did you know Marie Antoinette and King Louis XVI's marriage was arranged? She married him when she was *fourteen*! That's younger than me." I cross my arms over my chest. "Bet she wished her parents hadn't done *that*."

My grandfather kind of smiles, one side of his mouth turning up. "I don't think there was any political gain for our families in the case of our marriage."

"Right. Because Birdie was an orphan. No family. No money." I know I should let it go, but I just can't. Birdie and Grandpop are so different; I could never figure out why someone like him would marry someone like her. "So . . . did you guys fall in love, or did Mom Brodie and your dad kind of push you two together?"

"We married because we wanted to, Sarah. People get married for different reasons."

"Were you in love with her?"

258

He holds up a piece of paper that's about half the size of a piece of notebook paper. "Knew it was here somewhere."

He didn't answer my question. Duly noted. I take the paper; it's so old and delicate that I'm afraid it's going to disintegrate in my hands. The words *Certificate and Record of Marriage* are printed across the top; it's a preprinted form with the information handwritten in. There's a place for the husband's name, the wife's name, where the marriage took place, the name of the person who officiated, and then there's information on each of the people getting married. All of the actual information is written with slanty cursive that's hard to read. I read it out loud. "Sarah Agnes Hafland married Joseph James Brodie, May 23, 1933, in . . ." I squint. "Teton . . . Trenton, maybe. Trenton, New Jersey." I look up. "Were they married in Trenton?"

Grandpop nods. "I guess so." He sits down.

I return my attention to the document. "Says he was born in Brodie, Maryland, and was thirty years old." I look up. "That's old for getting married in those days, wasn't it?"

"He was briefly married in his early twenties. A girl from Baltimore, but she died, giving birth. Baby died, too."

"That's so sad. He must have really loved her to wait so long to marry again." I carry the marriage certificate to the couch and sit down and prop my bare feet up on a pile of seed catalogs. "Mom Brodie was eighteen, born in Chicago, Illinois." I look up. "I thought she was born in Indiana."

He nods. "She was."

"Then why does this say Chicago?" I hold it up.

"Someone made a mistake, I guess."

"Eww." I point at the paper. "It says they're both white." I look up again. "Why would you write the color of someone's skin on a *marriage* certificate?"

"There were rules in those days, laws about who could marry whom."

"You mean white people weren't supposed to marry black people?" I'm so disgusted by the idea that it takes me a second to realize I'm treading on touchy ground. Uncle Joseph's birth mother was an African-American woman. Grandpop cheated on Birdie with a black woman. And even though, by then, the 1980s, the United States was supposed to be way past the whole race discrimination thing, I know they weren't on Brodie Island. Celeste once told me that everyone talked about it for years after.

My grandfather nods, but he doesn't say anything. I return my attention to the marriage certificate. He and I have never talked about the fact that Uncle Joseph isn't Birdie's son. It's not the kind of conversation you have with your grandfather. Maybe someday I will, but today's not the day.

"There's the name of the minister who married them here." I squint. "Reverend Allen or Albert . . . Cummings. But what . . . What are these names on the other side of the paper?" I get up and walk around Grandpop's desk to show him.

He studies the place where I point. "Looks like those were their witnesses."

"Witnesses?"

"You have to have two witnesses to a marriage. Usually the man has one and the woman has one. It's usually the people who stand up with you. Like, your best man and the maid of honor. In those days there wasn't usually a big wedding. People just got married."

"James Brodie," I read. "Obviously a relative. You know him?" I smile. "Of him?" If Grandpop Big Joe was still alive, he'd be like 112.

Grandpop shakes his head. "No, but my dad had second cousins in New Jersey. On the shore. Fishermen. Gotta be a cousin. It's likely that's who my father was visiting when he met Mama."

I nod, walking back to the couch to sit down again. "So her witness was . . . Billie . . . no, *Bilis* . . . looks like . . . Allsop." I glance up, making a face. "*Bilis?* What kind of name is that for a girl?"

He shakes his head, rising from behind his desk. "No idea."

"And Mom Brodie never mentioned her?"

He comes around his desk, grabbing a ball cap and pulling it down over his mostly bald head. "Can't say that she did."

I'm trying not to be perturbed with him. Why doesn't he know any of this stuff? She's his *mother.* And she's going to die; someone needs to know these things.

"I gotta go see Jesse Junior about the crabs. He'll probably steam 'em for me. Your grandmother doesn't like the smell in her house. Be back around three for crabs." He gets to the door. "You're welcome to stay put." I get a half smile from him that's pretty close to a smirk. "Hide out in here, where it's safe."

"Thanks." I look down at the marriage certificate in my hand. "You think Birdie would know anything about Mom Brodie's cousin, or friend, Bilis?"

262

He shrugs and taps his thigh. Duke leaps up and bounds toward him. "Maybe. Hard to say. You know how the two of them were sometimes. They could get each other worked up. But they talked. Women who live in the same house. They get close. Even when they don't want to." He hesitates. "You know, your grandmother . . . Birdie, she . . ." He exhales slowly. "She loves you. She loves you all so much. She just . . . she doesn't know how to show it. She's got a good heart. She just says the wrong things, sometimes. But none of us are perfect, Sarah. Good Lord makes that clear."

He nods. I nod. Then he smiles at me. Meeting my gaze. Really looking at me.

I like that about my grandfather. I think he really sees me for who I am. He gets me. I wish I came here more often. I wish I could remember how this feels when Mom asks me if I want to come for the weekend and I say no because I want to hang out with my friends. Hanging out with my grandfather, with Uncle Joseph, even with Celeste and her craziness is way better than hanging out with my friends. Most of the time. I mean, my friends are fun, but I don't think about them later, or about what we talked about. Not like I do with my family.

"Thanks," I say. "I might. Internet's way

faster in here." I point at a little table behind his desk. "Router."

"Yup." Duke goes out the door ahead of him. "These old walls. I think they block the signal."

He closes the door behind him. I stare at the marriage certificate. I trace Mom Brodie's signature with my finger. "Born in Illinois and not Indiana. Or Indiana and not Illinois," I murmur. "With a cousin . . . or possibly a friend named Bilis. So who are you, grandmother with a tat? And whom did you lie to?"

I reach for my laptop.

21
ABBY

"Has she been restless?" Gail, the hospice nurse, gently wraps the blood pressure cuff around my grandmother's bird-like arm.

Gail looks nothing like what I expected a hospice nurse to look like. I was expecting . . . I don't know. Someone more grandmotherly-like? Or maybe nun-like? She's neither. Gail is a six-foot-tall, curvaceous-leaning-toward-chubby brunette with almost as many tattoos as my brother. She's got bumblebees circling one arm leading to a *Star Wars* rebel symbol and something that looks like Sanskrit on the other forearm. She wears jeans and a white, short-sleeved T-shirt with a badge identifying that she works for Coastal Hospice and Palliative Care. Her hair is super long and piled on top of her head the way Sarah wears hers. Gail can't be thirty.

"Not restless at all," I respond. "I don't think she's moved of her own volition since

I arrived Thursday afternoon. Birdie . . . my mom . . . said she was restless Tuesday, after the ambulance brought her here, but . . . she just seems to be sleeping now."

Gail nods and lifts her purple stethoscope ear tips to her ears. She presses the drum to the crook of my grandmother's elbow. I know she's listening, so I'm quiet. When she's done, she pulls her stethoscope down to hang around her neck and removes the blood pressure cuff. "Seventy over forty-four."

I cross my arms over my chest. I thought I was ready for this, but I . . . It's harder than I thought it would be. To sit here and watch Mom Brodie die. "That's low, right? For blood pressure? And it's lower than yesterday."

"It is lower, but that's to be expected. All part of the process." She checks my grandmother's pulse. Again I wait. "Is she in any pain?"

I'm just standing there by the bed, looking down at my grandmother. I'm in the same clothes I wore yesterday. We're going to pick crabs. Why would I put on clean clothes? I did, however, shower to get the smell of The Gull off me. Celeste sprayed beer in my hair last night while telling a story about a guy trying to pick her up on the subway. "I don't think so." I shake my head, thinking. "No, she's not in any pain, which is kind of weird because she was in the hospital. She was getting pain meds through her IV."

Gail nods and opens Mom Brodie's medical file on the nightstand next to the bottles of pills Mom Brodie won't be taking, and the teacup my mother put there, and Sarah's little blue scroll. "It happens sometimes. Patients get home, in familiar surroundings, and they settle down." She looks at me and smiles. She has a gorgeous smile, one that makes you think everything is going to be all right. Which of course it isn't. It never is, in her line of work. Or at least *all right* has to be reinterpreted.

"I'm glad she's comfortable and pain free, but should she become restless, there's medication in the comfort pack in the refrigerator. All you have to do is give us a call, and we'll walk you through what to give her and how much. Birdie said you'd be the one administering it?" Gail looks at me, waiting for a response.

I feel like I'm a beat behind in the conversation. I'm trying to wrap my head around the moment. Mom Brodie's blood pressure is dropping. She's moving closer to the end. "Right." I nod. I didn't open the *comfort pack,* but I know morphine is one of the drugs in there. Now that I realize I might actually have to give it to her . . . The idea is a little overwhelming. Not that I can't. Or won't give it to her. I'd do anything to keep Mom Brodie from suffering. But saying you can do something like that is different from actually having to do it.

"Don't be afraid to give the medication to her if she needs it, Abby." Gail's tone is kind, but not in any way condescending. "I know this is hard. But you have to remember, this is her choice. To die in her own home, surrounded by her loved ones. We're here to help her make that journey, and we want her to be comfortable in it. We want all of you to be as comfortable as possible." The smile again. "It's a good thing you're doing for your grandmother. Being here with her. Remember that. It's the right thing to do, Abby."

I smile, feeling myself tear up. I reach for a tissue from a box on the old sewing machine cabinet against the wall. "My grandmother was a great one for being present for births and deaths. I can't tell you how many people on Brodie Island she's seen come into this world or leave it. She said it was important to be a witness to both."

"A wise woman, your grandmother." Gail removes her stethoscope and tucks it into a canvas tote bag that says, THIS IS WHAT AN AWESOME NURSE LOOKS LIKE, with a big thumbs-up in the background.

"I appreciate your coming, Gail." I cross the room to rest my hand on Mom Brodie's for a moment. It's cool and dry. "I know it's a long drive from Salisbury. Just to . . . check on her."

"It's what I'm here for. And it's a beautiful drive. This is the first time I've ever had a client on Brodie Island. Where have you been hiding this place? I feel like it's like Atlantis or something. A magical place, hiding in plain sight. I stopped for a cold drink on the way over. On Main Street. It looks like Mayberry. I almost asked the clerk what year it was." She laughs.

I chuckle, impressed she's heard of *The Andy Griffith Show*. It was certainly before my time, although I actually remember watching reruns of it when I was a kid. Mom Brodie loved Andy Griffith. "Brodie *is* quaint," I agree.

"And you grew up here?" Gail removes her blue disposable gloves and tosses them in a trash can.

"Born upstairs in my parents' bedroom." I point over my head. "It was before the bridge was built. We had to take the ferry or a boat to the mainland, so most women just had their babies at home. My sister and I were both born here. Delivered by the same midwife."

"So, let's see, who's here with Mrs. Brodie? Your dad and mom and your sister?"

"And my daughter. Sarah. Named after . . ." I open my hand to indicate my grandmother. "The first Sarah. And also my brother. He's here, too. In and out. He lives about a mile from here."

"I didn't realize you had a brother. Your mother didn't mention him when we met for intake. I'm glad he's here. The more support Mrs. Brodie has, the better. Most families find it comforting to be together, go through the process together."

I keep nodding my head like I'm one of those dog statues on the dashboard of a Chrysler.

"Abs?" Joseph calls from down the hall.

"Speak of the devil," I say. It was what Mom Brodie used to say all of the time when the person she was talking about appeared. "That's my brother." Then I answer him. "Down here. With Mom Brodie." I hear Joseph's footsteps. "Thought you went to Salisbury to get Ainslie."

He stops in the doorway. "Change of

plans. Her mother's dropping her off."

"Long ride," I comment.

He shrugs. "Whatever. Saves me the trip."

Gail is standing there checking out my brother. It's obvious she thinks he's good-looking.

"This is Gail, our hospice nurse," I introduce. "Gail, my brother Joseph."

He nods. Smiles. "Nice to meet you, Gail."

"You too, Joe." She's grinning ear to ear.

"Nah, it's Joseph. My dad's Joe, or Little Joe. If you ask anyone on Brodie Island for Joe Brodie, you'll get a seventy-one-year-old farmer. Gotta ask for Joseph."

"I'll keep that in mind, Joseph."

They check each other out long enough for me to feel awkward. I pick up the crocheted afghan on Daddy's chair and refold it, just to have something to do while my brother makes eyes with our home-care nurse.

Gail finally says, "Well, I'm done here, Abby. Unless you need me to do something else. Give your grandmother a bath, help you change her?"

"No, no." It comes out louder than I intend, and Joseph and Gail both look at me as if I'm loony tunes. But all I can think of is that this stranger will see her tattoo, and I know Mom Brodie wouldn't want

271

that. "I can do all that. *We* can . . . my sister and I. We don't mind bathing her. And her . . . diaper" — I hate using the word — "hasn't even been wet."

"Normal, too," Gail says gently. Then she lowers her voice, brushing her hand against my arm. "Go ahead and leave the Depends on, though. She might need it when she passes."

I swallow and nod, thinking to myself that it's a good thing Mom Brodie is unconscious. She wouldn't like people standing around discussing her bodily functions. It wasn't that my grandmother was a prude; she just . . . She was a private woman, at least when it came to herself. And definitely not crude like me and mine. When I excuse myself from the table, I say, "Be right back; gotta pee." Not Mom Brodie. To my knowledge, she never peed. Which is interesting because she was the one who told me about getting my period and sex and even about birth control. Daddy told Joseph. I think Celeste learned most of what she knew in her early years off bathroom walls. And fact-finding missions.

"Okay. I'll be on my way, then," Gail says cheerfully, slinging her tote over her shoulder. "You have the number to call if you have any questions, or when she passes. If

I'm not available, Mary or Tiffany will be. And they're terrific. You'll like them both. But I'm working tomorrow, so I'll see you then. Like one thirty? Your mom said you'd all be going to church in the morning and a friend would be staying with Mrs. Brodie. That I was to come after church."

Joseph and I look at each other, and we both roll our eyes.

"I'm not going to church with you all tomorrow," he says.

"Oh, you're going," I warn him. "If I'm going, *you're* going, buster." I return my attention to Gail and smile. "One thirty is fine."

She shifts the bag on her shoulder. "Super. I'll see you tomorrow."

"I'll walk you out," Joseph offers.

"I'd like that." Big, bright smile.

Joseph and I make eye contact again as he lets Gail pass him in the doorway. I raise my eyebrows as high as I can, in an exaggerated motion. He grins.

Joseph is gone long enough for me to settle in Daddy's chair with my iPad. I'm reading my book-club book for next month. Erik Larson on the sinking of the *Lusitania*. Another cheerful selection. We've been on a dead or dying kick for months. I was just telling Drum the other day that I needed to

273

do some research and make a couple of suggestions just to get us out of this rut. I could use a book about a woman in her forties who finally figures out who she is and what she wants to do when she grows up. Or maybe about a woman who writes a novel in a year, sells it, and it goes *New York Times* bestseller. A fantasy of mine that will never come to pass. Mostly because I don't have a creative bone in my body.

When Joseph walks in, I lower the iPad to my lap.

He walks over to the bed, pulls something from his pocket, and sets it down on the nightstand next to the teacup. When he draws back his hand, I see that it's an oyster shell. None of us have spoken about it, but it appears that we're making some sort of altar for Mom Brodie. Only *altar*'s not really the right word because the objects are as much for her as in honor of her. I want to add something, but I'm not sure what. Maybe one of her favorite books?

Joseph surprises me by leaning over and kissing Mom Brodie's forehead. It's the first time I've seen him touch her since I arrived. "How is she?"

I get the idea he doesn't want to discuss the oyster shell. What it means to him. To her. "Same. But her blood pressure is lower."

He turns to me. "That mean it's going to be soon?"

I shrug. "Gail says no way to tell how soon. I mean, clearly she's dying. She *will* die. But, basically, in her own time." I switch gears then. "Speaking of Gail . . ." This time I lift just one brow. "Were you flirting with your grandmother's nurse, or was I reading something wrong?"

The grin. He whips his cell phone out of the back pocket of his jeans. It doesn't matter how hot it gets, Joseph wears jeans. And work boots. But he mixes it up with an assortment of black and navy blue T-shirts. It's black today. Just a little tight to show off his buff chest, arms, and abs. He runs, and he has weightlifting equipment in his house. He actually uses it.

I lean forward to see the screen of his phone. It's his contacts, and Gail's name and number have been added. "What? You asked our dying great-grandmother's hospice nurse for her phone number?" I'm actually a little shocked. But not as shocked as I'm acting.

"She pulled my phone out of my pocket and put in her name and number." He returns the phone to his pocket.

"Cheeky. I like it." I look up at him. "So, you're dating now?"

He shrugs and walks over to pick up one of Mom Brodie's pill bottles and read the label. "I haven't been, but I guess I should. Marly filed."

"For divorce?" I ask.

"No, Abs, for social security benefits. Yes, for *divorce.* And she's dating some doctor she works with." He waves his hands, waggling his fingers, hanging on to a pill bottle with one thumb. "He's a plastic surgeon."

I hesitate to ask what I want to. I ask anyway. "Was she seeing him before . . . before she left?"

"She sure was. Hey, this is an opiate." He holds on to the bottle. "You probably shouldn't leave it out in the open. Sticky fingers."

I get out of the chair, completely taken off guard by his statement about Marly. "Celeste wouldn't take our grandmother's painkiller." I make a face. "Drugs aren't her analgesic of choice, anyway."

"She could sell them. I think they go for like thirty dollars a pill. This county's got a serious prescription-pill addiction."

I frown. "How do you know about such things?"

"What? You think I live under a big oyster

shell? Just because I never left home doesn't mean I don't know anything. I read, Abs. I watch television."

"The Hunting Channel."

"Not just the Hunting Channel. I watch Lisa Ling." He points at me. "And I just binge-watched three seasons of *Downton Abbey* in one weekend."

I meet his gaze. "Marly cheated on you? I'm surprised to hear that."

"Because you thought I was the one who did it?"

I hesitate. Do I lie? Because now that I know it was her and not him, I feel guilty. And he looks hurt.

"I'm the illegitimate child of a married man. I'd never cheat on my wife, Abs."

I look down. "I'm sorry. You're right. I don't know what I was thinking. You're not that guy. I know that."

He thinks for a minute. "I guess people thought the same thing about Dad. He doesn't seem like that guy, either."

"I'm really sorry," I say again. Then I let the subject drop. Though I've got another one to upset us both. "You get a chance to talk to Daddy?"

He nods. "For a couple of minutes. In the yard a few minutes ago. He was on his way to get the crabs. Was going to make a stop on his way. We've got a problem with an irrigation system over on Custom House Road. Jimmy D. called it in. I told Dad I'd take care of it, but he said, "Go help your mother."

I wait.

"Yeah, so the will. Dad thinks we shouldn't say anything to Blondie. That there's no sense in getting her riled up now. He thinks we should let Mom Brodie die," Joseph says softly, as if she can hear him. "After the funeral, we tell her, and let hell fly then."

"Hell will fly, all right," I agree, pacing. "But I don't agree with Daddy. You?"

"I think *I'd* want to know now," he says.

"We're not talking about you; we're talking about Celeste."

He tugs his ball cap off and runs his hand over his short-cropped hair. He looks younger than thirty-two. I bet Gail thinks he's younger than she is.

"She home?"

"Yup. But she didn't get home until dawn. Birdie was already up. I got an earful on the subject. Of course it's our fault, yours and mine. It was *our* responsibility to bring her home."

"Not mine. Yours. I'm just the little mixed-breed bastard of the family." He laughs.

I don't.

He rolls his eyes. "Come on, Abs. It's funny. It's never *not* funny. The Brodie heir apparent having been born on the wrong side of the sheets."

I cross my arms over my chest. I don't like it when Joseph makes fun of himself like this. "I don't think it's funny. You're as much a Brodie as Celeste and I are."

"Absolutely." He walks to the window. "I didn't know the view from this window was so beautiful. Guess I never came in here that often," he muses. He turns away from the window. "Was Blondie with that old guy she was talking to at the bar? She was trying pretty hard to pretend she wasn't interested."

"No idea." I walk over to the bed. I think about Mom Brodie's tattoo. I want to tell him about it. I turn around. "Daddy say how much money we're talking about? I mean, maybe all this worry is needless. Maybe it's not enough money to matter."

"Oh, it's enough to matter." He names a number without blinking.

I blink twice, certain I didn't hear correctly. I repeat the number with a question mark.

Joseph nods.

"You've got to be kidding me," I murmur.

I look up at my little brother's face. He's not kidding. "She left all that to us?" I say, feeling like all of the blood has drained from my face. "Where did she get it?"

Joseph shrugs.

Then, against my will, my brain starts turning. Flying in ten directions at once. I don't want to think these things. I don't want to be greedy. Feel greed. I'm *not* a greedy person. I've got a lot of faults, but that's not one of them. But with that kind of inheritance, Drum can quit his job. He can quit it this week, before the semester even starts, if he wants to. We can sell the house and buy one at the beach. He can be a glassblower if that's what he wants. Hell, he can be a candlestick maker if we're careful with our money and there's a market for candlesticks. . . .

"And all of that is just for you and me?" I ask, still not totally able to believe it. "She didn't leave anything to anyone else?"

"Actually she did. Added to the Brodie education fund. Ainslie can go to Harvard if she wants. Hell, there will be tuition for your grandchildren and their grandchildren if we continue to invest well." He tugs on the brim of his ball cap. "She also left a nice chunk to the church and to a couple of old ladies in town. Mrs. Smith. Mrs. Freeman.

I don't remember who else. Just a thousand dollars here and a thousand there."

"But nothing for Birdie?"

Joseph looks at me strangely. "Why would she leave money to Mom? She and Dad have more money than they know what to do with. And what difference would it make how much money Mom had? She'd still buy her sneakers at Walmart."

I sigh. He's right, I guess; my mother owns half of everything my father owns. Half of Brodie Island. At least the money. The land is in some kind of trust, so it can't be sold. It just gets passed down generation to generation. And no amount of money would change how my mother lives. But I can't help thinking Birdie would have been tickled, at least secretly, had Mom Brodie left her just a little pin money. A token of her appreciation.

I look down at my grandmother, lying there looking innocent. I wonder why she didn't tell me. She should have told me. About all of it. Warned me. I'm actually annoyed with her. "You couldn't have left Birdie a few dollars?" I say softly. "All that money and you couldn't leave her anything?" I sigh again and walk away. It's probably not good etiquette to criticize a dying person to her face. Even if she is in a coma. And she just left you a bajillion dollars. Or what seems like it right this minute.

I start pacing again. Joseph just stands there. He's gone back to looking out the window, leaning so he can see the bay to the far left. The Chesapeake Bay holds some sort of spell over us Brodies, or so my husband says. She mesmerizes us, calls to us in our sleep. No matter how many times we take in the view in a day, we lay our heads to our pillows wishing we could see her one more time.

I wonder if Mom Brodie is wishing right now that she'd seen the bay one more time before she closed her eyes for the last time. It's funny; she wasn't born here, but she loved this island as fiercely as those of us who were.

"Did Daddy tell you what he told me? That he thinks that Celeste borrowed money from her and didn't pay it back?" I chew on my lower lip when he doesn't respond. "You think it's true?"

"I don't know why it's so hard for you to believe." He stares out the window. "She certainly borrowed money from me and never paid *me* back. You?" he asks.

I don't want to be a tattletale, but I nod. Mom Brodie, unlike Birdie, never liked tattletales. She liked us kids to settle matters amongst ourselves. Police ourselves, unless someone was in danger or something big was on fire. I look at him. "But that's still no reason to —"

Joseph meets my gaze, and I don't finish. Of course that's a good reason not to leave someone an inheritance. Surely Mom Brodie didn't loan *that* kind of money to Celeste. I never gave her more than a couple of hundred dollars at a time. Well, maybe a thousand once or twice, but only when she was about to be evicted. Or the time she went to some island in the South Pacific with a guy who was supposed to be the love of her life and then dumped her there . . . without a plane ticket home.

And then there's Mom Brodie's opinion of Celeste's lifestyle. And how she spends her money. And other people's. I can't deny that my sister is irresponsible with money. Worse than irresponsible. Wasteful. Negligent.

I sigh. Long and hard, feeling it to my toes. "Did Daddy say if he told Birdie?"

He nods.

I cringe. "How'd it go?"

Joseph gives me a look that says, *Are you kidding me? How do you think it went?*

"Birdie's got to be devastated," I muse. "Probably more than Celeste will be."

"You think?"

We're both talking quietly now.

"You know how Birdie is about Celeste. Her little girl can do no wrong. She deserves the best."

He crosses his arms over his chest. "Little jealousy there, sister?"

"Are you kidding me?"

"No?" His eyebrows go up.

"Of *course* I'm jealous," I scoff. "I don't want to be. I don't like how it feels. But I am. As long as I can remember, everything has been about Celeste. It doesn't matter what I do: education, good job, perfect husband, perfect kids. Birdie barely notices me. She's too busy looking at our *movie star sister.*"

"Really?" Joseph grimaces. "You're kidding, right? You've got everything, and Blondie has nothing. She hasn't even got her looks anymore. How can you be jealous of her?"

I cross my arms over my chest so that we look like some sort of dueling sibling pair. He looks at me. I look at him.

"Abs," he murmurs. "You shouldn't be jealous of her. You should feel empathy for her." He reaches out and takes me in his arms. Kisses the top of my head. I hold onto him, afraid I'm going to cry. "She'd give anything to be you," he tells me. "Don't you know that? To have just a little bit of what you have. You have so many people who love you."

I sniff, feeling silly. "You're right." I give him a squeeze, breathing in his scent. I remember the first time I held him and smelled the sweetness of his little head. It was the night Daddy brought him home to Brodie from the hospital in Salisbury where his mother died. To this house. I was fourteen years old, sitting at the kitchen table doing my homework, and Birdie just plopped him in my arms. I loved him from that moment on.

I let go of Joseph and grab a tissue. "Did Daddy say if Birdie thinks Celeste should be told?"

"Dad didn't —" Joseph goes quiet and lifts his chin in the direction of the hall. I hear silence, then footsteps. Birdie's.

She walks into the room and looks at me and then Joseph. I dab at my eyes and then blow my nose with the tissue, wondering if she was standing out there listening.

"What?" she asks, taking in my red eyes. Then she looks at Mom Brodie, an emotion in her face I can't read. "She's not —"

"No," we both say at the same time.

She looks at us both again, pointing at Joseph. "What's going on?" She points at me. "I know something's going on."

"I'm going to go ahead and dispose of these." Joseph scoops up the pill bottles off the nightstand. "Should I get the steam pot out of the shed, or is Dad getting them steamed?"

"Getting them steamed," Birdie answers. "Get newspapers for the table. Not too hot to eat outside. I don't want the whole house smelling like crabs. This house will be full of people after the funeral. I don't want anyone saying this house smells of days-old fish."

"Nobody liked the smell of crabs covered in Old Bay better than Mom Brodie," Joseph points out.

Birdie ignores him. It's a clever ploy of hers, really. She just pretends that things she doesn't want to hear were never said. I don't know why I don't try it.

Joseph is making his retreat with the pill bottles. I'm surprised Birdie isn't putting up a fight over them. She's got expired drugs squirreled away in a drawer in her bedroom, *just in case.* "Newspapers. Right. I'll get paper towels and vinegar, too," he says. "You have saltines in the house?"

"Have you ever known me not to have a box of saltines?" Birdie asks. "Where's Ain-

286

slie? I thought you went to go get her. She should make her good-byes to her great-grandmother."

"Marly's dropping her off, Mom."

Birdie looks over her shoulder at him. "You ask Marly to stay for crabs?"

"Nope," my brother answers. He's almost out the door, the bottles in both hands.

"Good," Birdie says loudly enough for me to hear her, though possibly not Joseph. She's at Mom Brodie's bedside now, fussing with her pillow. "Think we should change the sheets?" she asks me.

"I don't think we need to today." I speak to her gently. I know she's upset, whether she's letting on or not. She's got to be devastated about the will. "Let's do it tomorrow."

"She needs to be bathed," my mother says.

I go to stand beside her, and I actually feel the urge to put my arm around her. She's got to be upset about Celeste being cut from Mom Brodie's will. I'm upset, too, though not for the same reasons. I just can't get myself all that worked up right now about Celeste not getting the money, now that I know she owes Mom Brodie. But I am upset that Mom Brodie left Joseph and me all that money and didn't leave Birdie, the person who's cared for Mom Brodie the longest, after Daddy, a single cent. Mom Brodie left an old lady who lives in a shack on our property money, but she didn't leave any to Birdie?

I don't put my arm around my mother, though. It will just make her uncomfortable. It'll make *me* uncomfortable.

Suddenly I want to talk to Drum. I *need* to talk to him, to tell him about the money. To tell him I'm angry with Mom Brodie and feeling guilty about being angry with my favorite person in the world. Who left me a ton of money and didn't even tell me.

"I'll bathe her," I tell my mother. Even though I don't think it's necessary to wash her. She's not perspiring. There are no bodily functions to clean up. Mom Brodie doesn't have a smell anymore. Mostly I smell the clean sheets.

It's like she's fading away.

Birdie smooths the pillowcase one last time and turns to go. Joseph is already gone. "Time your sister got out of bed. She needs to be with her family, a time like this."

"I thought we were going to let her sleep —"

"You going to wake her or should I?" our mother interrupts.

I stare at the blue carpet. My sister's just been disinherited. And I know she's been counting on that money. The least we can do is let her sleep in. But I keep my mouth shut.

Birdie turns to go again. "And you better look in on Sarah. Been locked up in your father's office. No tellin' what she's getting into."

In a split second, I go from feeling sorry for my mother to feeling like banging my head on the wall. Instead, I go to wake my sister before Birdie beats me to it.

22
SARAH AGNES

Four months after I left Bakersville, I'm sitting in the food tent in Nowhere, Tennessee, talking to my best friend, Minnie. It's a hot morning, and we got into town late last night. We have a lot of work to do if we are going to be up and running by suppertime. Already, I can hear the ring of sledgehammers hitting iron tent poles. But it's beginning to rain, and the ground's already a swamp from rain that fell over the last couple of days. It's so hot and humid that it feels to me like what I imagine the jungle must feel like. I just finished reading *Tarzan,* so the jungle is on my mind. Bilis loaned it to me. He drives his own truck, lives in back, and he's got more books in his truck than Mrs. Abbiati had at the market in her so-called town library back in Bakersville. And every town we pull into, big or small, Bilis goes out looking to buy books, old and new.

"I'm real sorry about Hank," Minnie tells me in that Southern drawl that I love. She's sewing a tiny skirt that one of the dancing dogs is going to wear. A new act Jacko picked up in Dayton.

Minnie's my age. My fake age. She and her sister Millie are coochie girls. They dress like they're identical twins. They're not. Millie's a year older. And I don't think they look all that much alike, except they both have jet-black hair, and they wear the same hairdo. But they do this act together, covering their private parts, after they strip down, with big black-and-white feathers. Minnie starts out all in black, and Millie in white, but then they start sharing feathers and swapping them out. The marks love it. Minnie makes so much money that she can buy anything she wants and still send money home every week to her mother and grandmother in Atlanta.

I groan. Henri. I was trying not to think about him. I caught him three nights ago in the back of the tent truck making business on our mattress with a local girl. He swore he hadn't done anything with her, but she was only half-dressed. She couldn't have been more than thirteen or fourteen. She ran when I started hollering at Henri. Actually, she ran when I threw her shoe at him and it bounced off his forehead. I don't know what scared her so bad. I didn't use language. I was mad at him, not her. Though I did tell her she best get home to her mama. But I just said that because I was so angry with him.

After I threw the rest of his stuff out of the truck, Henri got mad at me. *He* used language. Then he grabbed up a pillowcase, stuffed it with his things, and walked off. And he didn't come back. The next morning, we set out for here, and I drove the truck. First time ever. Wasn't hard. I've been watching him do it for months. And when the old truck got twitchy in second gear, instead of hollering and beating on the steering wheel, I was gentle, and she popped right into third with barely any effort.

The rain's starting to come down pretty heavy. It's not looking good to open tonight. I stare out into the falling rain, trying not to cry. After Henri left, I was so mad that I let my anger carry me. He cheated on me. He was supposed to love me. We were going to get married after he saved up some money. And he made business with another girl. But my righteousness wore off sometime around midnight last night when we took a wrong turn headed here. I tried to back the tent truck up, got stuck, and Jacko yelled at me. He called me stupid. Some of the boys helped me get it unstuck.

I told Henri good riddance when he stalked off the other night, but now I'm starting to miss him.

I sniff and wipe my nose with his handkerchief I keep in my pants pocket. I wear pants because of the work I have to do. Odd jobs for Jacko. I pick up trash. I grease gears that need greasing, and I clean up after the animals. We've got a couple of horses, one that's pink. And a lion. Lion manure smells pretty awful. Bilis calls it dung. But manure or dung, it's nasty. I get dirty doing this kind of work, and the pants keep me a little cleaner. It was Bilis who brought them to me about a week out of Bakersville when I was struggling to lug water and tore one of the two dresses I had, clear up to my drawers. He found me sitting on the ground crying, and he didn't say a thing. He just walked away and came back five minutes later with a pair of men's pants that fit me pretty well with a string around the waist to hold them up.

I bite down on my lower lip and look over at Minnie. "I thought Henri loved me," I say quietly. But I'm beginning to realize how little I know about love. I thought my father loved me. I thought he'd come looking for me. Put two and two together and guess I was with Rudebaker's. A few days after we were gone, I think I was actually hoping he'd show up. But he never did.

"Hank loves you. He does, sweetie." She bites the thread at a knot she's just made with her teeth. "Best he can."

I sniff, fighting back tears. I haven't cried in weeks. Crying is for little girls, and I'm certainly not a little girl anymore. Any little girl left in me was gone by the time we crossed from Indiana to Missouri. Funny thing is, it wasn't making business with Henri that did it. I don't mind the business; sometimes I even like it when Henri's being sweet to me. When he kisses me a lot. And tells me how pretty I am. But it wasn't that that made me grow up; it was life. It was earning my own keep. Seeing the good and the bad in people that I never noticed before because I guess I was too busy being a kid. It's funny; I've only been with Rudebaker's four months, and I feel like I'm years older than the night I snuck out of my father's house. I was such a silly girl. Such a foolish girl.

"If he loves me, Minnie, why would he do that? Why would he kiss on that girl? Why would he kiss her on *our* bed?" I ask.

She reaches out and squeezes my hand,

then reaches into her pocket and pulls out two peppermint candies. One for me. One for her. She pops hers in her mouth and goes back to threading her needle again. I don't know how she knows how to make a skirt that will fit a dog, but she's magic with a thread and needle. That's what Bilis says. Turns out, she was the one who made Bilis the suit I saw him in that first time we met. She made Spotty's red pants, too. Spotty's her boyfriend. Nicest guy you'd ever want to meet as long as he doesn't have money in his pocket and there's not a craps game to be had. Minnie keeps most of his money for him so he doesn't gamble away the farm, she says. Which is a pretty funny thing to say, since he doesn't have a farm.

"Men are different than women, Sarry. Don't you know that by now? They don't think with their heads all that much. Mostly just with their little johnnies." Minnie arches perfect eyebrows that she plucks every day. She keeps offering to help me with mine, but I think it must hurt, pulling them out like that, one hair at a time.

I laugh. Mostly so I won't cry. I put the peppermint in my mouth; I love peppermints, and Minnie always has a supply of them. "You think he'll be back? Bilis says he'll be back. Just like a bad penny." I realize that's not a very nice thing to say about someone. When I first joined Rudebaker's, I thought Bilis and Henri were friends. I think Henri thinks they are, but I've figured out pretty quickly that Bilis doesn't like him very much. Bilis is always telling me I can do better. (And correcting my grammar. Quick is an adjective, used to describe a noun. Quickly is an adverb, used to describe an action.)

Turns out Henri's not only *not* French, but he's never been to France or even anywhere in Canada where they speak French. I know as much French as he does from the little book I got from Mrs. Abbiati. He won the beret in a card game the winter before we met, and the accent is something he copied off a seasonal worker who had ridden with the carnival last summer. *His* name had been Henri, and *he* had been from France, Minnie says. The whole Frenchman thing was just a game with Henri, who's from Texas. But I don't hold it against him. I still think it's kind of sweet that he would like me enough to pretend he was a Frenchman to get me to like him.

"I think he'll be back." Minnie holds up the little dog skirt, and I catch a glimpse of her new tattoo on her arm. It's an exotic bird, like a parrot, with a long tail. It's the most beautiful picture I think I've ever seen, God bless my Presbyterian soul. There's an old Japanese man named Haru who does them. Minnie says he was the husband of a Japanese dwarf who used to travel with the carnival. After she died, Haru just stayed on. When he feels like it, he'll let Jacko put him in the sideshow. He wears a piece of a bedsheet wrapped around him, kind of like a big diaper, and sits solemnly, letting people pay a penny to see his body covered in tattoos. And I mean *covered.* He's even got them on his face. Most of them he's done himself, Minnie says, but I don't know if I should believe her or not because carnies, even the good ones, I've learned, lie a lot.

I look out at the rain, watching it run off the tent sides, and sigh. There's a group of men and women in the far corner playing cards and laughing and drinking coffee. I smell their coffee. I never drank coffee until I ran off with Henri. Now I love it. I love it so hot it burns my tongue. I love the smell of it in the morning in the food tent the best. "I guess I should get to work hauling water for the horses," I tell Minnie. I can't work up much energy for it, though. I'll be covered in mud in twenty minutes.

Minnie shakes her head. "I don't know

why you keep doing it. Shoveling poo."

I slowly rise, crunching on what's left of the peppermint in my mouth. I don't want the horses going without water. "Henri says I have to work. Everyone pulls their share."

She shakes her head, looking down at the little skirt. She's sewing on sequins now. "You could join the coochies. Jacko hasn't replaced Alice yet."

Jacko sent Alice packing because she got in the family way and wouldn't *get rid of it.* I hadn't known her well, but she'd seemed like a nice girl. I wouldn't have gotten rid of my baby, either. But I'd have done what I could to keep a baby out of my belly to begin with. Of course I hadn't known about such things when I left Bakersville. I hadn't even understood what making business was or how it was done. It was Minnie who saved me from Alice's fate, probably. She brought me a little rubber thing to put inside me. I was so embarrassed when she tried to explain how it worked and where it went that I was in tears. But Minnie ignored my girlish behavior and even offered to help me put it in the first time. I thank God for Minnie. And I don't care if it's a sin for one girl to help another girl not have a baby. I don't know what I'd have done without her.

"I don't think I could do what you do,

Minnie." I feel myself blush. I've seen Minnie and Millie's act dozens of times. I don't think it's so terrible. But I can't imagine myself on that painted stage. All those men looking at me. Hollering and whistling. "And . . . I don't know how to dance. Not like you. I can't even do the fox-trot."

Minnie sets down her sewing and gets off the bench to come around to me. She takes both my hands and pulls me to my feet. "I could teach you."

I shake my head. "I should probably talk to Henri."

"It's not Hank who makes decisions for you, Sarry. It's you." She squeezes my hands in hers. "You could save a lot of money."

"I don't have anyone to send it to," I tell her, looking into her big, dark eyes.

"Then save it for yourself. And when you're ready to move on, you'll have it."

"But I love Henri. I could never . . . entertain men after, the way you and Millie do." Jacko has a private area set up behind the stage where for an extra fee a gentleman can spend a few minutes with one of the coochie girls. What the girl does on her time is her business, Jacko says, as long as Jacko gets his cut. I don't even want to think about what the girls are doing back there.

"Not required for the job," Minnie says firmly. Then she goes on, talking fast. "The dancing is easy. You just sway your hips and move your arms. And I could make your costumes. We could get fabric in town this week. And I've got plenty of feathers. Rudebaker's girls are known for their feathers, now."

"I can't buy fabric. I don't have any money," I whisper. "What I make barely covers what I have to pay Jacko to eat and sleep in the truck."

"So I'll front you the money. You pay me back. No interest."

"Sarry!"

I hear Jacko's voice calling from somewhere outside the tent. I keep my gaze locked with Minnie's.

"You planning on working today or you running off after Hank?" Jacko shouts.

"Think about it," Minnie whispers. "Things don't work out with you and Hank, you could make enough money to go anywhere you want in a year."

I try to pull my hands from hers. She smells good. Like French toilet water. Men bring her things like that. She has regular marks because this is her third summer passing through these towns. "I have to go, Minnie," I tell her.

She gives me a quick peck on the cheek and lets go of me. "A carny girl's got to take care of herself, Sarry. And have a plan for when she's ready to move on. You best think about your plan now, while you got the chance. And the pretty face."

I press my lips together and nod.

"Sarry!" Jacko yells. Then he lets out a string of curse words that would have made me blush two months ago. Not anymore.

I flash Minnie a quick smile and rush off in my heavy rubber boots. "Hold your horses, Jacko!" I shout. "I'm comin'!"

23
ABBY

I listen to Drum's cell ring, wondering why he hasn't picked up. It's the third time I've called. Not that I'm worried. At least not yet. I'm not that person who thinks every time someone is late getting home from work or school that he's been flattened by a tractor trailer. Still, it's not like him not to pick up. Even when he's running.

I'm seated on the end of the dock in our backyard. It's a nice dock. Daddy replaced the old wood and pitch dock three or four years ago with one made from composite decking. Daddy is so old-school about so many things; I love it when he surprises me this way. He said he did some Internet research about the environmental issues of chemical-treated wood for docks and decided to give this more expensive version a try. The dock is picturesquely beautiful with what looks like weathered gray, wide planks. It's prettier than any dock one of the guys in town built us over the years, and I don't get splinters in my shorts sitting on the end anymore.

Drum's cell rings three times, and I'm just about to hang up so I don't get his "leave a message" message, when I hear his voice on the other end.

"Abby?"

"Drum." I laugh, so relieved that I feel silly. I guess I *was* worried. "Hey, where you been? I called you a couple of times."

"Nobody expects the Spanish Inquisition?" he asks. It's a line from a Monty Python skit from a million years ago. Our code for *why are you being so nosy?*

I look up, across the bay, at the glistening, blue-green water. When I was a little girl, Mom Brodie used to tell me that the surface was littered with diamonds, and that was why it sparkled. I believed her for a long time, maybe because it certainly seemed, growing up, as if I lived in a magical place.

I'm quiet for a second. Drum's voice sounds strange. He doesn't sound like himself. "You okay?" I ask.

He doesn't say, "Sure, I'm fine." In fact, he doesn't say anything for a long beat.

The concern creeps back. "Drum?"

He exhales. "Sorry. I was asleep. Trying to sleep. Take a nap."

I wait for further explanation. Drum's not a napper. Me? I love a good nap on a rainy Sunday afternoon, but Drum doesn't want to waste the precious minutes he has on this earth sleeping them away. Which means he only sleeps about five hours a night and he never, ever naps. He didn't even nap when the kids were babies, keeping us up all night. But that was the old Drum. Lately, he's been sleeping more. A sign of depression, I'm afraid.

"Should I come home?" I ask.

"No." He makes a derisive sound. "Of course not. I'm fine, Abs."

"You don't sound fine." Emotion wells in my throat. It's not just Drum. It's everything. It's Mom Brodie's dying, the will, my awkward relationship with my mother, my concern for Celeste. I was worried about my sister even before all this. She's been so sad lately. When I talk to her on the phone. In person, she's always performing. I think I get the real Celeste late at night, when I sit in the dark in my living room and talk with her. I'm afraid of what losing the money she thought she was inheriting might do to her.

"You want to come here?" I ask.

"You need me to come?"

I watch a sailboat glide by in the distance.

It's not a local sailboat. Sail is too white. Hull is too pristine. It irritates me that some stranger is marring my view of the open water, though I certainly don't have that right. It's not as if Brodie Island has some sort of moratorium against strangers in these waters.

"No, I don't *need* you to come," I tell my husband. "But . . . it would be nice to have you here." I take a breath. Exhale slowly. "This is harder than I thought it was going to be. She's just lying there, fading away right in front of us." I hesitate and then go on. He's such a good listener. He's known me so long; he knows when I'm trying to gather my thoughts, and he's okay giving me that time. "I keep wondering what's going on in her head. Does she know we're there? What's she thinking? Is she here with us, or is she lost in her memories? Is she with us at all or has her brain shut off, and we're just waiting for her body to catch up?"

"Aw, baby, I'm so sorry. I'm supposed to go have dinner with Reed tonight. I could come tomorrow. I can take a couple of days off. Take some personal time. If they don't like it, tough tacos."

I have to chuckle. My husband has to be the only sixty-year-old man who says "tough tacos." "No, it's fine," I say, feeling better

305

already. I just needed to hear his voice. "We should stick to the original plan. You and Reed will come for the funeral." I lean forward and dip my toes in the water. The tide's low, so I have to stretch to reach. Slack tide. I can tell by the waterline on the shore. "I'm fine. We're fine. I just miss you," I say wistfully. "And, things are . . . the way they always are here. Awful and wonderful."

I think about Mom Brodie's will. I wasn't sure when I was going to tell Drum about my impending inheritance. It makes me uncomfortable talking about the money before Mom Brodie's dead. It makes me even more uncomfortable to think that her death is going to significantly change our lives, in a good way. But Drum seems so down that I think I'll tell him. Then I feel awkward. Where do you start with something like this? "I . . . I won't keep you," I hear myself say. Gulls circle over my head and call. "I know you have to get on the road, but I have a . . . surprise." I hesitate.

"Okay." He doesn't say it with much enthusiasm. He *really* isn't himself, and I wonder if counseling wouldn't be such a bad idea. But maybe he doesn't need professional psychological advice. Maybe he just needs enough money to allow him to make the changes in his life that he wants. Maybe he just needs to pursue his dream.

"I'm inheriting some money from Mom Brodie. A lot of money," I blurt.

"What?" He says it as if exhaling. "You're kidding. How much — no. I'm sorry. That was so not cool. Your grandmother is dying. We shouldn't even be talking about this."

I name the amount of money I stand to inherit.

For a moment I think he hasn't heard me and I'm going to have to repeat it. Then I hear a sound, like he's sat down.

"Wow," he says at last. "Wow."

"Yeah." I lean over the water and watch a blue claw crab move lazily along the bottom, through the waving green grass. It's a small one, not big enough legally to catch. And a smart crab, I suppose, because he's safe here. We never crab off our home dock. Other docks we've got on Brodie, sure. When we were kids we used to crab off the old cannery docks all the time. But never here. Daddy calls it his crab sanctuary. He swears they bed down here because they know they won't get caught, be covered with Old Bay seasoning, and be thrown into a steamer basket.

"Wow," Drum says again. "I didn't know she . . . I didn't realize Mom Brodie had money of her own to leave anyone. I just assumed everything was locked up in a trust the way the land is. You've always joked about being the pauper heiress."

"I was shocked when Daddy told me. Still in shock. I don't think any of us knew she had money. You know my family. No one ever talks about money. Not Brodies." I think on that for a moment and then go on. "You realize what this means, Drum. You can retire." I give a little laugh, excited and scared at the same time. I can't believe I'm going to be able to give him his dream. How many people can ever say that? How many people can ever give this kind of gift to someone they love so dearly? "We can sell the house and buy something near the water. You can open your studio. Drum, you can go in Monday and resign. You never have to teach again if you don't want to."

"I . . . don't know what to say, Abs." His voice is full of emotion. I think he might be crying, which makes me want to cry. "You sure you want to do this with your money? Because . . . it's yours."

"Ours," I say. "Or it will be."

"I . . . I don't even know how to wrap my head around this. I . . . I'm speechless."

I smile, so happy he's so happy. "So you might as well start making plans," I say. "We've got to get the house ready to sell and —"

"Whoa, let's go easy, here, babe. We need to talk to the kids. To Sarah at least, before we talk about moving."

"Sure, sure, but you know her. She's always up for an adventure. That's how we'll present it."

"You think she wants to move this year? She's just going to be a sophomore in high school."

"Don't you remember last year when she wanted us all to move to Costa Rica so she could learn how to surf? Sure, we'll talk to her, but I think she'll go for it, Drum. I really do."

He's quiet for a minute on the other end of the phone before he says, "I think we should table this whole discussion until after the funeral."

"You're right," I agree. "It's weird to talk about spending her money before she's dead. Disrespectful, almost. But I wanted you to know. Because I'm so happy for you, Drum. For us."

"Wow," he says again. "It's a lot to think about. Fairly overwhelming. I mean people talk about changing their lives, really changing, but we don't usually do it."

I shift my cell phone to my other ear. "Um . . . but there is a weird little . . . I guess I can't even call it a snag," I say. "I don't know what to call it."

"Okay. What's that?"

"She didn't leave Celeste anything, just Joseph. And me. Apparently Celeste *was* in the will, then at some point, fairly recently, Mom Brodie went to the family lawyer and removed her name."

"Holy shit, Batman."

Another one of his phrases. I smile. My sixty-year-old, ponytailed, vegetarian husband doesn't look like the kind of guy who says "Holy shit, Batman." But maybe he does. After all, he does say "tough tacos." "So yeah, we've got that going on here, along with the hospice nurse's stopping by to tell us Mom Brodie's blood pressure is dropping, but that's to be expected. Before she dies."

"You sure you don't want me to come down?" Drum asks me in the sweetest voice. He's almost whispering. "I can reschedule with Reed."

"No. No." I stand up and push my hair out of my face. I should have worn my ball cap. I can feel my nose burning. I'm not one of those super-pale redheads like Sarah is. I actually tan a little. Mom Brodie always said it was the Native American blood in the Brodies, but I do try to protect my skin.

I don't want cancer eating off my nose. "You go see Reed. I know he's looking forward to it. I get the idea Mom Brodie could die anytime, now. So I'll see you when you come for the funeral."

"Okay. But you know I'll come, Abs. I'll come right now if you need me. I don't mind."

Again, I smile. And I wonder what I did to deserve this guy.

"So . . . how's your sister taking it?" Drum asks. He already seems like a new man. A man with hope. "Being dispossessed?"

"Um . . . she doesn't know."

"She *doesn't know*?" he repeats.

"Daddy wants to wait until after the funeral to tell her. I think he's worried about her making a scene."

"I can understand that. Blondie can sure make a scene when she wants to. It's not really my business, but why do you think your grandmother didn't leave her anything when she left her other two grandchildren all that? Certainly enough to go around."

I look back at the house and squint into the afternoon sun. It's a sprawling, turn-of-the-century, two-story farmhouse. White. From the backyard, you can't see the two-story veranda that makes it so grand. But it's the back of the house I see in my dreams. The house and the dock. Mom Brodie said that back in the days when the house was built, most families faced the front of the house to the water, but old Joe Brodie, Daddy's grandfather, had a different idea. He wanted the private, family area to be on the water, where it could be enjoyed on lazy Sunday afternoons after church.

I spot Daddy and Joseph near one of the two picnic tables under the Granddaddy Oak. That's what we all grew up calling the tree that was supposedly here when the Brodies came here in the seventeenth century. It's a white oak, the same species as the Wye Oak, which was the oldest oak in the US, dating back to the 1500s, until it toppled in a thunderstorm when I was in my twenties.

I feel like I've spent half of my life under Granddaddy Oak. I played superheroes under it when I was a little girl. Celeste and I learned to dance a waltz under those trees under Daddy's tutelage. Drum asked me to marry him under that tree. And I can't imagine how many bushels of crabs I've eaten . . . how many *hundreds* of bushels my family has eaten there over the last three centuries.

"You've got a lot of secrets going on there, babe," Drum says in my ear.

I see Celeste come out of the house, spot me, and start the hike toward me. "Not really," I tell Drum. "Just the two."

He chuckles. "Right, just that your squeaky-clean grandmother has a naughty tattoo and a past that I presume no one knows about. And the will drama."

I watch Celeste walking toward me. As always, she's overdressed. Who dresses for picking crabs? She's wearing a tight little jean skirt that suggests she's waxing her nether region, and a pink sequined tank top. Her hair is teased up in some kind of crazy topknot that looks like cotton candy, with a glittery headband. She isn't wearing the glittery heels, at least. She's barefoot, but I bet the crazy shoes are within reach.

"I gotta go," I tell Drum. "Blondie fifty yards off my bow and coming in fast."

"I kind of wish I was there," he says. "I have a feeling things are going to get exciting before they get boring again."

"Give Reed a hug for me. And a kiss." I feel myself choking up again. It seems like a week ago our son was a baby in my arms. Or at least a toddler on my lap. Now he's going to be a sophomore in college.

Celeste waves to me. She's also wearing a chiffon scarf around her neck that looks like a watercolor in green and yellow. It's quite the outfit. Especially on a Saturday after-noon in August in our backyard. I wave to her and smile. "Call me tonight on your way home," I say into the phone, walking toward my sister.

"Might be late."

"That's fine. I'm probably going to sleep with Mom Brodie. I did last night. In Dad-dy's chair."

"You're a good granddaughter, Abs."

I smile sadly. "I just don't want her to be alone when she dies. I want her to know how much we all love her."

Drum tells me he loves me; I tell him I love him, and we end the call. I slip my cell into the back pocket of my jean shorts as Celeste walks onto the dock. She's got enough blush on her cheeks to share with every woman on the island. I wish she knew how the heavy makeup ages her, but we don't have the kind of relationship that I can even bring up the subject. She'd take the advice all wrong. Think I was criticizing her. She always jumps to that conclusion. Of course, in all fairness, maybe sometimes my *advice* has been criticism, but not when it comes to her looks. I understand how sensitive she's become about aging. And I get it. My bare bottom and my breasts sure don't look like they used to.

"Where you headed, all gussied up?" I ask, thinking maybe I can steal a little of that blush and rub it on *my* cheeks. I didn't bother to put any makeup on today, and I probably look pretty scary.

"Nowhere."

I raise my eyebrows.

She lifts one undernourished shoulder and lets it fall. "Might go in to The Gull later. Wanna come with?"

"Two nights in a bar in the same moon cycle?" I shake my head. "No thanks."

She walks past me to go out on the end of the dock. "Come on. It'll be fun."

I turn to watch. "You go home with that guy you were talking to last night? The older, distinguished man?"

"Birdie's been spying on me again."

"I don't think any spying was necessary." I cross my arms over my chest. "Apparently, she was making Daddy's coffee when you came in this morning."

"Are you talking about Bartholomew?" Celeste redirects, her back to me.

"Didn't catch his name." Someone goes by in a dinghy with an outboard motor and waves. He's too far out for me to recognize. I smile and wave back. "I'm talking about the guy with the ascot. I'm pretty sure he was the only one in the The Gull in a suit jacket and ascot." I indicate my neck. "I saw you flirting with him."

Reaching the end of the dock, Celeste turns and sashays toward me, swaying to a tune I can't hear. She's always been a performer, even when we were kids. I'd play the bongos, beating on a half-bushel basket or a pot we stole from the kitchen, and she'd do these dances which, thinking back, were pretty risqué for a ten-year-old. And she wrote plays, specifically tailored to what she saw as her own talents. She always got to be Queen Nefertiti or the plantation mistress. I was usually the slave girl or an elephant.

"I was thinking," my sister says, swaying her hips, using her scarf as a boa, "a man like Bartholomew could set me up for life. He's got a house in Atlanta and one in the Keys in Florida. Another in Vale. A business-man. Exports some kind of machine parts. Widowed. Kids live on the West Coast. Busy with their own lives. He's lonely. I bet he knows how to appreciate a woman."

"So, you're looking for a sugar daddy?" I ask. I guess I shouldn't be surprised. Nothing Celeste says or does surprises me.

Instead of being insulted, she laughs. "The thought's crossed my mind." She walks by me. "Birdie's looking for you. She said to fetch you. And Sarah." She starts for the

316

house and then turns back. "And Joseph is looking for you, too."

I open my arms. "I've been right here. Plain as day."

"It must be a terrible thing to be the family favorite," she calls over her shoulder.

"I thought *you* were the favorite," I holler back.

This time neither of us laughs.

24
BIRDIE

"It's not right," I say very quietly, so only Mrs. Brodie can hear me. "It's not right, and you know it." I gently push the brush through her crown of white hair. I know she wouldn't want anyone to see it a mess. She was always so neat in her appearance, and she took extra care with her hair. It used to be the prettiest red.

When I first came to Brodie Island, I remember lying in my own little bed in my very own bedroom at night in this house, wondering if, when I grew up, my hair would be red like Mrs. Brodie's. Not just because it was the prettiest hair I'd ever seen, but because I was sure it was her red hair that made people like her. People like pretty women. And the red hair made people listen to her. Trust her. Especially other Brodies. Little Joe wasn't the only one who took in every word that came out of his mother's mouth as gospel. Big Joe did, too. That man thought the sun rose and set in Mrs. Brodie. She could do no wrong, and once in a while when I did hear them have a spat, one minute Mrs. Brodie would be raising her voice; the next minute I'd hear the two of them laughing. Big Joe adored this woman. Did until the day he died in bed with her.

When it was decided Little Joe and I would get married, I laid in my same bed and imagined my Joe talking to me the way Big Joe did to Mrs. Brodie. I imagined us laughing, our heads together, holding hands when we thought no one was looking. It was a foolish girl's dream. I should have known better. I should never have let my expectations grow like that. Nothing good ever comes of those kind of dreams. Nothing but disappointment. I wasn't a redhead. No one was ever going to love me that way.

My mother didn't love me. Obviously. Otherwise, she wouldn't have left me on the steps of the orphanage, still bloody from being born. No note. No gold locket with a lock of her hair. One of the girls at the orphanage with me, Lilith, she had a locket her mother left with her with a lock of blond hair, the same sandy white as Lilith's. I used to dream the locket was mine when I was a little girl, sleeping under the eaves in the orphanage. Only my locket had brown hair like mine. But prettier, shinier. That locket was my hope that my mother would come back for me.

She never did.

I go on brushing Mrs. Brodie's hair, gentle as I can. I asked the nurse if Mrs. Brodie could hear me. I asked if she could understand me or if her brain is already dead. Gail said there was no way to know what Mrs. Brodie can hear or how much she can think, so we ought to speak to her, and it's best we assume she can hear us.

I think Mrs. Brodie can hear me. I think she knows exactly what I'm saying. I think she's enjoying lying here in bed like this, letting us take care of her, putting the house in such a state. I think she cut Celeste out of her will just because she could and she knew how it would upset everyone in the house. Upset me.

I lean over and whisper in her ear. "Celeste ought to have her fair share of that money. What's Joseph need with money? He's got this whole island, and that's all he cares about. He's just like his father. As long as he's got a place to rest his head and a decent truck, he's got no need for money."

I lean back to look at her. "Now, I'm not sayin' you ought to cut Abby out, but Joseph, he . . . I'm just going to say it. He's getting a lot for a boy born on the wrong side of the sheets." I chew on my lip for a second, looking at her. Her eyes are still closed. If she heard me, she's pretending she didn't. "Celeste needs that money," I go on. "Not just for what it can buy her, but to know you care about her. That she matters. Everybody knows Abby was always your favorite. And you were her favorite from the hour I pushed her onto this earth. She was always more yours than mine, our Abby. And Celeste could see that. It hurt her. Don't you know how much it hurt her?"

My thoughts drift back to Abby's birth. And my overall failure as a mother. What a fool I was. I thought God gave you a baby and the love for that baby with it. I thought when Abby was born, I'd know how to love her. Only I didn't. I mean, I *did* love her. In my own way, but not the way Mrs. Brodie loved her. Mrs. Brodie's love came right out of her heart, always full of joy and optimism. I always felt like my love for my children was too tinged with fear. The enormous, overwhelming fear that I wasn't what my girls needed. I wasn't enough. And I'd never be enough.

Looking back, I guess that was the same problem between me and Joe, too. I *did* love him. The best I knew how. But it wasn't enough. It wasn't good enough. *I* wasn't good enough. And that's why he strayed. My inability to love Joe the way he deserved to be loved is what brought Joseph into this world.

I fluff Mrs. Brodie's hair over one ear. She just got her hair cut the week before she went into the hospital that last time, but I wonder if I ought to call the hairdresser to come out to the house. It's looking a little long over her ears. She won't want the undertaker's wife messing with it. Ruby likes to think she's a hairdresser, but I don't think you can call yourself one if you only do dead people. Because who's going to notice if you do a bad job? And if they do notice, who's going to complain?

"Celeste needs to understand that for all the mistakes she's made, she's still a Brodie, same as Abby." I look down at Mrs. Brodie. Her chest keeps rising and falling, but I don't see her twitch a muscle. I go on before I lose my nerve because that's what usually happens with me. I plan out what I want to say to people, but then I can't say it. "What I was thinking is, maybe you could wake up for a few minutes. I know you're tired, and you're ready to go to the Lord." I exhale, putting the brush back in the nightstand drawer.

There's an oyster shell and a piece of blue paper with one of Sarah's palindromes on the nightstand now, with the teacup and saucer I set there. And a handful of red and white peppermint Starlight mints, each in their own cellophane wrapper. The mints are Abby's work. Mrs. Brodie and Abby were always munching on those mints together.

"Can't say I'm not envious, Him calling you home," I tell Mrs. Brodie, looking down at her. "But if you could just see your way to wake up for a little while, we could send for Clancy, and you could tell him you made a mistake. And you could set it right. You could give Celeste her share. Fair is fair."

I hesitate, on the outside chance she's going to answer me. I listen to the sound of the air whooshing out of the vent on the floor, and then I hear Duke barking outside the window. I have half a mind to throw up the window and holler at him to stop his barking. Doesn't he know Mrs. Brodie's trying to die in here in some peace and quiet?

I look back at Mrs. Brodie. "I even thought about giving Celeste my pin money, but you made me promise not to touch it until the time was right. And I don't think this is the time, else you'd have told me." I think for a minute. "This isn't just about money. It's not about Celeste being able to make her rent and get a face-lift, or whatever nonsense she's been talking about. This isn't just about money, Mrs. Brodie. It's about you. And Celeste and her needing to belong here. To belong to you."

Because we all need to belong to you, I think. But I don't say it. I feel like I'm going to cry, all of sudden, so I shut up. A part of me wants to tell her, while we're on the subject, that it wouldn't have hurt her to throw me a few dollars. Or her car. Or her fake diamond brooch that looks like a palm tree. I always liked that brooch. The girls won't want it. It'll end up getting sold for a dollar at the next church bazaar. But I would have liked her to have given it to me. Just to show me that I matter to her. But I'm too ashamed to say it. Too scared to think maybe she knew what she was doing when she didn't leave me the brooch.

I'm not worth a dollar brooch.

I stand there for what seems like a long time, and finally I let out a long breath.

"So that's your final word on it, is it?" I ask her. "You're not going to wake up and call Clancy, and you're not going to change your will, are you?" I reach down and smooth the sheet over her, wondering if I should get her a blanket. Wondering if this air conditioning of hers might be making her too cool. I take her hand to see if it's cold. It's not, and I arrange the side of the bed so she's comfortable.

"All right . . . Well, fine. Soon enough I'll be the lady of the house, won't I?" I take a stubborn tone with her. "And it'll be me to set things right. The way you always did." I look down at her face. It looks like a death mask I once saw in a magazine. "So that's what I'll do. I'll set it right myself."

I turn so fast to walk away from her that I don't see Little Joe coming into the room. I practically run right into him, and he has to put his hands on my shoulders to slow me down. It startles me. Him so close, touching me. I can't remember when the last time was he had both hands on me. Oh, he gives me his hand getting in and out of the car on Sunday mornings. But this is different. More . . . *intimate* I think the word might be. I've never been a big one for words or for reading, not like Mrs. Brodie. But I learn things. Words. Mostly on my soaps.

"Who you talking to?" my husband asks me.

I can feel his hands, warm on my shoulders. Almost like they're burning. There was a time when I wanted him to touch me. I don't mean I ever wanted him to be all lovey-dovey the way Abby and Drum can be. Kissing hello and good-bye can take up a lot of a woman's day. I don't have time for that nonsense. But Mrs. Brodie was always one for hugging people, coming and going. Not me, of course. She never hugged me. I never came and went. I was always here. But anyone else who came into the house, or left, Mrs. Brodie would hug him or her. I never understood the need for it. But there was a time when I wanted Little Joe to act like he liked me. Like he married me for some reason other than because his mother told him to.

That's worn off.

I take a step back from Joe, looking down at the floor. I hope he didn't hear what I was saying to his mother. I wouldn't want him to know I was cross with her. "I was talking to Mrs. Brodie." I go to his recliner. It looks strange in the room. Takes up too much room. I shake out the afghan Abby left laying on the back, just to keep my hands busy. "The nurse says she might still be able to hear us, even if she can't talk back."

He stares at her. I don't think he thinks

she can hear us. He looks uncomfortable standing there. Like he feels he doesn't belong.

"You ought to talk to her," I tell him. I start refolding the afghan. Abby made a mess of it. She was never much for folding right. "You ought to tell her anything you still got left to tell her. Blood pressure's down. She's goin', Joe. I don't think it will be much longer."

He just stands there, closer to being out of the room than fully in it, looking at his mother. I take a good look at him as I fold the crocheted afghan. He looks small to me. And old. Little Joe was never a big man; Brodie men aren't. But he had a way of filling a room, making you know he was here. I guess that made him seem like a bigger man than he was. Today, though, he seems small and wrinkled and older than his seventy-one years. He seems a little bit lost.

"She doesn't look like she's dying," he says. His voice sounds like he's far away. "I don't think she'll die yet."

"You know your mother. There won't be a hullaballoo. It's not her way. One minute she's going to be with us, Joe, and the next she won't. So you best say anything you've got to say to her, or you'll be saying it to her stone in the cemetery."

He seems to think on that for a minute before he speaks. "Already said my good-byes." His tone is gruff.

I can't tell if he's talking to me or her. I nod anyway.

He stands there a little longer. I throw the afghan over the chair and plump the back cushion.

"Seems like Abby's set on sleeping in here with her," I say. "I wonder if we should bring one of those single beds down from the blue room. Get Joseph to carry it down while he's here."

"She say she wants a bed down here?"

I point to his chair. "Guess she wants to sleep in your chair. Where do you want her sleeping?"

He rubs his temples with his finger and thumb like he's working on a headache. I'll get him some aspirin when I get back to the kitchen. "Whatever you think best, Birdie. I came to tell you . . ." He exhales like he can't exactly remember why he's here. I think this mess with his mother's will is upsetting him more than he's letting on.

"Marly's here with Ainslie. To drop her off. I thought you might want to say hello."

"I got nothing to say to Marly."

He's about to walk out, but then he turns slowly toward me, like it pains him to speak to me. "Birdie, what's between them is as much Joseph as her. He said so himself. No matter what happened, Marly's still Ainslie's mother. And she's been good to us. She was always good to Mama. Mama would want us to treat her kindly."

So that's what it comes to. Always does. Lying in a coma, one foot in the grave, and Mrs. Brodie's still commanding our every word, our every move.

I look down at the floor. It needs vacuuming. Little bits of dust on the carpet. "I'll be out directly."

"Good. Because we're ready to eat when you are."

"Start without me. I'll be out. Just have to put the tea on ice," I call after him. He's already in the hall.

I'm checking to be sure Mrs. Brodie doesn't need anything else when Abby comes in. Like a bus station this room is today.

"Celeste said you were looking for me."

I glance at her. It takes me a second to remember why I was looking for her. "Wanted your dirty clothes so I could do your wash."

"You don't need to do my wash." She gives a little laugh as she walks over and takes Mrs. Brodie's hand between hers.

"I've only been here two days. How much wash could I have?"

"You can bring it down later. Towels, too." I put my hands together, realizing I have to say something about the will. Because Mrs. Brodie has pushed me to it. Her lying there so quiet. "Something else I need to talk to you about."

Abby looks surprised. I guess because I don't usually tell people I need to talk to them. I just talk to them. "It's about Mrs. Brodie's will." The second it comes out of my mouth, I wonder if we shouldn't talk in the hall. Just in case Mrs. Brodie can hear us. But I decide to stay put. If she doesn't like what I have to say, she can just get up out of that bed and tell me herself. And while she's up, she can call Clancy and set things right.

I take the afghan off the chair again. Shake it out again. My daughter's watching me. I guess I shocked her with my boldness. *Bold* isn't a word a person would use to describe me. Somebody might say I'm a hard worker, or I'm loyal, or I'm plain, but no one would say I was bold.

Truth is, I'm surprising myself. "Where's your brother?" I ask.

She looks at me funny. "Um . . . in the bathroom, I think."

I lift my head in that direction. "Go get him. No need for me to say this twice."

"What?" She lets go of Mrs. Brodie's hand.

I point in the direction of the door. "Go get Joseph and come back with him. Where's your sister?"

Abby's still looking at me funny. "Um . . . I think she and Ainslie were walking down to the dock. Marly couldn't stay. She said to tell you she said hello, and she'll see you tomorrow when she comes back for Ainslie."

"She ask how Mrs. Brodie was?"

Abby shakes her head. "No, but I think Joseph —"

"Go on, then." I don't give her the chance to finish. She told me what I already knew; Marly's not all that interested in this family. Never was. Now I want to hurry up with this before I lose my nerve. "Fetch your brother and bring him back and not a word to your father or your sister," I warn, the afghan in one hand so I can hold up a finger with the other.

She takes one more look at me, and out she goes.

I glance at Mrs. Brodie. "I know you're not going to like what I have to say to them, but . . . this is a mess of your own making.

You didn't think I was going to just let you leave Celeste out without putting up a fuss, did you?" I listen to her not say a word. Then I realize what I've said. "No, I don't guess you did expect me to do anything about it, did you?" I whisper, a lump rising in my throat. "Because when did I ever?"

It's not long before Abby is standing in the doorway with Joseph right behind her, tugging on the brim of his ball cap, looking like he'd like to be anywhere but here. Just like his father, that one.

"Close the door," I tell them.

They come in and close the door behind them. They look so puzzled, I almost smile. Not often that anyone can say I surprise them.

I clear my throat, taking my time, wondering how Mrs. Brodie would say this. She'd come right out and just say it, I guess, so I do. "Your father told me what's in Mrs. Brodie's will." I nod politely in her direction. "About leaving money to you two but not Celeste." Even though the door is shut, I say it quiet, on the outside chance Celeste is in the house. Because I'm sure not going to be the one to break the news. If she has to be told, it can be Little Joe who does the telling. It's his mother who's made this mess.

332

Abby glances over her shoulder at her brother. She almost looks like a teenager, with no makeup and her hair all messy. She's got what I'd call natural beauty. She doesn't need face powder and lipstick like Celeste does.

Abby meets her brother's gaze, and they seem to communicate without words. The two were always close. She was like a little mother to him. I cared for him the best I could, but I think she filled in the gaps. I was always thankful for that.

Abby speaks first. "We had no idea about the will until Daddy told us."

"Mrs. Brodie didn't tell you she was leaving you a truckload of money?" I ask. Sounds just like her. To give somebody something without giving him or her the opportunity to at least say thank you.

"She . . ." Abby comes closer. "She mentioned her will a couple of weeks ago to me. She said something about pin money, but I didn't . . . I had no idea she was leaving me that kind of money, and I certainly didn't know that Celeste wasn't getting anything."

I don't like having nothing to do with my hands, so I start lining up the peppermints on the nightstand. There are five. "What about you?" I ask Joseph. "She tell you?"

"No, ma'am."

I look down at Mrs. Brodie, giving her one last chance to speak up. She doesn't.

"It's not right," I tell them. "Celeste needs her inheritance."

"Daddy says maybe Mom Brodie thought Celeste already got hers. More or less," my daughter pipes up.

"She borrowed money from Mom Brodie that she never paid back." Joseph.

"You don't know that," I say. "I don't know that. I don't see any IOUs." I point to the bedside table. "You see any IOUs?"

Joseph looks at his sister. She's always been the ringleader, that one. Joseph's a good boy, but he's a follower. I worry that when his daddy can't run this farm . . . the island, Joseph won't be able to step into his work boots. I don't know if he'll be able to make the decisions that have to be made to keep a business running. Hard decisions. He's got such a soft heart. Sometimes that's a good thing, but sometimes it makes a person weak. Weak people don't make good leaders. I know Joseph's the male heir and all that, but Abby's the one to give the job of keeping the Brodies going. I think Little Joe knows it. Maybe Joseph does, too. But it's not something we've talked about.

"And I think," Abby goes on, "that Mom Brodie might have worried the money would just . . . go to waste."

"Not our business to say how Celeste spends it," I counter. "Who's to say buying whatever you intend to buy with the money is any better than what she'll buy?"

"I don't know what we could do about the money if we wanted to." Abby rests her hands on her hips. "The will is legal. Mom Brodie has the right to leave her money to whomever she likes."

"Don't tell me she can leave it to that dog," I threaten, holding up my finger.

Abby cuts her eyes at her brother like I'm talking crazy.

I ignore them. "I know what you can do. This is what you do. You put your money together" — I put my hands together — "the two of you, and you split it three ways." I pull my hands apart. "Celeste doesn't even have to know. She won't ask to see the will. You tell her she's getting money. She'll ask how much. All she need know is that she's getting a third of what Mrs. Brodie left to her grandchildren."

The two of them are looking at each other again.

"Mom," Joseph says slowly. "I have no idea how we would do that, tax-wise. It would be like giving her a big chunk of money. It's different from inheriting money.

335

The tax implications are different."

I shrug, moving toward the door. I've talked more today than I talk in a week, and I'm about talked out. Besides, I need to get the iced tea poured and find Little Joe some aspirin. "Figure it out. The two of you are smart. We've got an accountant and a lawyer, and there's plenty more where they came from. I think between all of you, you'll be able to work it out."

"What's Daddy think of this idea?" Abby asks me.

I shrug as I walk out of the room. "Don't know. And don't know that I care."

As I walk down the hall, I hear Joseph speak, then Abby, but they're talking quiet enough that I can't understand what they're saying.

For once I don't think I care about that, either.

25
SARAH

I catch Mom as she's coming out of the big downstairs bathroom. "Mom?" I don't say it too loud because I don't want anyone else to hear me. "You can't guess what I found." I'm so excited; I'm bouncing on my bare feet like I'm a little kid. This place makes me feel that way, sometimes. This house. Not in a bad way, though. Maybe because I spent so much time here when I was little, and I was so happy here. Maybe because Mom did, too? I don't know.

Mom looks up at me. She has her worried face on. She comes toward me. She looks so young she could almost be my sister.

My excitement falls off, and I hold my closed laptop to my chest, hugging it. "Oh, no. Mom Brodie didn't —"

Mom shakes her head.

Then I see Uncle Joseph come out of the bathroom behind her, and I look at him and then at her. He slips past us like he's trying to escape.

"Ainslie's here," he tells me, walking backwards down the hall. "She was so excited when she heard you were here."

I smile because that seems like the right thing to do. "Are you staying for a sleepover?" Sometimes Ainslie spends the night when we're here, and Uncle Joseph stays, too. I love it when they both stay. Breakfast is so much fun I actually get up for it. If Dad and Reed were here, that would make it perfect.

It's kind of weird that Mom Brodie's impending death means a good time for me. I'm not sure what to do with that. Think about it later.

"We'll see about the sleepover."

The minute he turns into the kitchen, I look at Mom again. "Were you and Uncle Joseph just in the bathroom together? *With the door closed?*"

When she doesn't respond right away, I know something is up. "What's going on? I know you two weren't peeing together."

Mom exhales and pushes some loose pieces of hair back off her forehead like she's hot. "Family business."

I stand there for a minute. I don't believe her. Well . . . it might be *family business,* but it's not about the price of soy beans or

338

buying a house on the island to use as a rental property. It's about us. I can see it in the little lines at the corners of her eyes. Which are what make her look like my mom and *not* my sister.

I think about pushing the subject. I'm a Brodie, too, and I'm old enough to start being included in family dramas. This one obviously has to do with my aunt Celeste, because most of the dramas in this family revolve around her. Uncle Joseph gets the occasional one, like when he married Marly. And when he told everyone they were separating. But that died down pretty quickly, mostly because Birdie never liked Marly anyway. There's never any drama with Mom, except when she gets into a fight with Birdie or Celeste, but she always ends up apologizing, even when she shouldn't, and it blows over pretty quickly.

"We should go outside. Your grandfather's feelings will be hurt if we don't make a fuss over the crabs."

"I got it; I got it," I say, trying to lighten things up. "Wow, Grandpop, these are huge. And heavy." I pretend like I'm lifting a crab. I *am* a vegetarian, but I eat crab. Not at a restaurant, but if it's fresh and someone I'm related to by blood makes it or it comes out of water touched by Brodie soil. I also eat fish, and sometimes mussels when Dad brings them home from Mom's favorite seafood place at home. Well, her second favorite seafood place. Her favorite is the public dock in town. Anyone with the last name Brodie walks down the dock, and people just hand us free fish and clams and stuff. People act like we're these benevolent ladies and lords or something. Like on *Downton Abbey.* Mom and I binge-watched all the seasons in one weekend last winter when we got snowed in. I guess Grandpop and Mom Brodie are kind of like the Crawley family. *Were* . . . Mom Brodie won't be bestowing any more acts of kindness on anyone.

Mom looks like she wants to get by me, but I don't let her. "Guess what I found out." My excitement comes back to me.

She presses her lips together. She's really upset about whatever is going on. "What?"

"Mom Brodie lied."

She blinks. Like her head was somewhere else, and now she's trying to find her way to what I'm saying. "Lied about what?"

"All kinds of things." I lower my voice. I still don't know where my snoopy grandmother is.

Now Mom's annoyed with me. She's getting her hackles up. That's what Dad calls it when she gets all stiff and her voice gets tight. "I'm looking for an example, here, Sarah." Now it's the Mom voice I rarely hear. The one that's critical and judgey.

"Her name, for one thing."

Mom's looking at me like she doesn't believe me.

"There's no Sarah Agnes *Hafland* born in Indiana in 1915, Mom. Or Chicago. The marriage certificate says she was born in Chicago."

"It was probably just a mistake."

"Right, because we all know she was born in Indiana. But there's no Sarah Agnes Hafland born in Gary, Indiana, in that *decade*. Sarah Hafland doesn't exist."

She frowns. "How do you know?"

"The Internet, Mom." I try not to get impatient. She and I have had this exchange a million times. I'm always saying "Google it" or "YouTube it." "You can look up anything."

She glances past me, down the hall. "We need to be outside," she says quietly.

I nod. But I'm not going anywhere until I tell her what I found out. "Her name was Sarah *Han*-fland. She always told us it was Hafland. And that's what's on her marriage certificate. But I found her birth certificate, Mom. It was online. And she wasn't born in 1915, either. She was born in 1917. Which means —"

"She's not a hundred and two," my mother interrupts.

"She's not a hundred and two," I repeat slowly as I meet my mother's gaze. "It also means she married Great-Grandpop —"

"When she was sixteen," my mother murmurs, looking down at the floor, "not eighteen."

We both let that settle in for a minute. That means Mom Brodie was a year older than I am right now when she married Great-Grandpop and moved to Brodie Island. The idea is so unbelievable that it makes me a little dizzy thinking about it.

Mom's frowning so hard that her forehead is wrinkled. "How'd you find her birth certificate?" She turns and leans her back on the wall. "And don't tell me *the Internet*. It might not be hers," she adds.

I lean on the opposite wall so we're facing each other in the hall. "I'm telling you, Mom, this birth certificate is hers, and her name is Sarah Agnes Hanfland, and she was born in 1917. First I just Googled her name and nothing came up, but then I started Googling birth records in Indiana, and I was *still* not coming up with anything. But then this ad popped up about researching

342

your heritage. There's this online company that has access to all these records, birth records, immigration records, death records, and if you pay an annual fee you can see any records they have for a whole year. And you can also see all the records and information other members have found and posted."

"You bought a year's subscription to Ancestry.com? How did you pay for it? You better not have used my credit card."

"I didn't use your credit card," I defend. "I *was* going to call Dad and ask for his number, but then I remembered that this girl on my hockey team was talking about how her mom used it to track down her birth mother and how now her mom's all into it. So I texted the girl and got her mom's password and stuff."

"You hacked into someone's account?"

I make a face. "I didn't *hack* in, Mom. I had the user name and password. That's not *hacking.*"

"To-may-to, to-mah-to," she says.

I exhale in a huff. Now *I'm* getting annoyed with *her.* I thought she would think this was cool. Cool that Mom Brodie's life was more interesting than we thought, which was obvious when the tattoo showed up. But I guess I was also hoping Mom was going to be impressed that I'd used my Benedict Cumberbatch (I'm secretly in love with Bennie) Sherlock powers of deduction to find Mom Brodie's birth certificate from 1917.

"I'll prove it to you," I tell her. "Don't you want to see it?"

"What I want to do, Sarah, is go sit outside under Granddaddy Oak and pick crabs and have a beer with my family."

"Mom —" I cut myself off. "Fine." I huff again. Then I turn and head for the kitchen, the laptop still in my arms.

"We'll talk about this later," she calls after me.

I try to think of a good palindrome for the way I'm feeling, and I say it as I go. "Parcel bare ferret up mock computer-referable *crap.*" It's not a great one, but I feel better because I say "crap" really loud.

26
SARAH AGNES

My heart is beating so hard that I feel like it's going to fly out of my chest. And then I'll just die because you can't live without your heart. Which might be okay because right now I feel like I want to die. "I can't do this," I pant, pressing my hand to my chest. I can't breathe. I feel like someone's thrown a feed sack over my head.

"Sure you can, *mon cher amour.*" Henri is relaxing on a pile of crates, whittling on a stick. He came up with this harebrained scheme that he was going to whittle barnyard animals from sticks and sell them to people waiting in line for the Ferris wheel. Sticks are free, he told me. And they're everywhere. The only problem is, he's been whittling going on two weeks and still hasn't come up with a single thing that resembles an animal.

Henri came back about a week after he took off. I didn't say anything about the girl he was making business with, and he didn't say anything about her either, but he hasn't done it since. I don't know that I can trust him, though. Both Minnie and Bilis have hinted it would be a mistake to think he won't do it again. " 'Can the Ethiopian change his skin, or the leopard his spots?' " Bilis asked. It comes from the Bible, from Jeremiah, he told me.

Being with Henri has been what Minnie calls an "eye opener."

When I left Bakersville, I had this crazy idea Henri and I were going to get married and settle down and have babies. I thought the carnival was just us sowing oats and that he was going to get some great job, or maybe buy a general store or something so we'd always have plenty of food to eat and shoes for our babies. I've learned a lot in the last six months, more than in my previous fourteen years on this earth, I think. Among other things, I've realized that men like Henri who work carnivals aren't the kind of men who marry and settle down. I'm not saying some of them aren't fine people, because they are. Bilis has been better to me than anyone in my life, my blood kin included. And I'm not just saying that because he loans me books and sometimes brings me little presents from the towns we pass through, like a china teacup and saucer with bluebirds with ribbons in their beaks. He really cares about me. He cares about what I think, and we talk about stuff. Important stuff, like how poor the country has gotten and whose fault it is and how much more complicated the whole thing is than most people think. I've learned about stuff like the stock market and what it meant when the papers said it crashed and how Post and Gatty's flight around the world in a fixed-wing aircraft is going to change everything. But Bilis and I talk about silly stuff, too. Yesterday, we laid on our backs in the grass and watched the clouds drift by in shapes like an umbrella and an anteater. I didn't even know what an anteater was until he took me back to his truck and showed me a picture in an encyclopedia.

I glance at Henri and pull the front of my robe together, trying to cover as much of my bare skin as I can. The other girls, including Minnie, are walking around in their costumes, more naked than not, for anyone in the tent to see. Anyone who works backstage, that is. They've seen it all before. The marks are out front, filing in after they pay Bilis their hard-earned nickels and dimes. We can hear their excited talk and nervous laughter. MJ and JJ and Sparky are already playing music in the pit. That's what Bilis calls it. I don't know why. There's not a hole.

Henri offers me the fag hanging from his mouth, but I shake my head. He's not as good-looking without his beret. He lost it the week he was gone. I take a puff of a cigarette once in a while, but I'm not going to do it now, mostly because I'm annoyed with him. I was surprised he didn't put up any fuss when I told him I was going to be a coochie. I don't know why I thought he would care if I danced practically naked in front of men, but it still hurt that he didn't. Not only did he not protest, but he actually said something that made me think he thought he ought to have part of the money I'm going to be making. I set him straight on that quick enough. I already have to give Jacko a cut of my tips. Henri's not getting a penny. And I'm not dumb enough to keep my money hidden in a sock in my trunk in the truck, either. Bilis keeps it for me. I thought about asking Minnie, but her Spotty helps himself to her stash when he's down on his luck at craps. If I'm going to shake my bubs for nickel tips, I'm sure not giving my money to anyone, and if I were, Henri would be last in line.

The music is working up to the first act, and JJ is clashing his cymbals. Minnie pats my bottom through the robe as she goes by to go onstage. I can hear Bilis, calling the last marks into the tent.

"You're going to be great," Minnie assures me.

"Sure I am," I tell her. I've learned that the best way to do something you've never done before, even if you're scared stiff, is to pretend to know what you're doing until you know what you're doing. And the same goes for almost-nudie dancing. I've been telling myself that since I told Jacko I'd rather dance naked behind a fan of red feathers than pick up one more shovelful of lion dung.

Minnie throws me a kiss and sidesteps through a curtain and onto the stage, and all of a sudden I'm breathing so fast that I'm starting to feel light-headed. And then Bilis is beside me. He's in a blue and white seersucker suit and straw boater's hat that makes him look quite dandy. It's funny, but now that I've gotten to know him, I forget he's a dwarf. He's just Bilis. I told him that one day, and he said he felt the same way about me; most of the time he forgets I'm a redhead.

"You don't have to do this if you don't

want to," Bilis tells me, taking my hand in his. He's talking quiet so no one else can hear him. So Henri can't hear him, I think.

"I want to do it." My voice sounds shaky. I'm more scared now than I was when I sneaked out of my house the night I ran away. "I gotta make more money than I'm making," I tell him.

"Move in with me," he whispers, looking up at me, into my eyes. "Move in with me, and I'll show you what a real man is like."

I almost laugh, but then I realize he's serious.

"I'll take care of you, Sarry. We could have a good life together, you and me. I've got a lot of money saved. We could get married, and I'll take you to Paris for a honeymoon. I'll take you to London and introduce you to my mother and to Big Ben."

My breath is starting to come slower now. I can hear men clapping and hooting out front. Minnie and Millie must be knocking them dead out there. "Who's Big Ben?" I ask Bilis.

He smiles at me like I'm a child. But I know he doesn't think I'm a child; otherwise he wouldn't be offering to marry me. He wouldn't want to make business with me, which clearly he does. It doesn't offend me, though. In fact, I think it's sweet. I almost wish I felt that way about him. Because I'd really like to go to Paris.

"I can't marry you, Bilis," I whisper back to him. "Henri and I are getting married."

"Are you?" he asks me. "When's that going to happen?" He's still got my hand, holding me tight.

"I'm sorry, Bilis." I look down at him and smile, feeling sad. Because I really am sorry. "But I don't feel that way about you."

He brings my hand to his lips and kisses it. Just like a gentleman. "I think you could learn, Sarry."

My gaze goes to Henri, who's still sitting on the crates. He's looking at us, but there's no reaction on his face. He doesn't care that Bilis has my hand, kissing on it.

I look back at Bilis. "I should get in place. I don't want to make a late entrance, my first time."

"You absolutely sure you want to do this?" He's still holding my hand.

"I have to, Bilis." When I look down at him, he looks so sad that I lean over and brush my lips against his. I kiss him right on his kisser. In front of Henri.

Bilis squeezes my hand and lets go. "You just say when you've had enough of this, Sarry, and we're out of here. Alrighty?"

I wipe a tear from the corner of my eye,

but it's not a sad tear. It's a happy tear. Because at this second I feel like I can do anything. I can be anyone I want to be. Because Bilis believes in me. Because he loves me.

"Alrighty," I tell him, and then I throw off my robe and grab my feather fans and walk up the stage stairs to the entrance, just like I know what I'm doing.

27
ABBY

"Wow, Grandpop," Sarah says from across the picnic table from me. She's sucking crab meat from the carpus of a claw. "I think these are the fattest crabs we've had all summer." She reaches for her hammer to open the claw and rubs a smudge of Old Bay seasoning off her chin. Like me, she likes to dip lumps of crabmeat into the salty spice. "Heavy." She makes eye contact with me, and her blue eyes sparkle with mischief.

Some days I could thump my daughter, but sometimes . . . I just want to hug her and cover her sweet, freckled face with kisses.

"Think so?" my dad asks, using the tip of his penknife to work some meat out of the body of his crab. He doesn't crack a smile. He takes his crabs very seriously. "I got a light one, two back."

Sarah and I grin at each other.

"Wanna chase grasshoppers?" Ainslie asks

Sarah, jumping up and down behind her, tugging at her elbow. The four-year-old is adorable, with her father's gorgeous eyes and her mother's dimples.

"Let me finish this crab, and then we will," Sarah answers. "Why don't you pick some flowers for Mom Brodie while you're waiting for me?" She points at some dandelions in the grass, and Ainslie bounces off.

"Anyone else want another beer?" Joseph stands and tips his beer bottle back to get the last drop.

"I'll take one," Celeste says. She's sitting beside Daddy, whacking a claw with one of the wooden mallets. I can't believe she doesn't have any crab goo on her.

Self-consciously I blot my T-shirt with a balled-up piece of paper towel.

"Abs?" Joseph asks. There's something in his tone that makes me look up at him. He tilts his head ever so slightly in the direction of the back door.

"I'll get it. Bathroom break." I hop up from the picnic table bench, wiping my hands on the paper towel. I'll wash them when I get inside. Picking crabs is the one event that requires washing your hands *before* you pee. "I'll check on Mom Brodie," I tell our mother, even though we've brought the baby monitor receiver out. Even though

354

Mom Brodie hasn't moved or said a word in days.

Birdie had just sat down at the end of the table in one of those old-school lawn chairs made with the nylon webbing, and was eating coleslaw from a paper plate with a plastic fork. She's been in and out of the house ten times. I don't know what she's been doing. She makes such a fuss about us all sitting down together for a meal, then won't sit with us. I've never understood it. Drum thinks we make her uncomfortable, which seems silly to me. We're her family, for heaven's sake. We love her, and she loves us. How can we make her uncomfortable?

"Anyone else need anything?" I ask. I point to Celeste's plastic cup that I know very well doesn't have water in it. I'd bet the money due me for editing that freshman organic biology textbook I just finished that what's in her pink cup is coming from a bottle out of her suitcase.

Celeste smiles sweetly and shakes her head.

In the kitchen, Joseph turns to me, two empty beer bottles in each hand. "She's right, you know."

It takes me a second to realize what he's talking about. Selective memory, I guess. Or maybe I'm learning my mother's MO. What

I don't like, I just don't retain.

I walk to the sink, the linoleum floor cool on my bare feet. I don't know where else in the country there's still linoleum on kitchen floors. I find it appalling and comforting at the same time. The flooring must be thirty years old, the pattern faded from my mother's mop. I gingerly hit the handle of the faucet with the back of my hand and thrust my hands under the water.

Joseph comes up behind me. "Come on, Abs, could you really enjoy that money, knowing Blondie might be getting evicted?"

"She always lands on her feet." I pump soap from a dispenser into my hand.

He bumps my hip with one of the beer bottles, and I move to let him get under the sink where he keeps a plastic bucket for recycling. Birdie's not really on the recycling bandwagon, but she tolerates Joseph's bucket as long as he empties it. He collects the recycling in a bin in one of the sheds and hauls it to the city recycling depot, which he established.

The bottles clink as they hit the bottom of the bucket, and when he steps back, I close the cabinet door and rinse my hands again. "What if she's right?" I say.

"Mom? That's what I'm saying. She *is* right. Celeste deserves her share."

I shake my head. "Mom Brodie. What if *she's* right? What if giving Celeste the money will be a waste? What if we're just fueling the Celeste problem by giving her money to throw away?"

He shakes his head. "Doesn't matter."

I grab a tea towel that's hanging from the handle of the oven. It's got a big red rooster on it. It goes with the salt and pepper shakers, I guess. I dry my hands. "The money Mom Brodie left me could change my life." I think for a minute. "No. I'm perfectly happy with my life. But it could change Drum's life."

He goes to the fridge, grabs a cold bottle of beer, and holds it up. I shake my head. He gets a second and closes the door.

"Drum's not happy teaching anymore. He hasn't been for a while. He wants to make changes. Big changes." I lean the small of my back against the counter, still drying my hands with the rooster. "He wants to quit his job. Sell the house. Move to a place on the water. Open his own glassblowing studio."

"I get that. But why do you need money? Why don't you move here? You know Drum wants to."

"He's never said that," I say quickly. "Not exactly," I add.

"Because he knows you don't want to."

I press the heel of my hand to my forehead. "Can you imagine me living in this house with Birdie?"

I look up to see him with what Celeste refers to as a shit-eating grin.

"I already do, practically," he says. "Hasn't killed me." He waggles one of the beer bottles at me. "What doesn't kill you makes you stronger. And what about what Mom Brodie wants?" he goes on, faster. "You know you're the one she wanted to pass this farm to. Not me. She thinks I'm slow-witted."

"Well, you are," I tell him. "But not any more slow-witted than any other man."

The grin again. But there's also pleading in his eyes. And I thought the middle child was supposed to be the peacekeeper. In this family, the middle child has always been the rabble-rouser.

I close my eyes. "Joseph, I cannot live with Birdie," I say quietly. "She'd be the ruination of my marriage. Of my relationship with my children. Of me. I'd throw myself off the bridge in six months."

He sets one of the beers on the counter and opens the other with a bottle opener. "Fine. We'll table that discussion for later."

"No, we're not tabling it until later. We're

358

tabling it until . . . forever," I say, hearing how ridiculous I sound as it comes out of my mouth.

"Okay, so back to the money. It's simple, Abs. It should be split three ways."

I rest one hand on my hip. More of me agrees with him than I want to admit. But I want this money so badly for Drum. He deserves it. He deserves all the happiness I can find for him because of the happiness he's given me. "You don't think Mom Brodie has a right to do with her money what she wants?"

"She'll be dead. It will be our money. We can do with it what *we* want." He tips the bottle to his mouth.

I toss the towel on the counter, annoyed with him, annoyed with myself. I want the money. But I want to do what's right, too. I'm so torn. Mom Brodie must know best, right? She always does what's right, doesn't she? But then I see the image of her tattoo in my mind, and I wonder about the choices that led to her lying on a bed in the early 1930s and letting someone tattoo her upper thigh. And then there's the matter of her age. There's a really good possibility that she lied to Big Joe, and he married a teenager instead of the consenting adult he thought he married.

It's pretty naïve of me to think that Mom Brodie *always* made the right decision.

"Think about it." He opens his arms wide, a beer in each hand. "All I'm asking is that you think about it. Call Drum. See what he thinks."

The back door opens, and Celeste walks into the kitchen. "What are we getting Drum's opinion on?" she asks. She's holding her hands out as if she's a surgeon about to put on sterile gloves.

"You don't want to hear about their boring domestic life," Joseph responds without missing a beat.

I'm impressed with my little brother's quick thinking.

"Probably not," Celeste says. "Marly cheated on you with a hunky doctor. Happens all the time." At the kitchen sink and pumping soap into her hands. "I've got to get this smell off. I knew I should have skipped the crabs." She hits the faucet, and the water comes on. "You tell him?" she asks, looking over her shoulder at me.

I meet his gaze, knitting my eyebrows questioningly. He lifts his hand ever so slightly and lets it fall. Later, he's telling me.

"So did you?" Celeste demands.

"Did I what?"

360

"Tell him." She rolls her eyes at me and then looks over the other shoulder. "Mom Brodie has a tattoo."

"Get out." Joseph swears. He sets the open beer bottle on the counter for her. "You saw it?"

"When we were giving her a sponge bath." Celeste reaches into the little drawer under the sink and pulls out the nail brush. We keep it in the drawer just to use after eating crabs. If you're not careful, the smell can follow you for days. Which is fine on Brodie, but once you cross that bridge, nobody appreciates the smell of crabs and Old Bay seasoning wafting from someone's hands.

"Get out of here," he repeats. "What is it?" He holds up his hand. "Wait. Please don't tell me she's got a butterfly tramp stamp. No, no wait." Now he's laughing. "Grandpop's name on her bicep?"

"Better than that." Celeste grins. No one likes to tell a secret better than our sister. "Way better."

I cross my arms over my chest. "I thought we agreed we weren't going to say anything."

She shuts off the water and reaches for the rooster towel. "*We* didn't agree to anything. You told me not to say anything in one of your usual, big sister, we-have-to-do-

361

whatever-Abby-says declarations."

Her words smart. Do I really make *declarations*? I thought it would be wrong to tell Mom Brodie's secret. If she'd wanted anyone to know about the tattoo, she'd have shown it to us.

"What is it?" Joseph asks. Then he glances at me. He's laughing. "Sorry, but come on. Now that I know she's got one, I have to know what it is. You know how I am with tats." He indicates his left bicep, covered in an amazing vine and flower pattern. Somewhere, woven in the greenery, is Ainslie's name, but you'd never know it unless you were really looking for it.

Celeste reaches for the beer on the counter. "You want to see it?"

"No," I say. "Absolutely not." I look at him. "It's on her upper thigh. Do you really want to see your grandmother's thigh? Your *dying* grandmother's thigh?"

"Hell, yes."

Celeste giggles. "Come on."

I don't go with them. Joseph is back in a minute. I hear Celeste's footsteps on the staircase.

"It's beautiful, Abs," he tells me.

I nod. "But I don't think Birdie and Daddy need to know about it. She didn't want us to see it, Joseph."

362

He's quiet for a minute as he goes to the refrigerator for another beer. "You're right. You're absolutely right." He turns to me. "Anyone else know?"

"Just Sarah, but she's as good with secrets as Mom Brodie. She'll take it to her grave."

He smiles, and I can tell he's sad. He's feeling the same loss I am, even though our grandmother isn't quite gone yet. "You know, I almost got suspended in high school," he recalls. "Eleventh grade. I'd have gotten kicked off the football team if I'd been expelled. School called here, and I got lucky because Mom Brodie answered the phone. She came in. Talked the principal into a bunch of detentions instead of the expulsion. I had to do weeks of housework as punishment. I think I cleaned every attic in this house, and I did several old ladies', too. Mom B's Methodist Circle cronies. But she never told Mom and Dad."

I nod and smile, and we're quiet for a moment, lost in our own memories.

"Where did she get it?" Joseph asks.

I shrug.

"Had to have been before she came to Brodie. Hell, before she was eighteen."

I let that slide. I might tell him later about what Sarah found out about the incorrect birthday, but not today. Not until I have time to verify the information, and, even then, I don't know if I'll tell anyone. Because, to what end? Again, is my grandmother's secret mine to tell, even after she's dead?

He shakes his head. "I always knew she was a hell of a woman, but this . . . It adds a whole new dimension, doesn't it?"

"Sure does," I agree.

He takes a sip of his beer. "Guess I best get outside. You coming?"

"Be out in a minute."

After he's gone, I slip into Mom Brodie's room. The sun is bright coming through the window, so I adjust the blinds. Then I stand over my grandmother, holding her hand. I look at the photo of her and Grandpop Joe. My gaze drifts from the teacup to the oyster shell and the peppermints I left on the nightstand and then to her wrinkled face.

"Can you hear me?" I say softly. Her hand is cool and seems a little . . . stiff. But she's definitely still breathing, so that's got to be my imagination, right?

"Mom, it's Abby." Tears fill my eyes. I feel like she's drifting away. Like I can actually feel her spirit moving away from me. I don't know what heaven is going to be like, but I like the idea that we go to a place we want to go to. I'm not interested in puffy clouds and cherubs singing. I want to be right here on this shore, gazing out at the Chesapeake Bay. And I think she does, too.

I wonder if Grandpop Joe is waiting for her. I'm not sure I really remember him, or if it's something I've imagined from things Mom Brodie has told me. I was two when he died. But I have an image of him in a rowboat off our dock. Mom Brodie is holding my hand, and we're waving. And he's laughing and waving.

Maybe he's in that old wooden rowboat, waiting for her now.

"I don't know how much you've heard about what's going on here. Clancy told about your will. Daddy feels like we need to follow through with your wishes. Money for Joseph and me. Nothing for Celeste. But Birdie says Celeste deserves her share, and Joseph agrees. He wants us to split the money three ways, Mom." I exhale. "With the money you've left me, I think I can make all Drum's dreams come true. If I share with my sister . . . I don't know that I can."

I'm quiet for a moment. Then I ask, "What do you think?" Then I smile because that's a silly question. I already know what she thinks. What I don't know is what she would do if she were in my place.

I let go of her hand and lift the sheet and cotton blanket and stare at the tattoo. It's so beautiful, so . . . startling on my grandmother's wrinkled thigh that I still can't believe it's real. Who was Sarah Brodie before she became Sarah Brodie? How did she end up with this tattoo? A bigger question than that, how did a woman with this tattoo end up on Brodie Island, married to Big Joe Brodie?

I gently take her hand again. "I wish we could talk again. Just one more time," I tell her. I sniff, fighting my tears. "Because I could really use some advice right now." I squeeze her hand, hoping she'll squeeze it back. But she doesn't.

I kiss her hand and lay it on the bed. I slip my phone out of my pocket and call Drum. As it rings, I go down the hall and hang a left into the big front hall. I'm just stepping out on the broad front porch that we never use when Drum picks up. I can tell by the sound that he's in his car.

"Hey," he says. His voice is warm and gentle, and I seriously consider telling him to turn his little car around and start driving this way.

"Hey," I say, instead.

"What's up?"

"I've been talking to Joseph and . . ." I

stare out at the immense, green front lawn and the long, tree-lined lane that leads to the road. They're poplars, as old as I am, tall and strong. I don't feel tall or strong right now. "He thinks Celeste has a right to part of the money," I blurt.

"Which would mean less for you," Drum says, his tone still calm.

"Less for *us,* Drum. I don't know if we can make it happen on that."

"What do your parents think?"

I sit on the top step and watch an old pickup slowly make its way down the road, far in the distance. Most people don't drive fast on Brodie, even though no one really enforces any kind of speed limit. I guess we feel like we've got all the time in the world to go where we want to go, to do what we want to do. Which, of course, isn't true. Mom Brodie's proof of that.

"Divided. You know Daddy. Basically, he says it's Mom Brodie's money and she has a right to do with it what she pleases. And we should do what she says. And of course you know Birdie. She disagrees with Daddy and Mom Brodie. She thinks Celeste has a right to part of the money. I think if she had it her way, Joseph wouldn't get squat."

Drum chuckles.

I smile. "Joseph feels that if Celeste wastes

the money, as I guess Mom Brodie thought she would, then that's her prerogative."

I hesitate, resting the cell phone against my ear. "You're not saying anything."

"I'm thinking."

I watch a tiny praying mantis crawl up the step's rail. They always fascinated me when I was a kid. The way they looked like a leaf. On closer inspection I see that there's a whole bunch of them. Hatchlings.

"What are you thinking?" I ask.

"About how much I love teaching, and how I could never just up and quit."

I laugh, but I want to cry. "There's got to be a way we can do this."

"Maybe there is, but I have to go with Birdie and Joseph on this one, babe. Sorry. You have me and the kids. Joseph has Ainslie and the whole island. What's Celeste got?" He doesn't wait for me to answer. "She should get her cut of the money. Who knows, maybe she'll do something smart with it."

We both laugh at that. And then we're quiet for a few moments. The good kind of quiet that makes you feel closer to someone, not further away.

"Should we think on this? Mom Brodie's not dead yet."

"It's your money, babe. You should think

on it, but I'm not sure I can take Celeste's money."

I want to holler that it's not Celeste's. It's mine, mine and Joseph's because Mom Brodie left it to *us*. But I can't say it. Maybe I feel guilty that Mom Brodie always favored me over Celeste. She even favored Joseph over Celeste. The fact that Celeste has never tried to be particularly likable doesn't really matter. Birdie's right. Celeste is still one of us. She's still a Brodie.

"I was hoping you'd say 'take the money and run,' " I tell him.

He chuckles. "Would you do it?"

I groan and close my eyes. The sun is still warm, and the grass smells like it's been recently cut. When I'm very still, I can hear bees buzzing . . . and the very faint voices of my family. "I don't know, Drum. I guess I need to think on it a few days. I just . . . I want it so badly for you. For us."

"Babe, do you know how lucky we are? We've got kids who are healthy and smart —"

"Smartasses," I interrupt.

"Smartasses," he agrees.

"And weird," I tell him. "I mean, palindromes? Really? There was a time when people were put in insane asylums for walking around blurting those kinds of things in public."

He laughs. "We've got parents who are still in good health and still married."

"To *each other*," I interrupt. It's a joke between us because so many couples our age are already on their second or even third marriages.

"And we've got each other," he says so sweetly that it brings tears to my eyes. "I love you. All I want is you. Glassblowing is silly anyway."

I wipe my eyes. "I should go. Daddy brought crabs from town. Everyone's out back. I'm sitting on the front porch, hiding. Feeling sorry for myself because I was thinking I was sort of rich for a few hours."

"I think you need to sit on it for a few days. Try to figure out what you really want to do. Okay?"

"Okay," I concede.

"Okay. Mom Brodie still hanging in there?"

"Yeah, I guess, but . . . I feel like . . ." I exhale. "This is going to sound silly, but I get the feeling she's drifting away. Like . . . not as much of her is here as there was when I got here two days ago." I pause. "Crazy?"

"Not at all."

"Call me later?" I ask. "And give Reed a big hug for me."

"Will do."

I slip my phone into my pocket and go back to Mom Brodie's room to give her hand another squeeze before I return to the loving bosom of my family.

28
Sarah Agnes

Bilis squeezes my hand. "It's going to be all right, luv," he says in his dreamy British accent. "You don't need him. You're going to be all right, Sarry."

I hold his little hand tightly. I'm not crying so much because Henri is leaving, for good this time, but because I feel like he's taking little Sarah Agnes Hanfland with him. Not that I blame him for taking her innocence or anything like that. Fourteen or not, I knew what I was doing when I climbed into that truck that morning and left Bakersville forever. It was my choice and mine alone. Looking back, it was certainly more my idea than his. But somehow this seems so . . . final. Like that girl I knew will never be back. It's been a year. A year, where has the time gone?

Henri is making the rounds, kissing the girls. He lays a big, wet one on Minnie's mouth. He shakes hands with the men.

Even Jacko pumps his hand, punches his shoulder. Henri's always been a likable guy. No one can argue with that; what fourteen-year-old wouldn't have fallen in love with him, in that beret he used to wear? But he's not trustworthy. Not with your money. Not with facts. Certainly not with your heart. I learned that pretty fast. I caught him making business with enough girls over the last year to finally cut him off from business with me. And now Rudebaker's is headed to Ohio, and Henri has decided to stay put in Tennessee. Some widow he met at our last stop, old enough to be his mother, has hired him as a handyman. Room and board included. I have a feeling he'll be all kinds of handy around her house.

It was Bilis who made me realize I was getting off easy here. No big breakup or blowup. No having to move from one truck to another. Jacko's already said I can drive the tent truck and stay put, living in the back. Just wish Hank the best, Bilis told me, and he'll be out of your hair and drawers for good. Bilis made me laugh when he said that because he rarely cracks off-color jokes. He's the gentleman of Rudebaker's for sure, even if he does call the coochie show. He's a rare man, my Bilis. I learned that pretty quickly. He's the one who protected me and looked after me for the last year. Not Henri. Bilis.

I wish I could give back to Bilis just half of what he's given me. A hundred times I've wished I could feel more for him than I do. It doesn't seem right that I'd leave my whole life and any security I had for the likes of a loser like Henri, but I can't love the finest man I've ever met. The feelings aren't there. And it's not because he's a dwarf. That doesn't bother me a bit. But I just can't do it. I can't love Bilis the way he wants me to love him. The way he deserves to be loved. Which makes me way sadder than Henri's leaving me for an old widow woman.

Henri offers his hand to Bilis, and Bilis accepts it, shakes it, but he's still holding onto me. Then Henri is standing in front of me.

"Mon chéri," he coos. It's the first time I've heard the French accent in a while. He's been trying out an Italian one. I wonder which he used on the widow.

I smile because I'm not the kind of girl who's going to go through life carrying grudges. They get too heavy. That's what Bilis says. I let go of Bilis's hand, and I hug Henri, but I don't let him kiss me on the lips. I turn my head so all he gets is my cheek. "Good luck, Hank," I tell him.

He steps back, winks, and makes a motion like he's pulling a trigger on a pistol. "You too, kiddo."

I turn away from him first and walk off to climb behind the wheel of the big tent truck, excited to move on to the next town.

29
CELESTE

I turn at the front step and bestow Bartholomew with one more kiss, this one on the cheek, and then I give him my flirtiest smile.

"I'll see you tomorrow night?" he asks. "Dinner at my place?"

"I don't know." I use my breathy, sad voice. The one I used when I did that commercial selling recliners. I rest my hand on his arm. "She may not live through the night."

He takes my hand in the darkness. The front lights are out because we never use the front door. I'll go around to the back after he's gone. But I want Bartholomew to see where I come from. What it means to be a Brodie; how important we are. Of course that should be obvious to him; the island is, after all, named after us.

"I'm so sorry, Celeste. Are you sure there's nothin' I can do for you?" He has a kind voice, and the slight Southern drawl makes it sexy. He seems genuine, which is a nice change from the losers I've been going out with lately. Who am I kidding? Most men I date/sleep with are losers. Or dicks. Or both.

I shake my head ever so slowly. "It's all in God's hands, now." I pause. Count the beats. The idea is to let what you've said sink in with the audience. But you can't be quiet too long or you'll lose their attention. "You should go." This time I rest my hand on his chest. He doesn't have a bad body for his age. Barely a gut. "I need to go in and sit with her."

He takes my hand and kisses it. Just like in the movies. I don't think a man has ever kissed my hand. Unless there was something kinky going on along with it.

"I'll call you tomorrow," he tells me. "But if you need me, if you need *anything,* darlin', call me."

I watch him walk to his car, this year's E-Class sedan. He's got a pretty good spring in his step for a man in his late sixties. He told me he works out; I think he was telling the truth. And he said he just got a clean bill of health from his doctor. No cardiac issues in his family. I got the feeling he was offering some sort of dating résumé. Which was kind of sweet, because he is twenty-five years older than me. His health would certainly be an issue if we got serious. As to whether a girl wants a man twenty-five years her senior, in good health or poor, I guess that depends on the girl and what she's looking for.

I stand at the door and watch him get into his car. He's wearing his ascot again and a navy blazer. Despite the fact that it was in the high eighties today. He looked very sporty in The Gull, though. I like sporty. He told me he'd been waiting for me, hoping I'd come. And he said that he was determined to get my phone number this time. Sweet. He didn't seem to mind my thinning hair or my crow's feet. And he was actually interesting. He talked about something other than his ex-wife or his ED refill. He wanted to hear about my career as an actress, but he didn't press for too many details, which made the conversation easy. The older I get, the harder it is to keep up with the lies.

He waves at me. He's smitten, all right.

I wave back, fluttering my scarf. I give him my best pose; it's the one that doesn't show off my double chin. I wait until his headlights show him making the turn from our long lane, onto the road back toward town. He's staying in one of the pricey condos on the east side of the island. A client offered it to him for the week.

When he's finally gone, I slip off my Jimmy Choos that are killing me (corns). I go down the steps and around to the back door. I let myself in and lock the door behind me. The light is on over the stove. Birdie. I check the clock on the wall. It's one thirty-six. Bartholomew invited me to go back to his place, but I decided to play things a little differently than usual. Draw out his anticipation. He talked tonight about making a trip to Paris. I could use a trip to Paris. Besides, I'm beat. It takes a lot of energy to look as good as I do and keep smiling.

I go down the hall. There's a soft glow of light coming from Mom Brodie's dying room. I find Abby asleep in Daddy's recliner, an ugly afghan pulled over her. I think about waking her to tell her about Bartholomew because I kind of like him. I can't remember the last time I liked a guy. I mean actually *liked* him. The fact that Bartholomew has money is just a bonus.

I decide to let her sleep. My Spanx are starting to cut off my circulation. I'm halfway up the hall when I realize I never even looked at Mom Brodie. I consider going back, but decide against it. What's the point? She doesn't even know we're here. Worst case scenario, she's dead. And if she's dead, she'll still be dead in the morning, and we'll all have gotten a good night's sleep.

I'm about to go up the stairs when I notice Daddy's office door is slightly open, and there's a light on. Which is weird this time of the morning. He always shuts the door on his way out. Sometimes he locks it and takes the key. I guess he doesn't know that Birdie and I figured out how to pick the lock years ago.

I leave my heels and bag on the bottom step and continue along the hall toward the other end of the house. "Daddy?" I push the door open slowly. Duke looks up from his favorite spot on the rug, sees it's me, and lowers his head again. I see Daddy right away, laid out on the couch. For a second, he scares me. His head is half off a crocheted pillow, and his mouth is open. Is he dead?

Wouldn't that be a hell of a thing if we were all sitting around waiting for the old lady to die and he beat her to it? But as I walk toward him, he lets out a big, long snore. I lay my hand on my chest, feeling my heart pounding. I don't want to ever find anyone dead. *Ever.*

I stand there for a minute looking at him.

I wonder if I should wake him up and tell him to go to bed. I decide against it. He's probably here for a good reason. Probably directly related to Birdie and the beer Daddy was knocking back this afternoon. When Joseph and I left so he could drop me off at The Gull, Daddy and Birdie were getting into it over his beer. Well, as getting into it as they ever do. She was collecting beer bottles and mumbling under her breath. He was quietly saying, "Let it go, Birdie. Let it go."

As I turn to head to bed, I spot a big pile of paperwork on his desk. It's a white envelope on top that catches my attention. LAST WILL AND TESTAMENT it says in gold lettering. I walk over and pick it up, and when I do, I see a business-size envelope with my name written across it that was underneath. It's written in Mom Brodie's distinct, old-school cursive.

My stomach lurches, and for a second I think I'm going to be sick. I knew I shouldn't have had that last vodka and cranberry.

I drop the will and pick up the envelope. It's sealed. I stare at it in my hand for a long moment. There are no other envelopes here. Not one for Abby or Joseph. This is not good. Not good at all.

I stare at the envelope in my hand. I look at Daddy. If he has it in here, that means I'm not supposed to have it. Not yet. Not until Mom Brodie dies.

I ease open the envelope. Inside is a piece of paper.

My dear granddaughter Celeste . . .

By the time you read this . . . blah, blah, blah.

My eyes dart as I speed read.

Given great thought . . . blah, blah, blah.

Irresponsibly . . . Dishonesty . . . Poor judgment.

Her diatribe goes on for a quarter of a page as she lists not just general bad qualities she sees in me, but includes specific details. . . .

The pyramid scheme when you lost the $5000 you borrowed from me, the arrest writing those bad checks, the unwanted pregnancies . . .

Blah.

Blah.

Blah.

It's not until she gets to the very bottom of the page that she comes out with what she should have just said first off. With great sadness, I've made the decision not to leave you any money because frankly, you don't deserve it, and you'll only waste it.

Know that I have always loved you and will continue to love you unto my death, she finishes off.

"Bitch," I say out loud.

Duke lifts his head and stares at me. Daddy groans and rolls over, but he doesn't wake.

"Bitch," I repeat. I throw the letter down. Then pick it up again. Against my will, tears fill my eyes. "Bitch." I say it again, but with less enthusiasm. I wipe my nose, that's starting to run, with the back of my hand.

"I don't know why you always thought you were better than us. Better than me," I say aloud, not caring if anyone hears me. "I need that money. How am I supposed to get my hair plugs? How am I supposed to make myself beautiful again?"

A sob escapes my lips.

Without her inheritance, I'm sunk. It's over. Not only can I not get my hair implants, I can't get the face-lift. I can't get the watch Daddy gave me for my fortieth out of hock. And I can't pay my rent this month. Again. September one, I'm out. I'm evicted. Again.

I slump into Daddy's chair. Throw the letter on the desk. What am I going to do now? A shuddering sob bubbles up my throat and out of my mouth. *What am I going to do?*

No one in this house will loan me any more money.

My eyes are stinging. My mascara and eyeliner are running. I wipe at my eyes, not caring if I look like a raccoon.

Another sob rises, and I try to push it down. What am I going to do?

And then I know.

I think about the bridge.

The cool water of the bay.

Of how easy it will be to just step off the rail.

And a strange calmness comes over me.

Because then it will be over. All of this will be over.

And everyone who's been mean to me? Everyone who's tried to *help* me with what they see as good intentions? They'll all feel so guilty. They'll be wracked with remorse. Everyone is waiting for Mom Brodie to die, but they're expecting it. People who are a hundred and two aren't supposed to be alive.

But no one will be expecting me to die.

I rise out of Daddy's leather chair. I'm not shaking anymore. I carefully return the letter to the envelope and press down to reseal it smoothly.

Duke looks at me one last time, then

closes his eyes. As if he's resigned to it too.

I'll kill myself, and then everyone on Brodie Island will be talking about me. Everyone in this house will be sobbing. Wishing they had treated me better. Wishing they hadn't said mean things behind my back all these years.

It's too bad Mom Brodie is in a coma. If she wasn't, she'd feel guilty for cutting me out of her will and making me kill myself.

Everyone will come to my funeral. Everyone likes a funeral for someone who committed suicide. I bet the church ladies will have to have two sittings for my funeral luncheon. And everyone will cry. And talk about how good I looked in the casket. How peaceful. How beautiful. I bet Bartholomew will postpone his trip to Paris to come to my funeral. And he'll wear a blue jacket and maybe his ascot.

It suddenly occurs to me that I might not have brought a dress suitable to be laid out in, in my casket. I packed and left New York quickly to avoid the landlady. I've had a green chiffon hanging in my closet for a couple of years, thinking it would be my funeral dress. But it would be a toss-up between it and a gorgeous navy Halston I got at a flea market last year.

I have to have a decent dress. And maybe

my wig. But I brought a wig. I just haven't worn it because it's so damned hot here.

I grab the envelope and slip it back under the will, exactly the way I found it, slightly turned to the right. I'm good at putting things back the way I found them so no one notices. I've had a lifetime of practice. And an excellent teacher. Birdie knows a little bit about the art of snooping without getting caught.

I do have the pink and green dress with the fluttery sleeves. That might look nice on me. Especially since I got a little sun yesterday. I walk out of Daddy's office.

I consider going now to the bridge. Maybe taking Abby's car. Or Daddy's truck. No . . . Mom Brodie's Cadillac. Everyone on Brodie knows her 1992 white Caddy. It will add to the tragedy.

I can hear them whispering, crammed into the pews.

"They say she took her grandmother's Caddy to the top of the bridge."

"Such a shame."

"Such a gorgeous woman."

"So tragic."

I decide against doing it tonight. I'm too tired. There are too many things to be done to stage the whole thing. I have to hang the dress that's balled up in my suitcase to get the wrinkles out. And the wig will have to be spritzed and fluffed. And then there's the matter of the suicide note. Do I write one to the whole family, or do I write individual ones? I've been writing and rewriting my suicide notes in my head for years. I know just what I want to say to everyone. But Mom Brodie's might have to be revised, now that she's unconscious.

At the staircase, I pick up my shoes and bag and slowly climb the steps, thinking about everything I need to do tomorrow. And I'll have to think through my behavior. Do I act like everything is fine, thus shocking everyone even further? Do I tell them I found Mom Brodie's letter and how devastated I am? That would really dial up the guilt when someone finds me floating the next morning.

I smile to myself in the dark as I slowly make my way up the stairs. Come Monday morning everyone is going to be sorry for the way they've treated me. And I'm going to look so beautiful in my coffin.

30
BIRDIE

I stand over Mrs. Brodie, in my nightie, watching her chest rise and fall. It's almost three in the morning. Everyone else is asleep. Abby is here in the chair. Little Joe's on his sofa in his office. Snoring. I can hear him all the way in here.

He got cross with me tonight, but I don't care. The doctor told him to cut back on his salt, which means Old Bay seasoning, and he certainly shouldn't be drinking a six-pack. I don't care if it is light beer. Too many people around here depending on him for him to up and have a heart attack and die on us the way his daddy did.

Me fussing with him turned out to be a good thing though, because he ended up convincing his boy to stay. Because Brodie men have to stick together, Little Joe told him. So Joseph is upstairs in his old room, and his little Ainslie is sleeping with Sarah. Even Celeste is home and in bed. Home at a decent hour, for once. I like the feel of this old house in the middle of the night when I know that everyone I care about is here, safe and asleep. Not looking at me, so I can look at them.

I glance down at Mrs. Brodie.

She's definitely breathing slower than she was earlier. It's not just my imagination. I stand here for a minute, my scrapbook tucked under my arm. I was in bed upstairs reading, but then I got this feeling I needed to come down. Like she needed me. I knew Abby was here with Mrs. Brodie, but I just felt like I needed to be here, too.

I look over my shoulder. Abby's out. She had two glasses of wine while she played Monopoly with Sarah and Joseph and Little Joe last night. Wine makes her sleep hard. I wish I liked it. Wish I could sleep hard like that.

I slowly walk over to the far side of the room. Lift an old ladder-back chair, one Mrs. Brodie and I bought at a yard sale over on Deal Island, and carry it to the bed. I settle down into the chair slowly. My feet hurt. My knees hurt, and the one hip is giving me a fit with the arthritis.

I study the nightstand for a minute. I look at the picture of Mrs. Brodie and Big Joe and them smiling like they've got everything

389

in the world. Because they do. I run my fingertips over the oyster shell and feel its bumpy solidness. I pick up one of the peppermints and smell it. Mrs. Brodie always smelled of peppermints. I bet she bought thousands of pounds of them over the years. It's a wonder her teeth didn't rot right out of her head. She carried them in her apron pockets, her coat pockets, even Big Joe's pockets. And she kept them in the glove compartment of her Cadillac. I think about eating the peppermint, but it doesn't seem right with her lying here dying, so I put it back. Then I pick up the little, curled-up piece of blue paper. I don't have to squint to see the tiny writing because I've already read it a couple of times. *Sniff'um muffins,* it says. I like it. This palindrome is way better than some of the ones Sarah's always mumbling under her breath. She really likes that one about sluts in Tulsa.

I sit back in my chair, set my scrapbook on my lap, and open it. I flip through a couple of pages until I get to the section on the Grand Canyon. For some reason, tonight I feel like gazing at the Grand Canyon. I smooth the postcards I've taped to the pages. Bought them on eBay. You can buy anything on eBay. Even old postcards. Funny that Little Joe has never asked me what I'm buying by mail order. Even when he carries an envelope in from the mailbox. Guess he thinks they're more chicken tea towels.

I clear my throat.

"The Grand Canyon National Park," I read quietly to Mrs. Brodie. "Unique combinations of geologic color and erosional forms decorate a canyon that is two hundred and seventy-seven miles long, up to eighteen miles wide, and a mile deep. The Grand Canyon overwhelms our senses through its immense size."

I look over at her. She once told me she'd seen the Grand Canyon. It was a long time ago, back when I actually thought I'd get to go someday. When I truly thought Joe would take me there. I wanted to ride the burros from the rim down, all the way to the bottom of the canyon. Maybe camp out down there. I've never been camping.

Mrs. Brodie told me the north rim was the thing to see, not the south rim. I asked her when she'd been there. She told me in another lifetime. While I was considering what she might mean, she handed me a half-bushel basket of lima beans to shuck, and that was the end of that. She never brought it up again, and neither did I. For a long time, I told myself she was lying. That she really hadn't ever seen the Grand Canyon. That she just wanted to tell me she had because she knew I wanted to see it and I never would.

But that wasn't true. Because Mrs. Brodie never lies. Even when the truth hurts you. A lot of her truths have hurt me over the years. She once told me the reason Little Joe strayed from my marriage was because I couldn't make him happy. She didn't have to say that. I already knew it. Just like I know I'm fat. And ugly. Truth still hurts.

I turn the page.

"Sitting atop the Kaibab Plateau," I read, thinking she might want to hear this, since she's been there, "eight thousand to nine thousand feet above sea level with lush green meadows surrounded by a mixed conifer forest sprinkled with white-barked aspen, the north rim is an oasis in the desert. Here you may observe deer feeding, or a coyote chasing mice in a meadow." I look up at her again. "I've never seen a coyote. Seen pictures. Watched a YouTube video of one hunting on Little Joe's computer. You know, you can see almost anything on YouTube. Sarah told me about it." I look down at the scrapbook again.

It's late, and I'm tired, so the words are hard to see. I need my readers, but I didn't bring them down with me. I think for a minute, then, glancing over my shoulder to see that Abby's still asleep, I open the bedside drawer. I pull out Mrs. Brodie's readers, and I feel like a naughty child. Ordinarily, I'd never do something like this. The glasses are fancy, with plastic jewels glued on them and a long, sparkly chain. They didn't come from the five-and-dime like mine do. Mrs. Brodie bought them at some fancy department store when she went shopping with her friends in Salisbury.

I loop the chain around my neck and settle the glasses on my nose. The words come into focus better. "Here you may observe deer feeding, or a coyote chasing mice in a meadow," I read. "A mother turkey leading her young across the road, or a mountain lion slinking into the cover of the forest."

I look at Mrs. Brodie again. "Did you see a mountain lion when you were at the Grand Canyon? Bet you did. You're lucky like that. Always were." I think about how many times she won at Bingo at the fire hall. She won all kinds of things: Longaberger baskets, handbags, a set of dishes with strawberries on them. And money. She was always winning the 50/50 somewhere.

Guess I know now where all that money went all these years.

I turn the page to look at the pictures of all the wildlife you can see in the Grand Canyon. Pictures I've cut from magazines. I've got pages and pages of them. I'm looking for the one of the mountain lion I cut out of a *Smithsonian Magazine* at the doctor's office when I hear Mrs. Brodie make a funny sound. Like a snort.

I peer over the sparkly glasses. Her mouth is open, and her lips are moving. Just a little. Like quivering. I set the scrapbook under my chair and stand up, taking her hand, looking down. "Mrs. Brodie?" I whisper.

Her whole body twitches . . . just a little. And it scares me. I'm just wondering if I should wake up Abby, or call the hospice number, or something, when I feel Mrs. Brodie's hand move in mine. Almost like she's trying to hold my hand. Trying to tell me it's okay. That everything is going to be okay. Tears fill my eyes so suddenly that it startles me. I can't remember the last time I cried.

I squeeze her hand back. And watch her chest. It doesn't seem to be moving up and down like it was. But just when I'm starting to get scared that she's gone, really gone, I see it slowly rise.

I exhale because I realize I was holding my breath when Mrs. Brodie was, and I sit down in the chair hard. I wipe away my tears with one hand, but I still hold her hand with the other. "It's all right," I whisper, not sure where the words are coming from inside me. I pull off the glasses and let them fall so they hang around my neck, against my nightie. "Don't be afraid. You stay as long as you want."

My lower lip trembles, and I bite it. "You stay as long as you want, Mrs. Brodie. I'll watch over you. I'll change your diaper. I don't mind. Not one bit. Because . . . you know why. Because you saved me from that orphanage. And you brought me here. You gave me a roof over my head and a fine man for a husband. And you . . ."

It's on the tip of my tongue to say "you loved me," but it seems like too much. So I just say again, "You stay on this earth as long as you want, and I'll stay right here with you. But . . . but you feel like the good Lord is calling you, and you're ready to go. . . ." My voice catches in my throat, and my eyes fill with tears again. This time I don't wipe them away. I just let them roll down my cheeks. "You go on. Because I'm sure Big Joe is waiting for you in that rowboat of his. Right out in the bay. And I bet he'll have that big straw hat of yours you used to love to wear. The one with the blue ribbon. And I bet he'll be happy to see you because I know he's missed you. I know he's missed you," I repeat.

And then I settle down in the chair, her hand in mine, to wait to see what she wants to do.

31
SARAH AGNES

"Is he there?" I ask Bilis.

I stand with my back against the shabby curtain, trying to peer out into the audience without anybody's seeing me. I'm still stripped down to my drawers and pasties tassels from the last show because it's so darned hot in Jersey in August. Whatever sense of decorum I once had is gone, though I'm always decently dressed when I leave this tent. It's funny how quickly and easily I've fallen into the life of a hoochie-coochie dancer. I went from being a scared girl shaking in my shoes to a woman who can dance with the kind of confidence that brings the money in. Last month, I made more money than any of the other girls, and Jacko officially made me the lead act, meaning I go on last.

I wouldn't say it's affected my dignity, though. Being a coochie girl. Which Minnie says is the way it has to be. Some women can't ever get past the idea that they show their bubbies to make a living, she says. But women like us, like Minnie and me, we're of a stronger nature. It's Bilis's belief that no one can make us feel anything. That we choose how to respond to life, the good and the bad. When I started doing this, I *chose* not to feel bad about myself, no matter what people in these little Podunk towns think of me. I know who I am and what I want in this world and what I can give, and that's what matters.

"Do you see him?" I ask Bilis again. He's standing on the stage, waiting for the marks to quiet down. He's wearing his top hat today and looking very smart.

"I don't know. They all look the same to me." He talks out of the side of his mouth so none of the men lined up on the benches can hear him. Bilis is being grumpy with me. I think he's jealous about Joe.

I met Joe a few days ago. He came to our first evening performance here in Hoboken and has come to two or three shows every night. Third night he came, after turning him away both nights before, I agreed to a private meeting in one of the little cubicles curtained off in the back of the tent. I had never done it before with a mark. Partially because I was scared. Partially because having a bunch of men watching me take off my clothes onstage is one thing. Doing it alone with one man is another. And Jacko said I didn't have to do it, so I don't do it.

But there was something about Joe's handsome, rugged face and his kind voice that just . . . it got to me. And the fact that he offered double the usual tip didn't hurt. Because I'm saving money. Hoarding it, Minnie says. For what, I don't know.

I didn't take my clothes off for Joe. In fact, I wore a silk dressing gown over my costume. I told him I wouldn't show him my bubs, and he said he'd pay anyway. He just wanted to talk, he said.

So we talked. Until Bilis sent Junior T in to tell us time was up. Joe tried to pay again to stay with me longer, but Junior T sent him packing. Said Bilis wouldn't like it. Besides, it's not safe, he said. You spend too much time with a mark, and they start getting possessive, and those are the kind that end up having to be *taught a lesson* with the tent stake he keeps in his pocket.

Only Joe turned out to be safe. He really did just want to talk, though last night I got a little silly and sat on his lap and even kissed him. Fact of the matter is, I realized that I'm lonely. Lonely for a man who tells me I'm pretty and smiles at me the way any girl wants to be smiled at. A man I can feel the same way about him that he feels about me. There hasn't been a boy in my life since Henri took off a year ago. My choosing. I really did love Henri, and I feel like I lost a piece of myself to him. I just decided I couldn't let myself fall for too many men, otherwise, when the right one came along, I wouldn't have any heart left to give.

And I want to have a heart to give someone someday. Rudebaker's has been an adventure from the first day I took off with Henri. And I've liked it, for the most part. I've met amazing people and seen more of the country in two years than most girls do in a lifetime. But I know this isn't going to be my life. Not like it's been Bilis's and Jacko's and the bearded lady's, who I've really gotten close to. I know it's not for me because, at heart, I'm still an old-fashioned girl from Indiana. I want to marry and have babies. I want a house and a bed to call my own that's not in the back of a tent truck. I want to love and be loved. And I want to grow old with the person I love.

"He's got to be here," I mutter, trying not to be annoyed with Bilis. I know he just wants what's best for me. Only he can't accept that he might not necessarily know what's best for me.

I peek around the corner as the cymbals clash in the pit and Bilis walks to the middle of the stage to introduce the new girl. Mousy brushes past me on tiptoes and onto the stage, her little hands high in front of her, pressed together like she's praying. It's part of her act. She's wearing fuzzy ears and a long tail pinned to sparkly underdrawers, too. I think it's silly, but what do I care if she wants to act like a mouse?

The men go crazy, stomping their feet and whistling catcalls.

I peek around the curtain again, and this time I see Joe. He's on one of the far benches, on the end. He's a tall, medium-built man with brown hair and the nicest brown eyes you ever did see. And there he is, sitting there quietly like he's on the front pew at church. Waiting for me.

And I smile.

After the show, it doesn't take Junior T more than five minutes to come backstage to me carrying a crisp dollar bill. Tells me Joe wants to see me.

My eyes get big. "A dollar?"

He's grinning ear to ear as he hands it over. "He gave me a nickel just to come tell you he wants to buy you some cotton candy. Go for a walk on the midway. With your clothes on," he adds.

I don't know why, but that makes me laugh. And I say yes.

And a week later, I'm sitting on the bumper of my truck, watching Bilis pace in front of me, smoking a store-bought cigarette. "I think you should go with him," he tells me.

I tuck of lock of hair that's slipped from the scarf on my head behind my ear. It's late at night, and Joe's just dropped me off. I told him to go for a ride and come back in a while. Because I have to talk to Bilis. Because I feel like I'm standing on the edge of a cliff, trying to see what's below. Trying to decide if I'm brave enough to step off the edge.

We had the best day together. Joe and I. The best day of my life. Joe came for me in his cousin's car this morning and took me to the ocean. It's the first time I ever saw water that big, and I fell in love so fast, so hard, that I actually cried when we packed up so he could bring me back. Because I'm afraid I'll never see, never smell the sea again. Because we're pulling up stakes in two days. And we're headed to . . . I can't even remember where. I just drive behind the monkey-boy truck. Because all these towns are the same. The men and the boys who come to watch me dance, practically in my birthday suit, are the same.

Except Joe.

Joe's different. At least I think he is. I want him to be.

Joe asked me tonight to marry him. He's known me less than two weeks, and he asked me to marry him. He says we can get married tomorrow. And then he wants to take me home to his family, to a place in Maryland. It's an island. Joe says his family has been farming and fishing the Chesapeake Bay for hundreds of years. I've never seen the Chesapeake Bay, but he says it's big. Not as big as the Atlantic Ocean, but every bit as beautiful. And magical. That was the word Joe used. He said the place is *magical*.

And I want to go to a magical place.

I tried to point out to Joe that a good Methodist man like him couldn't marry a girl like me. Not a girl with a tattoo. That's one of the reasons I think I liked Joe, right from the start. Because he liked my tattoo. Because even though a good church man like him shouldn't like it, he does. He had to have the whole story behind it, of course.

I told Joe about Haru, the old Japanese man, and about his dwarf wife who died before I joined Rudebaker's. And about how sad Haru is without his wife because he loved her so much. I told Joe about the English teacup and saucer set Bilis gave me that has bluebirds with ribbons in their beaks on it. About how it's my most prized possession. Joe didn't even get jealous when I told him about Bilis and how he's in love with me and wants to marry me. Joe seemed to understand that, for me, that teacup means I'm worth something. To someone. My bluebirds on my thigh remind me of that, every day. I think that's the best gift Bilis gave me, the sense of self-worth I have now, that I didn't have when I left Bakersville.

Actually getting the tattoo was an impulse. Kind of like running away from home and joining the carnival had been. And I wasn't even drinking hooch when I did it. I don't like hooch. We were all sitting around on a rainy night in the mess tent, the Rudebaker's crew. Everyone was comparing tattoos, and the girls started teasing me about my *virgin* skin. They all have tattoos, ones you see in plain daylight, ones you can only see in more intimate settings. Even our bearded lady has one: a little heart with the name of her little boy who died under it. Haru offered to do my tattoo for me. Free, he said. The garter was his idea. Classy tattoo for a classy lady, Haru said in his broken English.

But the bluebirds, they were my idea. Bilis warned me at the time that a tattoo was a bad idea, that it would make it hard for me to hide my carnival life when I got to the point in my life that I wanted to hide it. And he said I would, some day. But I wanted the bluebirds tattooed on my thigh so I would always remember who I am. That I can be somebody. And I don't regret getting it. Not for a second.

Joe said my tattoo wasn't a problem, though he agreed it would be where he was from. I guess his magical place doesn't include tattoos. But he had an answer for that. He said no one would ever have to know. Not about the tattoo, not about Rudebaker's or what I've been doing to pay my keep. He said no one would ever have to see my tattoo. That it would be our secret to share for the rest of our lives. Joe was supposed to be attending a gospel tent meeting with his cousins here in New Jersey. He said no one would ever have to know he met me in the coochie tent instead of a prayer meeting tent. And I believe him when he says he'll never tell a soul.

"I don't know," I tell Bilis. I shake my head. The skirt of my polka-dotted dress is blowing in the wind, flipping up and flashing Bilis with my bare thighs. I push down my skirt, imagining what it would be like to go to church and wear a nice hat. "What if I'm wrong about him? What if . . . what if he's just like Henri?"

"Not every man is like Henri," Bilis says.

"I guess that's true," I say. "Because you're not."

He gives me a half smile, and by the light of the kerosene lamp hanging on a pole, I can't tell if it's a happy smile or a sad one.

"He says he'll marry you?" Bilis asks.

"Tomorrow. He's not trying to trick me because he said I could bring you along to sign for me. And he didn't even try to get in my drawers, Bilis. Said it could wait until we were good and married."

"He ask you about other men you've been with? Henri?"

"Nope. I tried to tell him, but he said it didn't matter. He said we'd have our whole lives to talk about stuff like that."

Bilis throws his butt on the ground and grinds it out with one little polished shoe. "I think he's the real thing, Sarry. I think he means what he says." He comes to stand in front of me. "He tell you he loved you?"

I nod.

"You love him?"

Again, I nod.

He takes both my hands in his and holds

them tight. "And what do you see when you look in his eyes?"

I think for a minute. "I see . . . kindness . . . and laughter . . . and . . . I see happiness. The kind I want."

He stands there for a long time, looking up at me, and then he lets go of my hands and tugs on the hem of his seersucker vest. "Then you should marry your Joe."

"Yeah?" Suddenly I feel like I'm going to cry. Because I'm happy, and I'm sad. I want to marry Joe and go to his magical island, but I don't want to leave Bilis.

"Yeah," Bilis says. "You marry him, and you never tell him how old you are because that might make him feel bad. And you never tell anyone on that magic island about this grand escapade of yours." He motions to the carnival trucks around us.

"And what about you?" I ask. "Do I tell them about my best friend in the world, Bilis? Bilis who is a dwarf and has the biggest heart of anyone I ever knew?"

He reaches out and brushes away a tear from my cheek with his thumb. "You don't," he says in a whisper.

The headlights from an approaching car suddenly get bright in my face, and I squint, holding my hand up to shade my eyes.

"Sarah!" Joe hollers out the window of

the Studebaker.

The headlights are so bright that I can't see him. I just hear his voice.

"Go on with you," Bilis says.

I pretend not to see his tears. I get up from the bumper of the truck, and I walk into the light, hearing the sound of Joe's voice calling my name. And I wonder what great adventure will come next.

32
ABBY

"No, no, I don't think it's been long." I put my arm around my mother. I just woke up, and I'm groggy. Or I'm dreaming. I wish I could go with the dreaming scenario. I'm not ready for this. I'm just not ready. "She still feels warm," I whisper.

We're both standing beside the bed, looking down at Mom Brodie, who doesn't look any different than she did when I checked her around four this morning when I woke to find Birdie asleep in a chair beside the bed. Mom Brodie still looks like she's sleeping. Only maybe her face is more relaxed. And I'm probably just imagining it, but I think she looks like she's on the verge of one of her great big smiles. I swear I can smell peppermint in the room.

Birdie's whole body is shuddering. Her nose is running. But she doesn't make a sound.

Tears run down my cheeks. I'm relieved

that Mom Brodie's gone to be with Grand-pop. Relieved I can go home to Drum. And I'm sad for my loss. But mostly I'm crying because I feel so bad for Birdie. She seems devastated. As if she didn't realize Mom Brodie really was going to die.

"I just nodded off for a minute," Birdie tells me. She's gripping Mom Brodie's hand so hard that I think it would hurt. If Mom Brodie was still here with us. "I didn't mean to." She takes another shuddering breath. "I didn't mean to leave her to die alone."

I look down at my short, fat, ugly mother, and I feel like my heart is going to break. Like it's going to snap right in two. "Oh, Mom, she wasn't alone." I wrap my arms around her, and I cry like I haven't cried in . . . I don't know that I've ever cried like this.

All these years, I thought my mother was cold. I thought she didn't love me. Didn't love any of us. I thought she wasn't much of a mother to me or Celeste. She certainly wasn't the mother Joseph deserved. And I never thought she loved Daddy the way he wanted her to love him. But standing here with her and my dead grandmother, I have an epiphany, the kind you only experience a couple of times in your life. If you're lucky. I realize that if my mother didn't love us the way I thought she should, it wasn't because she didn't love anyone. It was because she loved my grandmother too much.

I've never thought that love could be a quantitative thing. I love so many people, so freely. I loved Reed with everything I had, and then, when Sarah was born, it wasn't that I had to divide my love; instead my love grew exponentially. But maybe that's not true for everyone. Maybe some people *can* only love a certain amount. My mother grew up in an orphanage. She was fed and kept dry, but she was never loved as a child. Maybe that limits a soul. Then Mom Brodie brought her to Brodie Island.

I think Mom Brodie got all of Birdie's love.

My mother clings to me, hugging me in a way she's never hugged me before. Letting me hug her. We hold each other for what seems like a very long time. Almost enough time to make up for all the years we haven't hugged. Almost.

It's my mother who puts an end to our little pity party in the early morning light of the sunny sewing room with too much furniture in it. She stiffens, lets go of me, and reaches around me to take a handful of tissues from the box. She blows her nose loud and hard, making a honking sound. I can't help myself. I laugh as I pluck one from the box.

"Hospice has to be called," she says, honking again. "And the funeral parlor."

I almost laugh again because *parlor* is such a funny word for it, but I don't. I bet Mom Brodie would have laughed, though. Or cut her eyes at me, laughing with her eyes. "I can do that."

"Your daddy has to get up. He slept in his office last night. He needs to get himself decent before they get here."

"We've got some time," I say gently. "The nurse will probably be coming from Salisbury." I close my eyes for a second, trying to remember if Gail said she was or wasn't working today. It seems like it was weeks ago that we stood here and talked. Joseph's here, so he'll get to see her again. It occurs to me how ridiculous it is to be playing matchmaker in the room where my grandmother just died.

"You want me to tell Daddy?" I ask. I called her Mom just a moment ago, and now it seems weird to call her Birdie. But I can't bring myself to call her Mom again. It just doesn't . . . fit right on my tongue.

She's fussing with Mom Brodie's bedsheets, and I feel a sudden moment of panic. What if she pulls the sheet down? What if she sees the tattoo? She can't see the tattoo. My mother isn't very broad-minded. I'm afraid she'll pass judgment about Mom Brodie if she knows. And the relationship between these two is already complicated enough. Birdie doesn't need added complications.

I understand now what people mean when they say love is sometimes close to hate. My whole life I thought my mother disliked my grandmother. I even thought, at times, that my grandmother disliked my mother. Which couldn't have been true because Mom Brodie was the one who decided Birdie would marry my dad, her only son. Her sun in her universe. If their relationship was confusing to me, observing it from the outside, I can't imagine how confusing it must have been to Mom Brodie and my mother, living it.

"We shouldn't disturb her until she's officially declared," I suggest gently. And by the time hospice does what they have to do, the funeral home will be here to get her. With a little luck, no one will ever know about the beautiful bluebirds but Angus at the funeral home, and I know he would never say a word, even to one of us.

Birdie smooths the sheet one last time,

sniffs, and steps back. "I'll put coffee on. Start some oatmeal. Then I'll wake your daddy."

I guess that means she's going to tell him, and I shouldn't.

I move toward the doorway. First things first, I need to go to the bathroom. Then I need to put on a bra. I'm not sure why I think I need to put on a bra to call hospice to have my grandmother declared dead. I'm definitely going to need a big cup of my mother's bad coffee.

I call Drum while I'm still in the bathroom and have another good cry. He says all the right things, and I feel better when I hang up. Then I wake Joseph, and together we wake our girls and tell them Mom Brodie is dead. Sarah's eyes fill with tears, and she gives me a hug. She seems to accept the death of the woman she is named after with the same aplomb with which she tackles everything else in the world. Ainslie is too young to really understand, but she throws herself into her daddy's arms for a bear hug, and the two head downstairs with her getting a piggyback ride.

"You think it's okay if I go for a run?" my Sarah asks me when they're gone. She's opened the French doors and walked out onto the balcony. A light breeze comes in off the bay, smelling briny and life-giving. "Before I see her?"

See Mom Brodie's body, she means. "You don't have to see her. It's not necessary."

"No, I want to." She turns her back to me to lean on the balcony rail. She's wearing a pair of very short pink shorts that say SCORE! across her butt cheeks. It doesn't look like something I would have bought, but I keep my mouth shut. *Pick your battles. And pick the time and place.* That's my new addition to the rule.

"I've never seen a dead person," she says, sounding scarily matter-of-fact.

"I'll go with you, if you want."

She turns to face me. "That's okay. I need to do it alone."

I meet her gaze, and we have *a moment.* And I feel so fortunate to have my daughter. *This* one. "I just called hospice. It'll be close to two hours before Gail gets here, so you have time."

She nods. "You going to wake up Celeste now?"

I groan. "I guess we have to tell her at some point." I make no attempt to keep the reluctance from my voice.

Sarah makes a face. "You really think she's going to be that upset, Mom? Because the only thing I've heard her say about Mom Brodie this weekend is that she can't wait to get her inheritance. Did you know she's getting a hair transplant?" This time, it's just her freckled nose that Sarah wrinkles. "I didn't even know there *was* such a thing."

"Hair transplant?" It sounds so crazy that it has to be true.

We're both quiet for a moment.

"Well, good luck with that." Sarah turns her back to me.

I walk slowly down the hall toward my sister's room. The phrase *dead man walking* goes through my head. Which is totally histrionic. I sound like my sister now. And Sarah's right. Celeste isn't going to be that broken up about Mom Brodie's dying. Specifically, when she finds out she's been cut out of the will.

So why am I dreading telling her?

Because Mom Brodie's death will instantly become all about Celeste. Because she'll pretend she gives two craps. Because Celeste loves a drama, and I hate providing one on a silver platter.

I don't knock on her bedroom door. I just walk in. Halfway through the door, I have second thoughts. What if she brought that old guy home? I don't know if I can look at Bartholomew's bare butt before I've had a cup of coffee.

Celeste is alone in the bed. Thank God for small favors. Another one of Mom Brodie's little sayings. I guess our loved ones really do carry on, in us.

I walk over to the heavy drapes that cover the French doors and push them open. Celeste doesn't move. She's sprawled on top of the bed wearing panties and a cami. She never made it under the sheets. Her hair is plastered to one side of her head, and in the morning light I can see how thin it's become. And I feel bad for her. And I feel bad for laughing at the idea of a hair transplant. If she wants it, if it makes her feel better about herself, who am I to judge? I know better. My grandmother taught me better.

As I walk over to the bed, I see a pink and green dress hanging on the front of her closet door. It's a pretty dress, chiffon with fluttery sleeves. In anticipation of the funeral? I also see her wig on her dresser. She's stuffed it with the scarf she was wearing yesterday, and propped it on an empty fifth of vodka. The girl's innovative; I'll give her that.

I sit down on the edge of her bed and look down at her. I never realized how much she looks like our mother — a skinny version, albeit. She didn't take her makeup off when she got home last night. I wonder if it has anything to do with the empty vodka bottle.

I feel a sudden tenderness for my little sister, and I want to reach out and brush the hair off her mascara-streaked cheek. I want to whisper that everything's going to be all right. But I don't.

I turn and gaze out the double doors. Celeste's room is at the front of the house, looking out over the acres of the front lawn Daddy keeps mowed. He doesn't do it himself, of course. He's got a grounds crew that works all of his properties, including this house and Joseph's. Celeste never minded having a front room, instead of one with a view of the bay. I'd have thrown a fit if Birdie ever decided to move me to the front of the house. Even when the doors are closed and the drapes pulled, I can hear the bay. Smell it. Feel it.

But Celeste's view is beautiful. From here, I can see acres and acres of soy beans and field corn and sorghum ready to be harvested soon. My love of farm fields comes second only to my love of the Chesapeake Bay. The view from here is so beautiful that tears well in my eyes. The older I get, the more I love this place. The more I feel Brodie Island pulling me into her arms.

Every time I come home, Daddy mentions how nice it would be to have me here again. Yesterday, while we were having crabs, he brought up, out of the blue, the idea of Drum's having a studio in the barn where we used to keep our ponies when we were kids. I wonder if Joseph said something to him about us splitting the money with Celeste.

I turn back to my sister. I need to wake her because I need to get dressed and go downstairs and be with Birdie and Daddy.

My thoughts and my heart go back to Mom Brodie, lying downstairs in the sewing room. I can't believe she's gone. . . .

I lay my hand on Celeste's bony shoulder. She's *so* thin that it's a little scary. I wonder for a moment if she has some awful disease and hasn't told us. But I know she's not sick; she'd be playing that card for all it was worth.

"Celeste," I whisper.

She doesn't start like I would if someone woke me this way. She just slowly opens her eyes and looks up at me. We have the same eyes. She looks like Birdie, but we all have the Brodie eyes.

"Hey," I say softly.

She blinks and pushes her hair off her face. Then she sits up and leans back against her headboard, wiping her mouth with the back of her hand. I know that look.

I hand her the half bottle of water sitting on her bedside nightstand. I reach for the bottle of ibuprofen. I have a feeling she's going to need that, too.

"What are you" — she twists off the cap and takes a long drink — "what are you doing here?" She reaches over, wakes her phone to see the time, and drops the phone back on the nightstand. "Christ, it's seven thirty in the morning."

"Mom Brodie died," I say softly, handing her four little white tablets.

She stares at me, seemingly confused. Maybe because she's not awake yet. "She died?"

I nod. "A little while ago."

"She *died*," she says a little more forcefully, as if she's annoyed. "God damn it." She looks away, shaking her head. She throws back the pain reliever and takes another long drink. A little of the water trickles from the side of her mouth. "So typical of her." She's past annoyed now and moved on to anger.

My own temper flares, but I keep it to myself. *"Typical?"* I get up off her bed. Any tenderness I felt for my sister is gone. This is so like her. Everything is about Celeste.

Always. "What's that supposed to mean? She's dead, Celeste." My voice chokes up.

"Right." She sets the water bottle back on the table and leans back and closes her eyes. "She's dead." She seems to think on it for a moment, and then her voice changes. "Mom Brodie's dead. I can't believe she's dead." Now she sounds likes she's going to burst into tears.

I'm confused. It's on the tip of my tongue to ask her if she's still drunk. I bite my tongue and turn for the door. No one has the right to judge how another grieves, I tell myself. I repeat it in my head, like a mantra. "You should come down and have breakfast with us. Daddy needs us. And Birdie, too," I add. "The nurse will be here to declare her dead in about an hour and a half. Angus says he can be here waiting to take her to the funeral home." I stop in the doorway and turn back to look at Celeste. "So, if you want to . . . see her. To say good-bye. You should do it now."

She mumbles something under her breath as I leave the room, but I don't hear it. And I don't ask because I don't want to know.

33
CELESTE

I watch Abby walk out of my bedroom and close the door with more than a little attitude. I don't know what she's being so pissy about. I bet she's got a big, fat pile of money coming to her as soon as Sarah Brodie's will is probated. And I'm getting a big, fat nothing.

I feel like throwing the water bottle at her, or at least at the door. But my head is pounding. I need the water.

I take another sip, and my gaze drifts to the green and pink dress hanging on my closet door. The wrinkles have come out of it nicely.

I stare at it. Now what the hell am I going to do? Mom Brodie's ruined my perfectly good plan. The nerve of her dying and ruining my carefully planned suicide.

Everyone on the island is going to be so worked up about Sarah Brodie's death. Queen Brodie's death. You can't have two funerals in one week. Because hers will be first. Attendance would be down for mine.

I guess they could bury us at the same time. I could request it in my suicide note.

But she'd still be stealing my thunder. People always liked her more than me. The funerals would all be about poor Miss Sarah. People might even talk about *thank goodness Miss Sarah died first and didn't have to go through Celeste's suicide.*

So my plan's ruined.

I finish the water and throw the empty bottle at the door. It hits and bounces off with a less-than-satisfying sound.

So now what?

I stare at the dress, my thoughts churning. It's pretty, and I look good in it. It makes me look young, I think.

I guess I could wear it to Mom Brodie's funeral. I could postpone my flight off the bridge, and then they could lay me out in it.

That plan has possibilities.

It could be seen as tragic. Especially if I can finagle a photo of me in the dress, in dark glasses and a hat in the weekly paper. The following week, I bet I'd make the front page. *Celeste Brodie is laid to rest in the dress she wore to her grandmother's funeral.*

That could work. It would certainly get

people talking.

I get out of bed because I really have to pee. I slip into my silk robe that has the flamingos on it and tie the silk sash.

Postponing would give me a little more time to make my plans, perfect the suicide note. I think I'll write only one to everyone rather than one to each member of my family. I'm not much of a writer.

I open the nightstand and pull out the pint bottle. It's empty. I drop it in the drawer and go to my bag, at the end of the bed. There's a few swallows left in a pint in there, and I unscrew the cap and tip the bottle. I close my eyes, relieved by the burn.

I imagine Mom Brodie's funeral will be Saturday. She rates a Saturday funeral. That will give out-of-towners a chance to get here.

I could do it Saturday night. If I get lucky and my body washes up early enough Sunday morning, everyone in the three churches on the island would be talking about it by the eleven o'clock service.

I screw the lid back on the empty bottle and drop it into my bag. I'll need to get into town this morning and restock.

I immediately start thinking about what I should wear today. Word will be getting around. People will want to talk. Pay their respects.

My irritation at Mom Brodie's ruining my plan eases. I can make this work.

I can totally make this work.

34
SARAH

I stand in the doorway, staring at her in the bed. I was expecting her face to be covered with a sheet, the way you see it in movies. It's not. But her eyes are closed, which is good because I don't know if I could go in if they weren't.

I'm all sweaty from my run. I wonder if it's disrespectful to go see your dead great-grandmother wearing running shorts and a sports-bra top and covered in sweat. I thought about going up for a shower first, but when I came down the hall, no one was in here. Mom's on the phone in the kitchen with someone. Celeste was smoking in her underwear on her balcony when I came up the driveway. Birdie's out hanging clothes on the clothesline, of all things.

I know we're not supposed to judge people. I realize we probably all handle loss in different ways. Who's to say my running four miles is an appropriate response? Or

Grandpop standing at the end of the dock for an hour, watching his dog swim?

But hanging clothes on a clothesline? That seems weird, even for Birdie. Like, it's any other day. Like Mom Brodie doesn't matter.

But it's kind of interesting how everyone is responding.

I stare at my great-grandmother, wondering what she would think.

She doesn't look any deader than she did when we got here three days ago.

I can't believe we've been here only three days. It seems like . . . I've always been here. Like my life back home isn't real. It's weird, but I don't miss that life. I don't even really miss my friends. Just Dad.

I take one step into the room.

I don't know what I'm afraid of. Dead people can't hurt you. Well . . . zombies can, but clearly Mom Brodie isn't a zombie, because if she was, she'd be jumping up out of that bed and snapping her teeth at me.

I take another step toward her. I can hear Mom's voice down the hall, in the kitchen. Birdie's in there now, too, talking to Uncle Joseph. I can't really hear what anyone is saying, but the sounds of their voices make me feel better. Feel safe.

I take another tentative step toward the

bed. "I'm really sorry you died," I whisper. The words sound stupid in my head, but my mom always says go with your gut instinct. My gut told me to tell Mom Brodie that I'm sorry. Because I *am* sorry. I wouldn't say I was really close to Mom Brodie. I mean, I think she liked me, and I liked her, but we never had any kind of deep conversations or anything.

But she did like my palindromes.

I take a couple of more quick steps toward the bed, and then I'm right there. Staring down at a dead person.

Now that I'm here, I'm not sure what to do. I'm not even sure *why* I'm here. Why I felt like I had to do this.

She's so wrinkled that it's hard to see the woman in the photograph on the nightstand in the face I'm looking at. It's like she's wearing a mask.

But then I think about the tattoo, and the pretty young woman comes more into focus on the wrinkly face. I think about the fact that once upon a time, she was barely older than me, and she got married to Great-Grandpop Joe. In New Jersey. And he knew about the tattoo. Or found out about it pretty fast. And he loved her anyway. Her and her tattoo. At a time when tattoos on women were totally *not* cool or accepted the way they are now.

I never knew my great-grandfather, but from the things people say about him, I've figured out he must have been a nice guy. And everyone agrees he adored Mom Brodie. Adored her until the day he died.

I look down at her. "My mom's really going to miss you," I say softly. "And . . . me too, I think. I mean . . . I know we were never like best friends or anything, but —" I'm feeling stupid again, and I don't know where this is going, so I stop talking.

I just stand there, looking at Mom Brodie. My gaze moves to the photo again. Then the oyster shell. Then the teacup. Then the mints and my little piece of blue paper with the palindrome.

I look back at her again. She's not scary, now that I'm here. It's like . . . I'm looking at an inanimate object. I don't get the same feeling I did when I was in the room before. When she was alive. I don't know where I stand with souls or even God. I've got a lot of mixed feelings about it all. But I'm pretty certain that whatever part of Mom Brodie, even though she was in a coma, was here last night, when I came in to say good night, isn't here now.

So talking to her is probably dumb.

But what if there is a heaven? What if I get

there in eighty-five years or so and there she is standing at her pearly gates I've heard her talk about. Will she ask me why I didn't talk to her when I was here today?

I look down at her hand and reach out slowly with the intention of touching her. Maybe not taking her hand, but just touching it. But my hand doesn't get all the way there before I drop it to the sheet.

I can't do it. If she's cold, it will freak me out.

I look at her face. Then the form of her body under the sheet. Somehow she looks smaller than she did the last time I was in here.

Which is impossible, of course.

When my gaze reaches the topography of her legs, I stare, thinking about the tattoo. I really, *really* want to see it one more time. Before the funeral guy comes for her body and they embalm her and stick her in a box and we stick her in the ground.

But I wonder if that's crossing the line, looking at the tattoo of your dead great-grandmother. The way hanging wet laundry out an hour after you find out your mother-in-law is dead is. I mean, in order for Birdie to have been hanging out wet clothes, she had to have woken up, found Mom Brodie dead, and then gone to the laundry room and thrown clothes in the washing machine.

I hope when I die, that won't be my daughter-in-law's first thought. Oh, Sarah's dead, I better get those bath towels in the wash.

I glance at Mom Brodie's face. "Do you . . . Would it be okay if I look? Just once more?" I wait, trying to let my gut instinct take over. My gut instinct tells me to go for it.

I reach out and tug at the sheet, lifting it, baring her bare foot, then her ankle, then her knee. I move the sheet slowly, as if this is some kind of unveiling of a priceless piece of art.

To me, I guess it sort of is. It's a piece of art that's about to be lost to the world forever.

When I pull the sheet high enough to reveal the tattoo, I don't see the wrinkly, saggy skin of an old lady's thigh. I just see the bluebirds and the ribbons. It makes me smile.

And then I feel like I'm going to cry.

I stare at the tattoo for a long minute, and then, using two hands, I gently, carefully lower the sheet, covering the tattoo, then her knee, then her ankle, and at last her wrinkly foot.

I feel better having seen the tattoo. I've

got it in my mind now, and I know, as long as I live, I'll never forget it.

I smile down at my great-grandmother. "If you're there when I die," I tell her, "at those gates, you know I'm going to ask you what the story with the tattoo is. And you're going to have to tell me."

A tear runs out of the corner of my eye and down my cheek, but I let it go.

I feel sad, but I have this weird sense of . . . not happiness exactly, but something that makes me want to smile while I'm crying. Maybe because I know how lucky I am to have known her. Most of my friends don't have great-grandparents, and, if they do, they live thousands of miles away. "You know I loved you," I whisper.

After I say that, I know I'm done. I've seen her. I've told her what I wanted to tell her, and now I feel like I can go.

As I turn away from her, the teacup in the saucer catches my eye. It's been there two days; I've seen it several times, but I never looked at it. It's the blue on the cup that catches my eye.

Bluebirds.

35
ABBY

"We'll let you know just as soon as we know," I tell my grandmother's friend Florence. Florence is — was — one of Mom Brodie's *young* friends. She'll be eighty-six on her next birthday, she just told me.

Through tears, Florence again says how sorry she is, and I hang up and slide the phone onto the kitchen table, almost taking out the rooster pepper shaker. I've been using the house phone to make calls so everyone on the island doesn't have my cell number.

"Is there more coffee?"

Birdie is making a cake. I have no idea why because by this evening we'll have enough cakes, cookies, casseroles, and trays of lunch meat to feed everyone on Brodie next week. Everyone on the island will bring us a dish. I'm seriously considering calling a homeless shelter on the mainland to see if they'd like a couple of dozen pans of lasagna. I don't mean to be ungrateful. I know making food is a way people express their sorrow and empathy, but we could never eat all the food that everyone is going to bring, and it will take weeks for my mother to sort out all the plates and bowls and get them returned.

"A cup left. I'll make another pot shortly." Birdie turns the hand mixer on.

I'm pouring the coffee into my commemorative mug from some Methodist conference when Celeste wanders in. She's wearing her silky robe and is barefoot. Her hair's still sticking up every which way. She looks awful. I push the mug of coffee into her hand. She needs it more than I do.

She plops down in Mom Brodie's chair. "When's the funeral?"

"Um. Not sure yet." We have to talk above the sound of the mixer.

"Do we have a —" Celeste throws Birdie a look and glances back at me, raising her voice. "A *guess* when the funeral will be?"

"Friday or Saturday." I slide into Daddy's chair.

"So is it Friday or is it Saturday? You know, some people have to make plans." She's clearly annoyed by the inconvenience of Mom Brodie's death.

I try not to get testy. "I don't know yet."

434

Each word is clipped. I'm not in the mood for Celeste's nonsense today.

She takes a sip of the black coffee, makes a face, and takes another sip. "What are we waiting for? It's not as if no one knew this was coming."

"Can you postpone . . . whatever you need to be back in New York for?" I ask. I assumed she'd been lying when she said she had to get back for an audition. But maybe she really does have an audition.

"It's fine." She exhales. "I just — you think it's safe to get my hair done in town?" She looks up at me. "Or should I go to Salisbury? I was thinking I'd have it washed and styled this morning. You know, people will be coming over."

"I think you'd be fine going into Bertie's." We are still talking over the sound of the mixer. "Or . . . I could help you." I don't know why I'm offering. I'm not particularly good with hair. I guess I feel bad for her about the will. I talked briefly with Joseph a few minutes ago. He was on his way out to take Ainslie back to her mother, afraid there would be too much confusion in the house today. He said he wanted to talk to Clancy and go see our CPA to find out how we would go about handling Mom Brodie's money and splitting it three ways instead two. Which I guess means we're seriously considering doing it.

Celeste looks at me over the coffee mug. "No offense, but you're not exactly great with hair."

I get up. "None taken." I walk over to my mother, who's staring into the red bowl of batter, watching the beaters spin, and say in her ear, "I think you've whipped that into shape." My tone is kind.

She shuts off the mixer and sets it on the counter. "I'll make more coffee." She meets my gaze, and her eyes are red.

"Daddy still outside?" I ask.

She nods. "Said he was taking Duke for a walk. I don't know why. The dog's got the run of this whole place."

I shrug. "Maybe he just needed a walk. Daddy."

She grabs the old percolator off the stove and carries it to the sink.

I glance at the clock on the wall. "Gail should be here soon." I rest my hand on my mother's shoulder, and she doesn't flinch.

"I might go on to church." Birdie glances at me over her shoulder, as if waiting for my permission.

"I think that's a good idea," I say softly. "Celeste and I will hold down the fort while you're gone."

"People will be calling." Birdie dumps the coffee grinds into a compost pail on the counter.

"I'll take messages. Or let the answering machine pick up."

"Gotta find clothes to take to the funeral parlor."

"I can do that. You have something in mind?"

"Panties." My mother's now filling the percolator with water from the sink. "She'll need clean panties."

"She doesn't need panties," Celeste pipes up. "No one's going to hike up her dress at the viewing." She looks at me, but is talking to herself now. "Hell, I forgot about the viewing. What am I going to wear?"

"Panties," Birdie repeats more softly.

I cut my eyes at my sister. "I'll take care of it," I tell my mother, whose back is to me.

"Birdie?" Sarah comes rushing into the kitchen. She's still in her running clothes. "Where did that teacup come from?"

Birdie turns from the sink, fitting the metal basket back into the coffee pot. "What?"

"Mom Brodie's teacup. The one next to her bed."

"Don't know." Birdie's brow furrows.

"She's always had it."

Sarah looks at me. "She couldn't have *always* had it. She wasn't born with it."

It seems like everyone is testy this morning. It's funny; you'd think after a woman we all loved desperately just died, we'd be hugging and crying on one another's shoulders, not be at one another's throats. My gaze goes to Sarah. "Why do you ask?"

"You don't know where it came from, Birdie?" Sarah asks my mother. "Did she bring it with her? When she married Great-Grandpop?"

"I . . . I don't know. Maybe." Birdie sets the percolator on the counter and wipes her hands on the full apron she's wearing. I notice it's one of Mom Brodie's favorites. The one with blue and white morning glories all over it. I don't remember ever seeing my mother wear it before. I wonder if she's trying out the new position. Mom Brodie's. After all, she's now the oldest Brodie woman on the island. She's the Queen of Everything, as Celeste would say. My mother, after living here fifty-odd years, is finally the matriarch.

"She kept it on her dresser," Birdie goes on. "But there's a box it goes in."

"There's a box where?"

Birdie seems to think on that for a mo-

438

ment; I suspect it has to do with her snooping gene.

"In her closet. A tin box, yea big." She squares off something about twelve by twelve with her hands. "The cardboard box for the teacup and saucer is in there."

"Can I check it out?" Sarah asks eagerly. The question is for me.

I look to Birdie. Mom Brodie's been dead less than three hours. I don't know how appropriate it is for us to be picking through her belongings.

Birdie reaches for the can of coffee on the counter. "Makes no matter to me. She won't be using it anymore." Her words seem cold, but her tone doesn't.

Sarah is still looking to me for the final okay. I nod. "It's okay if you look, but be respectful."

Sarah darts out of the room.

"What's that all about?" Celeste asks. I guess she's going to be irritated about everything we say or do today.

I shrug. "She's fifteen."

Gail texts me to tell me she's running a little late, so after I get my cup of coffee, I leave my mother to her cake baking and go upstairs to my grandmother's bedroom. I find Sarah sitting on her bed. I haven't been in the room since I came home. I've been avoiding it, I think.

It's as neat as a pin. Sparse and simple, but cozy, with a double bed, a dresser, two nightstands, and an overstuffed chair with a floor lamp behind it, for reading. There's blue everywhere: blue and white curtains, a blue chenille bedspread, blue terry-cloth slippers sticking out from beneath the bed. The room is on the bay side. And smells of peppermint.

"Hey," I say from the doorway.

Sarah doesn't look up. She's digging in an old tin box that advertises a baking powder I've never heard of. I vaguely remember seeing the box, sometime over the years. "Hey," she says.

"What's up?"

She glances up at me. "The teacup," she whispers.

I have no idea what she's talking about. I almost feel as if I'm hungover. Like everything is taking too long to process. The funny thing is, I didn't even have too much to drink yesterday; two beers with the crabs, two glasses of wine last night when I was playing Monopoly.

"Next to Mom Brodie's bed. On the nightstand. With the bluebirds," she says meaningfully.

It takes me a moment to realize what she's

saying. "Wait. There are bluebirds on the teacup?"

She nods and whispers, "Like the ones on the tattoo. I was hoping there would be something in her things, pictures maybe from before she came. But I can't find anything." She indicates a pile of papers, a few photographs, and a cheap little Kewpie doll with red lips. "There's nothing here."

"You find the box Birdie said the teacup was in?"

She holds it up. The old cardboard box is just the size to hold a teacup and saucer. "It was inside this tin box. Just like Birdie said."

"Anything in there?"

Sarah shrugs as she removes the lid. She pulls out shredded bits of newspaper that appear to have been wrapping, and then something else. A little card that's been folded to fit into the bottom of the box.

"What is it?" I ask, walking over to the bed.

"I don't know. It's . . ." She smooths it out on her bare leg. "It's a valentine card, I guess." She holds it up. It features an old-style, cartoonish picture of a boy and a girl, a big heart in the background, and he's helping her climb up the side of a big pear. On it is printed, WE MAKE A GREAT PAIR.

"Must be from your great-grandfather," I say.

Sarah flips it over to read the back. "Nope," she murmurs. "It's not."

"It's not?" I take the card from her and look on the back. The handwriting is faded, but it appears to say *To Sarry, with all my love.* The signed name is hard to make out. "Billy?" I read.

"No," Sarah says with great satisfaction. "Bilis."

I look at her, handing over the valentine, which looks like it's from the thirties. "Bilis?"

"Yup. She was Mom Brodie's witness when she got married. Only I bet Bilis isn't a girl." Sarah gets to her feet, sets the valentine aside, and starts repacking the other items. "You think Birdie will let me have the teacup and saucer?"

"I don't know. Maybe."

"Is it okay if I ask?"

I look at the valentine on the chenille bedspread. "I'm not sure she needs to know about the valentine."

"Mom." She says it like I'm an idiot. "I'm not going to tell Birdie about the valentine." Sarah scoops up the little cardboard box and carefully puts the valentine inside. "I think Bilis gave her the teacup, and that's

where she got the idea for the tattoo."

I lift my brows. Mom Brodie had a beau before she married my grandfather when she was sixteen years old. And he gave her a gift that she chose to remember with a tattoo on her thigh? She chose a tattoo to remember *him* by? I'm floored. Practically shocked. "Who do you think he was?" I murmur.

"Don't know. But I'm going to try to find out."

"How?"

She puts the little box back in the larger tin box. "Mom, he signed the marriage certificate. I know his last name. How many Bilises can there be?"

"The Internet," I say.

"I tell you all the time, Mom," she says, walking past me, headed for the door. "You can Google anything."

36

BIRDIE

I sit on the edge of my bed, staring at the time glowing red on the nightstand. The baby monitor is still plugged in, but the little light isn't green anymore. I turned the thing off. I should give it back to Joseph. Don't need it now that Mrs. Brodie's gone.

It's 2:16. I can't sleep. I just sit here in the dark. Staring into the dark. Joe's snoring, but that's not what's keeping me up. It's my head. All the stuff that keeps going around and around in my brain. I can't shut it off.

I sit there on the bed and listen to Joe snore. Listen to the quiet in the rest of the house. Sarah and Abby are asleep in their bedroom. I peeked through the door that was open just a crack. They were both sleeping on their backs. Abby had her arm around Sarah, kind of the way they used to sleep when Sarah was a little thing.

Joseph went home to sleep in his own house. Said he'd be back in the morning to run errands. I don't know what he thinks needs doing. Mrs. Brodie's dead and gone. Lying on a table in the cellar at the funeral parlor. That's where Angus gets the body ready. I've never been down there, but I know that's where they do it. I don't know what Joseph thinks he can do for her. There'll be a luncheon after the services Saturday, but that's days away. He thinks he's going to make up a potato salad?

Celeste went out tonight. Her grand-mother died, and she went out. To God knows where. Had Joseph drop her off. At The Gull, I'm sure. At least I don't have to worry about her driving home drunk. But The Gull's closed by this time. She should be home. I don't know where she is. With some man, I guess. I try not to think about it. I try not to worry that she's going to go home with some crazy killer some night and end up in a ditch, thrown out like garbage. Or worse, planted in a grave in the wetlands where no one will ever find her. Be bad enough for her to get murdered, but it would be worse never knowing what hap-pened to her.

I think about getting dressed and going downstairs and making myself useful. There's always things to be done around this house: toilets to clean, tomatoes to can, floors to be mopped. But then if someone catches me, there'll be talk. I'll have to explain myself. I don't want talk. And I don't want to scrub any darn toilets.

So I'll just sit here.

I reach for my water glass and take a sip. Mrs. Brodie had a little glass water carafe with a bee on it that she took up to bed with her every night. There's a matching glass. I always liked that little bee on the carafe. A water carafe is something fancy, but secretly, I wish I had one, too, even though I'm not fancy. It's next to her bed right now.

I guess I can have it.

But I don't want it. I don't want any of her things. I thought I would, but I don't. Maybe it's my sin of envy boomeranging back onto me. I know it wasn't right to be jealous of her all these years. My whole life. Whatever I've got, she gave me. And I should have been thankful. But I wasn't. Instead of liking the good things about Mrs. Brodie, I hung on to the bad things. I carried them around in my apron pocket every day, all day.

And now I'm sorry.

But it's too late for sorries because she's gone. And I have to live with my mistakes. I can ask the good Lord to forgive me, but I still have to live with them.

I take a sip of water, and I set the glass with the roosters on it back on the nightstand. A gift from Abby, or maybe Joseph. I don't even like chickens that much. I just . . . Mrs. Brodie collected her Hummels and her books, and I wanted to collect something, too. So, somehow, I ended up collecting chickens. It just crept up on me. I bought something with a chicken on it, and then someone bought me something else with a chicken on it. And then I got another chicken for my birthday or Mother's Day or something. And now they're everywhere in the house: on my curtains, on the powder room towels; they're even on my kitchen glasses.

Guess I'm stuck with them now.

As I pull my hand back from the water glass, I hit the corner of my Arizona scrapbook. I was looking at it before I went to bed. Joe didn't pay it any mind. I've had it for years, and he's never once asked me about it.

I pick up the book and lay it on my lap. I can't see it in the dark, but I don't have to see it. I have the pages memorized. My favorite is the section on the red cliffs of Sedona. I don't know why but I've always thought they were so beautiful; I just do. Some people say when you go to heaven, you see what you want to see, go where you want to go. I know Mrs. Brodie is still right here on this bay. But if I fell over dead tonight, it would be those red cliffs I'd see when I opened my eyes again. They would be my heaven.

Mrs. Brodie knew about my scrapbook. She'd even give me clippings once in a while, if she came across something in a newspaper or a magazine. She never asked me why I was keeping it, but she didn't seem to think there was anything wrong with it. I hug the old album in my arms and choke back a lump that rises in my throat, and all of a sudden I feel like I can't listen to Joe snore one more time.

I get up and walk out of the bedroom in my bare feet. I never go anywhere in bare feet except the shower, but I don't go back for my slippers. I don't even know where I'm going. I just walk down the dark hall. I don't need any light. I know this house inside and out. I don't need lights; my feet know the way. Even bare.

I go downstairs. Up the hall to the sewing room. Inside the door, I flip on the light. Somebody made the bed after the funeral parlor took Mrs. Brodie. Abby, I suspect. Celeste's not much for making beds.

I go over and sit on the edge of the

hospital bed. I'll have to call the medical supply company to come get it. I still have to pay for the thirty days. It was the only way they would rent it.

I look at the nightstand. The teacup and saucer with the bluebirds are still there. And the oyster shell and the little piece of blue paper rolled up and the peppermints. I reach out and snatch up one of the peppermints and start to untwist one end of the wrapper. The cellophane sounds really loud in the quiet of the house.

I pop the mint in my mouth and suck on it.

Mrs. Brodie was always eating peppermints. Passing them out to people, to anyone and everyone: people at church, kids in line at the bank, even strangers at the market. She'd offer them to me, but I never took them. I don't like peppermint.

I suck on the white and red mint, moving it around in my mouth. It tastes cold and hot at the same time and sweet. Really sweet.

It's good. I hate to admit it, but it's good.

So how many of my sixty-six years have I gone, thinking I didn't like peppermint? Why did I think I didn't like it to begin with? I can't remember. But I have a feeling it had more to do with Mrs. Brodie than the candy.

Cutting off your nose to spite your face. That's the phrase that comes to mind. Mrs. Brodie used to say it. She was a big one for phrases. *A good deed is never lost. A man warned is half saved. Every path has a puddle.* She had one for every situation. I think if she didn't know what to say, she just repeated one of her sayings.

I bite down on the peppermint. Crunching it between my teeth, I lean back and throw my legs onto the bed. I hold my Arizona scrapbook tight in my arms against my chest and lie back to rest my head on the pillow. I close my eyes and think about Mrs. Brodie lying here dead and chew up her peppermint.

I can't believe she's gone. That's what's been going through my head all day. That's why I can't sleep. Because she's gone. I know she's gone, but . . . I still can't believe it's really happened.

I thought I'd be glad when she was gone. For months, years, I've been thinking about what would happen when she died. I know that seems ghoulish, but who lives to be a hundred and two?

I can sit in her chair at the kitchen table now. I can drive her Cadillac. Little Joe gave me the keys after supper. Said it wasn't worth enough to bother to sell and that I should have it. That *Mama* wanted me to have it.

Then why didn't she say so when she was still livin'? I wanted to ask him that, but I didn't. I just took the keys. I had the idea I'd put them in my handbag. I actually carried them around in my apron pocket while I cleaned up the supper dishes. But they didn't feel right in my pocket. They were too heavy. I hung them on the hook near the back door where they've always hung.

But even if I don't drive the Caddy, I'm still the woman of the house, now. The only woman. I can make what I like for supper without asking her what she would like. I can sit on the back porch with Little Joe as the sun is setting, talking about crops or a new piece of farm equipment he's thinking of buying.

I imagined what it would be like to sit in her place on the second pew on the left side in church. The place she'd been sitting since I was girl and came to Brodie Island. Only when I went to church today, I couldn't sit in her seat. I tried to, but things didn't look right from there. I ended up sliding over to the place I always sit and left her spot on the aisle empty.

Because I can't take her place. Not at

church. Not on the island. Not in the house. Not with my children. And certainly not with Little Joe.

I sit up, suddenly wishing I was anywhere but here. I stare at my scrapbook in my lap. I think of the basalt and limestone cliffs of Sedona. I could go there now. Mrs. Brodie doesn't need me anymore. Joe could get on well enough if I left a bunch of meals in the freezer for him to heat up in the microwave. Joseph would keep an eye on him for me; I know he would.

For a moment I'm excited. My heart is beating faster, and a smile lifts the corners of my mouth. I could go online in Joe's office right now, and I bet I could buy a plane ticket. I've never bought a ticket. I've never flown on a plane. But I've gone to airline sites hundreds of times and pretended I was buying a ticket. I could fly into Flagstaff and rent a car. I even know what hotel I want to stay at in Sedona. It's just a chain hotel, but all the reviews online say the view is spectacular and the rooms are clean and comfortable.

I've got my own money. I could go. I could do it.

I move my tongue around in my mouth. The peppermint is gone now, and I can only taste the memory of it.

I stare at the scrapbook in my lap.

Who am I kidding?

I'm never going to Arizona. I'll never see the red cliffs of Sedona. I'm not brave enough or strong enough. Mrs. Brodie, she could have done it. Would have, if she'd wanted to. But not me.

I stand up, angry now, and throw the big book into the trash can. I pull up the bag and tie the top and carry it out of the room, flipping the light off behind me. I walk into the kitchen, in the dark, step on the pedal on the trash can with my bare foot, and open the lid. I drop the bag in and let the lid fall.

Then I stand in the dark kitchen, not sure what I'm going to do after the funeral Saturday. Because I realize I can't live here anymore. I can't live without her because without her, I'm no one. I'm nothing.

37
ABBY

"This feels so weird," I whisper. I'm curled up in Drum's arm in my bed, my cheek on his chest. There's a glow of light from the lamp on the nightstand that I threw a scarf over to diffuse the brightness. I thought we were going to make love when we came upstairs, relegating Sarah to her own room. I feel like we've been apart for weeks, rather than days, Drum and I. But once we finally made it to bed, I suddenly felt so drained that I don't think I would have had the strength to slip off my own clothes.

"What's weird?" Drum murmurs. His eyes are closed. I can tell he's almost asleep.

He doesn't really like talking at this point of the day. He just wants to go to sleep and mull things over in the morning over his cup of green tea. But I'm not like him. I can't sleep with matters unsettled in my mind. Thank goodness he tolerates me.

"Everything," I say. "The whole day. The

whole week. It feels weird to be in this house without her. Standing there at the graveside today, I kept thinking it's all a dream. That I was going to wake up, and Mom Brodie was still going to be alive. That she was going to be down the hall in her bedroom, staying up too late, reading a good book."

"That's normal." Drum smiles faintly. "And I guess, in a way, she *is* still down the hall, reading her book." He opens his eyes to meet my gaze. "Because as long as she's still here" — he taps my forehead — "and here" — he taps just above my left breast — "she *is* still alive."

I close my eyes and groan. "That sounds like something she would say."

He chuckles.

"No, I'm serious." I open my eyes again. "All of this, it's so surreal. Her death. The whopping inheritance."

"Celeste throwing herself on the coffin at the church service and having to be led away. Don't forget that," he reminds me, amusement in his voice.

I laugh. I can't help it. Celeste is such a bad actress. It was so fake. Her tears. The sobbing. And the hat with the veil. The big sunglasses. *Way* over the top. She was even worse than I expected. It was as if she was performing some awful finale.

455

"I warned you, didn't I?"

"That you did," he agrees. "But I thought you were kidding. Exaggerating."

"I don't think it's possible to exaggerate with Celeste." I smooth his bare chest with my hand. He's not very hairy, which I like, but the chest hair he does have is turning so gray. He's aging. Which I am, too, but I'm suddenly becoming conscious of our age difference. In five years, Drum will be eligible for social security benefits. And that thought scares me. Which brings me back to the money.

Drum and I spoke with Joseph, after the graveside service, after everyone had headed back to the church for the luncheon. After Celeste had allowed herself to be led away on the arms of two good-looking guys from town. We talked about Joseph's proposal concerning our inheritance.

Drum and I told Joseph we'd do it. *I'd* do it. I'd give Celeste part of my money. I agreed to go against Mom Brodie's wishes and split it three ways. We discussed when to tell Celeste and agreed it could wait until next week, after Clancy got back to town. After Joseph talks to our accountant.

"So what are you going to do with it?" Drum asks. "The money? It's still a hefty sum."

I had just closed my eyes, but I open them and push up in the bed to look down at him. "You mean, what are *we* going to do with it? Do you think there's any way you can still retire with it?"

He reaches up and strokes my cheek, looking into my eyes. "I don't know, hon. I don't think so." His voice is so gentle and sweet that no one would ever suspect that he's giving up his dream with his words. "Not with our mortgage."

I lie down again, closing my eyes. Not if we stay in our house, he's saying, without actually saying it. But we *could* swing it if we moved to Brodie. If we moved in here. He didn't say it, but it's got to be on his mind.

But I can't do it. I know I can't. My mother and I . . . It would be a bigger disaster than Celeste's moving home. Way bigger. I'd end up resenting Drum, resenting all of them.

Seeming to sense my thoughts, Drum tightens his arm around me. "Stop worrying; it'll all work out."

"Work out?" I whisper. "How?"

"I don't know." He kisses the top of my head and lies back, sounding drowsy again. "But it always does. What happens in our lives is what's supposed to happen."

457

I'm tempted to call him on his philosophical bullshit, but I don't. Because I don't want to argue with him. I don't even want to disagree. Not tonight. "Shut out the light?" I whisper.

He reaches, still holding me, and flips off the lamp.

In minutes, he's asleep.

I'm just drifting off when I hear a tap at the door. For a second I think I'm imagining it. Then I hear the door open. "Mom?"

"Sarah?" I sit up, a moment of panic making my heart beat a little faster.

Drum sleeps on.

"Mom, I'm sorry to wake you, but —"

"You didn't wake me. You okay?"

"Fine." She walks around to my side of the bed. She's carrying her laptop, and the light from the screen illuminates her face. "Mom, you have to see this." She sounds like she did on Christmas morning when she was a little girl.

"Okay." It doesn't occur to me to send her away. One of the things I learned with Reed when he was a teen was that you talk when they want to talk. Which often means late at night because their internal clocks seem to run differently than ours. The best conversations I've had with Reed, over the years, took place in the wee hours of the night.

"Let's go to your room." I slip out from under the sheet. "So we don't wake your dad." I grab my readers from the nightstand and follow her out of the room.

"Celeste still out?" I ask as we go down the hall.

Sarah glances over her shoulder at me. One of her *are you stupid?* looks. She's wearing the SCORE! booty shorts again, and I make a mental note to accidentally leave them here in the morning, if I can wrangle it without her seeing me.

"Didn't you see how dressed up she was in her sleazy skirt and that yellow and green silk scarf she wears? And those crazy heels?" Sarah rolls her eyes. "She's out, all right."

I sigh. "We'll be lucky if she comes home in the next couple of days." *Already out spending the inheritance she's not getting. Or wouldn't be getting if it weren't for Joseph's good heart.*

"So, what's up?" I ask.

"I told you I could find it," Sarah whispers, the excitement in her voice again.

"Find what?" I follow her into her room, and she perches on the side of the bed. I sit beside her and slide on my glasses.

"The tattoo. But I hit the jackpot. Mom, look."

My daughter turns her laptop so I can see it, and the screen is filled with a grainy, black-and-white photo of a group of people, men and women, in front of a big white tent with a striped roof. The photo is obviously from decades ago, the twenties, maybe thirties? I'm not good with that sort of thing. The first person I notice is a little person. A man, in smart clothes and a top hat. The next thing I see is something printed on the tent, behind their heads. It says RUDEBAKER'S in flaking paint.

"There she is," Sarah breathes. And points.

I look at the woman she's pointing to. It takes me a second for the synapses in my brain to fire. I'm just about to say *who?* when I recognize the grainy face looking back at me. Because she looks like me. And Sarah.

"Oh, my God," I whisper, pulling the laptop onto my own lap. The young woman is in some sort of risqué costume, bare-legged, holding a fan of feathers that covers her breasts, which appear to be bare.

"It's Mom Brodie!" Sarah whispers excitedly. "See. There's the tattoo. There can't be another like it."

She reaches over and hits a key, and the screen zooms in to the young woman with the feathers. And there's the bluebird tattoo on her upper thigh. Identical to the one on my grandmother's thigh.

"It's her, Mom," Sarah whispers. "It's our Mom Brodie."

"It sure is," I breathe. I can't stop staring. I'm shocked. And thrilled to see the woman I never knew, who I've known all my life. "Can you zoom out a little? So I can see all of her?"

Sarah does her magic, and my grandmother comes into view again.

Mom Brodie looks so beautiful. And so young. She doesn't look any older than Sarah, even with the heavy eye makeup.

"How did you find it?" I whisper. Though why we're whispering, I don't know. Everyone else in the house is asleep.

"The valentine," she tells me. "And the marriage certificate."

I hit the same keys she did and zoom out until the whole picture fills the screen again. There are thirteen people, including a woman with a beard and an old Asian man covered in tattoos. Then I spot a tiger on the edge of the photo. A live tiger. At least I think it's a tiger because a piece of the corner of the photo is gone. "I don't understand."

"The name on the valentine in the teacup box was Bilis. Remember? And a Bilis also signed the marriage certificate. Only I thought Mom Brodie had a *girlfriend* witness her marriage to Great-Grandpop. It was her *boyfriend,* Mom." She giggles. "I found Mom Brodie through *him.*"

I'm fascinated by the little man in the top hat, and the tiger, the woman with the beard, and several other young women dressed scantily with feathers, but my gaze keeps going back to my grandmother. Never, in a million years, would I have believed this if I wasn't seeing the proof. Mom Brodie was a carny before she came to Brodie Island.

"I Googled Bilis. Did you know Bilis was a dwarf in the King Arthur legends? Bilis, the dwarf king of the Antipodes. This guy's parents named him after the dwarf king." She points at him in the photo. "This Bilis, Bilis Allsop, was born in 1900 in London. His parents were super wealthy; he was educated in Europe. Had some kind of English title. But he came to the US, and he joined a carnival. He worked a couple of different carnivals in the late twenties and into the thirties, through the Depression.

He was with Rudebaker's Carnival for nine years. Rudebaker's." She points to the words on the screen as if I can't read. "I found this picture of him, and there she was!"

"And he's identified in this photo?"

She sighs, obviously trying to be patient with me, but not doing a good job of it. "No; there're no names. But how many dwarfs could there have been in a carnival in the early thirties? And it doesn't matter if that's her Bilis or not; that's definitely Mom Brodie." She points again.

I look at the screen. "Sure is."

We sit side by side and stare at the computer screen. "So now what?" I say, eventually.

She looks at me. "What do you mean?"

I shrug. "Do we tell anyone? If so, who?"

Sarah makes a face. "Obviously we don't tell Grandpop or Birdie." She hesitates. "I don't even think we should tell Uncle Joseph or Celeste."

"Why not?"

"Mom, look at her." My daughter points at the screen. "It's 1934, and she's half-naked. I don't think she was a cotton-candy girl."

The way she says it makes me smile.

"As I see it, you and I are cool with this. Because we know who Mom Brodie was on

Brodie Island. This picture doesn't change how we feel about her. No matter what she was doing in those feathers," Sarah says meaningfully. "But what if Uncle Joseph doesn't get that? That would be our fault for telling him. And you know your sister. I don't mean to be mean or anything, but she'd use this to try to make herself look better and Mom Brodie worse."

We meet each other's gazes.

"I think this should be our secret," Sarah says.

I look at the photo again. "I have to tell your father."

She rolls her eyes and takes the laptop back. "*Obviously.* I know how you two are. It's like you've only got one brain." Her words sound critical, but her tone isn't.

"Okay, then," I say, getting up. "I guess . . . I'll go back to bed."

Sarah has crawled into the middle of her bed and is leaning against the headboard. She's staring at the computer. " 'Night," she says, not looking at me. "Love you."

In the doorway I stop and look back at her again. My eyes are full of tears. I'm so sad, and I feel so blessed. "And I love you, Sarah Brodie MacLean."

38
CELESTE

At the foot of the bridge, I slip off one shoe and then the other and sigh with pleasure as my feet sink into the soft, cool grass beside the road. I hold my shoes on the end of my finger, by the ankle straps, debating whether to take them up or not. I gaze up at the highest point of the bridge. The moon is still out, a big half-dollar, low in the sky. By the moonlight, I can make out the structure of the bridge. It's twice as tall as the Deal Island Bridge, which is a good thing because I'm not sure you can jump off the Deal Island Bridge and expect, with any confidence, to actually die. I figure, if I stand on the rail, it's a good seventy-five feet to the waterline. Farther, because the tide is low.

I look at my shoes again. They sparkle in the moonlight.

It seems a shame for Jimmy Choos to end up at the bottom of the bay. It's likely they'll fall off on the way down, or maybe when I hit the water. Of course, if I leave them here, who will find them? It's not like we've got a lot of homeless people on Brodie. Anyone who has the potential for being homeless is cared for by the Brodie family. Mom Brodie was always a big one for handouts. Which pisses me off because I don't understand why she'd give a drunk like my dad's second cousin money to pay his rent, but she couldn't leave me money to pay mine.

I look up at the moon, the shoes still dangling from my finger.

If I leave them here, the police will find them when they search the area. They'll return them to my family. Birdie's so thrifty, I know she won't toss them. They'll end up for sale at the fall church bazaar. The idea makes me laugh out loud. I can just imagine somebody finding Jimmy Choos on the three-dollar table. Of course, the question is, will anyone here even know what they are? I can imagine some chick walking around in my shoes, thinking they came from some cheap, mall shoe store, when they're probably worth a thousand dollars, even with the one loose strap and the nicks in the heels.

I set them down carefully and arrange them, toes out, in the grass beside the road.

I rewrap my favorite scarf around my neck and start up the bridge, walking right down the middle of the road. There's a sidewalk on one side, but there's no need for me to walk over there. There are no cars coming from either direction.

I had Bartholomew leave me at the end of our drive because I didn't want him to be suspicious. I told him I wanted to walk up to the house. That I needed some time alone. He seemed hesitant to leave me there, thinking I was upset about Mom Brodie, which was sweet. He got out of the car and kissed me and invited me, again, to go to Paris with him. I think he was actually serious this time.

We had a fun evening together. He took me for dinner at the little yacht club on the bay near the condo where he's staying. I had surf and turf, and it was amazing. Then we went back to his place for drinks and sat on his balcony with our bare feet on the rail and stared at the water. I didn't even have sex with him. We made out, but he said he was looking for something more than a fling. I couldn't decide if his not wanting to have sex with me made him weird, or endearing. Maybe a little of both.

He's a good kisser. Which surprised me because who would think an old guy like him would be? Maybe it has to do with experience? Which makes me wonder if I've been missing out on something all these years. That makes me laugh, too.

I walk on one of the two solid yellow lines, as if it's a balance beam. I can almost do it. I'm not super drunk. I was, but I've sobered up. Luckily, I've got my flask in my bag. Just in case I need a little encouragement when I get to the top. I don't think I will. I think I'm ready. I left the dress I wore to the funeral hanging on my closet door; anyone who walks into my bedroom will see it. They'd have to be idiots not to see it and say to themselves, "Let's bury her in that." I seriously thought about throwing Mom Brodie's mink stole over it. No way Sarah would want it if she thought I meant to be buried in it. But I couldn't find it. I bet the little shit hid it, just so I couldn't get it. I guess I should have left the Jimmy Choos with the dress. But I wanted to wear them one more time. Maybe they'll end up burying me in them anyway. I guess it depends on how quickly the police return the "evidence."

I ended up not leaving a suicide note. After about a dozen drafts I wrote over the week (all of which I burned on my balcony in a flowerpot), I decided it might be better to not say why I did it. What if they dismissed what I wrote in my letter as Crazy Celeste and her crazy talk? This way, they'll talk together about all the possibilities as to why I did it. Everyone in the town will be talking. My family members. They'll go over and over in their heads all the conversations they've had with me, *ever,* wondering if something they said made me do it. They'll be wracked with guilt, all of them: Birdie, Daddy, Joseph, Abby, even Drum.

Abby will feel so guilty. The guiltiest of all. She's like that. She'll be sure it was all her fault. She'll feel guilty for years, thinking she caused my suicide. She'll be so sorry for all the mean things she ever said to me. Ever did to me, real or imagined.

It's too bad Mom Brodie is already dead. Even she would feel like my suicide was her fault. Well, maybe just a little.

At the top of the bridge, I walk to the rail on the north side. It's surprisingly windy for late summer, and my scarf whips behind me. I reach into my bag and pull out my cigarettes. It won't be sunrise for another hour, but it already seems as if the sky is getting lighter. I can't wait too long. Some fool will be headed out early for church in Pocomoke or Princess Anne and will be calling Daddy from their cell to tell him "your Celeste's on top of the bridge again. Looks like she might be thinking about jumping again."

Which sounds like I've been up here a bunch of times to do it. Which I haven't.

I actually got the idea from Birdie. When I was a kid, she was always threatening to drive up to the Bay Bridge and jump off there. She never meant it. She just used to say it when Mom Brodie or Daddy made her really mad. I used to think it was funny. Mostly because I knew she'd never do it. She's such a coward. Not like me. I've been saying I'm going to kill myself, and now I'm going to do it. And then everyone will feel bad for not listening to me.

I light up and enjoy the cigarette like I've never enjoyed one before, taking one deep drag after another.

I look toward the island. There are a few lights on, here and there. I can't see home in the dark, but I know exactly where it is. I imagine Birdie will be getting up soon, making coffee, having her cold cereal, alone. I don't know what she'll do with herself without Mom Brodie to fuss over and fuss with. They were such an interesting pair. They had one of those can't-live-with-her, can't-live-without-her relationships. I have a feeling that Birdie is going to have a hard

470

time without Mom Brodie. So I guess this morning Birdie will sit over her mushy cornflakes, then make Daddy breakfast before she goes off to the early service. She often rides with Mrs. Larson, from down the street. They'll go early to church to set up coffee and tea and talk about what kind of donuts people will bring for fellowship after service. Donuts are better after the second service. Late risers are better at picking out donuts, according to my mother. They understand the value of sprinkles and chocolate icing.

I breathe the smoke of the cigarette deep in my lungs and think about how many cigarettes I didn't smoke because of the whole lung cancer thing. I could have smoked them. Of course, there have been times when I didn't have the money to buy a pack of cigarettes, and I had to bum them. That thought makes me angry all over again about the inheritance I'm not getting.

I reach into my bag and pull out the letter Mom Brodie wrote to me. I left it on Daddy's desk that night because I didn't want him to know I'd read it. He put it, along with the will, in his safe the next day, I guess. After she died. It took me about two minutes to get into the safe yesterday. He uses the last two digits of his children's birthday years, oldest to youngest. I guess he's never read one of those articles about all the dates and words you shouldn't use for passwords, which applies to safes.

I stare at the envelope in my hand. I know my name is on it in Mom Brodie's handwriting, even though I can't really make it out. She always had the prettiest handwriting. I start to pull out the letter to read it one more time, but then I realize, why should I? What's the point? I don't need to read about all my failings. I know them better than anyone. I open my hand, and the envelope flutters downward. I lose sight of it before it hits the water. I take another drag, enjoying the burn of the smoke in my lungs.

All too soon I'm at the end of my cigarette. As I drop it over the steel rail and watch it fall, I wish I had a joint. I didn't have one of my own, but I imagine I could have bummed one from my brother-in-law or one of my brother's friends.

With my cigarette out, there's nothing left to do but climb up on the rail that's supposed to keep idiots from falling or driving off the bridge. It takes me a minute to get up and sit down on the rail; it's skinnier than it looks. My bare feet swing free, and I'm glad I left my Jimmy Choos down on the road. I'd be heartbroken if one fell off my foot and into the water.

I look down. It's seems farther to the water than I thought it would be. Surely the fall will kill me. Though I've heard drowning isn't so bad, once you give up.

I wonder what I should do with my handbag. Take it with me?

I think about having a sip from my flask, but I don't pull it out.

It's a strange sensation not to want a drink. I can't remember when I last felt this way.

I spot headlights, coming from the mainland. It's a long, dark, rural road to the bridge. It's called Brodie Road. Of course.

So it's now or never.

I look up into the sky as I slowly come to my feet on the rail. There are no stars. Just that big moon.

I wonder if Mom Brodie is watching me.

I wonder if she'll meet me at the bottom.

39
BIRDIE

The sun's up in the eastern sky when I park the white Caddy on the mainland side of the bridge in a little wooded spot where no one will notice it. I take my time walking up the bridge, following the little sidewalk. I don't get off Brodie Island much, but I do once in a while. I don't remember ever noticing the sidewalk. I wonder why they put it here when they built the bridge. It's a good fifteen miles from here to Princess Anne or Pocomoke, with nothing between here and there. Who's gonna come walking over the bridge, coming or going in either direction? Another big waste of government money.

But it's a nice sidewalk.

I'm wearing my new black sneakers. I've been keeping them in my closet in the shoebox since I got them on sale, saving them for something. I realized when I was getting dressed, careful not to wake up Joe, that if I was ever going to wear them, this was the day.

I didn't say a word to my Joe. Nothing left for us to say to each other. And I didn't leave a note. No point. Duke looked at me as I walked out of the bedroom, and I looked at him. I told him to be a good boy and look after Joe.

I think he understood.

I checked on Sarah before I went downstairs. She was asleep, her computer lying on the bed beside her. I wanted to go in and kiss the top of her head, say good-bye, but I was afraid I would wake her. I checked on Reed, too. And I looked in on Abby and Drum, too. Opened the door real quiet; I know how to do it. They were asleep in each other's arms, which brought tears right to my eyes. He loves her so much. She'll be fine. Better off without me.

I didn't go to Celeste's room because I knew she wasn't there. She never came home last night. Out with some man, I suspect. Her men have always been more important to her than any of us. Certainly more important to her than I am.

I didn't want to wake anyone; I just walked out of the house. It didn't seem right to put that burden on them. Because my mind's made up. I've read that once a person's mind is made up, you can't change it. You think you can, but you can't. You can sometimes delay it, even for years, but in the end, a person does what she wants to do.

As I walk up the incline of the bridge, huffing and puffing, I realize this might be the first time I've ever done what I wanted to do. Taking nobody else into account.

I wonder what Mrs. Brodie would think.

Oh, I know what she would *say*. She'd go on about how wrong it is. She might even bring up sin. But I wonder if, secretly, she'd admire my decision. Admire me for making a choice and seeing it through.

I reach the top of the bridge and still not a car in sight. I guess it was meant to be.

I go to the rail on the north side and look over toward the house where I've lived since I was nine. It's a beautiful property with the big house and all the outbuildings and the lawn that runs down to the bay. I can even make out my chicken house, I think.

It's funny, but I don't even feel sad. I just . . . I feel done.

I look down at the water, and it seems darker than it ought to. Farther away than I expected.

But it doesn't scare me. Because I'm done being scared.

I look up at the sky that's getting brighter by the moment with the coming of the new day. I wonder if Mrs. Brodie is looking down on me from heaven. Or maybe she's looking up at me from the bay, her and Mr. Brodie in that rowboat of his. In my mind's eye, I see her wearing that big hat, and I hear her laughing.

The idea makes me smile.

I look at the water again. Something catches my eye. Something colorful that doesn't belong. Something yellow and green. It looks like fabric, but maybe it's just a piece of trash. My eyesight's not what it once was.

I sigh, and, for the first time since I made up my mind, I feel sad. I press my hand to the rail and look down again. Then back at the house.

And say my good-byes.

40

ABBY

I take a shower in the morning, and, by the time I get downstairs, Drum, Sarah, Reed, Daddy, and Joseph are all around the kitchen table eating pancakes and scrapple. It looks like a farmhouse scene right out of Norman Rockwell's world. The table is set with white dishes and pitchers of orange juice and maple syrup. I bet he would have painted in the rooster and hen salt and pepper shakers.

"Mmm, smells good."

"Want coffee, babe?" Drum asks. He's sitting in my chair. Mom Brodie's and Birdie's are both empty.

"I'll get it." The fertilizer mug is the only one left in the cupboard. "Where's Birdie?" I walk to the stove for the percolator.

"Went to church early I guess," Daddy answers, slurping coffee from his Labrador retriever mug. "Didn't even make coffee," he adds, sounding a little put out.

478

"Daddy, I think you can make your own coffee," I chastise gently. I start to pour my coffee, then upright the pot to turn back to the table. "Wait, so who made the pancakes?" No one ever makes breakfast in the kitchen but Birdie, at least not without taking a lot of crap for it.

"I did. Blueberry," Drum says over his shoulder. "Saved you some, still warm in the oven. I was afraid these fiends were going to eat them all before you came down." He points to our children with his fork. "Your dad made the scrapple."

"Thanks." I fill my cup and walk over to stand beside him. I reach for half-and-half and sugar for my coffee and use Drum's fork to stir it. It tastes better than usual, not so . . . thick.

"If you don't want your pancakes, I'll eat them," Sarah tells me, stuffing a forkful in her mouth.

"I got first dibs," Reed announces, his mouth full. "Great pancakes, Dad. Way better than those frozen ones I buy."

"Easy enough to make," father tells son. "I'll write down the recipe. Girls like a man who can whip up pancakes from scratch. Good for breakfast, lunch, or supper."

"You seen my hat?" my dad asks me. "My John Deere?"

I see he's got a spanking new Dekalb ball cap beside his plate on the table. I don't think my father could physically leave the house without a ball cap, unless he was going to church. "No. Maybe Birdie washed it?"

"She knows better," my dad says, taking another bite of pancake.

I sit down in Birdie's chair and nibble on a piece of a pancake Drum fetches for me. I also have two slices of fried scrapple; I don't get it at our house. It's so crispy I'm actually tempted to roll it up in a pancake, or worse, a slice of soft, white bread, but I don't because I know it will gross out Drum and Sarah. Reed's on my side of the debate. I think he eats half a pound of scrapple.

All too soon, breakfast is over, dishes are loaded in the dishwasher, and it's time we scatter to the winds. Joseph heads to Salisbury, and Drum and Sarah are taking his car home. I'm going to run Reed back up to Philly and then meet them at home. It will be a long day of driving, but I'm looking forward to a little alone time with my son. I feel like we haven't talked in ages.

Sarah kisses her grandfather good-bye and leaves him with a promise to be back as soon as she gets a break in her weekend field hockey schedule and the palindrome, a

Santa dog lived as a devil god at NASA. Which Daddy seems to appreciate.

I give Drum a kiss good-bye. Reed runs upstairs for a *super-quick* shower.

When Daddy and I are alone in the kitchen, I pour him another cup of coffee, even though he doesn't ask for it. He's back in his chair at the head of the kitchen table, looking a little small. And lost. I slide into Birdie's chair, watching him stroke Duke's head. The dog seems to sense the abrupt shift in the world that's taken place since Mom Brodie's death. He appears as uncertain as we are at the changes in our roles in the family.

"You going to be okay, Daddy?" I ask. "I need to take Reed to Philly, but I can turn right around and come back if you want me to."

He shakes his head. "Go home to your husband. We'll be fine, your mother and I. Just going to take some getting used to, not having Mama here." His voice takes on a gruff tone, but I think he's fighting tears.

I rub the back of his hand that's now resting on the kitchen table. It looks like an old hand today. The hand of an old man. "Daddy, I know you're not thrilled with Joseph's and my decision to give Celeste part of Mom Brodie's money, but . . ." I meet his gaze. "We feel like it's the right thing to do."

"Your mother will be happy about it." He reaches for his coffee, but he doesn't pick up the mug. Instead he fiddles with the handle. "You tell her? Celeste?"

I shake my head. "Not yet. She'll want the money yesterday. Joseph says Clancy will be back sometime this week. Joseph wants to talk to him and the accountant, see the best way to go about it. I think you should just keep the will and the letter in your safe for now."

"It's going to cost you money," he says. "Taxes, likely. You can't just *give* money away, even to family. Government wants a piece. They always want a piece."

I want to avoid the conversation about taxes this morning; otherwise we'll never get on the road. "I know."

He exhales. "Sarah said she didn't come home last night. Celeste."

"I imagine she'll be dragging in any time."

He half smiles. "Sleep all day, probably. She didn't say when she was going back to New York. Maybe she'll stay a few more days."

I lean back in the chair. "Maybe. So what have you got planned for today? I guess you're not going to church."

"Nah. Got things I want to get done. Fire department is coming midweek to burn the cannery. Joe thought we could salvage some wood. Loopy's meeting me over there later, see what we can do with a couple of crowbars." He hesitates, picking at a cuticle. "It was sure nice having everyone here this week. I know Mama would have enjoyed it. She always liked having a houseful."

I smile with him. It's bittersweet. "She certainly would have." I rise from my mother's chair. "I'll be back in a week or so."

He stares into his coffee cup. "I don't want you to put yourself out, but . . . your mother will appreciate it. I know she and Mama didn't always see eye to eye, but . . . but Mama loved her like she was her own daughter, and this is gonna hit Birdie hard. Once it sinks in."

I lean down and kiss him on the cheek. "Have a good day. Tell Birdie I'll talk to her tonight or tomorrow."

He slurps his coffee and reaches for his Sunday paper. "Will do."

Reed and I are probably twenty minutes behind Drum and Sarah, so I'm surprised to see Drum's car at the top of the Brodie bridge. Parked, flashers on. Reed and I both jump out. Drum and Sarah are just standing at the rail, looking down at something in the water.

"Everything okay?" I call. Against my will, I feel a little flutter in my chest. I'm not a worrier, but it's not normal to see a car parked on the bridge. And certainly not one of *our* cars. There's just one narrow lane going in each direction, no passing lane or shoulders. The bridge was constructed only as wide as necessary, to save on construction costs, I'm sure.

"Everything's fine," Drum answers over his shoulder.

"You can't park on the bridge." I cross the other lane. "It's dangerous."

"It's Sunday," he argues good-naturedly. "There's almost no traffic. Only one car's gone by. One of your dad's cousins. Jim? John? I can't keep them straight. He just went around."

Sarah is staring intently over the rail at the water below. Reed and I both join her.

"What you looking at?" Reed beats me to the question. He's a carbon copy of his dad, but instead of being a Mini-Me, he's a Big Me, now. He's got Drum by at least an inch in height, and I'm not sure Reed's done growing.

"Nothing," Sarah says dreamily. "Everything. I felt like we needed to stop."

"Wow, I didn't know you could see the farm so well from here." Reed shades his eyes from the sun. "Why haven't we ever stopped up here before? The view's incredible. You can see all the way across the island."

"Because it's dangerous," I say testily. I look to Drum.

He makes kissy lips at me and taps on the steel rail with his palm. "Okay, let's load up. See you at home this afternoon," he tells me. I get another kiss.

"Later, Dad," Reed calls as he lopes across the street.

"Have a good week. Don't worry about the physics class. I know it's not your thing, but you'll do fine. You've got the groundwork."

Reed bobs his head. We climb back into the cars, and we're soon on our way. After Reed makes a call to a girl who I suspect is either his girlfriend, or a potential girlfriend, he starts telling me about some kind of drama going on in the lab where he works.

We have a nice drive up to Philly, without hitting too much beach traffic from the Delaware shore. We stop for an omnivore's lunch of spicy wings and salads. It's late afternoon, getting on to suppertime by the time I arrive home. When I walk in, carry-

485

ing my overnight bag, I find Drum on the phone.

"Here she is, Joe; just walked in."

I make a face of inquiry at Drum. My dad's calling? My dad never calls. I call him. Or Birdie calls me and puts him on the phone.

I set my bag on the kitchen floor and take the phone. "Dad?"

"Abby." His voice sounds strange. "I'm worried about your mother. She didn't come home. I was wondering if you talked to her."

"Didn't come home from where?"

"Church."

"From this morning?" I look at the clock on the kitchen stove. "Dad, it's almost six o'clock."

"I came home for supper, and she wasn't here."

"Did you see her at lunchtime?" I ask.

"She didn't bring my lunch to the warehouse, but Loopy had plenty. We got some nice wide planks from the floor in the office. Not sure what I'll do —"

"Daddy," I interrupt. I'm not worried yet. It's Sunday. She's busy some Sundays with various church events. I'm more concerned about my father's memory; he hasn't demonstrated any issues with it before, but he *is*

486

seventy-one. "Think back. Did Birdie say she had something going on today? Did she tell you supper would be late?"

"Not that I recall."

Now the slightest worry is beginning to creep into my chest. "Look in the fridge. Is there something there for you to heat up? It will probably have a sticky note on it." My mother rarely misses meals. When she and Mom Brodie would occasionally have a commitment at church, Birdie would leave leftovers for Daddy with detailed instructions as to what he was to eat and how he was to reheat it in the microwave. "With all that food everyone's been bringing all week, she probably left you something. She probably told you, and you forgot."

"She didn't tell me she'd be home late," he argues. "Let me look in the refrigerator, though." There's a pause, then he's back. "Plenty of food in there, but no note. I was expecting her home, Abby. Been waiting for her about two hours."

I keep my tone even. "Daddy, why didn't you call me sooner?"

"You were driving Reed to Philadelphia."

"I have a cell phone. You have a cell phone."

"I didn't think anything of it. Got home, she wasn't here, and I laid down a few minutes. Just woke up and no supper."

Something about the way he says it ticks me off. He seems more concerned about supper than Birdie. "Did Celeste come home?"

"Nope. Checked her room."

"You try *her* cell?" I ask. My mother doesn't have one. No need, she's always told us when we wanted to get her one. She doesn't go anywhere to need a cell phone.

"I don't call Celeste much," my father says, sounding short with me now. "I'm not interested in what she's up to, or with who," he adds meaningfully.

I sit down on the edge of a barstool at the kitchen counter. Suddenly I'm bone-weary. "Did you call Mrs. Larson? Birdie must have ridden to church with her. Birdie's car was in the driveway when I left."

"Didn't want to bother her," he tells me.

I take a breath. "Please call her, Daddy. I'll call Celeste. Did you talk to Joseph?"

"Been gone all day to Salisbury. Don't know what he was getting into. Some kind of preseason football or something on TV. Meeting up with friends, I think."

I rub my temple. My father is always so sharp of mind that I'm a little disconcerted by the way he seems to be thinking. It's as if he doesn't understand that he should be concerned about his wife. *Very* concerned. Because never once, in my life, has my father not known where my mother is. Exactly where she is. She's big on giving a full itinerary to anyone who will listen. Not only will she tell you she's going to the market, but she'll tell you what's on the grocery list.

"Call Mrs. Larson. Do you have her cell?"

"Don't know that I do. But I can call the house. Likely she'll answer this time of day."

"Unless she's at the church, Daddy. *Working. With Birdie.*" I make eye contact with Drum and roll my eyes. He's busy at the stove, making something in the wok that smells delicious. "I'll see if I can get ahold of Celeste. Call me back, Daddy, after you talk to Mrs. Larson." I hang up and look at Drum. "My mother hasn't been home all day."

"So I gather." He turns to the kitchen island and begins chopping mushrooms. "And your dad hasn't seen her all day?"

I shake my head. "Of course, he didn't notice she was missing until no one plopped his supper down in front of him." I don't hide my annoyance now. I get off the stool. "Sarah here?"

"Upstairs."

"I have to pee," I tell him. I call my sister

on the way to the bathroom. It goes to voice mail. I don't leave a message. Then I text her. No response. Next, I call Joseph. No answer there, either. I text him, **Seen Birdie today?**

I'm on my way back to kitchen when he texts back, **No.**

Where are you?

Date with Gail.

I scowl. Then feel guilty. Why would I be annoyed with him? I'm glad he asked her out. I saw them talking for quite a while after the funeral, longer than a hospice nurse talks with a client's family member.

I'm just frustrated with my father. And with my mother for not leaving a note or calling Daddy or something. Or telling someone her plans for today, last night. But last night, after the funeral, *was* crazy. People ended up coming back to the house. Maybe she did tell Daddy, or even me, and we just don't remember.

It all seems logical. She's probably at the church. Or someone's house. But I'm still worried. Somewhere in the back of my head, in the pit of my stomach, I have this nagging feeling that something's wrong.

Birdie's missing, I text my brother.

My cell rings thirty seconds later. "Missing?" Joseph says when I answer. "What do you mean, *missing*?" I can hear music in the background. And voices. It sounds like he's in a bar. Or maybe a restaurant.

"She never came home from church, and Daddy doesn't remember her saying she'd be home late. She wasn't there to make him supper."

"She's probably still at the church," Joseph says dismissively. "At a spaghetti dinner or something."

"Probably," I agree. "Maybe. You hear from Celeste? She never came home either."

"That's a little less surprising than Mom's being late for supper."

"Right."

"You want me to go home? I can cut this short. Gail will be cool with it."

Drum brings me a glass of water with a slice of lemon in it. I smile my thanks. "Um . . . no, not yet. Daddy was calling Mrs. Larson. Birdie went to church with her this morning. He didn't think to call her. So, I'll text you after Daddy calls back. Let you know he found her."

While I'm waiting on Daddy, I call my sister again. This time, I leave a message. "Hey, can you call me when you get this?" I decide not to leave a message that Daddy's misplaced Birdie. It will be moot in five minutes. Instead, I surprise myself by say-

491

ing, "We need to talk about Mom Brodie's will. There's money, Celeste. A lot of money. I know you've been worried about your finances, but" — I find myself tearing up, and I have no idea why — "you won't have to worry anymore. Call me. Love you."

It takes way too long for my father to call me back. I pick up on the first ring.

"Nope," he says in my ear.

"Nope, what?" I come off sounding annoyed, but really I'm just scared.

"She didn't go with Mrs. Larson to church this morning. Didn't go to church at all. Nobody's seen her."

"Nobody's seen her *all day*?" I'm perched on one of the barstools again, but I get to my feet. Something terrible has happened. I just know it. Birdie doesn't skip church. And she would never *not* make Daddy's supper. It's not in her DNA.

Drum comes around the counter, his face creased with concern.

"Daddy, I'm headed back." I walk to the back door where I left my flip-flops, trying to think. But I'm so scared that I feel like my brain is sludge. "How could she have gone anywhere? Her car's in the driveway. Right? Her car *is* in the driveway?"

"Sure is."

"And you're sure she's not somewhere in

the house? Taking a nap maybe?"

"Not in the living room or our bedroom or the den."

"Check all the other rooms, Daddy. Maybe she's in Mom Brodie's room."

Drum has picked up my overnight bag and is now following me out the door.

"Why would she be in Mama's room?" my father asks me.

"I don't know. Go check. I'll wait. And check the sewing room, too," I add. Then I cover the mouthpiece with my hand and look up at Drum. "I have to go back. He can't find her. She didn't go to church. Where the hell can she be, Drum?"

"Want me to come with?" He opens my car door for me in the driveway.

"No, you stay here with Sarah. She's got practice in the morning. You'll have to take her." I put my hand on his shoulder. "Would you go get Sarah? I want to give her a hug before I go. I don't know how long I'll be gone. Drum, what if she's fallen somewhere, broken her hip or something, and can't get up. What if —"

"There's got to be an explanation."

While Drum is gone, Daddy comes back on the line. "She's not here, Abby. Duke and I looked everywhere. She's nowhere in the house." Now, finally, at long last, he

493

sounds worried.

"Okay, listen, I'm on my way. Joseph will be there in an hour. Less than an hour. I want you to call everyone on the contact list in your cell. Somebody has to have seen her today. And while you're calling, go out and check the chicken house. Maybe she went out to feed the chickens, and, I don't know . . . And check the dock," I add.

"You mother never goes down to the dock."

"My mother never misses supper either, Daddy. Please. Just do it. Call me on my cell. I'm leaving now."

We hang up, and I call Joseph back. He says he's walking out of the bar. He'll drop Gail off at her place and be on the road in ten minutes. I hand the house phone to Drum when he and Sarah come out to the car. I give Sarah a big hug.

"Want me to come with you?" she asks, clearly understanding the potential gravity of the situation.

"No," I murmur, close to tears. Where could Birdie be? How did she leave? She couldn't have just walked. Not with her feet. Her arthritic hips. I know something bad has happened. She's too dependable. She'd never just go to a movie or something without telling us. And how would she go if

494

she wanted to, if she didn't take her car?

The thought that Birdie could have been kidnapped, maybe even murdered, crosses my mind, but the idea is ludicrous. I've been watching too many crime dramas on Netflix. There's been only one murder on Brodie in my forty-five years, and that was a wife doing in her abusive husband in what was basically hand-to-hand combat with oyster knives. She wasn't even arrested.

I just can't fathom where Birdie could be. So I guess we're going to have to look everywhere on the island.

I kiss Sarah good-bye, then Drum. I'm at the end of my street when I think of something. Using the Bluetooth in my car, I call my father's cell.

"Is your old truck in the driveway?" I ask when he answers.

"Sure is."

"Then go check the Caddy," I say.

"The Caddy?" he asks me.

"Yes, Mom Brodie's Caddy. Maybe Birdie . . . I don't know, went for a drive. And took Mom Brodie's Caddy. You told her she could have it, right?"

"It's in the back shed. Shut up. Covered."

"Please, Daddy." I speak slowly, as if he's a child. "Go look to see if Mom Brodie's Cadillac is still there."

I'm out on Route 50 by the time he calls me back. "Damned if you weren't right," he says, sounding relieved. "She took off the canvas cover and backed her right out of the shed and closed the door again. She took Mama's Caddy."

"Okay . . ." My heart rate, for the first time in half an hour, is starting to slow down. "So where do you think she might have gone? You're absolutely positive she didn't leave a note?"

"No note. And I don't know where she'd go." He sounds frustrated now. "She doesn't go anywhere but the market, church, and the hairdresser. And around to visit the sick."

"Start making phone calls, Daddy. Someone had to have seen her today. Nothing happens on Brodie that someone doesn't see. And stay at the house until Joseph gets there. We'll find her."

But we don't find her. I think we call every single person on the island. Joseph and I drive all over, looking for the car. Looking in all the places we hid as teenagers when we wanted to make out, drink beer, or just escape from our parents. We checked parking lots and dirt roads and every property we own.

496

But the white Caddy is gone. It's just gone. And so is Birdie. I call Celeste several times, leaving messages, and I text her. I tell her Birdie is missing. No response.

I suggest to Daddy around one in the morning that we call the police chief and have him call the state police. What if Birdie decided to drive to Salisbury and got into an accident, and for some reason we couldn't be contacted. Maybe she's unconscious or . . . I don't know. I'm so tired I can't think anymore.

Daddy refuses to let me call the police. By then, he's not just tired; he's angry that Birdie would put us through this. He insists she's fine and she'll call. I'm not sure he's right, but I agree not to call the police until we talk again in the morning. We decide to get some sleep, and it's not until I'm in my bed in the same boxers and T-shirt I slept in the night before that I realize Celeste *still* never called me back. Or even texted me.

Now I'm worried about her. It's true she comes and goes as she pleases without any regard to us, but I called her like six times. My texts have to be blowing up her phone. She's not a monster. She would call if she knew our mother was missing. Unless something has happened to her, too. Did they go off together? I wonder.

But that's even less likely than Birdie's not making Daddy his supper.

The last time I saw Celeste, it was after the funeral. She was wearing those sparkly heels of hers and the green and yellow scarf and a short skirt. I assumed she was going to The Gull because it's what she does every night she's here.

I get out of bed and go down the hall to Celeste's room. I turn on the light. Her stuff is all still here. The organza dress she wore to the funeral is hanging on a hanger on the closet door, and her wig is on the dresser. Her gigantic bag of makeup is on the floor near the dresser. She didn't go back to New York. She wouldn't leave without her makeup. The only thing odd is that she's left a pretty pair of red panties and matching bra on the bed. Like she intended to wear them and didn't.

I flip out the light, wondering if that means she went out of the house last night with no underwear. Which would be odd, even for her.

Back in my room, I collapse. I'm sure I won't be able to sleep, but I drift off.

41
ABBY

When my phone rings, it startles me. I was sound asleep. Eyes half-open, I feel for my cell, plugged in on the nightstand. It's barely dawn; a thin, pale light comes through the openings in the drapes. I don't know the number, but it has a Maryland area code. Which really scares me. I know I'm Celeste's emergency contact.

"Hello?"

The line is open, but no one speaks on the other end. "Hello?" I say again.

I'm half expecting a deep male voice to identify himself as a state trooper. Ask if he's reached Abigail MacLean. "Hello," I say again, panic rising in my voice.

"Abby."

It's my mother. I sit straight up in bed. "Where are you? Are you all right?" My hair falls over my eyes; it's a tangled mess. I push it away impatiently. "Mom, you scared us to death," I murmur.

"Just wanted to tell you I'm okay," she says.

She sounds hesitant. It's her, but it doesn't *sound* like her. Her voice is almost robotic. The kidnapping scenario goes through my mind again. My parents are rich, though to look at them, you'd never know it. But what if someone *does* know they're rich? What if she's been kidnapped for ransom?

"Mom, where are you? Are you alone? Are you *sure* you're okay? You don't sound okay."

"I'm fine. Better than I've ever been," she says calmly. Now she sounds more like herself.

"When . . . when are you coming home? I'm at the house with Daddy and Joseph. We've been worried sick. We thought you'd been hurt or —"

"I just wanted you to know I was safe," she interrupts. "I have to go. Plane to catch."

"Plane? Plane to where?" My mother's never been on an airplane in her life. I can't imagine her being able to buy a ticket and navigate an airport.

"Tell your father the car is at BWI. Economy Lot A. It's near the M1 sign. Near the fence. He'll see it well enough."

"But . . . where are you going?" My eyes fill with tears. This can't be my mother. My mother would never do something like this. "I don't understand."

"Have to go. There's a line to get on the plane."

"Wait, wait," I say desperately. "Is there some way for me to call you?"

"Nope. This is a pay phone. Nice one, near the ladies' room. I'll call you in a few days." She hesitates. "Don't worry about me. I'm good."

"Don't worry about you? Mom —"

She hangs up.

My mother hangs up on me.

I sit there on the edge of the bed staring at the cell phone in my hand. My mother is in an airport, flying somewhere. She's lost her mind. What other explanation can there be? That, or the world has tilted on its axis. Which is definitely true. My world.

I offer to take Daddy to the airport to get the Cadillac, but he insists Joseph can do it. And Joseph goes along with the plan, saying privately to me that he'd feel better following Daddy home. My father doesn't say much about Birdie's having flown the coop. He pretty much refuses to talk about it. All he says is that she'll come home when she's ready. And he tells me to go home to Drum.

So home I go, feeling more lost in my life

than I think I've ever felt. Mom Brodie is gone. My mother might as well be gone, because I don't know this woman who would take my grandmother's car, drive to the airport, and fly somewhere. Without telling us where she was going.

And I still haven't heard from Celeste. So all day Monday, I split up my time equally, worrying about my mother and my sister.

I get another call from an unknown number early two mornings later. This time, I bolt upright in my bed and rip my cell from the cord. It's got to be my mother. I already have in my head what I'm going to say to her. I'm going to insist she tell me where she is and that I'm flying there, wherever she is. I'm going to get to the bottom of this.

"Abby?"

I'm so surprised it's not my mother that it takes me a moment to switch gears mentally. "Celeste," I heave. "Where the hell have you been?"

"Sorry," she says cheerfully. "My phone won't make calls to the US."

"What?" I get out of bed and begin to pace in the semidarkness. It's almost dawn. Drum sleeps on. "Where are you?" I repeat each word sharply.

"Paris! Oh, God, Abs, it's beautiful here.

I'm thinking about taking French lessons. You know, so I can speak it."

"So you didn't get any of my messages?"

"Just the one about the money. How am I getting money? Mom Brodie cut me out of the will," she says cheerfully.

"You know about that?"

"Read the letter she left me. Nobody noticed it was gone?"

We've been a little busy. I think it, but I don't say it. I exhale, my anger with her sandwiching my relief that she's okay. "It's going to be complicated, but you're getting money. How the hell did you get to Paris?" I ask, pretty certain I'm going to wake up any minute and still be at home in Brodie, sleeping in my bed, maybe with Mom Brodie asleep in her room down the hall. Because this is just too wild to be real.

"Bartholomew." She giggles. "He asked me to marry him. But I told him not yet." Another giggle.

"So you didn't get any of my messages about Birdie?"

I hear her talking, but clearly not to me. The sounds are muffled. "No, no, I didn't get any messages after we took off. Hey, listen, I have to run —"

"No, wait! Celeste, Mom's gone. She left. She called to say she's okay, but we don't know where she is. She flew somewhere."

"Well, that's the silliest thing I've ever heard. Look, I really have to run. We have a lunch reservation at a restaurant in the Eiffel Tower! Bartholomew says we can just straighten out my money business when we get back. If you need me, you can call me at this number. It's Bartholomew's. We might fly to Greece next week; we're not sure. But I should be back in a month. Talk to you then." She makes a kissing sound into the phone.

And then she's gone.

I'm standing in my bedroom in nothing but one of Drum's T-shirts when he rolls over in bed. "That your mom?" he asks, only half-awake.

"No. My sister." I slide the phone onto the nightstand and climb into bed. "Go back to sleep. It's just too crazy." I raise my hand. "Too crazy for a conversation this early in the morning."

42
CELESTE

"You talk to your sister?" Bartholomew walks past me, planting a kiss on my bare shoulder.

"Mmmhm." I smile up at him as he walks by me, tying his ascot. I'm standing in a silk slip over serious French Spanx. On the dressing table (the hotel where we're staying actually has a dressing table!) is a box with a new pair of Christian Louboutin kitten heels and a box with a new Chanel dress in it. A day dress. There's another box under it with a slinky black number for tonight. And I'm wearing a divine new wig. We're going to look into hair transplantation when we get back, but for now, I'm glorying in the feel and look of this beauty that's prettier than my own hair could ever be. I guess that's the difference between a mail-order wig and one from a shop on a French street where you have to ring a doorbell to be let in.

"Everything okay?" he asks.

"Perfect." There's no need to say anything about Birdie missing. I'm sure he doesn't want to get involved in any Brodie family dramas. I don't. I flash another smile that's a combination of one of the many in my arsenal . . . and my own.

"Car will be here in half an hour," he warns as he walks out of the boudoir and into the living room. Our suite has a living room!

"I'll be ready," I promise.

I sit in the cushioned velvet chair in front of the dressing table and pick up my new eyelash curler from the bag of outrageously expensive makeup I bought yesterday on our shopping spree. I'm beginning to realize that Bart's not rich; he's *filthy* rich. And he doesn't mind spending his money on me.

I lean closer to the mirror and slip my lashes into the curler and give it a good squeeze.

I can't believe I almost jumped off that stupid bridge.

I curl the eyelashes on my other eye and dig in the bag for the Dior mascara in jet-black.

I was really going to do it.

I think I *really* was going to kill myself.

Standing on that bridge rail, I actually got as far as trying to decide if I should hold my breath on the way down.

Only then a breeze picked up. It seemed to come out of nowhere, and, for a second, I thought I was going to be blown off the rail and into the water. And suddenly I was scared. Scared to death. Which is funny since I was contemplating death.

That was when I realized I didn't want to do it.

What if I didn't die in the fall? What if it hurt when I hit the water? What if drowning hurt?

So I climbed down from the rail, and I lit another cigarette, and I walked off that bridge. I walked off that bridge because I realized Mom Brodie was right. She always said I was selfish, and I am. I'm too selfish to kill myself and spare my family from the embarrassment I am. From the pain I know I cause every day.

So what if Mom Brodie didn't leave me any money? Screw her.

That's what I told myself as I rescued my Jimmy Choos at the foot of the Brodie bridge. So what if the old bitch gypped me out of my inheritance? I don't need her money. I can get my own. I can make my own. That's what I told myself. And then I called Bartholomew and asked him to pick me up. I didn't say a word about where I'd just been or what I'd been contemplating. I told him I'd go to Paris with him, but only if we went today. That's what I said. And ten minutes later he was there.

The second coat of mascara applied, I lean back to get a good look at my face. I can't help but smile. With expensive makeup and the new wig, I look younger than I have in years.

With Mom Brodie's money, I guess I don't need Bartholomew. But I kind of like him. And I sure like Paris, and Chanel dresses and black limos. So maybe I *will* marry him, just to spite Mom Brodie, because I know what she'd say. She'd call me a gold digger.

But maybe I won't marry him. I don't have to if I have my own money.

I study my pretty face in the mirror and try not to listen to her faint voice in my ear.

I taught you right from wrong, girl, Mom Brodie whispers from the grave. *If you want the life he can give you, grab it with both hands. But remember, nobody rides the Ferris wheel for free. Be certain you're willing to pay the price. Marry him, if that's what you want, but be the wife he deserves.*

I shiver and wonder if Mom Brodie will ever really be gone.

43
ABBY & BIRDIE

A week later I'm sitting in my office, staring at my computer screen. I'm having a hard time getting back into the swing of things. Sarah has started the new school year. Drum's fall semester is under way. Reed's too. I talk to Daddy every day; he'll be cutting soy beans soon. He doesn't want to talk about my mother. He just keeps saying she'll be back when she's good and ready. Mostly we talk about Mom Brodie, sharing memories. We laugh. Sometimes there are a few tears. But all in all, my father seems to be adjusting to the new normal for him. I can't decide if that's good or bad. He and my mother have been married almost fifty years, and it appears that she's walked out on him. And he wants to talk about what soy beans are bringing at auction.

I'm the one who's not adjusting. I miss Mom Brodie. It isn't as if I talked to her every day, but I miss knowing she's there if

I need her. Strangely enough, I think I miss my mother more. Which seems irrational because what do I miss? The time we spent together or talking on the phone, I was mostly annoyed with her. She wasn't my kind of person. But she was . . . *is* my mother.

I'm still staring at the first page of the textbook I'm supposed to be editing when my cell rings. It's not a number in my contacts. I hope beyond hope that it's Birdie. She said she'd call, but she hasn't.

"Hello?"

"Abby."

I smile. "Mom."

I like the way she says it. *Mom.* I don't know why Abby's decided to call me that now, after all these years. Maybe because she called Mrs. Brodie Mom. And now that Mrs. Brodie's gone, there's room for me? Doesn't much matter why. I like it.

I take a sip of coffee from a Styrofoam cup and look out the window of my hotel room. The cliffs of Sedona are even prettier than in the photos in my scrapbook that went out with the trash. I could sit here all day and look at those red rock formations. But I'm not going to sit here all day. I'm going for a hike later. A walk, really. With two old ladies I met downstairs at the buffet breakfast. The food's free with the room and half-decent, though their hot cakes are a bit heavy. I doubt they use buttermilk; buttermilk's what makes a decent hot cake.

"I'm glad you called," Abby says. "I've been worried about you."

"I told you not to worry. I'm fine."

"I can't stop worrying just because you tell me to."

She does sound worried. And a little scared, which makes me feel bad. But not bad enough to regret doing what I've done.

"Where are you?" Abby asks me.

I've been going back and forth as to whether or not to tell her where I've gone. I wouldn't want anyone coming here, making a fuss, trying to get me to come home. Because I'm not going back to Brodie Island. Not ever. I had decided that by the time I drove over the bridge in the Caddy. I don't know if I ever belonged there, but I know I don't belong there anymore. Not with Mrs. Brodie gone.

"Arizona," I tell her.

"Arizona?" She says it like I said I was on the moon. But then she gentles her tone. "Mom, what are you doing in Arizona?"

I slurp my coffee that's just the right temperature. They've got a coffee pot right in the room here. You can make your own, day or night. "Always wanted to see it."

"So . . . you decided to take a vacation?"

"Nope." I set down the coffee cup, my gaze focused on the red wall of basalt and limestone out my window. "Decided to move here."

Abby's quiet long enough on the other end of the phone that I pull it away from my ear and look at it. I've never had a cell phone before. I got one of the fancy Apple ones like my kids have, so I can search things on the Internet on it. Nothing on the screen says she hung up. I put it back to my ear.

"You've left Daddy?" she says finally. Then, "Does he know that?"

"If he doesn't, I suppose he'll figure it out in good time."

"Mom —" She stops and starts again. "You can't just . . . walk away from your life."

"Why not?" I reach for the coffee again. I don't go on because I'm not ready to talk about it. I wouldn't say I regret marrying Little Joe because I got Abby and Celeste out of that marriage. And Joseph. Who, when push comes to shove, I love as much as I love my girls. Maybe more, in some ways, because even though he didn't come from my body, I think he understands me better than they do.

My daughter sputters on the other end of the phone, like she doesn't know what to say. It makes me smile. I've never baffled anyone before. No one thought I was unpredictable. Because I never was. I'm enjoying it. "Your daddy get the car at the airport?" I ask.

"Yes."

"I guess he found the ticket to get out. I left it right on the dash with one hundred dollars in cash in an envelope. Wrote *ticket to get out of the parking lot* on the envelope."

"Mom, where did you get the money to leave one hundred dollars for parking? How did you pay for a plane ticket? Where are you staying?"

"Hotel I found on the Internet. It's a nice place with a pool and a breakfast buffet," I tell her. "Not cheap, but the view's worth every penny." I pause to take a sip of coffee, thinking I might just have another cup before I head out for the day. I've never had time to drink two cups of coffee in one sitting. "Don't you worry about me. I have money of my own," I tell her. "Been saving my whole life. Well, since I was twelve or so. From eggs I sold. Jams and jellies. Stuff I returned. A penny pinched here or there.

Money your father gave me to buy stuff that didn't need buyin'. Got my own bank account with just my name on it. And a credit card of my own. Mrs. Brodie, she's the one who told me a woman needs her own money."

"I don't understand," Abby says. She almost sounds like she's going to cry.

I hold the cell phone tight in my hand. I'm glad I'm here. This is the best place I've ever been in my life, but I don't want to hurt Abby. I don't want to hurt my kids. "I'm going to live on my pin money," I say. "I got a lot of pin money."

Again, she's quiet longer than I expect her to be. But I wait.

"You mean . . . you've been saving money for fifty-some years, in anticipation of running away from home?"

"I didn't run away from home. That makes it sound like I'm coming back. I'm not coming back. My time there is done. I'm done."

"Mom . . ." Now I can hear that she's crying, but not loud, sobby crying. The quiet kind. The deep kind. "I don't understand," she whispers.

"Can't say I do, either," I tell her, sighing. "But when I do . . . I'll tell you." I feel a strange calm come over me, calm like I've never felt before. And I feel a connection to my girl that I never felt before, either. "That be okay?" I ask. "If I tell you once I figure it out?"

"Yeah." She sniffs. "Of course."

I nod. "Good." I take a breath. It never occurred to me I might be able to have a better relationship with my Abby away from Brodie Island than on it, but all of a sudden I feel the possibility. "You talk to your sister? I tried to call her. Just goes to voice mail. I didn't leave a message. She won't listen to it."

Abby laughs. Which makes me smile.

"She's in Paris," she tells me. "She says she's getting married."

"Married!" That's as surprising as my flying off to Arizona. "To who?"

"Some guy she met at The Gull the week Mom Brodie died. His name's Bartholomew. He took her to Paris."

"He a nice man?"

"I don't know, but . . . Celeste seems happy. I told her about the money. Apparently she knew she'd been cut out of the will, but she didn't seem that upset."

"She still want money from you and Joseph?" I ask.

"Of course."

We both laugh. Then I sigh again. I feel

like we have a lot to say to each other, but we can't just pour it out in one sitting. It's going to take time. "I have to go, but if it's okay, I might call you tonight I need to talk to you about you and Drum and Sarah moving to Brodie Island. I've been thinking on it a while. Mrs. Brodie and I talked about it, and she thought it was a good idea, too."

"Mom —"

"I said I don't have time to talk about it now," I interrupt. "I just want you to start thinking about it. Because . . . you and I both know it's where you belong. 'Specially now that I'm gone. It's where you've always belonged, Abby."

She's crying again, and I feel bad again. But Abby's strong. She'll be okay. I know she will.

"I have to go," I say gently. "But I'll call you. And you can call me. At this number. Only . . . don't give this number to your daddy. I'll call him. I'll explain everything to him. I'm just . . . I'm not ready. I've still got things to work out in my own mind."

"You're really not coming home?" Abby whispers.

"No." Now I'm tearing up. I didn't even know I had tears. "But maybe you could come here to visit. You and Drum and Sarah and Reed. Maybe Joseph and Celeste and her husband might want to come too, sometime. It's so beautiful." I press my lips together and gaze out at the red cliffs again. "I'd like it if you come to see me, Abby. Will you come? Not now. I need to be by myself now. Never been alone. But maybe . . . maybe in a few months?"

"I'll come."

We're both quiet. And then I say, "I always loved you. You know that, right?"

"I know," she whispers.

When we hang up, I get to my feet and adjust the sparkly palm tree brooch on my sweater. Once it suits me, I reach for Joe's John Deere ball cap on the bed and head out to see my red cliffs up close.

A Reading Group Guide: What Makes a Family

COLLEEN FAULKNER

About This Guide

The suggested questions are included to enhance your group's reading of Colleen Faulkner's *What Makes a Family*!

DISCUSSION QUESTIONS

1. How did Mom Brodie's impending death affect Birdie, Abby, Celeste, and Sarah? How did it affect Joe and Joseph?

2. Do you think it was a good idea for Abby to bring Sarah to Brodie Island? Why did Abby bring her? What did Sarah's character add to the dynamics of the family?

3. Though Mom Brodie wasn't born a Brodie, she became the family matriarch. How did the Brodies operate as a matriarchal family? In what ways were the Brodies different from families that are patriarchal?

4. How well do you think Abby dealt with Celeste? Do you have someone in your family or know someone like Celeste? How do you deal with him/her? How does

she/he affect you negatively? Positively?

5. Do you think Mom Brodie loved Birdie? Why do you think she always had Birdie call her Mrs. Brodie? Who was Birdie to Mom Brodie? Do you think Birdie saw her relationship with Mrs. Brodie accurately?

6. Do you think Birdie and Joe could have had a better marriage? Who was responsible for the poor state of their marriage? How did bringing Joseph into the house affect the marriage? Why do you think Birdie accepted Joseph to raise?

7. Why do you think Birdie had such a difficult time being a mother and loving her children? Why was Abby able to be a better mother than her own?

8. What do you think about Mom Brodie's decision to leave her old life behind when she married Big Joe Brodie? Do you think she was wrong to keep her past from her family? In what ways did she keep her past with her?

9. Why do you think Abby and Drum had such a good marriage when Abby's parents

didn't? Do we base our adult relationships on the ones we saw as children? Do you think Abby and Drum moved to Brodie Island? Why or why not?

10. Were you surprised by what Birdie did at the end of the book? Why or why not? Do you think she ever changed her mind? Was it strength or weakness that made her do it? Who influenced Birdie's decision to make the change so late in her life? Do you think she'll ever find happiness?